Aria Knew What It Meant to Be a Royal Princess . . .

J.T. lifted the limp woman from the water and made his way to the shore. Gently, he began to try to pump the water from her lungs. Her dress clung to her, revealing slim hips, a waist he could span with his hands, and breasts that swelled against the fabric. Her eyes were closed, thick, dark lashes lying against a cheek as pure and pale as porcelain.

"Sweet lady," he said, squeezing her ribs in a way that was half caress, "breathe."

After what seemed to be hours, he felt a shudder run through her body. She was alive! He kissed her fragile-looking cheek, felt the cold skin, then resumed pumping with increased vigor.

Another shudder passed through her body and she began to cough violently. When the spell passed, he pulled her into his lap and rocked her.

"You—." She coughed.

"Don't talk, just rest. Get all the water out and I'll take you home."

"You may not"—cough, cough—"touch _____—cough, cough. "I am" _____

"I'll be damned," _____

J. _____
Would Teac _____
to Be _____ . . .

JUDE DEVERAUX

THE PRINCESS

POCKET BOOKS

New York   London   Toronto   Sydney   Tokyo

Cover photograph by Paccione Photography Inc.
Illustration by Lisa Falkenstern

Another *Original* Publication of POCKET BOOKS

POCKET BOOKS, a division of Simon & Schuster Inc.
1230 Avenue of the Americas, New York, NY 10020

ISBN: 0-671-67386-6

First Pocket Books printing November 1987

10 9 8 7 6 5 4

POCKET and colophon are trademarks of
Simon & Schuster Inc.

Printed in the U.S.A.

Chapter One

Key West, Florida
1942

J. T. Montgomery stretched his long legs out in the motorboat, resting his injured calf against one of the crates in the bottom of the boat. He was the remarkably handsome product of generations of remarkably handsome people. His dark hair had been cut too short by the navy but that did not detract from his good looks: brilliant blue eyes, lips that could be as cold as marble or as soft and sweet as the balmy air surrounding him, a slight cleft in his chin, and a nose that on a smaller man would have been too large. His mother called it the Montgomery nose and said it was God's attempt to protect their faces from all the fists aimed by people who didn't like the Montgomery hardheadedness.

"It still doesn't make sense to me," Bill Frazier was saying as he maneuvered the stick on the motor. Bill was a striking contrast to J.T. Bill was six inches shorter, hair already thinning at age twenty-three, and built like a stack of concrete blocks. Bill was grateful to have J.T. as a friend because, wherever J.T. went, the chicks followed. Six months ago, Bill had married the pick of the bunch.

J.T. didn't bother answering his friend, but just closed his eyes for a moment and smelled the clean salt air around him. It was heaven to get away from the smell of oil, from the noise of machinery, and away from the responsibility of taking care of others, of answering questions, of—

"If I were a bachelor like you," Bill was saying, "I'd be down on Duval Street having the time of my life. I can't understand anybody wanting to spend time alone on one of these godforsaken islands."

J.T. opened one eye at Bill then turned and looked out over the ocean at several mangrove islands surrounding them. He couldn't explain what he felt to Bill, who had grown up in a city. J.T. had grown up in Maine, away from the noise and confusion of people and their machines. And there had always been the sea. When other boys had bought their first cars at sixteen, J.T. had received a sailboat. By eighteen he had been sailing three-day trips alone. He had even dreamed of sailing around the world alone. But then the Japanese bombed Pearl Harbor and the war began and—

"Hey!" Bill was calling. "Don't leave this world yet. Are you sure that's enough provisions? Don't look like much to eat to me. Dolly says you're too skinny as it is."

J.T. smiled at the mention of Bill's pretty little wife. "It's enough," he said, and closed his eyes again. City people were never able to look at the sea as one long banquet table. He had brought a net, a fishing pole and hooks, a couple of pots, a small box of vegetables, and his mess kit. He planned to live like a king for the next few days. The thought of the silence, the solitude, and the lack of responsibility made him shift on the hard seat.

Bill laughed, his very ordinary face crinkling. He was a man who would have made an excellent spy since he could have faded into any crowd. "All right, point taken. But I still think you're crazy. Anyway, it's your life. The commander wants you back next Monday and I'll be here to pick you up. And Dolly said to tell you that if you don't swear you'll use that burn salve she'll be out here tomorrow to apply it herself."

Bill snorted when J.T.'s eyes flew open with a look of horror on his face. "Now that would be *my* idea of a visit to a island," Bill said. "I'd lay in a hammock and have two beautiful—no, three—gorgeous dames feeding me mangoes."

"No women," J.T. said, his blue eyes darkening. "No women, please."

Bill laughed again. "What happened with that little WAVE was your own fault. Anybody could see marriage was in her eyes. And why *didn't* you marry her? I can highly recommend the state."

"That's my island over there," J.T. said, ignoring Bill's comments about marriage.

"Beats me how you can tell one island from another, but it's your funeral. One good thing is you'll be so lonely out here you'll be glad to get back to work."

J.T. grimaced at that. Peace, he thought, that's all he wanted. Nothing but the sound of the wind and the rain beating down on his tarp. And the food! No more navy chow, just fish, lobster, shrimp, conch, and—"Cut your motor," he half shouted at Bill. "You're going to hit the beach."

Bill obeyed and eased the motorboat onto the narrow white sand beach.

Holding his left leg stiff in order to minimize the

pulling of the burned skin, J.T. untangled his six-foot-long body and stepped out of the boat and into the shallow water. The heavy navy boots felt awkward on the slippery bottom and he suddenly couldn't wait for Bill to be gone so he could get out of the stiff uniform.

"Last chance," Bill said, handing J.T. the first crate. "You can still change your mind. If I had time off, I'd get drunk and stay that way until I had to sober up."

J.T. grinned, showing even white teeth and making the cleft in his chin almost disappear. "Thanks for the offer and tell Dolly I swear I'll use the salve and try my best to fatten up," he said as he took the second crate ashore.

"She'll probably still worry about you and when you get back she'll no doubt have twenty pretty girls lined up to meet you."

"I'll be ready for them by then. You'd better go, it looks like it might rain." J.T. couldn't keep the eagerness out of his voice.

"I can take a hint, you want me gone. I'll pick you up on Sunday."

"Sunday night," J.T. said.

"All right, Sunday night. But you don't have to live with Dolly. She's going to worry me to death about you."

"All right," J.T. said, stepping toward the boat. "Now you've made me a decent offer. I'll live with Dolly and you stay here."

"Some joker," Bill said, the smile leaving his face. His buxom little wife was the love of his life; each day he still marveled that she had married someone like him. For all that J.T. was his friend and had even introduced them, J.T.'s looks aroused Bill's jealousy.

J.T. laughed at his friend's expression. "Go on, get out of here and don't get lost on the way back."

Bill revved the engine and backed off the narrow beach with J.T.'s help.

J.T. stood at the edge of the water and watched his friend until Bill rounded another island and was lost to sight, then J.T. opened his arms and breathed deeply. The smell of decaying sea matter, the salt air, the wind on the mangrove trees behind him made him feel almost at home.

In another minute he had grabbed most of his things and was heading north along the beach. Nearly a year ago when the navy had first sent him to Key West to supervise their ship repair operation, he had seen this island through binoculars from the deck of a ship. He had known then it was a place where he would like to spend time.

Over the past year he had read a few books about the land around Key West and he had gotten an idea of what was involved in camping on a hostile mangrove island.

Saying that the interior of a mangrove island was impenetrable was an understatement. The branches of the trees that had formed the island hung down to the ground, creating a prison of woody stems.

J.T. removed his shirt, took up his machete, and began slashing a narrow path through the growth. He meant to reach the freshwater cut in the center of the island.

It took him four hours of hard work to reach the cut and by that time he was down to his skivvies. Dolly was right in saying that he was too thin. He had lost weight in his three weeks in the hospital and the burns on the left side of his body were still pink and now beginning to itch from sweat. He stood panting for a moment and looked about him. He was completely enclosed on three sides by the short, glossy-leaved mangrove trees, but in front of him was the cut of water and a small area of land and sea debris. The water flowed out before him, its source hidden under the trees. There was room here for his tarp tent, a campfire, and his few provisions; it was all he needed.

He wiped the sweat from his face and turned back down the path he had just made. The track had many twists and turns, and twice he had let it lapse, crawling under the looping, low branches for a while before starting to hack away again. He didn't want a freshly made path leading to his sleeping area. Several times German submarines had come into the Keys and J.T. had no desire to awaken one night to a bayonet at his throat.

It was sundown by the time he dragged all his things down the serpentine path, then, wearing only his shorts, boots, and a knife about his waist, he grabbed a johnny mop from his kit and went back to the beach. He removed his boots and walked into the warm water.

"There are definitely things to recommend this place," he said aloud, remembering the cold Maine water of his hometown.

When he was in water to his chest, he dove and easily swam underwater to the nearest bit of wreckage protruding from the water. Unfortunately, the war had left the shallow water near Key West littered with debris. The water was dark but J.T. could see the deeper shadows. He stuck the mop into a hole in what had once been part of a ship and twisted. When he pulled the mop out, the antennae of four lobsters were entangled in the threads of the mop.

One lobster got free before he got it to shore but he quickly pegged the claws of the other three and carried them back down the path.

Moments later he had a fire going and a pot of water boiling. Deftly, with a practiced gesture, he pierced the spine of each lobster before dumping it into the water. These lobsters were different from the ones he had grown up with, smaller, with spotted shells, but they turned red when cooked just the same.

An hour later he tossed the empty shells into the water and smiled as he climbed into his hammock strung between two trees. The air was balmy, the wind just barely moving. The water was lapping at the shore and his belly was full. For the first time since he had left home, he was at peace.

He slept soundly, more soundly than he had in a year, and dreamed of mounds of shrimp for breakfast. For the first time in weeks he didn't dream of the night he had been burned, didn't dream of being surrounded by fire.

The sun rose and J.T. kept sleeping. Somewhere his mind was rejoicing that there were no starched nurses shoving stainless steel trays under his nose at five A.M. and saying, "And how are we this morning?" He smiled in his sleep and dreamed of yellowtail snapper roasted over an open fire.

When the shots came, he was too deeply asleep to even hear them, much less recognize them. He had slept knowing that he was safe and now he somehow knew the shots were not aimed at him.

When he did awake, it was with a jolt, sitting upright. Something was wrong, he knew it, but he didn't know what it was. He leaped from the hammock, ignoring the pain on the left side of his body, pulled on his boots, laced them as fast as possible, grabbed his rifle, and left the clearing, wearing his shorts and knife.

When he reached the beach and he still had heard

or seen nothing, he began to laugh at himself for being skittish. "It was a dream," he muttered, then started back toward the path.

He heard another round of shots before he could take another step.

Crouching low, staying at the far edge of the beach, he began to run toward the sound. He had not gone far when he saw them. Two men were in a motorboat, one sitting by the motor, the other standing, aiming a rifle at something in the water.

J.T. blinked a few times then saw the dark, round shape in the water dive. It was a human head.

J.T. didn't consider what he was doing. After all, it was wartime and perhaps the head in the water was a German spy who deserved to die. All he thought was that two against one was unfair. He put his rifle behind a tree, flung off his boots, and eased into the water.

J.T. swam as quietly as he could, trying to watch the men and the head. When the head went down and didn't surface, he dove, swimming under the tip of the boat and heading downward.

"There!" he heard above him just as he dove. Moments later bullets came zinging through the water, one of them cutting into his shoulder.

He kept diving down, down, his eyes wide as he searched.

Just when he knew he was going to have to resurface for air, he saw the body, limp, bent over, and floating downward. He kicked harder as he dove deeper.

He caught the body about the waist and started clawing his way upward. He could see mangrove roots to his right and tried to reach them. His lungs were burning, his heart pounding in his ears.

When his head broke the surface, his only concern

was air, not the men. Fumbling, he grabbed the hair of the person he held and pulled the head out of the water. As he tried to determine his position, he knew he heard no gasping of air from the body he held. The men had shut off their motor and were now only a few feet from J.T. but their backs were to him.

Silently, J.T. swam into the tree roots. Involuntarily, he gasped as a razor clam clinging to the roots cut into his burned side. But he made no more sound as he backed further into the roots, the clams cutting into his skin. The men used oars to maneuver the boat.

"You got her," one man said. "Let's get out of here."

"I just want to make sure," the man with the rifle said.

Her? J.T. thought, then turned to look at the face of the head lolling on his shoulder. She was a delicate-featured young woman, quite pretty actually—and she didn't seem to be alive.

For the first time J.T. felt anger. He wanted to attack the two men in the boat who would shoot at a woman, but he had no weapon except a small knife, his body was covered with half-healed burns, and he had no idea how deep the bullet wound in his shoulder was.

Impulsively, he pulled the woman closer to him, shielding her slim body from the razor clams, and encountered the curve of a female breast. He suddenly felt even more protective of her, holding her to him in a loving way.

He glared at the backs of the men who searched the water.

"I hear something. It sounds like a motor," the seated one said. "She's dead. Let's get out of here."

The other one shouldered his rifle, sat down, and nodded as the first man started the motor and they sped away.

J.T. waited until the boat was out of sight then protected the woman's body as best he could with his own as he made his way out of the jungle of roots and into the open water. He held her with his injured arm while swimming with the other until he reached the beach.

"Don't be dead, honey," he kept saying as he carried her to the shore. "Don't be dead."

As gently as he could, he put her on her stomach on the beach and began to try to pump the water from her lungs. She was wearing a long-sleeved, high-necked, full-skirted dress, her dark hair coiled and pinned about her head. The dress clung to her in a way that allowed him to see that she had a beautiful body: tall, slim-hipped, a waist he could span with his hands, and big breasts that swelled against the fabric. Her face was turned to one side, her eyes closed, thick, dark lashes lying against a cheek as pure and pale as porcelain. She looked like some rare, precious flower that had never been exposed to sunlight. How could anyone have tried to kill this delicate beauty, he thought with anger. All his protective instincts rose within him.

"Sweet lady," he said, squeezing on her ribs in a way that was half caress then lifting her arms. "Breathe, baby, breathe for Daddy Montgomery. Come on, sweetheart."

Blood ran down his shoulder from the bullet wound and more blood flowed from half a dozen cuts from the razor clams, but he didn't notice. His only concern was the life of this beautiful young woman.

He prayed, asking God to spare her.

"Come on, sweetheart, please try," he begged. "You

10

can't give up now. You're safe now. I'll protect you. Please, baby. For me."

After what seemed to be hours, he felt a shudder run through her body. She was alive!

He kissed her fragile-looking cheek, felt the cold skin, then resumed pumping with increased vigor. "That's it, honey, just a little more. Take a big deep breath for Daddy. Breathe, goddamn you!"

Another shudder passed through her body and she gave a great gagging heave. J.T. felt so much empathy for her that his own sides tightened. A huge amount of water came from her mouth and she began to cough as she struggled to pull herself upright.

J.T. smiled, feeling a great joy flood through his veins, and thanked God as he pulled her into his lap. "That's it, baby, get it all out." He stroked her damp hair, caressed her small, frail back, and felt as God must have when He created man. J.T. didn't know when anything had made him feel as good as saving this girl. He caressed her pretty cheek with the back of his fingers, cradled her like a child, and soothed her more. "You're safe now, sweetheart. Perfectly safe." He held her face against his neck.

"You—" She coughed.

"Don't talk, honey, just rest. Get all the water out and I'll take you home." He began to rock her.

"You"—cough, cough—"may"—cough, cough.

"Yes, love? You can thank me later. Let's get you into dry clothes for right now. How about some hot fish soup?" His voice was deep and loving.

The girl seemed to want desperately to say something so J.T. allowed her to move back a few inches so she could look at him.

He pulled her back into his arms, cradling her as if she were the most precious object on earth. "It's all right, baby. No one will try to hurt you again."

She struggled against him and he let her pull away again as he smiled at her indulgently.

Again he was struck with the sheer prettiness of her. Not beautiful in a modern sense but in an old-fashioned way. Her small features and perfectly shaped head made her look as if she had stepped out of an old photograph. She reminded him of the ladies in the fairy-tale books his mother read to him as a child. She was a damsel in distress and he was her rescuer. Warmth flooded him.

He kept his hands lightly at her back in a protective way. "All right, honey, what is it you want to say?" he said caressingly.

Trying to talk made her cough again but he waited patiently, his eyes filled with tenderness while she made the effort to gain control.

"You may not"—cough, cough—"touch me"—cough, cough—"I am"—cough, cough—"royalty."

By the time she finished, her back was ramrod stiff.

It took J.T. a moment to comprehend what she had said. He stared at her stupidly.

"I am a royal princess and you"—she looked down her nose at his bare chest—"may not touch me."

"I'll be damned," J.T. breathed, and dropped his hands from her back. Never in his life had he felt such betrayal. He was on his feet in seconds, leaving her sitting. "You ungrateful little—" he began, then stopped. His jaw hardened and his eyes glittered like blue fire as he looked at her before turning away and leaving her where she was. "Find your own breakfast, Princess," he muttered, and stalked away from her.

Chapter Two

❧

ARIA sat where she was on the beach. Her head hurt, her lungs hurt, her legs ached, and what she most wanted to do was lie down on the beach and cry. But a royal princess must never cry. A princess must never show anyone what she is feeling. To the outside world she must always smile even when she is in pain. She had been taught these things until they were second nature to her.

Once when she was a little girl, she had fallen from her pony and broken her arm. Even though she was only eight years old, she didn't cry, but stood, holding her arm close to her body, and went inside to her mother. Neither her groom nor her governess knew that she was in pain. Later, after her arm had been set—through which ordeal Aria shed not one tear—her mother had congratulated her.

Now here she sat in a strange country after having had to fight for her life all night and the man who had rescued her was behaving very oddly. She glanced toward the tangle of trees and wondered when he was going to return with that fish stew he had promised. Of course she would have to insist that he clothe himself. Mama had told her never to allow a man to appear before her unclothed, whether he was a servant, a husband, or a native of some strange island.

There was a single palm tree a few feet down the beach and she slowly rose and started walking toward it. Her head swam with the effort and her legs were weak from exertion, but she pulled herself up as stiff as possible and began to walk—no slouching or staggering for someone of the blood royal. A princess is always a princess, Mama had said, no matter where she is or how people around her are behaving. She must remain a princess and let others know of their status or else they'll take advantage.

Take advantage, Aria thought, such as that man did this morning. The names he had called her! She willed her cheeks not to blush in memory. And the way he had touched her! No one, ever, in all her life had touched her like that. Didn't he understand that he wasn't supposed to touch a royal princess?

She sat down under the tree in the shade. She wanted to lean against the trunk and rest but she didn't dare. She would probably fall asleep and it wouldn't do for that man to see her sleeping when he returned with her meal.

Instead, she sat up straight and looked out at the ocean and, without willing them to, the events of the last twenty-four hours came back to her.

This past night had been the worst of her life, perhaps the worst night of anyone's life. Three days ago she had left her country of Lanconia for the first time in her life. She was to be the guest of the American government, and while the officials were talking to her ministers, the Americans planned to take Aria on a round of official engagements. Her grandfather the king had explained that their hospitality was merely an effort to persuade him to sell Lanconia's vanadium but he thought Aria might benefit from the experience.

There had been a long, tiring journey on trains then an army plane that had hastily been outfitted with antique chairs and brocade that was taped to the walls. Some of the tape came unstuck but Aria did not let the Americans know that she saw. Later she planned to laugh about it with her sister.

The Americans had treated her well if a bit strangely. One minute someone would bow to her and the next minute some man would take her elbow and say, "Watch your step, honey."

They landed in a place called Miami and immediately she was led to a small plane that was to take them to the southernmost tip of America, Key West. Here Aria was to be escorted about the big naval base and see where ships that had been injured in the war were repaired. Unfortunately, her two-week itinerary was full of visits to naval bases and army hospitals and luncheons with dowager societies. She wished that one afternoon could have included a gallop on a good horse but there didn't seem to be any time. Grandpapa had said the Americans wanted to impress upon her the need their country had for the vanadium and they didn't think that parties with handsome young men were likely to do that.

Straight off the plane Aria was greeted with a red carpet, and several overweight ladies wearing dresses of pastel chiffon—dresses that were indecently short —and carrying heavy bouquets of flowers. Aria accepted the flowers, smiling even though her feet were killing her and the heat of Key West made her feel light-headed. Three times she had to stifle a yawn as she handed the flowers to her lady-in-waiting who handed them to an American officer who handed them to an enlisted man who handed them to the chauffeur who put them in the trunk of a long black limousine.

Aria was escorted to a room in a building on the naval base that made her gasp. It looked as if the Americans had scoured the island for every piece of gilt furniture they could find and had put it all in the room. The hastily built, plain building with its purely functional rooms looked incongruous with the carnivallike carved, gilt furniture.

Aria gave her lady-in-waiting a quelling look lest the woman offend the Americans, but she was afraid the room would give her nightmares. There was an hour for her two dressers to ready her for a banquet.

At the banquet, she sat at a long table set on a dais surrounded by generals and town officials wearing suits smelling of mothballs. Every one of them had to give a speech and Aria tried not to show her sleepiness. She was also hungry but could not eat because the Americans had allowed photographers into the room for the entire meal. Royalty could not be photographed while ingesting food. So she sat, her plate taken away barely touched.

By the time she got back to her room, her long black heavy dress was weighing her down and she knew that even though it was midnight she had to be up at six A.M. for breakfast with a politician, then at seven she was to see something called a gyro compass laboratory.

Standing in the middle of the room, waiting for her dresser to come and remove her dress, waiting for her maid to draw her bath, in those few minutes when she was alone, someone threw something heavy over her head and carried her out of the room, and, as far as she could tell, out of the building.

She was nearly suffocated before the two men removed the covering.

"You will be paid if I am returned unharmed," she had begun, but a gag was put over her mouth then her hands and ankles tied. She was shoved into the backseat of a car and driven away.

Her mother and grandfather had often lectured her on the hazards of being royal, and once before, when she was twelve, there had been an attempt on her life. Aria lay quietly in the back of the car but she never lost her wits. She began to work the cords on her wrists, wriggling them looser and looser.

The men in the front seat didn't speak, just drove. They stopped, got out, and Aria could smell the ocean. She had freed her hands then untied her feet, but she had wrapped the cords lightly back around them. By now she thought the alarm would have been given and people would be looking for her, but she had to wait until there was a good opportunity to escape.

The men returned, but before she could see where she was, they covered her with a cloth again. This time she was put into what felt like a boat.

"Let her breathe," one of the men said as he started the motor, and the cloth was removed from her face.

Aria had a good look at the men. With a jolt, she realized that if they allowed her to see them, then they did not mean for her to live. She could smell the ocean and see the sky but nothing else.

After an hour or more one of the men said, "We're out far enough. Let's get it over with." He slowed the motor and over her feet, Aria thought she could see tree leaves.

She saw the other man lift a rifle and check to see if it was loaded.

Aria made her move as quickly as possible. Under the cover she had removed the loose bindings and now she jumped up and over the side of the little motorboat. The action rocked the boat and startled the two men, giving her a few precious seconds. She dove, but when she came up for air the man was shooting at her. She dove again. After she dove the fourth time, she remembered nothing until that man was holding her and saying outrageous things to her.

So here she was now, sitting under a palm tree in a country that was entirely too hot, having had no sleep and no food, and the only other person who seemed to be on this island was a half-naked commoner.

She stood, tried to straighten her dress, smoothed her hair back, and decided to look for him. Americans certainly didn't seem to know how to act. Why hadn't he apologized for touching her? And why wasn't he bringing her food? She would have to find him then allow him to return her to the American government. They would be frantic by now.

He wasn't easy to find. It took her an hour to walk around the narrow, smelly little beach but there was no sign of him. What a very odd way to treat royalty. Of course she had read that America had never had a king but surely even that couldn't excuse this man's behavior. In her own country the commoners were anxious to please her. Every time she left the palace they lined the streets to wave at her and present her with gifts. Perhaps this man was a prince and that was why he acted as if he had rights of familiarity. She dismissed that idea. He was an American and all Americans were equal—they were all commoners—no royalty, no aristocrats, just a nation full of commoners.

She sat down on the beach. So why wasn't he bringing her food? Even an American should know enough to bring a princess *food*.

At noon she moved back to the palm tree. The heat, her hunger, and the lack of sleep were too much for her. She stretched out on the sand and went to sleep.

When she woke it was dark. There were the calls of strange birds and she could hear movement in the bushes behind her. She moved nearer the palm tree and drew her knees up, wrapping her arms around them. She dozed a bit but mostly she stayed awake and wondered what was happening on the naval base. If they told her grandfather the king she was missing, he would be very worried. She had to get back as soon as possible and let the world know she was safe.

The sun rose and she sat up straight. Perhaps the naked man had left the island and she was alone here. Perhaps she would die after all.

A shadow blocked the sun and she looked up to see the man standing over her. He wore an unbuttoned shirt that exposed a great deal of his chest which was covered with dark hair. She could not possibly look directly at him.

"Hungry?" he asked.

"Yes," she answered.

He held a string of fish in front of her but she looked away. He tossed the fish onto a patch of grass then began gathering wood.

"Look, I guess we got off to a bad start," he said. "Maybe I *was* a little too friendly and maybe getting shot before breakfast doesn't put me in the best of

temper, so what do you say we start again? My name's
J. T. Montgomery."

She turned to look at him as he squatted over a fire,
the fish on sticks as he turned them. With his shirt
open and hair on his chest and black whiskers on his
face, he looked very primitive, more like something
out of a history book about Attila the Hun than what a
proper man should look like. Her mother had warned
her about men like him, or at least her mother had
warned her about improperly attired men. She
doubted if her mother had ever imagined that men
such as this one existed. Such men were never to be
allowed to take liberties.

"What's your name?" he asked, smiling at her.

She didn't like that overly familiar smile. It was
imperative to stop it at once. "Your Royal Highness
will do," she answered, her jaw set.

The man looked away, his smile gone. "Okay,
Princess, have it your way. Here." He thrust a fish on
a stick at her.

She looked at it in bewilderment. A princess was to
eat whatever was offered to her, but exactly *how* did
one eat this?

"Here," J.T. said, and dumped the fish on a leaf of
the palm tree. "Have at it."

Aria looked at the fish with horror, then, to add to
her horror, she saw the man was about to sit down on
the other side of the fire and eat his fish.

"You cannot," she gasped.

"Can't what?" he asked, squinting at her, a piece of
fish halfway to his mouth.

"You cannot sit with me. You are a commoner and I
am—"

"That's *it!*" he shouted, coming to his feet and
towering over her. "I've had it with you. First I risk
my life to save you and all the thanks I get is a 'you

can't touch me, I'm royalty!'" he mocked. "Then I bring you food that you won't eat and I'm told to call you Your Serene Highness and now—"

"Royal," she said.

"What?" he sputtered.

"I am a Royal Highness, not Serene. I am a crown princess. Someday I will be queen. You must address me as Your Royal Highness and you must take me to the naval base immediately. Also, I need a knife and fork."

The man said a few English words her tutor had not taught her.

Was it possible, Aria thought, that the man was angry? She couldn't imagine why. He would have the honor of escorting her back to the base—it would be something he could tell his grandchildren about.

It was better to ignore commoners' outbursts. It was their lack of breeding and training that made them so emotional. "I should like to leave as soon as I've eaten. If you wash that knife you're carrying, I will eat with it."

The man removed his knife from his belt, opened it, and tossed it blade down so that it stuck into the ground an inch from her hand. She didn't flinch. Commoners were so unpredictable—and their tempers made them dangerous. One must take the upper hand.

She took the knife from the ground and waved it at him in dismissal. "You may go now and prepare the boat. I will be ready."

Above her, she heard the man give a little laugh. Good, she thought, at least he was in better humor. Even he had to see how childish his temper was.

"Yeah, Princess, you just sit there and wait." With that he turned away.

21

Aria waited until he was out of sight before looking back at the fish. "Princess," she murmured, "makes me sound like a collie."

It took her a while to figure out how to eat the fish. Food was not something to be touched with one's hands. She found a stick, cleaned it in the dying fire, and at last tackled the cold fish with the stick and the knife. To her amazement, she ate all three fish the man had left behind.

Noon came and the man did not reappear with the boat. He certainly took long enough to do things, she thought. It had taken him an entire day to catch three fish so it would probably take two days to bring a boat around. The day wore on and still he did not return. Were all Americans like this? Her grandfather would not tolerate such behavior in a palace servant. America was very young compared to Lanconia and she wondered about the survival of the country if all Americans were as slow and uneducated as this one. How could they possibly win their war with men as undisciplined as this one? The Americans needed more than vanadium—they needed a new population.

In the afternoon it began to rain. It was a light, warm drizzle at first but the wind rose and it grew colder. Aria huddled under the tree and wrapped her skirt about her legs.

"I'm not going to recommend him for a medal," she said, rain pouring down her face, her teeth beginning to chatter. "He is failing in his duties to me."

Lightning flashed and the rain began to come down in lashing sheets.

"Don't you know enough to get out of the rain?"

She looked up to see the man standing over her. He was still wearing very little clothing and his cheeks

22

had even more black whiskers on them. "Where is the boat?" she called up at him, over the rain.

"There *is* no boat. We're stuck here together for three more days."

"But I can't stay here. People will be looking for me."

"Could we discuss this another time? Much as I dislike the idea, you have to come back to my camp. Get up and follow me."

She stood, using the tree for support. "You must walk behind me."

"Lady, I don't know how you've lived so long without somebody murdering you. Go ahead, then, lead."

Immediately, she realized she had no idea which way to go. "You may go first," she said graciously.

"How kind you are," he replied, the first decent thing he had said to her.

He turned away and she waited until he was several feet ahead then followed. It would not do to get too close to him. He didn't seem to be a trustworthy man. She followed him a few yards behind then the rain obscured him and she lost sight of him. She stood absolutely still and waited, willing even her eyes not to blink against the driving rain.

He returned after several long minutes. "Stay close to me," he shouted over the rain. Shouted unnecessarily loudly, she thought. He turned away then looked back and grabbed her hand.

Aria was horrified. He had *touched* her after she had told him he could not. She tried to pull away from him but he held fast.

"You may not have any sense but I do," he yelled, and began to pull on her arm.

Really, she thought, the man was too insolent for

23

words. He plunged ahead, hanging on to Aria's hand as a dog holds on to a bone. Once in a while he shouted orders at her, telling her to duck, and one time he grabbed her shoulders and pushed her to the ground. He expected her to *crawl* through the underbrush! She tried to tell him he had to cut the growth away but the man didn't listen to her. She was faced with being dragged, on her stomach, through the swampy land or crawling. Disgusting sort of nonchoice.

When they at last reached the clearing, it took a moment to get her bearings. She was completely disoriented after her treatment by this man. She stood in the rain and rubbed her wrist where he had held her. Was this where this man *lived*? There was no house, nothing but a few crates and a piece of black fabric forming a little tent. No one in Lanconia lived this poorly.

"In there," he shouted, pointing to the piece of fabric draped over tree branches.

It was the most humble type of shelter, but it was dry. She knelt and crawled inside. As she was wiping water from her face, to her utter disbelief, the man crawled in beside her. This was too ridiculous even for an American.

"Out," she said, and there was an edge to her voice. "You will not be allowed—"

He put his face nose to nose with hers. "Listen to me, lady," he said as quietly as he could over the rain. "I've had more than enough from you. I'm cold, I'm wet, I'm hungry, I got a bullet wound in my arm, I got cuts on top of burns, and you've ruined the first vacation I've had in this war. You got a choice: you can stay in here *with me* or you can sit out there in the rain on your royal ass. That's it. And so help me, if you say one more word about what I'm allowed or not

24

allowed to do, I will take great pleasure in throwing you out."

Aria blinked at him. So far, America was not what she had imagined. Perhaps she had better try a different tack because this man seemed to have an extraordinarily violent nature. Perhaps he would begin shooting at her as the other men had done. "May I have some dry clothes?" she asked, and gave him the smile she gave to one of her subjects who had just pleased her.

The man groaned, twisted toward a corner of the tarp, and opened a metal chest. "I got navy whites and that's it." He tossed them into her lap, then turned away, lay down on the rubber floor, stretched out, pulled a blanket over himself, and closed his eyes.

Aria had difficulty hiding her shock. Was *all* of America like this? Full of men who abducted one, then shot at one, other men who called one honey and tossed knives at one's hand? She would not cry, under no circumstance would she cry.

She knew it was no use trying to unbutton her dress. She had never undressed herself and had no idea how to do it. She clutched the dry clothes to her and lay down, as far away from the man as possible, but she could not control the shivering.

"Now what?" he muttered, and sat up. "If you're afraid I'll attack you, don't be. I've never found a woman less interesting than you."

Aria kept shivering.

"If I go outside in the rain, will you get out of that piece of sail you're wearing and into dry clothes?"

"I don't know how," she said, clenching her teeth to still the chattering.

"Don't know how to what?"

"Would you mind not shouting at me?" she said, sitting up. "I have never undressed myself. The

25

buttons . . . I don't know how . . ." The man's mouth fell open. Really, what did he expect? What did he think royal princesses did anyway? Did he think they polished silver and darned stockings? She sat up straighter. "I have never needed to dress myself. I'm sure I could learn. Perhaps if you told me the rudiments I—"

"Turn around," he said, then shoved her shoulder until her back was turned to him. He began unbuttoning her dress.

"I think that your touching of me is more than I can allow—what was your name again?"

"J. T. Montgomery."

"Yes, Montgomery, I believe—"

He turned her around to face him. *"Lieutenant* Montgomery of the United States Navy, not just Montgomery like your damned butler, but lieutenant. Got that, Princess?"

Did this man shout every word he spoke? "Yes, of course. I understand that you wish to use your title. Is it hereditary?"

"Better than that, it's *earned.* I got it for . . . for buttoning my own shirt. Now, get out of that dress— or do you want me to undress you?"

"I can manage."

"Good." With that, he turned away from her and lay back down.

Aria kept watching him as she removed her dress. She didn't dare remove her several layers of wet underwear, so she was still uncomfortable as she pulled his white uniform on over her head—and that took some concentrated effort to figure out. All in all, it took quite some time before she was able to lie down.

The rubber ground cover was damp, her underwear

was soggy against her skin, and her hair was wet. In minutes she was shivering again.

"Damn," Lieutenant Montgomery said, then rolled over, flung the blanket over her, and pulled her to him, her back against his front.

"I cannot possibly—" she began.

"Shut up," he said. "Shut up and go to sleep."

His big body felt so warm that she didn't offer any more protests. Her last thoughts before she fell asleep were a prayer of hope that her mother in heaven would not see her like this.

Chapter Three

WHEN Aria woke in the morning, she was alone. For a few moments she lay still and went over the events of the previous hideous day. She had to get back to the naval base and let the world, and especially her grandfather, know that she was safe. She crawled out of the little shelter and stood. There was a small fire made, but no sign of the man. His uniform, which she wore, hung past her hands, the top reaching to her knees and the cuffs under her feet. Tripping on the thing, she turned back to pull her damp dress from the ground.

It had stopped raining and it was a clear morning that was already beginning to grow hot. The clearing was really very small and hemmed in by the shiny-leaved trees. There was no sign of the man.

Cautiously, after listening for him, she removed the naval uniform.

"It's too hot for all that underwear," said the man from behind her.

Aria gasped and clutched her dress to her.

J.T. picked up his white uniform from the ground at her feet, frowning at the stains. "You sure don't respect other people's property, lady."

"Not 'lady.' I am a—"

"Yeah, I know. You're my royal burden, that's what. Why couldn't you have waited until Sunday morning to get yourself shot at? Are you going to put that rig on or stand there and hold it?"

"You must leave here. I cannot dress in front of a man."

"Princess, you overestimate your charms by a long way. You could parade stark naked in front of me and I wouldn't be interested. Hurry up and get dressed. You can peel the shrimp."

It took Aria a moment to recover. "You cannot be allowed to talk to me like that."

He stopped in front of her then grabbed the heavy black dress she was clutching. As she watched, horrified, he took his knife and slashed away the long sleeves then tore off about a foot of the skirt. He handed it back to her. "That should help. And you ought to throw away about half of that underwear. You pass out from the heat, don't expect me to rescue you. I learned my lesson the first time."

He took a fishing net from the ground, walked away, and stood at the end of the little stream.

Aria could not believe what had just happened. Her aunt had told her that Americans were barbarians, that they had no manners, and that the men were not to be trusted, but surely this man was worse than the rest. Surely the whole country was not populated by men like him—men who had no respect for authority.

Ten minutes later Aria was still standing there when he turned back with a net full of wriggling shrimp.

"You waiting for your maid? Here, let me help." He tossed the shrimp down then grabbed the dress from her and roughly pulled it down over her head, scraping her nose on the buckram in the waist. He jerked it into place, shoved her arms through the now-short sleeves, then buttoned the back with as much gentleness as a shark attacking its prey.

Throughout this, Aria kept her back rigid. This man was insane. This man's mind was not functioning properly. She moved away from him and sat down on a wooden crate. Her dress was quite short now, to the middle of her calves, and her arms were bare. "You may serve me breakfast now," she said as politely as possible.

He didn't look at her but threw the net of squirming shrimp into her lap.

Aria did not scream, did not jump up, did not show the revulsion she felt. "May I borrow your knife?" she whispered.

He turned toward her, a look of interest on his face, and handed her the knife.

A princess ate whatever was put before her, she chanted. One must never offend one's subjects by refusing to eat their food. She carefully opened the net, her stomach backing up at the sight of the bug-eyed creatures with their many legs. Taking a deep breath to still her churning stomach, she speared a shrimp with the knife point then brought it slowly, ever so slowly to her mouth. A leg touched her lip and she closed her eyes, her stomach rebelling.

The man's hand clamped down on hers just as she was about to put the shrimp into her mouth. She opened her eyes to look at him.

"Are you that hungry?" he asked softly.

"I'm sure your food is delicious. It's just that I've never eaten it before. I'm sure that I'll enjoy it just as much as you do."

He looked at her oddly then took the skewered

shrimp and the netful from her. "First they have to be cleaned then cooked."

She watched as he dumped the load of shrimp into a pot of boiling water.

"Have you never seen a shrimp before?"

"Of course, but they have been served to me on a plate and they bore no resemblance to those pink wiggling things. I did not recognize them."

"Yet you were going to eat it raw. Where do you come from?"

"Lanconia."

"Ah yes, I've heard of it. Mountains and goats and grapes, right? What are you doing in America?"

"Your government invited me. I'm sure they are frantic since I have disappeared. You must—"

"Don't start that again. If there was any way to get you off this island, I would. Believe me, sister."

"I am not your sister, I am—"

"A royal pain in the neck. Here, cut the heads off these and shell them while I make a sauce."

"I beg your pardon. I am not a scullery maid, nor am I your personal maid."

He was standing over her, blocking the sunlight. Once again he had on shorts and an unbuttoned shirt. His legs were in front of her face and they were too large, too brown, too hairy.

"You're in America now, Princess, and we're all equal here. You eat; you work. I'm not serving you meals on a gold plate." He tossed the knife and a flat piece of driftwood at her feet. "Cut and shell."

"I don't think your government will like the way you're treating me, Lieutenant Montgomery. They very much want the vanadium my country has and I'm not sure I'll sell it to America if I'm not treated well."

"Treated well!" he sputtered. "I saved your skinny

ass and look what it cost me." He pulled his shirt from his left shoulder and she saw a deep, puffy, ugly furrow across his skin and around that were half-healed scars that ran down his upper arm, his ribs, and into his shorts. His leg was also scarred and the wounds there looked deeper and not as well healed.

She turned away from the sight. "You should not show me such things. Please keep yourself dressed in my presence."

"You *expect* people to risk their lives for you, don't you?"

"My subjects—"

"Subjects, hell! Here, get busy on these shrimp. If I have to do them, you don't eat them."

"I cannot believe you'd refuse me food."

"Baby, you just try me."

"Lieutenant Montgomery, you cannot call me—"

"Cut!" he yelled at her.

She picked up a boiled shrimp with the knife, put it on the piece of wood, then tried to slice downward with the knife. The shrimp moved but did not cut.

"Don't you know how to do *anything?*" He took the knife, grabbed a shrimp in his left hand, and deftly cut off the head then broke the tail off and slipped the shrimp from its shell. "See? Easy."

Aria was looking at him with all the horror she felt. "You touched it."

"The shrimp? Of course I touched it."

"I cannot do that. One does not touch food with one's hands."

He looked at her in disbelief. "How do you eat corn on the cob? Hot dogs? Hamburgers?"

"I have never eaten any of those things, and if one must touch them I do not plan to eat them."

"Apples?"

"With a knife and fork, of course."

He didn't say anything for a moment but looked at her as if she were an alien from outer space. He took her hand in his, turned it palm up, and dumped a fat shrimp in it. He kept holding even when she tried to jerk away from him. He forced her to hold the shrimp in one hand, the knife in the other, and guided her through the motions of cleaning the shrimp.

Aria willed herself not to gag. She tried to close her eyes but the horrid man waited until she opened them before proceeding.

"Got it, Princess? When I get back, I expect the lot of them to be done."

She breathed a sigh of relief when he was gone but the mound of shrimp looked enormous. She felt like the princess who had to spin straw into gold or be beheaded in the morning. Tentatively, she picked up another shrimp. It took her a full five minutes to get the thing cleaned and then there wasn't much of it left.

"The American government will not like this," she said under her breath. "When they hear of this, they will no doubt use their trial system to condemn this man to a long prison term. He will wear chains about his ankles and live in a rat-infested dungeon. Or better yet, they'll send him to Lanconia. Grandpapa will know how to deal with him."

The man's snort from directly overhead made her jump.

"You must announce yourself. You cannot enter my chamber without my permission."

"This is *my* chamber. You haven't done ten shrimp. At this rate we'll starve."

She expected him to take the knife and finish them but he didn't. Instead, he had another string of fish. He used a big knife to remove the heads then tied a string to the heads and secured them so they dangled in the water.

"We'll have blue crab for lunch—that is, if we ever have breakfast."

He made her so nervous that she cut her thumb. In shock, she sat there staring at the blood welling from the cut.

He grabbed her hand and looked at it. "What do you know? It's red like the rest of us peons. Go stick your hand in the water."

When she didn't move, he pulled her upright and dragged her toward the stream and pushed her down until her hand was in the water. "Lady, you are the most useless human I ever met. You're not good for much but living in an ivory tower. What do you people do, just marry each other and produce more useless brats?"

Aria's hand was beginning to throb. "I am engaged to marry Count Julian of Borgan-Hessia."

"Oh?" J.T. lifted her hand and inspected the cut. "Ever met him?"

"Of course. I've met him three times and danced with him four times."

"Four times! It's a wonder you didn't get pregnant. Don't look so shocked, get over there and finish the shrimp."

Crude, vulgar man. The dungeon would be too good for him. She'd have to come up with a better punishment, something humiliating and disgusting. "My hand is injured. I cannot . . . Where are your . . . your . . . private facilities."

"See all these trees? They are one big toilet."

Trying to keep her composure, she walked away toward the narrow path. Once she started, she didn't stop. The man was hideous. No one had ever spoken

35

to her as he had. She had never realized anyone ever spoke to anyone else as this man did. But she would not stoop to his level of crudity. She was hungry, thirsty, tired, and hot but at least she was away from him.

It wasn't easy for her to find her way to the beach but she finally made it. Perhaps there would be a boat to come by the island and she could hail it. She walked along the beach, stepping into ankle-deep mounds of rotting seaweed and straining her eyes to see across the ocean's horizon.

There were few shells on the beach but she did see what looked to be long, narrow blue balloons. She stopped to pick one up.

"Don't touch that!"

Her hand came away and she turned to glare up at him. He was on the rise of land above the beach. "Are you following me?"

He had his military rifle with him and he dropped it, butt down on the ground. "You say your country has vanadium?"

"A great deal of it." She bent again to touch the balloon.

"That's a man of war," he said quickly, "and on the bottom are tentacles that can sting. The pain often kills people."

"Oh," she said, straightening and starting back down the beach. "You may leave me now."

He followed her. "Leave you to get yourself killed? You have a propensity for getting into trouble. I don't want you on the beach. Those two jokers who tried to kill you before might come back."

"Perhaps your navy will send ships looking for me."

They were at the palm tree now and he sat down,

leaning his rifle against the tree. "I've just thought about it and I figure it's my duty to protect you—or at least to protect the vanadium you own. You'll have to come back to the clearing."

The edge of the beach disappeared into water. "No thank you, Lieutenant Montgomery. I would rather sit here and watch for ships." She sat down on the edge of the beach, her back straight, her hands in her lap.

J.T. leaned against the palm tree. "Suits me, just don't get out of my sight. We have three more long days here and I plan to deliver you to the U.S. government safe and sound. When you get tired of eating your pride, let me know. I got blue crabs at the camp."

Aria ignored him as he lay down and appeared to be dozing. The sun was hot and her stomach was growling with hunger. She imagined spring lamb and green beans with thyme. The sun flashed off the water but there was no sign of any sailing vessel.

Before her, swimming lazily in the water, was a large fish. She remembered how the man had speared a fish and cooked it over an open fire. It was the last meal she had had, so very many hours ago. She thought maybe she could make a fire, but how did one catch a fish?

She looked back at the man and saw he was sleeping. A foot from him rested his rifle. Rifles were something she understood since she had hunted game since she was a child.

Quietly, so as not to wake him, she climbed up the bank and had her hand on the rifle before he grabbed her wrist.

"What are you planning to do with that? Get rid of me?"

"I was going to catch a fish."

He blinked a couple of times before he grinned. "What? Use a rifle as a fishing pole? Bullets for bait?"

"I have never met a man more absurd than you. I am planning to shoot a fish."

He grinned broader. "Shoot a fish. With an M-1 rifle? Lady, you couldn't even fire the thing, much less hit anything with it. The recoil would knock you flat."

"Oh?" she said, and raised the rifle, drew back the bolt to check if it were loaded, and before he could speak, she had tossed it to her shoulder, aimed, and fired. "Another bullet," she said, stretching out her hand to him.

Speechless, J.T. put one of the long M-1 cartridges in her hand.

She loaded again, but this time she swung the rifle overhead, aiming at a flock of ducks. She fired and a duck fell a few feet out into the ocean. She put the rifle down and turned to look at him.

J.T. walked past her, down the bank, and stepped into the water. He picked up a large red snapper, the tip of its head blown cleanly off. Turning, he walked a few more feet out and retrieved a duck, its head missing.

"Princesses *can* do some things," Aria said, turning on her heel and starting down the path toward camp. "You may serve them to me for luncheon."

He caught up with her, the rifle slung at his back. He pulled her arms up and dumped the duck and fish into them. "You eat what you kill and you clean it. You're going to learn that I'm not your servant if I have to beat it into you."

She smiled at him. "Men are always angry when I outshoot them. Tell me, Lieutenant Montgomery, can you ride a horse?"

"I can dress myself and I'm not starving. Now go to

38

the camp and start plucking feathers. And this time you finish the job."

"I hate him now," Aria said as she pulled out a duck feather. "I hate him tomorrow." She plucked another feather. "I hate him yesterday."

"You haven't finished that yet?"

Aria jumped. "You *must* announce your presence."

"I did." He looked at her bare arms. "Do you realize that you're sitting in the sun again?"

"I will sit where I please."

J.T. shrugged, bent over the crabs, and began to clean them.

"I hate him for always," Aria said under her breath. "I think this is complete," she said, standing; then, to her consternation, the land began to twirl about her.

When she woke, she was lying in the hammock, Lieutenant Montgomery looming over her with a frown on his face.

"Damned dame," he muttered, then louder, he said as he glowered at her, "you're too hot in that damned dress, you're sunburned, and you're hungry." He turned away, muttering to himself, "I ought to get a Silver Star after this."

Aria did feel awful, and as she looked at her arms, she saw the pinkening flesh. In minutes he returned with a metal plate full of fish and crab. She had some difficulty trying to sit up in the hammock, so after a few more mumbled curses, Lieutenant Montgomery set the plate of food down, bent, and picked her up in his arms.

"You cannot be allowed to do this," she gasped, sitting rigid in his arms.

He set her down on the wooden crate and shoved the food into her lap. "I could have brought three kids with me and they would have been less trouble than you." When she didn't start eating, he groaned and handed her his knife. "Aren't the words 'thank you' in your vocabulary?"

Aria ignored him but began to eat. It was difficult to remember her manners and not eat with the gusto she felt. She sat absolutely rigid, daintily picking up the knife, eating one bite, and putting the knife down. The man huddled over the fire, doing things to the spitted duck.

Before she had finished the crab, he dumped a quarter of the roasted duck on her plate. It took her a few moments to figure out how to do it, but by using the knife and the tip of one finger to hold the meat, she managed to eat all of it.

The man seemed surprised when he saw her empty plate but she gave him a look that dared him to say anything.

"Now we get you out of those clothes."

"I beg your pardon."

"You fainted, remember? Florida is too hot to wear that many clothes. I'll unbutton you then you go into the trees and remove your underwear. Don't look at me like that; if I wanted a woman it would be one with a little meat on her and one with a sweeter temper." He turned her around and unfastened the back of her dress then pointed her toward the trees.

As Aria went into the trees she kept her head high. She knew he was right, she couldn't continue fainting, but right had nothing to do with his ordering her about.

She removed her dress then stood and looked down at her layers of underwear. She removed her petticoat first, which she had had to roll up at the waist to keep from showing below her abruptly shortened skirt. The silk camisole came off next and that left her with a pink satin corset laced in tightly over a girdle, under-pants, and hose.

She could not reach the laces of the corset, twist and turn as she might. She put her dress back on, picked up her slip and camisole, and left the trees.

He took one quick look at her and said, "Not enough off."

"I will not—"

He turned her around, opened her dress at the back and cut away the fasteners on her corset. He pointed toward the trees.

Aria removed the rest of her undergarments and felt heavenly. The tight, restricting girdle, which left marks on her skin, came off, and the removal of her hosiery allowed her skin to breathe. When she put her dress and low-heeled slippers back on, she felt absolutely decadent. The silk of the dress against her bare skin felt marvelous.

Of course now the dress was a little snug in places. Without the heavy elastic confining her, she seemed to be larger in places—both top and bottom. She had never appeared in public without her foundation garments before. At fourteen, at the first sign of growing breasts, her mother had ordered foundation garments made for her. "A princess does not move about under her clothes" was what she had told her daughters. Except at night, in bed, Aria had worn them ever since.

She hesitated before leaving the cover of the trees, but then she put her head up, her back straight—and her eyes widened. More of her protruded than before. Well, if she ignored this fact, she was sure that dreadful man would also.

She was mistaken. He glanced at her as she entered the clearing, turned away, then looked back for a long, hard look. Aria ignored him. She turned toward the path to the beach.

"Where do you think you're going?"

"To the beach to watch for boats."

"No you're not. You're staying here."

"Lieutenant Montgomery, I do not take orders from anyone lower than a king."

"Well, baby, I'm king here. I figure that if you have something the American government wants, then it's my duty as a sailor to protect it. You stay here where I can see you and you don't get out of my sight."

Aria just looked at him then turned toward the path again.

He grabbed her arm. "Maybe your hearing doesn't work too well. There aren't just Americans out there. German submarines have been spotted in this area."

She jerked away from him. "My cousins are Germans. Perhaps they will take me home to my grandfather. I don't think I care for America anymore."

The man stepped back from her and looked as if she were a monster. "We are at *war* with Germany," he whispered.

"Your country is at war with Germany, mine is not." She took a few steps down the path before he caught her.

"Look, you little traitor, you're staying here with me whether you like it or not. And tomorrow when my friend comes, I'm delivering you to the government—to the United States government." He took her arm and pulled her back into the clearing, then proceeded to ignore her as if there was nothing more to be discussed after his order was given.

She sat on the ground against a tree and waited. She wasn't going to try to explain to this man who saw only his side of a problem, but every minute she delayed was taking months off her grandfather's life. He would know by now of her disappearance and he would be very worried. He had trained his only son, Aria's father, to take his place as king but he had had to survive the tragedy of the young man's death when Aria was five. From then on, his hopes had centered on his young granddaughter. Aria had been trained to be queen. She had been immersed in history and politics and economics.

This man who now lay in his hammock reading thought he understood patriotism, but here he was enjoying himself while his country fought a war. No king or queen ever rested while his or her country was at war. The people looked to their royal family to set examples.

Her grandfather had been able to keep his country out of this awful war that waged through most of the world and he dreaded what the Germans were going to do if he sold the vanadium to the Americans, but Lanconia so needed the money. When Lanconia declared itself neutral in this war, it had cut itself off from the imports of the outside world.

This Montgomery had said Lanconia was mountains, goats, and grapes—and now the grapes were dying. Knowing how valuable she was, how likely a kidnap attempt was, her grandfather had still sent her to America—selling the vanadium was that important.

Yet here she sat, a virtual prisoner of this stupid man who was much too provincial to understand, and she could not get off the island.

She hoped the Americans would delay telling her grandfather that she was missing—but the American papers seemed to love telling *everything*.

She glanced up at the man and saw that he was

sleeping. As quietly as she could, she left the clearing and went down the path.

She made it to the beach but the sun was going down and she couldn't see very far.

Suddenly, she heard what was distinctly the sound of a motor. She took off running as fast as her feet would move. Around the curve of the island was a motorboat just docking, three men hauling it onto the sand. She raised her hand and opened her mouth to hail them but the next minute she was flat in the sand, a weight on her that could only be the lieutenant's body.

"Don't say a word," he said in her ear. "Not one word. I don't know who they are but they aren't picnickers."

Aria was chiefly concerned with catching her breath. She lifted one hand and waved it.

He rolled off of her but pulled her close to him so that she was still half under him.

"You cannot be allowed—"

He clamped his hand over her mouth. "Quiet! They're looking this way."

She pried his fingers away then looked at the men. One stood by the boat and lit a cigarette while the other two, carrying a heavy crate, disappeared into the trees. When they returned, they were empty-handed.

J.T. held Aria tightly while the men climbed into the boat and motored away.

"You may release me now," she said when the men were gone.

J.T. kept holding her, his one hand creeping down toward her hip. "What kind of underwear did you have on? It sure made a difference."

Her mother's training had not included this situation. She reacted out of a primitive female instinct:

she elbowed him in the ribs then rolled away and stood.

The man lay there rubbing his ribs. "I've been here too long if *you're* starting to look good. Go back to the camp."

"What did the men leave in the box?"

He rolled up on his feet. "Well, well, the princess is curious. I should have let you tell them you'll not allow them to litter your island."

"This is an *American* island," she said, confused.

"Come on," he said, groaning. "Does anyone in your country have a sense of humor?" He started down the beach and she followed.

"Only when they are not being held prisoner. Keep your hands off of me."

"Someone should have put his hands on you long ago. How old are you?"

"I don't think—" she began, then sighed. "Twenty-four."

"That's an old maid in wartime America. What's this prince you're going to marry like?"

"He's a count and he's related to the English and Norwegian thrones."

"Ah, I see, you'll breed pure-blood brats. Is he related to you?"

She hated his tone. "Just barely. We are fourth cousins."

"No blithering idiots out of that. Who picked him out?"

"Lieutenant Montgomery, I very much resent these personal questions."

"Maybe I'm just trying to find out about your country, your customs and such. Aren't you curious about Americans?"

"I have studied your customs. Your Pilgrims arrived in the seventeenth century, all the Texans were

45

killed at the Alamo, your government is based on a constitution, your—"

"No, I mean about us."

She was quiet a moment. "I find Americans to be a very strange sort of people. So far, this has not been the most pleasant of trips."

He gave a laugh at that and stopped where the boat had landed. "Stay here—and I mean that. *Stay here.*" He disappeared into the trees, returning a moment later.

"Stolen navy property. There's a big stash of it. I'm sure they're black-marketing it."

"Black market?"

He grabbed her arm. "Let's get out of here. They could make a couple of more trips tonight. When I get back, the navy will hear of this."

Aria pulled out of his grasp and walked ahead of him down the beach.

"Only kings walk *with* you, is that right? Tell me, does Count Julius walk beside you?"

She stopped, turned, and glared at him in the moonlight. "He is Count Julian, and in public, no, he does not walk beside me."

She turned and started walking away.

"What about when he's your husband and king?"

"He'll not be king unless I decree it, which I will not do. I will be queen and he will be made a prince consort."

"If he's not going to be king, then why's he marrying you?"

Aria clenched her fists inside her skirts. This man had a way of making her forget that she was not to show emotion. "Lanconia," she answered simply. "And he loves me."

"After four meetings?"

"Three," she corrected. "That will be all the questions I will answer. I'm sure there must be some books on Lanconia in your libraries. What are you serving for dinner?"

"*We* are preparing seviche. Ever cut up onions, Princess? You're going to love the job."

Chapter Four

ARIA sniffed her hands and they did indeed smell as bad as she remembered. No amount of washing would rid them of the awful smell of those onions. She turned back to the campsite and saw Lieutenant Montgomery settled in his hammock for the night. There was no bed for her.

"Where am I going to sleep?"

He didn't bother opening his eyes. "Wherever you want, Princess. Ours is a free country."

It was beginning to turn cool and she rubbed her arms. "I would like to sleep in the hammock."

Eyes still closed, he stretched out his arm. "Be my guest, baby. I'm willing."

Aria gave a sigh. "I suppose it's too much to hope that you'd leave that and let me have it."

"Much too much. I came prepared for one camper —one bed, one blanket. You can share what I have, though, and be assured that I won't do anything except sleep."

Aria sat on the ground against a tree, feeling the

night grow cooler. A breeze came up and chills broke out on her arms. She looked at him, warm and sleepy in the hammock. She leaned back and closed her eyes but her chattering teeth kept her from relaxing. She stood and walked about the camp.

When she looked back at him again, he seemed to be sleeping but he extended his arm out to her. Without thinking what she was doing, she climbed into the hammock beside him. She tried to turn her back to him but the hammock pulled them together and the stiff, cramped position made her back ache.

"Pardon me," she said, as if she were passing him on the street, and turned so that her head was on his shoulder. She made an attempt to pull his shirt closed but it was caught under him so she had to put her head against his chest. To her surprise, the sensation wasn't unpleasant at all.

He curled both arms around her and she heard him chuckle softly. It was better not to think seriously about what she was doing. A desperate situation called for desperate measures. Besides, his big warm body felt so very good. She moved her leg by his, then crooked one knee and put it over his leg. She sighed happily and went to sleep.

"Wake up, it's morning," said a cross voice in her ear.

She had no desire to wake up, so she just snuggled closer to the man.

He grabbed her shoulders and pushed her away to stare at her. "I told you to get up. And fix your hair! It's come down."

She wasn't fully awake. Her eyes were half open, her hair falling over her shoulders. She gave him a soft smile. "Good morning."

The next minute he pushed her out of the hammock

and onto the ground. Wide-awake now, she rubbed her bruised posterior.

"You're the dumbest broad I ever met," he muttered angrily. "Didn't you ever go to school and learn the facts of life?"

"If you are referring to a public school, I have never attended. I had tutors and governesses." She stretched. "I slept very well, did you?"

"No!" he snapped. "I slept rotten. In fact, I didn't sleep much at all. Thank God this is our last day together. After this 'vacation' I am going back to the war to rest. I told you to go fix your hair. Pull it back the way you had it, just as tight as you can get it. And put your underwear back on." With that he stomped away down the path.

Aria stared after him for a moment then began to smile. She wasn't sure what was wrong with him but it was making her feel absolutely heavenly. She walked to the water and looked at her reflection in a clear little pool.

Many men had asked for her hand in marriage but quite often they had done so without having met her. They wanted to marry a queen, regardless of what she looked like. Count Julian, sixteen years her senior, had asked her grandfather's permission to marry her when Aria was eight.

Aria felt her hair. It was dirty right now but when it was clean . . . She glanced down the path, didn't see the man, so she looked inside his crate of provisions. There was no shampoo but she did find a fat bar of soap and a skimpy towel.

Hurriedly, she undressed and stepped into the stream. She was lathering her hair when he returned. He stopped and stared, eyes wide, mouth dropped open.

She grabbed the tiny towel and tried to hide her

nude body behind a tree branch. "Go away. Get out of here."

With a look of dumb obedience, he turned and left the camp.

Aria smiled and then she grinned. She began humming. That odious man and the awful things he had said to her: "skinny ass," "you could walk stark naked in front of me and you wouldn't interest me." How utterly lovely his stares had made her feel. Of course he wasn't really anyone, but sometimes that type of man . . . She wasn't supposed to know about it but a cousin of hers had borne a child without being married and it was said that the father was the footman who wound her bedroom clock each night. Aria had heard her mother say that of course the footman had hypnotized the poor girl. Smiling even more broadly, Aria wondered.

She took her time dressing—and didn't put her underwear back on—and began to comb her hair. She was still combing when he returned.

"I got lobster for breakfast and there's crackers in the crate."

He stopped talking and she was aware that he was watching her. She smiled slightly as she played with her long, dark hair in the early morning breeze.

Suddenly, he grabbed her shoulders and hauled her up to face him. "Lady, you are playing with fire. You may think I'm some servant of yours you can tease and still be safe with but you're wrong."

With his fingers digging into her shoulders, he pulled her to him and kissed her in a fierce, hungry way. When he had finished, he pushed her away.

"You're a twenty-four-year-old child, an innocent little girl, and I'm willing to leave you that way for your Duke Julian, but baby, don't push me. I'm not your servant and I'm not safe. Now get over there and haul up that net and give me those shrimp."

It took Aria a moment to react. She put her hand to her mouth. Julian had kissed her once but only gently and only after asking her permission. It was not a raw, hot thing like this man's kiss.

"I hate you," she whispered.

"Good! I don't feel any love for you either. Now scat!"

Breakfast was a quiet, sullen thing with neither of them talking.

After they had eaten, he lit a cigarette. Aria opened her mouth to tell him he didn't have her permission to smoke but closed it again.

She didn't feel inclined to speak to him and now she was somewhat afraid of him. How very much she wished she could get off this island and away from him.

After his cigarette, he stood, gruffly told her to stay in the camp, then disappeared down the pathway.

Aria sat for a long while, hugging her knees to her and thinking of her grandfather. How she wished she could go home where people and places were familiar.

After a few hours, when the man didn't return, she made her way down the path to the beach. He was lying under the single palm tree, his eyes closed, his shirt open, his rifle leaning against the tree.

"Planning to go fishing again?" he asked, not opening his eyes.

She did not reply as just then they heard a motorboat.

J.T. was on his feet in seconds. "Get down," he commanded. "And stay there. Don't come out until I say it's okay." He grabbed his rifle and started running along the beach.

Aria crouched behind the tree and watched, but then she saw the man stand up straight and wave his arm in greeting. Feeling a bit foolish, she stood, smoothed her skirt, and tidied her hair. With a dress with no sleeves, a too short skirt, and hair that had not seen a hairdresser for a week, she did the best she could.

With all the grace of her years of training, she walked down the beach toward Lieutenant Montgomery and the man who was not getting out of the motorboat.

"I've never been so glad to see anybody in my life," J.T. was saying to the man, who was a great deal smaller than Lieutenant Montgomery.

"Dolly made me come early. She imagined all sorts of things happening to you. And besides, I thought I might stay here and do a little fishing before we go back."

"No thanks. I want to go back where it's nice and safe."

"You *did* get lonely then. I told you—" He broke off when he saw Aria. "Well, you devil," he said, chuckling and looking at Aria admiringly. She was obviously a classy dame, he thought. The way she walked, the way she stood, reeked with class. Bill knew J.T.'s family had some money and this was just the type of dish he had imagined J.T. would go for. He would like to see J.T. married—maybe he wouldn't be so jealous then of J.T.'s friendship with Dolly if J.T. had his own wife. "You certainly put one over on me."

"It's not what you think," J.T. snapped at Bill, then turned to Aria. "I told you to stay out of sight."

Bill smiled knowingly. A lovers' spat. Then he looked at Aria more intently. "Haven't I seen you somewhere?" Bill asked. "And, J.T., aren't you going to introduce us?"

J.T. sighed. "Bill Frazier, this is Her Royal Highness—" He whirled on Aria. "I don't know your name."

"Princess!" Bill gasped. *"That's* who you look like, that princess who visited the plant day before yesterday."

"But I was here," Aria said, eyes wide. "I have been here for many days." Years actually, she thought.

J.T. was frowning as he grabbed Aria's arm and pulled her toward the palm tree.

"Hey," Bill said nervously, "you think you ought to treat a princess like that? I mean, isn't her country valuable or something?"

"Yeah, something." J.T. stopped under the tree. "Now tell me why those men were shooting at you."

"Shooting?" Bill asked, running up behind them. "When I saw her, she was surrounded by about fifty servicemen. I never heard anything about any shooting."

"Bill," J.T. said. "When your princess was visiting the plant, *this* princess was here with me."

Bill looked confused. "You have a sister?"

"She does not look like me," Aria said, equally confused.

"Start talking," J.T. said.

As quickly as possible, Aria told of being kidnapped and of escaping.

"You can untie your hands but you can't unbutton your clothes?" J.T. said, one eyebrow arched.

"One does what one must." She glared at him.

"Ahem," Bill said, drawing their attention. "You think the guys that kidnapped you slipped in a double?"

"A double?" Aria asked.

"Someone is impersonating you," J.T. explained, and shocked Aria into silence.

Bill gave J.T. a hard look. "How do we know which one's fake?"

J.T. looked Aria up and down. *"This* one is the real princess. I'd stake my life and the lives of my family on that. *No* one could put on an act like hers."

Bill looked at Aria as if he had never seen her before. "My wife sure wanted to meet you. When I got home the other day, she asked me a hundred questions about you—her. She wanted to know what you were wearin', what you looked like, if you wore a crown." He stopped. "But I guess that wasn't you."

Aria gave him a hint of a smile. "Perhaps I will grant your wife an audience someday."

Bill looked back at J.T., his eyes wide. "Is she real?"

"More or less. We have to figure out what to do about this."

Aria thought the problem had an obvious solution. "You must take me back to your government officials. I will explain what has happened and they will remove this imposter."

"And how are they going to know which one is the real princess?" J.T. asked with the voice of a father talking to an annoying child.

"You will tell them. You are an American."

"I'm a commoner, remember?" J.T. said with anger.

"I thought all Americans were equal," she shot back at him. "According to my studies, each American is as important as another. You are each one a king."

"You—" J.T. began.

"Wait a minute," Bill interrupted. "Could we do this without you two fighting?"

J.T. looked at Aria. "Do you know any higher-ups in Washington? Generals? Senators?"

"Yes, General Brooks stayed a week in Lanconia

trying to persuade my grandfather to allow me to go on this trip. My grandfather will not like—"

"Her grandfather is the king," J.T. said to Bill. "Then what we have to do is get you to D.C. and General Brooks."

Aria straightened her back. "I am ready to go. As soon as I get my clothes, I will be ready to travel with you. Oh," she said, and for the first time she realized the enormity of what was happening. She couldn't go back to her clothes or her dressers or her ladies-in-waiting. She had no way to even get back to Lanconia. "Did the woman actually look like me?" Aria whispered.

"Come to think of it, she wasn't nearly as pretty as you," Bill said, grinning.

J.T. gave Bill a look of disgust. "Look, the important thing is to get the vanadium for America. I imagine that the reason you were replaced is so the imposter can turn the vanadium over to an enemy."

"Vanadium?" Bill asked.

"It's an alloy that you put in steel to make it harder," J.T. said impatiently. He gave Aria a critical look. "No general will see you looking like that. Bill, you think we can make it to Miami in that boat?"

"Miami! That'll take hours."

"That's all the time we have. We'll buy her some clothes, put her on a train to D.C., and that's the end of it. We've done our part."

"But she's a stranger in a strange country. Shouldn't someone go with her?" Bill asked.

"It's war, remember? We both have to report to work at nine tomorrow morning. In war, they don't dock you for being late, they shoot you. She'll be all right as soon as she gets to General Brooks." He hesitated. "Besides, I *can't* go with her." J.T. turned toward the path. "Come on, let's go shopping."

Bill gave Aria a nervous smile then ran after his friend. "J.T., you're crazy. It'll be midnight by the time we get to Miami and besides that it's Sunday. No stores will be open and how are you going to pay for clothes for her? She doesn't have any money and you can't very well buy her new clothes at Woolworth's, you know. And then there's clothing coupons. I think you're going to have to turn her over to the government and let them handle her."

"No," was all J.T. said.

"I don't guess you could give me a reason, could you? I mean, after all I'm in this too."

J.T. stopped and turned. "Somebody in Key West tried to kill her. If she walks up to this imposter princess and declares herself, I figure she'll be dead in two days. I've heard of General Brooks, he has some brains. He'll know what to do with her."

"You have more faith in the brass than I do." Bill followed J.T. as they crawled on all fours through the brush.

Thirty minutes later they had J.T.'s gear in the boat and were ready to go. Bill held out his hand to help Aria.

"She'll fall flat on her face before she touches you," J.T. said with disgust.

Aria concentrated on stepping into the swaying boat without falling.

"Oh hell," J.T. said, "we haven't got all night." He picked Aria up, and half tossed her over the side. "Now sit there and behave yourself."

Aria kept her back rigid and refused to look at him but she couldn't keep the blood from reddening her cheeks. A dungeon was going to be too good for this man.

They took off with more speed than she liked but she held on to the single seat in the boat as tightly as she could. It would no doubt give that odious man a good deal of satisfaction to see her tumble over the side of the boat.

After a few moments J.T. took the controls of the boat away from Bill and somehow got even more speed out of it. The salt air hit Aria's face, and after her initial shock, it began to feel good. Now and then Bill would ask her if she was all right, but Lieutenant Montgomery just kept his eyes on the water.

In the late afternoon they stopped in Key Largo for gas. Although her muscles were stiff from holding on for so long, Aria sat in her place on the boat. She had been trained to sit still for hours at a time.

"Where can I get some sandwiches?" J.T. asked the dock owner.

"Gertie's at the end of the pier."

Bill stayed with the boat and Aria while J.T. got the food.

"What's this?" Bill asked when J.T. returned. He was looking inside the bag of food. "A knife and fork for sandwiches? And a china plate?"

J.T. took the bags from Bill's hand. "You ready to go?" he snapped.

"Just waiting for you," Bill answered with a matching snap.

Bill boarded while J.T. shoved off then jumped in. As soon as they were headed north again, J.T. slammed an egg salad sandwich on the cheap plate he had had to pay dearly for and handed it to Aria with the knife and fork.

Aria, for the first time in days, felt comfortable eating. She didn't notice the way Bill kept gaping at her.

"A *real* princess," he said. "Wait'll Dolly hears about this."

"Dolly isn't going to hear about this," J.T. said

emphatically. *"Nobody* is going to hear about this. We keep it to ourselves."

Bill started to say something, but after looking at J.T., he closed his mouth.

They arrived in Miami at midnight.

"We'll have to wait until morning when the stores open," Bill said, then groaned. "The navy frowns on being late. Think we'll get the brig?"

J.T. leaped off the boat before it was fully docked. "Secure the boat and get her off. I have to make a phone call."

Aria unsteadily stepped onto the dock and made her way up the ladder. She was determined not to show her weariness.

"It's settled," J.T. said. "There'll be a cab here in a few minutes and my friend will meet us at a clothing store. There's a train out of here at four A.M. Come on, Princess, you're not too tired to buy clothes, are you?"

Aria straightened her shoulders. "I am not tired at all."

The taxi arrived with a squeal of brakes and J.T. lost no time in pushing Aria into the back seat.

"She seems awfully nice to me," she heard Bill saying. "Maybe you shouldn't treat her like that."

J.T. didn't answer as he climbed into the front seat and gave the driver the address. They rode through the deserted, dark streets.

"Are you sure this place is open, bub?" the taxi driver asked J.T.

"It will be by the time we get there."

They stopped in front of a small shop in a residential area of big, expensive mansions that were hidden behind vine-covered walls.

"Don't look like much to me," Bill said. "Maybe we oughtta try downtown."

J.T. got out of the car. "There he is," he said,

walking toward a long black Cadillac that was pulling to the curb.

Bill jumped out.

"Sorry for the inconvenience, Ed," J.T. was saying, hand outstretched. "If it weren't for helping with the war, I'd never have asked you."

"Think nothing of it," an older, gray-haired man said. He had the plump, well-cared-for look of a wealthy man. "The clerk isn't here yet?" he asked, frowning.

"No," J.T. answered. "How's your family?"

"Fine, one boy at Yale, the other in the air force. How's your mother?"

"Worried about her sons, of course."

The older man smiled and took out his wallet from his inside coat pocket. "I hope this is enough."

Bill's eyes widened as the man handed J.T. a four-inch-thick wad of money.

"It should be," J.T. said, grinning, "but you know ladies."

"May I meet her?"

J.T. went to the taxi door and opened it. Aria gracefully left the car.

"Your Royal Highness, I am honored," the older man said.

Aria would never get used to American manners. The man was not to speak until spoken to and he was to be presented to her. But considering the way she had been treated by the odious Lieutenant Montgomery on the island, this man's behavior was the height of protocol. She inclined her head in his direction.

J.T. seemed about to reprimand her about something when a dark Chevrolet pulled up beside them and a thin, hawk-nosed woman got out. She was obviously angry about something.

As every woman knows, there is no snob like a

saleswoman in an exclusive dress shop. And this particular clerk had been ordered from her bed in the middle of the night.

She looked at the men. "I don't appreciate this," she snapped. "I don't care if there *is* a war going on. I won't stand for this." She turned to Aria and looked down her long nose. *"This* is what I'm to work with?"

All three men opened their mouths to speak but Aria stepped in front of them. "You will open your little shop and show me your wares. If they are good enough, I will purchase an item or two." She said it in such an autocratic way, as if she were granting the woman a favor, that the men were stunned. "Now!" Aria said in a clipped voice.

"Yes, miss," the woman said meekly as she fumbled at her keys.

Aria entered the store as soon as the lights were turned on. It was the first store she had ever entered and it intrigued her. Rather than being presented with drawings of dresses and swatches of fabric, here were dresses already made. How very odd to think of wearing a dress that had not been designed for her alone.

Behind her the saleswoman was talking to the lieutenant and Aria touched a blouse hanging from a long rack. The ivory silk crepe was rather nice. Next to it was a yellow blouse with small black dots on it. She had always wanted to see how she looked in yellow. Perhaps she could see if the blouse fit.

She began to see possibilities in this idea of previously made clothes. She might be more inclined to be adventurous if she could see what something looked like before it was sewn.

"Here!" the saleswoman hissed at J.T., handing him a piece of paper with a telephone number on it. "Call this and tell Mavis to get over here instantly."

J.T., like all men, was out of place in the female atmosphere and docilely did as he was bid.

"Who is he?" Bill whispered as J.T. was dialing, nodding toward the older man who had managed to open the store in the middle of the night.

"A friend of my mother's. He owns a bank or two," J.T. said as he dialed. "Hello, Mavis?" he said into the telephone.

"I am waiting," Aria said impatiently from the dressing room.

The banker left, Mavis arrived, and Bill and J.T. sat down on little gold chairs to wait. Bill dozed while J.T. shifted on his chair impatiently.

"This will not do at all," Aria said, examining herself in the mirror.

"But it's a Mainbocher," the woman protested. "Perhaps a tuck taken in here and one here, and with the right gloves . . ."

"Perhaps. Now, about this one."

"The Schiaparelli?"

"I will take it. You must pack it carefully."

"Yes," the woman said hesitantly. "Does madam have her luggage here?"

"I have no luggage. You will have to provide it."

"But . . . but, madam, we do not sell luggage in this shop."

Aria found the woman quite tiresome. "Then you must obtain some. And I want the clothes packed carefully, with tissue paper." As far as Aria could tell, Americans were so odd, it was no telling what they would do with one's clothes.

The woman was backing from the dressing room. She whispered something to Mavis, who ran out of the shop. She turned to J.T. "This will take a while. There are alterations."

J.T. stood. "We don't have time. I have to report for

duty in Key West in a few hours. What size does she wear?"

"Six. She is a perfect six but sometimes the dresses are not perfect," the woman said diplomatically.

"Then give her one of every size six you have in the shop."

Her eyes widened. "But that will cost a great deal. And the clothing coupons—"

J.T. took the roll of money from his pocket. They were hundred-dollar bills. He began counting off bills. "Perhaps you can say that all your size sixes were damaged and they had to be discarded. Believe me, Uncle Sam won't mind giving up a few pieces of clothing for what this lady will bring him in return."

The woman's eyes were on the money. "There are shoes."

J.T. kept unrolling layers of bills.

"And gloves. And hosiery. And, of course, underwear. We also carry a line of costume jewelry."

J.T. stopped counting. "Princess," he yelled, startling Bill awake so that he nearly fell off the chair, "you want jewelry?"

"I'll need emeralds, and a few rubies, but only if they're deep red. And of course diamonds and pearls."

J.T. winked at the saleswoman. "I don't think she'll wear glass and gold paint, do you?"

"We do have a pair of diamond earrings."

J.T. unrolled a few more hundreds. "She'll take them. Give her whatever you have in her size."

At that moment Mavis appeared at the door. Behind her was a sleepy-looking man with a hand truck piled high with matching blue canvas luggage trimmed in white leather. "Where you want it?" he asked sullenly.

J.T. stepped back as the saleswoman took over.

"Beautiful, madam," the saleswoman said moments later to Aria in the dressing room. "You are utterly lovely."

Aria studied herself in the mirror. All her life she had been on display and how to look good was something she had learned at an early age. Yes, the clothes were beautiful, very little fabric used because of the war, of course, but they were cut well and they draped and clung to her body in a very pleasant way. But from her neck up she thought she looked very different from these Americans. Her long hair was scraped back and untidily wrapped into a knot and her face was pale and colorless.

"Your handsome young man is growing impatient," the saleswoman said, some apology in her voice.

"He is neither mine nor do I find him particularly handsome," Aria said, twisting to look at the seams in her stockings. "Are you sure American women wear dresses this short?" The clerk didn't answer so Aria looked at her and saw her staring.

"Not handsome?" the woman said at last.

It occurred to Aria that she had never actually looked at Lieutenant Montgomery. She opened the curtain to the dressing room and peered out.

He was sprawled across a small antique reproduction chair—and not a very good one at that—his legs stretched out across the floor so that Mavis had to walk around him, his hands deep in his pockets. He was broad-shouldered, flat-bellied, with long and surprisingly heavy legs. He had dark hair that waved back from his face, blue eyes under thick lashes, a straight thin nose, and perfectly cut lips above a slightly cleft chin.

Aria returned to the dressing room. "I believe this hat will do."

"Yes, madam. He *is* handsome, isn't he?"

"And I'll take all the hosiery. You may pack the dark green silk suit also."

"Yes, madam." The woman went away without an answer to her question.

When she was alone, Aria smiled at herself in the mirror. She had spent days alone on an island with an exquisitely handsome man—and she hadn't even noticed. Of course something had to be said for his despicable manner, which overrode any physical beauty. Before she had left Lanconia, her sister had teased her about spending time with the handsome American soldiers and here she had spent what would seem to be a romantic time alone on an island with a *very* handsome man and she had never once looked at him.

"Princess, we got to go. That train leaves in one hour and we have to drive there yet," J.T. said angrily from the other side of the screen.

Aria closed her eyes for a moment, braced herself, then left the dressing room. So much for handsome, she thought. She had heard the devil was handsome and now she knew it was true.

The man Bill gave a sort of whistle when she walked into the room that Aria found offensive, but before she could speak, it was echoed by the man who had delivered the luggage. As far as she could tell, the whistle seemed to be a type of compliment.

Of course Lieutenant Montgomery said nothing but grabbed her arm and started pulling her toward the door.

She jerked away from him—how good she had become at that motion since she had met him—and sat down. "I am not traveling with my hair like this."

"You'll do what you're told and be grateful that—"

The saleswoman cut him off by stepping between

Aria and him and removing a comb from her dress pocket. "If I may be so bold."

"We don't have time for anything fancy," J.T. said.

The woman combed Aria's tangled hair then quickly braided it and wrapped it atop Aria's head. "It looks like a crown," she said, pleased.

Aria looked in a hand mirror and saw the arrangement was neat but then she saw Mavis snickering at her. Mavis's hair was shoulder length, pulled back at her temples in a becoming way, and looked cool and very modern. Aria's hair, perfectly all right at home in Lanconia, looked old-fashioned here in America.

J.T. took the mirror from her. "You can admire yourself on the train. Come on. We got two taxis waiting, one for us and one for all your damned luggage." He pulled Aria from the store.

As he was shoving her into the taxi, the saleswoman came running out carrying a bottle of perfume. "For you," she said. "Good luck."

Aria held out her hand to the woman, palm downward.

Through some basic instinct that years of American freedom had not erased, the woman took Aria's fingertips then half curtsied. She caught herself in midbend and straightened, her face red. "I hope you enjoy your new clothes." She backed away.

J.T. started pushing Aria again but Bill stepped forward and placed himself between them. "Your carriage awaits, Your Royal Highness."

Aria gave him a dazzling smile then gracefully entered the taxi. Bill entered from the other side, J.T. next to him.

"I sure wish my wife could hear about this," Bill said as they sped away. "She'll never believe I met a real princess."

"Perhaps you could visit Lanconia one day. My house will be open to you."

"House? You don't live in a palace?" He sounded like a disappointed little boy.

"It is made of stone, is three hundred years old, and has two hundred and six rooms."

"That's a palace," Bill said, smiling in satisfaction.

Aria hid her own smile because she was glad she had not disappointed him. She vowed to greet his wife and him wearing the Aratone crown, the one with the ruby the size of a hen's egg in the center.

"If you two are finished playing old home week, we have some business to conduct," J.T. said. "Here, Princess." He held out a stack of green papers.

"What is that?" she asked, looking at them in the dim light.

"Money," he snapped.

Aria turned away. "I do not touch money."

"She *is* a princess," Bill gasped, obviously impressed.

J.T. leaned across his friend and grabbed the elegant little leather handbag from Aria's lap. It contained a lace-edged handkerchief and nothing else. "Look, I'm putting the money in here. When you get to D.C., get a porter to carry your bags and give him this bill, the one with the 'one' on it. No zeroes, understand? Get him to get you a taxi that'll take you to the Waverly Hotel. Give the driver a five. At the hotel ask for Leon Catton. If he's not there, have them call him. Tell him you are a friend of Amanda Montgomery."

"I do not know such a person."

"You know me and she's my mother. If you don't mention her name, you'll never get a room. Leon keeps a suite for emergencies, but you'll have to mention her name to get it. It won't hurt to show a little green either."

"Green?"

"Show them a hundred-dollar bill, that'll get their attention, and I imagine your attitude and all that luggage will make them take notice too. Oh, here." He pulled a box from his pocket and handed it to her.

She opened it to find a pair of earrings consisting of five small diamonds on each one. She held them up to the light of a passing car. Not very good quality at all, but she put them on.

"Don't you ever say 'thank you' for anything?"

"I will give America the vanadium," she said, looking straight ahead.

"You can't beat that, J.T.," Bill said.

If she gets back to her country. *If* she can persuade our government that there has indeed been a switch. *If* she can—"

Bill patted Aria's hand, making her start. "Don't you worry, honey, anybody can see you're the real princess."

"Don't touch her and don't call her honey. She is royalty," J.T. said sarcastically.

"Lay off, will you?" Bill snapped.

The rest of the journey was made in silence.

Chapter Five

Aria sat very still in the suite at the Waverly Hotel. Her ears were still ringing with the laughter of the hotel personnel. Never before had she been laughed at and it was not something she wanted to experience again.

The train had been dirty, cramped, and filled with hundreds of soldiers who kept trying to touch her. They had laughed uproariously when she had told them they were not allowed to touch her.

Upon arrival in Washington, she had been so flustered that she had become confused about the money. The porter nearly kissed her feet at the bill she had handed him, but the taxi driver had been abusive and yelled at her because of all the luggage she had.

There was a line at the hotel desk, and when she told the people to move out of her way, they became quite unpleasant. There were also many comments about her huge pile of luggage.

Aria had no idea how to wait in line but she soon learned. By the time she got to the desk, she was very tired and very impatient. Unfortunately, the hotel clerk was feeling the same way. He laughed in her face when she said she wanted a suite of rooms, then to further her embarrassment, he told the people in line behind her what she wanted. They had all laughed at her.

Remembering Lieutenant Montgomery's advice to show her "green," she thrust her purse at the awful little man. For some reason, this made him laugh harder.

By that time, after a night without sleep, Aria was feeling awful. She hated America and Americans and she couldn't remember half of what Lieutenant Montgomery had told her. Also, her command of the English language was failing. Her words became accented as she grew more tired and more confused.

"Amanda Montgomery," she managed to say.

"I can't understand you," the clerk said. "Are you German?"

The crowd had grown utterly silent at that and began to stare at her hostilely.

Aria repeated the name just as another man walked from the back.

The second man was the manager of the hotel and it seemed that the name Amanda Montgomery was magical. He berated the clerk, snapped his fingers at the bellboys, and within minutes was ushering Aria into an elevator. He apologized profusely for the clerk's rudeness, saying that the war made it impossible to get good help.

Now, alone in the room, Aria was still lost. How did one draw a bath? The manager, Mr. Catton, had said to ring if she needed anything but she could find no bellpull anywhere.

There was a knock at the door and when she did not

answer it a man walked in wheeling her baggage. Once the baggage was put in the closet, the man stood there looking at her. "You may go," she said. He gave her a little sneer and started toward the door.

"Wait!" she called, grabbing her purse. As far as she could tell, Americans would do anything for the green bills—and it made them so happy when the bills had zeroes on them. She pulled out a bill. "I need a maid. Do you know someone who can help me dress, draw my bath, unpack for me?"

The man's eyes bulged as he looked at the hundred-dollar bill. "For how long? My sister might do the work but she ain't nobody's maid forever."

It was Aria's turn to be stunned. In her country it was no disgrace to be someone's maid. Her ladies-in-waiting were aristocrats. "For a few days," she managed to say.

"I'll call her," the man said, and went to a black telephone on a table by the window.

Aria had used a telephone but someone else had always dialed it for her. She watched with interest as the man turned the dial. He turned away from her as he began to talk to his sister. Aria went to the bedroom.

The woman arrived two hours later. She was sullen, angry, and made it clear to Aria that she wasn't really a maid, that only because it was wartime was she willing to wait on anyone. She did what Aria asked but only reluctantly.

At four P.M. Aria lay down. She had bathed and washed her hair, eaten a mediocre meal, and now planned to sleep for several hours.

She had barely closed her eyes when the loud ringing of the telephone woke her. Groggily, she answered it. "Yes? This is Her Royal Highness."

"You don't lay off it even when you're asleep, do you?" said a familiar voice.

"What do you want, Lieutenant Montgomery?" She sat up straighter in bed.

"Bill wanted me to call to make sure you were all right."

"Of course I'm all right."

"No problems getting into the hotel?"

"None whatever. Everyone has been very kind," she lied.

"Did you see General Brooks yet?"

"I will see him tomorrow."

"Tomorrow? What did you do today?"

She wanted to scream at him that she had waited in line, been laughed at, had to deal with a maid who hated her, and been accused of being the enemy. "I washed my hair and spent hours in a tub of hot water."

"Of course. I should have known. A princess would put luxury before everything else. I'll call tomorrow night and see what he said."

"Please do not bother. I'm sure your government will rid itself of the imposter."

He paused a moment. "I guess you haven't seen the papers. That princess is a dead ringer for you and she's a hit wherever she goes. Maybe Americans will like her so much they won't want the real princess."

She glared at the telephone then slammed it down. "Hideous man!" she said as she left the bed and went into the living room of the suite. They had brought a newspaper with her dinner but she had left it where it lay.

On the second page was a photograph of a woman who looked very much like her, smiling at two men in uniform and cutting a wide ribbon. The caption told how Her Royal Highness, Princess Aria of Lanconia, was spreading peace across America. Instantly, she recognized her cousin Maude. "Were you always jealous of me, Cissy?" she asked in wonder, calling her cousin by the royal family's pet name. As she looked closer at the photo, she saw that in the background, smiling and hovering, was Lady Emere, Cissy's aunt. It was obvious that Lady Emere was protecting Cissy, probably keeping Aria's other attendants at a distance, but surely, Aria thought, one of them must be suspicious.

"Doesn't anyone know that's not *me?*" she said, blinking back tears.

She went back to bed but she didn't sleep very well.

Morning brought more problems. The woman she had hired to be her maid walked out when Aria held out her leg for her hose to be put on, so it took Aria three hours to get dressed. She was very glad for the black, veiled hat that covered her attempts at hairdressing.

When she left the hotel, she was feeling less than confident, but she kept her head high and her shoulders back. Once again she heard those low whistles from the men as she walked through the lobby, but she ignored them.

The doorman was someone she understood. She told him she wanted to see General Brooks, he blew a whistle, and a taxi came forward. Aria pointed at a long black Cadillac with a chauffeur leaning against the hood. "I want that car." The doorman walked across the traffic and talked to the chauffeur, who nodded.

"He'll take you to the Pentagon."

Aria had already realized that every American expected to be paid for everything he did. She handed the doorman one of the bills with the two zeroes on it, and he nodded gravely to her, then opened the door to the limousine.

Aria leaned back against the seat and closed her eyes. In the back of this luxurious car she felt at home for the first time since she had been kidnapped.

The chauffeur opened the car door for her and later, held the door that led into the Pentagon.

"I have been paid," he said solemnly when she offered him one of the few bills left in her purse.

She smiled at him, glad for any kindness from an American.

The time in the car was only a pause before the storm. Nothing she had experienced so far prepared her for the Pentagon during war. Everywhere people rushed back and forth, machines printed, people shouted orders, radios played news.

She stopped at a desk and asked for General Brooks.

"Over there," the woman said, her mouth full of pencils. "Ask over there."

Aria walked down the corridor and asked again.

"I'm not his secretary," a man snapped. "Don't you know there's a war going on?"

Aria asked a total of five people and they all shuffled her to someone else. Twice she started down hallways and men drew rifles on her. Someone told her to come back next week. Someone else told her to come back when the war was over. Someone else grabbed her arm and half shoved her out the door into a parking lot.

She straightened her suit jacket, squared her hat, and went back inside. If Americans didn't want to listen to the truth, then she would give them a good story. She walked into the middle of the busiest room and said in a normal voice: "I am a German spy and I will give my secrets only to General Brooks."

One by one the people stopped what they were doing and stared at her. After one brief second of absolute silence, all hell broke loose. Soldiers with guns came from every corridor and seized her.

"Do not touch me," she called, the men lifting her by her arms so her feet did not touch the ground.

"I knew she was German the minute I saw her," Aria heard a woman say.

She was pulled down a long corridor, people leaving their offices to have a look at her. Aria was glad her hat had slipped down to obscure half of her face. I am never leaving Lanconia again, she vowed to herself.

After what seemed to be ages, the soldiers dropped her into a chair.

"Let's have a look at her," said a voice with a great deal of anger in it.

Aria lifted her head, and pushed back her hat to look up at General Brooks. "So good to see you again," she said as if they were at a gala reception, and extended her hand to him.

General Brooks's eyes widened. "Out!" he commanded the many soldiers jammed in the room.

"But she may be dangerous," said a man holding an ugly black pistol aimed at Aria.

"I will somehow manage to fight her off," the general said sarcastically. When they were alone, he turned to Aria. "Your Royal Highness?" He took her hand, touching her fingers lightly. "The last I heard, you were in Virginia."

"Not me but someone who looks like me."

The general looked at her for a long while. "I'll send for tea and we can talk."

Aria ate everything that was on the tea tray, then

lunch was ordered, and still the general asked her questions. He made her repeat nearly every minute of their time together in Lanconia. He wanted to know anything that would make him *sure* she was the real princess.

At two he had her taken to a small sitting room where she could rest. At three-thirty she was led into a room where four generals and two plainclothesmen sat and had to tell everything over again.

Throughout this time she showed no impatience, no anger, no fatigue. The seriousness of the matter was coming through to her. If these men did not believe her and therefore did not help her get back to her country, she would lose everything. She would lose her identity, she would lose the people she loved, and she would lose her nationality. And Lanconia would have an imposter for queen—a woman eaten with jealousy who must want something besides the good of Lanconia.

She sat upright and answered their questions—over and over and over again.

At ten o'clock they sent her back to the hotel under armed guard. A WAC drew her bath and, Aria knew, searched her new clothes. Aria stayed in the tub until her skin wrinkled to give the woman plenty of time. At midnight, she was at last able to go to bed.

The big Pentagon room was filled with a blue haze of cigarette and cigar smoke. The mahogany table was littered with empty glasses, overflowing ashtrays, and crumbs from a meal of dried-out sandwiches. The preeminent smell was a mixture of sweat and anger.

"I don't like it!" General Lyons shouted as he shifted the wet cigar butt from one side of his mouth to the other.

"I think we have more than enough evidence that she's telling the truth," Congressman Smith said. He was the only one of the six men to still look somewhat fresh; nevertheless, there were dark circles of sleeplessness under his eyes. "Did you see the scar on her left hand? Our records say she fell while on a hunting trip when she was twelve years old."

"But who knows which princess is better for America?" General O'Connor said. "Lanconia doesn't really mean much to us except that now we need the vanadium. If the imposter princess will give us the vanadium, I don't think we should involve ourselves."

"Lanconia lies near Germany and Russia. Russia is our friend now but it is a communist country. After the war—"

"Who knows what will happen to Lanconia after the war? Say we restore this princess to the throne. Didn't that report say she was related to some German royals? What if she marries one?"

The six men began to talk at once.

General Brooks slammed his fist on the table. "I say we *need* her on the throne. You heard her promise to give America the vanadium if we help her. And she would be sure to give it to us if she were married to an American."

"An American?" Congressman Smith gasped. "Those bluebloods marry only bluebloods. We abolished monarchy in this country, remember? So where do we find an American prince?"

"That little girl will do *anything* for her country," General Brooks said. "You mark my words. If we told her we'd help her only if she married an American and later made him king, believe me, she'd do it."

"But didn't we hear she was already engaged?"

"I met him," General Brooks said. "A pompous little runt, old enough to be her father. He only wants our princess for her money."

"*Our* princess?" General Lyons snorted.

"She will be ours if we help her and put an American there beside her. Think of having military posts so near Russia and Germany."

The men considered this.

"So who do we choose to make king?" Congressman Smith asked.

"Someone we can trust. Someone who believes in America. None of these bleeding hearts."

"He has to have a good family history," General Brooks said. "We can't ask a princess to marry a gangster or an imbecile. We put only America's finest on the throne."

General Attenburgh yawned. "I vote we adjourn and present some names tomorrow."

The men readily agreed.

The next morning six sleepy-eyed men met. Four of them, without giving away the actual facts of the problem, had asked their wives what American would make a good king. Clark Gable won hands down, with Cary Grant a close second. Robert Taylor also received a few votes.

After four hours of arguing, six names were selected. Two of them were young congressmen, one a wealthy businessman not so young, and three were sons of America's oldest families, one of whose ancestors came over on the *Mayflower*.

Each name was given to a committee and rated as top priority. The men were to be researched as thoroughly as possible and it was made clear that the staff was to look for dirt. If this man was going to be crowned king, whatever skeletons were in his closet had better come out now.

"And check out that man Montgomery," Congressman Smith said as an afterthought. "Let's see if we can trust him to keep his mouth shut."

For three days Aria was kept as a prisoner in her hotel room. Two men with rifles were outside her door twenty-four hours a day and more soldiers were stationed on the street below her windows. On the morning of the second day a large package of magazines was delivered courtesy of General Brooks.

Aria sat down and got her first real look at Americans. They seemed to be a frivolous lot, interested mainly in movie stars and nightclub singers. A *Life* magazine had several pages neatly cut from it and the contents showed that it had been an article on Lanconia's regal princess.

At six A.M. on the fourth day, three WACs came to her room to help her dress. They were very professional and very cool, did what Aria asked, and made no complaint.

At eight she was again at the Pentagon, seated at the end of a long table with the same six men as before. They explained that she was to marry an American and crown him king.

Aria did not let her horror show. It seemed that these Americans believed they could ask *anything* of her. Patiently, she tried to explain why an American husband was an impossibility. "My husband will be prince consort and no American has a kingdom to unite with mine."

"You have the 'kingdom' of America," one man said sarcastically.

"It cannot be done," she answered with less patience. "I am engaged to be married. My people would not like my breaking my engagement, nor will my grandfather, the king." She was sure that would end the matter but it did not. A Congressman Smith began to explain to her an utterly preposterous plan.

"If we switch you with the imposter without first knowing who set this whole thing up, your life could be in danger. You make one error and you're a dead duck."

"Duck?"

"Dead princess, then. We have to find out who tried to kill you and who doesn't want America to have the vanadium. It had to be someone close to you."

Aria didn't respond to that but she knew the man was right. She tried to control the blood she could feel leaving her face. It was no use telling them her cousin was the imposter because she knew quite well that Cissy was not the instigator. Cissy was a nervous, easily frightened weakling, and if she was acting in Aria's place, it was because someone else was telling her what to do and how to do it.

"We have a few things going for us," said a large, gray-haired man with a chestful of medals. "First of all, they have no idea you're alive, so they won't be looking for you."

"So here's the plan we've come up with," said another man. "We let the imposter princess finish her tour, return to Lanconia, then we take her. At the same time you will appear in Lanconia and we figure someone will approach you to take the place of the missing princess."

"That way we can find out who engineered the switch," Congressman Smith said.

General Brooks cleared his throat. "The only catch is that you will have to be an American with an American husband."

Aria wasn't sure she was understanding. They were going too fast for her. "But I am not an American. How will they think I am American?"

"We'll teach you."

"But *why?*" she gasped. Suddenly, she just wanted to go home. She was tired of strange food, of strange customs, of using a language she had to think about before every word. She was tired of people acting as if she were a spy and maids who cursed her because she wanted her hose put on. She was tired of dealing with things and people that she did not understand. Desperately, she wanted to go *home.*

General Brooks took her hand and squeezed it and she didn't pull away. "If we take the imposter princess and then you show up talking as you do, walking as you do, eating cookies with a knife and fork, the men who first tried to kill you are going to do it again—but this time they may succeed. We want to create a need for another woman who looks like you, then we hand them an American who they'll probably want to train to be a princess."

"Train *me* to be a princess?" The absurdity of that statement brought her out of her homesickness.

General Brooks smiled at her but the others watched with faces of great seriousness.

Aria decided she had better try to comprehend their plan. "I am to learn to be an American and then learn to be a princess?"

"Think you can do it?" Congressman Smith snapped.

She looked down her nose at him. "I shall do quite well at the princess impersonation."

All the men except Congressman Smith laughed.

"But I do not need an American husband for this," Aria said. Perhaps if she went along with part of their plan, they would forget the more ridiculous aspects.

General Lyons leaned forward. "The fact is, the only way we're willing to risk our necks for you is if you put an American on the throne beside you. If you don't agree, you can walk out that door and we've never heard of you."

She took a moment to respond. They could *not* be serious. "But I have agreed to give you the vanadium."

Congressman Smith looked at her and his eyes were cold. "The truth is, we want more. The vanadium is for now, during the war. We want military bases in Lanconia after the war. We want a place where we can keep an eye on Germany and Russia."

"If you win this war," Aria said, some of her growing anger showing. "If Germany wins, then Lanconia will have an American prince consort—an enemy." She had to protect her own country.

"We won't lose and he's to be made king," Congressman Smith said in a cold, cutting voice.

"I cannot—" Aria began, but closed her mouth. They asked so *much.* They asked for diplomatic sacrifices and military sacrifices as well as personal sacrifices. She looked at her hands. But if she didn't agree, what did she have? America was the strangest place she had ever encountered and to have to live here forever . . .

She looked up and saw the men staring at her. The door opened and a woman in uniform came in and whispered something to General Brooks. He nodded at the others.

"Princess," he said, rising, "we have to leave you for a while. I will have someone escort you to a rest area."

The men walked out, leaving Aria sitting. She would never get over being horrified at American manners but at least they had given her time to think. She followed an armed guard to a waiting room.

* * *

The six men walked into a room that held fourteen tired, red-eyed enlisted personnel. None of them had had any sleep in the last three days as they had gathered information on the candidates for Princess Aria's husband. They had been given carte blanche for military transport to return to hometowns to talk to anyone who remembered a candidate. One woman had had three permanent waves in three days in three towns because she knew that the best place for gossip was the beauty parlor. Now, the fourteen researchers were too tired to do anything but sit and stare.

As the six men entered, the group wearily stood and saluted, and one lieutenant stepped forward, papers in hand.

"What did you find out?" Congressman Smith asked impatiently.

"I'm afraid it's not very good. Charles Thomas Walden," the lieutenant read. He told of the magnificent family tree of this young man.

"Sounds pretty good to me," General Brooks said. "What's wrong with him?"

"He's a homosexual, sir."

"Next one," the general barked.

The next man, the businessman, had married a woman from the wrong side of the tracks when he was sixteen and now paid her enormous sums to keep out of his life. There had been no divorce.

Another man was a compulsive gambler, another one's family was making a fortune off the war with black-market goods. One of the young congressmen was selling his votes.

"And the last man?" General Brooks asked wearily.

"German grandparents. We could never be sure of his loyalty."

"Now what do we do?" General Lyons asked.

"We're running out of time. The imposter returns to Lanconia in two weeks and she'll award the vanadium contract then. If she gives it to Germany, we'll have to take the war onto Lanconian soil and then no mining will be done."

"I have a brother," one of the WACs said, but no one laughed.

After a moment of silence, a young second lieutenant stood. "Sirs, I have a report that might be of interest to you. It's on the Lieutenant Montgomery who saved the princess's life."

"We don't have time—" Congressman Smith began.

"Read it," General Brooks barked.

"Jarl Tynan Montgomery grew up in a small town on the coast of Maine, a town which his family virtually owns. They are Warbrooke Shipping." The lieutenant paused a moment because he had the room's attention now. Warbrooke Shipping was vast, and when the war broke out the company was the first to convert its plants to making warships. The navy owed much to Warbrooke Shipping.

"His family first came to America during Elizabeth the First's reign—some of them were here to greet the Pilgrims. The family motto is 'Never sell the land,' and they've kept the vow. They still own land in England that once belonged to an ancestor, Ranulf de Warbrooke, who lived in the thirteenth century. In eighteenth-century America they were rich by any standards, but one of the men married a woman named Taggert and the two of them ended up owning half the state of Maine. In the early nineteenth century, some of the Taggerts left the East Coast to seek their fortunes and lost everything until in the 1880s one Kane Taggert made the money back in spades. An aunt of Lieutenant Montgomery's went to

Colorado around the turn of the century and ended up marrying the son of this Kane Taggert. They now live in a marble mansion and own Fenton-Taggert Steel." This was another supplier for the war.

The lieutenant took a breath. "Lieutenant Montgomery is also related to Tynan Mills in Washington State. Besides the money, which the Montgomery family is rolling in, he's got an ancestor who was a grand duchess in Russia, another one who was a French duchess, and several English earls as well as a few gunslingers. His ancestors have fought in—and been decorated in—every American war. Hell, even the *women* in his family have been decorated.

"As for Lieutenant Montgomery himself, I couldn't find a hint of scandal. He's worked in his father's shipyard with his three brothers since he was a kid. He's a loner, spent more time on his boats than on anything else. Good grades in school, three years captain of the local rowing team. Enlisted the morning after Pearl Harbor—as did his brothers—and after boot camp was sent to Italy. A year and a half ago he was brought back to the States, given a commission, and put in charge of converting civilian vessels to military use in Key West. Two months ago a PBM came in too low and hit an ammo igloo and caught fire. Eleven people were killed but Lieutenant Montgomery got the fire out before the ammo blew. He was badly burned, spent a few weeks in the hospital, and was recuperating on the island when he saved the princess."

The lieutenant put down his papers. "In conclusion, sirs, I'd say that this man Montgomery is about as blue blood as America has to offer."

"Absolutely not!" Aria gasped. "Under no circumstances will I marry that rude, boorish man. I will beg on the streets before I marry him." For once in her life she didn't bother trying to cover her emotions. She allowed her disgust, her horror, her repulsion to show to everyone. These Americans were *insane!*

Congressman Smith looked at her with contempt. "If it were only you involved, there would be no problem. I hate to think what this imposter princess and her advisers will do to your country. I hope they don't kill your grandfather." He closed his briefcase. "It was nice meeting you, Princess. I wish you well, whatever happens to you."

Images flew through Aria's mind: Cissy on the throne with someone—a murderer—controlling her. Lanconia had once been a warlike country. Would the murderer enter Lanconia in this war that raged around the world? Some Lanconians, usually older men without children to lose, said the lagging Lanconian economy would be helped greatly if the country joined the war.

Aria imagined living in some American hotel and reading about the war-bombed Lanconian countryside. All those deaths would be *her* fault. To prevent hundreds, maybe thousands of deaths, all she had to do was marry a man she disliked greatly.

"Wait!" she called to Congressman Smith.

He stopped at the door but didn't turn.

"I . . . I will do what you want," she whispered. She kept her back straight, her muscles tight. She felt that if she loosened one little bit, she would dissolve into a heap of tears.

"Lieutenant Montgomery has already been sent for," Congressman Smith said with a smirk before he left the room.

"Bastard," the WAC behind Aria muttered. She took Aria's arm. "Honey, what you need is a good cry. Come with me. I'll take you to General Gilchrist's office. He's away right now and you can be private in there. Is this Montgomery a real jerk?"

Aria allowed herself to be pulled along and the lump in her throat prevented her from talking. She managed to nod.

"Brother!" the WAC replied. "Am I glad I'm an American. Nobody tells an American what to do. I can marry whoever I want." She unlocked a door. "Now, you stay in here. Leave the lights off and nobody'll know you're here. I'll come pick you up at five. Until then I won't have any idea where you went." She winked at Aria and shut the door.

Aria sat down on a little leather-covered sofa and clasped her hands together tightly. If she started to cry, she was afraid she would never stop. She forced herself to visualize her country under attack, then she thought how she was saving it from destruction by this selfless, noble act of hers. Unfortunately, she also kept remembering Lieutenant Montgomery sneering at her, his rudeness, the way he pulled her about, tossed her into boats.

How could such a man be trained to be a prince consort?

The more she thought, the worse she felt. She prayed that her grandfather would understand that she had had to do this.

Chapter Six

Twenty-four hours later the six men who were working on what had become known as the Lanconia Project had dwindled to four. Two men pleaded that they had more pressing matters to attend to and left the conference room. The truth was that if they had found the princess difficult, they weren't prepared for the muleheaded stubbornness of Lieutenant Montgomery.

General Brooks's eyes were red and his throat raw from talking. "The son of a gun still laughing?"

Congressman Smith was too angry to do more than nod.

"What's the latest?" General Brooks asked the pretty young WAC. They had tried using men to talk some sense into Montgomery and that hadn't worked, so they had started using women. So far that had met with no success either.

"J.T. . . . er, ah, Lieutenant Montgomery says he'll stand a court-martial before he marries the princess. When I told him he was wanted because of his family history, he did, however, suggest that we offer Her Royal Highness to one of his brothers. He said that they might be tempted since they hadn't met the—" She looked up. "Expletive delted."

"His brothers?" General Brooks's face showed a little hope.

"I checked, sir," said a young captain. "The eldest brother is in intelligence, so far underground that only the president and two others know where he is. The second brother is now in a hospital. Last week his leg was nearly blown off by machine-gun fire. The third brother married an English girl last month. The family doesn't know of it yet."

General Brooks's face fell. "Any cousins?"

"We don't have *time!*" Congressman Smith said, slamming his fist on the table. "This Montgomery is perfect. He's about as American as a human can get, and he has the looks of a prince." He raised an eyebrow at the fervent agreement from the WAC. "His IQ tested out at one hundred forty-three and he's rich. According to our reports, Lanconia is barely surviving. The Montgomery family's money could put it on its feet."

"And spread American goodwill throughout the country," General Brooks added.

Congressman Smith stacked the papers in front of him. "We can't threaten him and risk losing the support of Warbrooke Shipping—"

"Or Tynan Mills or Fenton-Taggert Steel," the captain added.

"So we'll lie to him."

That succeeded in quieting the room.

Congressman Smith continued. "He can't stand the princess, right? He laughs at the idea of being king so we tell him the marriage is a sham, that he's to think of this as a temporary intelligence operation. He's to live with her, teach her to be an American, take her to Lanconia, then, when she's on the throne again, he can walk away."

"But in Lanconia he finds out the marriage is permanent and he's to be king?" General Brooks asked.

"Something of the sort. We do what we can now to get them married and America's foot in the door. We worry about the consequences later."

"Won't the princess give it away?" the captain asked.

Congressman Smith snorted. "She'd sell her soul for her country. She'll lie to him or do anything else to keep her country. I have a feeling that she has no plans to make Montgomery king. We shall see what he says about that. Well, shall we go? I don't want to give him time to think about this. How long has he been without sleep now?"

The captain looked at his watch. "Thirty-eight hours."

"And food?"

"He's had a sandwich and a Coke in twenty-two hours."

The congressman nodded. "Let's go."

Aria had difficulty concealing her astonishment. "Lieutenant Montgomery did not want to marry a royal princess? He does not want to be married to a queen?"

The WAC was not going to tell Aria the dreadful things J.T. had said about her, that she was inhuman, a piece of marble, that she wasn't anything like a woman, that he would much rather give his love to the statue of Venus de Milo. Instead, the WAC explained what they had had to do to get J.T. to agree to the marriage.

"He believes there will be a—what is that word?"

"Divorce, or annulment."

"But royalty is not permitted to separate—no matter what. A royal princess marries once and that is all." Aria looked at a picture of President Roosevelt on the wall. Too clearly she remembered the time on the island with this insolent, despicable man named Montgomery. For the sake of her country she had agreed to marry him, agreed to spend the rest of her life with him, but now he was saying he didn't want to marry *her*.

"I will not tell him we are to be married for always," she whispered.

"I'm afraid there's more." The WAC cursed Congressman Smith for detailing this job to her. She rather liked the princess, liked anyone who was willing to fight for her country.

"The army had rented a house for the two of you in Virginia, complete with horses and a butler, but the lieutenant refuses to have anything to do with it. He says he wants to return to his job in Key West and you two are to live in a single-family house—no servants, no special privileges. You're to live on his military pay also."

The WAC was well aware that no one had told the princess of J.T.'s wealth, and now, looking at her, the WAC thought she had no idea what J.T. was demanding of her. She couldn't imagine this elegant woman donning an apron and washing a sinkful of dishes. "He says that if you're to learn to be an American, he wants it done properly."

"The lieutenant certainly has many opinions, doesn't he?"

You don't know the half of it, the WAC thought.

"Then you agree to his terms?"

"Do I have a choice?"

"No, I guess not. If you're ready, the chaplain's waiting."

Aria didn't say a word but stood, her head held high. What she was doing was so much more important than the romantic nonsense of a white wedding gown and people wishing her joy and happiness. It didn't matter that the dress she was wearing was one she had had on for two days, that it was wrinkled and sagging in places.

She stood before the door until the WAC opened it.

Outside were waiting six other WACs, all of them smiling happily.

"They don't know who you are," the first WAC whispered. "They think the army's reunited you with your lover and you're to be married today."

"Something old," said one woman holding out a little gold locket. "It's also something borrowed. It was my grandmother's."

"Something new," said another, offering her a pretty little handkerchief.

"And something blue." A third woman gave Aria a corsage of blue-dyed carnations. She pinned it on Aria's shoulders as another woman took Aria's shoe and slipped a penny inside for good luck.

Aria was bewildered by this treatment. So far, the women in America had been very good to her, but the men . . .! She wondered how the women coped with the rude, ill-mannered men.

The conference room was to be used for the ceremony. No one had so much as bothered to push the table out of the way so there was no aisle for her to walk down, no older man to give her away. She walked along the wall beside the WAC toward the group of men at the far end. There were a few men in suits but about a dozen men wore uniforms, their chests resplendent with medals. It seemed that at least there was enough significance to this wedding that some of the higher officials attended.

Lieutenant Montgomery was sitting in a chair, half asleep, his head propped on his arm. His cheeks and chin were dark with unshaved whiskers. His uniform was dirty and rumpled.

Aria's anger rose immediately. Perhaps these men were afraid to tell him how disrespectful he was, but she wasn't afraid. She stood in front of him. "How dare you appear before me looking like that," she said, glaring down at him.

He didn't even open his eyes. "The dulcet tones of Her Royal Highness."

General Brooks took Aria's arm and pulled her to stand in front of the chaplain. "He's had a long few days. Perhaps we shouldn't annoy him until after the ceremony. He might change his mind again."

Aria clenched her hands at her sides. Was she worth so little that she had to beg a man to marry her?

Lazily, J.T. stood. "Want to change your mind, Princess? I'm willing."

She didn't look at him but instead concentrated on an image of Lanconia.

The chaplain hesitated over Aria's name.

"Who?" J.T. said, scratching at his whiskers.

"Victoria Jura Aria Cilean Xenita."

"Yeah, I take her," he said.

Aria glared at him. She promised to love and honor Jarl Tynan Montgomery but she left out the word "obey."

"Your Royal Highness," the chaplain said. "It's love, honor, and obey."

Aria looked at J.T. and didn't say a word.

"We have enough lies today," J.T. said. "Get on with it."

The chaplain sighed. "I now pronounce you man and wife. You may kiss the bride."

J.T. grabbed Aria's wrist. "Hell, I'm going to bed."

Aria barely had time to return the little gold locket to the WAC before J.T. pulled her out of the room.

General Brooks was chuckling. "It looks like they're off to a fine start."

Congressman Smith grunted.

Aria leaned back against the seat of the plain black car the army had provided and concentrated on controlling the smile that was threatening to escape. At the other end of the seat, as far from her as he could get, sat the man who was now her husband. His head was resting against the window and she couldn't see his face, but he had certainly made his feelings clear.

Again Aria had to control her smile. While they were marooned on the island together, he had pretended she wasn't a woman to him. He had also ignored the fact of her royal birth, but somehow that hadn't hurt as much as when he had told her he didn't think she was pretty or appealing. No matter how royal a woman was, she still wanted to be desirable.

Aria closed her eyes a moment. It had been a long two weeks since she had been kidnapped and many awful things had happened to her, but now it was over. She was married—she stole a look at Lieutenant Montgomery as he sprawled in the back seat—and she could have done worse. He might look all right in evening dress and he certainly looked strong enough to carry the heavy state robes. Of course she still had to learn how to be an American, but how difficult could that be? There seemed to be many people doing it with ease.

But first there was her wedding night. Her mother had talked to her about this night, had explained what men did to one and how they were driven to it by a passion not felt by women. Her mother said Aria was always to look her best for her husband and she was to encourage this desire in him—it perpetuated the line.

So tonight was to be her wedding night. Of course her husband was virtually a stranger but then Aria had always expected to marry a man she barely knew. Perhaps after tonight Lieutenant Montgomery wouldn't be so rude to her. Perhaps tomorrow morning he would kneel by her bed and kiss her hand and beg her forgiveness for the terrible things he had said to her. Perhaps after tonight . . .

She hadn't realized that the car had stopped until the driver opened her door. They were back at her hotel. She got out then waited while the driver opened the door for her husband. He had to catch J.T. before he fell.

"We're here, sir," the driver said as J.T. untangled his long body from the car.

J.T. looked at the hotel as if he had never seen one before. "Good," he mumbled, and went inside, leaving Aria standing. He returned a few seconds later, grabbed her arm, and pulled her along behind him.

"Which room is yours?"

"It is a pink one."

J.T. stopped and turned to look at her. His eyes were red and his beard was darkening by the minute. "When you get back here after being gone, how do you find your room?"

"I have to go there." She pointed to the desk. "Sometimes I have to wait, then someone escorts me."

"They didn't give you a key?"

98

"A key to the city? Why no, no one has mentioned it."

He closed his eyes a moment. "Stand right here. Don't move, understand?"

She nodded, then looked away to hide her smile. He was certainly anxious to keep her near him.

After some discussion at the desk and after shaking hands with Mr. Catton, J.T. returned and led her to the elevator. "I'll never be more glad to get into bed in my life," he said when the doors closed.

Aria did smile at that.

He unlocked the door to the room, went inside, leaving her standing in the hallway. A moment later his arm shot out, caught her hand, and pulled her inside. He stood very close to her as he locked the door and Aria modestly looked at her clasped hands. Now they were alone.

J.T. yawned and stretched. "Bed. I can see it," he said, and began to stagger through the living room into the bedroom. He got one shoe off then fell across the bed and was asleep.

Aria was still standing by the door. She waited a few minutes but heard no sound from the bedroom, so she timidly crossed the room. He was already in bed. He seemed to be asleep but she knew he was waiting for her.

"I'll . . . I'll get ready," she whispered, and went to the bureau to get a nightgown.

She saw immediately that there was nothing appropriate for her wedding night. This was a night that happened only once in a woman's life and she wanted to look her best.

She glanced at J.T. and thought he looked suspiciously as if he were asleep. A moment later he twitched and made a noise like a snore.

Glancing at the little clock by the bed, she saw that it was only four P.M. Perhaps she could go to one of those American stores she had seen on the way here and get a proper nightgown—one that would keep a new husband from sleeping.

Softly, she crept from the room after checking that her handbag had a clean handkerchief. All the green money papers Lieutenant Montgomery had given her were gone.

She did what she always did when she wanted to go out: she asked for Mr. Catton and he got a car for her and paid the driver. She had some difficulty explaining where she wanted to go without losing her dignity. He finally asked a pretty young girl who worked in the hotel and soon Aria was on her way.

The taxi driver let her off in front of a very large building; Aria had never seen a department store before. Perhaps it was the way she carried herself or perhaps it was the sight of a Paris original dress, but three women nearly ran to wait on her. She chose the oldest woman.

"I wish to be shown ladies' sleeping attire."

"Right this way, ma'am," said the saleswoman, feeling superior for having been chosen.

Two hours later, the woman was not so pleased. Aria had tried on every nightgown in the store and discarded most of them on the floor. The saleswoman had difficulty keeping up the supply and refolding them, as well as having to help Aria take them off and on.

At last Aria seemed to settle on a low-cut, off-the-shoulder, heavenly concoction of pink silk voile and satin.

The saleswoman sighed in relief. "If you'll come with me, I'll box it for you." When she found she had to help Aria dress, she also found she was losing her temper.

Moments later the saleswoman was slamming the nightgown into a box. "Expected me to wait on her like I was her damned servant or something."

"Shh," said her fellow employee. "The floor walker will hear you."

"I'll let *him* deal with her."

Aria came out of the dressing room just in time to see the clerk close the lid on the pink nightgown. As the woman turned away to make out the sales slip, Aria picked up the box and started walking toward the door.

"Oh my God!" the clerk gasped. "She's *stealing* it."

The telephone rang eleven times before J.T. awoke fully enough to answer it. "Yes?" he said groggily.

"You Lieutenant Montgomery?"

"Last I heard I was."

"Well, this is Sergeant Day at the Washington Police Department and we got a lady down here under arrest for shoplifting. Says she's your wife."

J.T. opened his eyes more fully. "Have you booked her?"

"Not yet. She says she's valuable to the war effort, but then she's sayin' a lot of things. She's too much of a screwball for us to make out. She says she has no last name and that she's a queen and we're to call her Your Majesty."

J.T. ran his hand over his face. "Princess, and it's Your Royal Highness."

"How's that?"

"Sergeant, it may seem hard to believe but she *is* valuable—at least to somebody. If you lock her up, it could cause a lot of problems with the government.

101

Could you just put her in a room and give her a cup of tea? And give her a saucer with her cup."

There was a pause from the sergeant. "You really *marry* this fruitcake?"

"Lord help me but I did. I'll be there as soon as I can."

"We'd sure appreciate your takin' her off our hands."

J.T. hung up the phone. "Who's going to take her off *my* hands?" he mumbled.

Chapter Seven

Aria sat in the chair in the glass-walled office in the police station and tried her best to ignore the gaping people on the other side of the glass. They had put a heavy white mug of what they had told her was tea beside her, but for some odd reason, they had put the cup in an ashtray. She hadn't considered touching it.

The last few hours had been miserable, what with people touching her, shouting at her, and asking the same questions over and over—and they hadn't believed her answers.

She was almost glad when she saw Lieutenant Montgomery's unshaven face appear in the room outside. He gave her one quick, angry glance then was surrounded by all the people who had moments before been shouting at Aria. She wanted to see how an American handled these other Americans. He distributed several of the green money papers, signed some white papers, and all the while talked to the people, but she couldn't hear what he was saying.

She was sure she could have done the same thing if she had just understood what they wanted. Perhaps it was going to be *very* easy to learn to be an American.

The crowd moved away from Lieutenant Montgomery and he strode toward her.

"Let's go," he growled after throwing open the door. "And not one word from you or I'll let them have you."

Aria held on to the box containing her nightgown and left the room, her head held high.

He didn't speak to her on the way back to the hotel and constantly he walked in front of her. Once inside the room, he went to the telephone.

"Room service?" he said. "I want dinner sent up to the Presidential Suite. No, I don't have a menu. Send me dinner for four, whatever you have, and a bottle of wine, the best you have in the cellar. Just hurry it up."

Aria stood there blinking at him when he had hung up.

"Could you keep out of trouble for a while? All I want is a decent meal, some sack time, a shower, and I'll be all right. Just give me that and maybe then I can tackle you and the U.S. government."

Aria didn't understand half of what he was saying, but she did understand that he planned to eat dinner now. She blushed. After dinner he would make her his wife.

"The woman who was my maid did not return. If you would draw my bath, I will ready myself," she said softly.

"Haven't even learned to fill your own bathtub yet?" he said with wonder in his voice. "Come on then and I'll show you."

She gave him a hesitant smile. "Don't the maids of American wives draw their baths? Perhaps we should call Mr. Catton and ask for someone?"

"Honey, American wives don't have maids, and from now on, neither do you. From now on you dress yourself, bathe yourself, and, what's more, I'm going to teach you how to take care of a husband."

Aria looked away to hide her red cheeks. He was a little rough, and more than a little rude as he showed her how to adjust the water, but she learned. He left her alone when room service knocked.

She took a long time in the tub, soaping herself and contemplating the coming event. Lieutenant Montgomery called to her twice that her food was getting cold but she still didn't rush.

It wasn't easy dressing alone, but the beautiful nightgown did just slip over her head so she managed. For several minutes she had not heard anything from the other side of the door and she supposed he was readying himself also.

Cautiously, she opened the door.

In the living room stood a large table with the remains of a banquet. The cad had eaten their wedding supper without her! Nose wrinkled, she looked at the dirty dishes, which seemed to be all that was left of the feast. This man might teach her how to fill a bathtub but she planned to teach him some manners.

She turned toward the bedroom. He was sprawled on his back on one side of the bed, a newspaper over his face. He didn't move when she tried to pull back the spread and get into the bed. Even when she gave an unladylike yank, he didn't move.

Taking a deep breath, she lay down on top of the spread beside him, her hands clenched at her side. "I am ready," she whispered.

He didn't move, so she repeated herself. He still didn't move.

Even for a husband, this man's conduct was beyond the limits of decent good taste. She pushed the newspaper off his face. He was sleeping with his mouth half open, and with his whiskers he looked like the town idiot.

"I am ready!" she bellowed into his face in a very unprincesslike fashion, then lay down again.

"Ready?" he mumbled, coming awake slowly, then sitting up with a jolt. "Fire!" he said, then seemed to realize where he was. He turned and looked at Aria, his eyes going up and down her lavishly clad body.

Aria kept her hands at her sides, her legs stiff, and her eyes on the ceiling. This was it. This was when men turned into basic animals—all men did this, her mother had said, whether king or chimney sweep. And now was her turn to be ravaged.

"Ready for what?" Lieutenant Montgomery asked groggily.

"The wedding night," she said, and closed her eyes against the coming pain. Would he hurt her terribly?

She opened her eyes when she heard him laugh.

"The wedding night?" he said, laughing. "You think that I . . . ? That you and me . . . ? That's a good one. Is that why you spent half the night in the bathroom?"

He was *laughing* at her.

"Listen, lady, I married you only to help with the war. No other reason. I don't have any designs on your body, no matter what silly thing you wear, but most of all, I don't want anything to stand in the way of our ending this marriage once you get back on your throne. I somehow think your Count Julie will frown on your carrying my brat. Now, will you go in the other room and let me get some sleep? But don't leave the hotel! Next time you'll probably do something that'll cause another country to declare war on us."

Aria was thankful for her years of schooling that had shown her how to control her emotions. To be rejected as a princess was one thing but to be rejected as a woman was hurting her deeply.

"Out!" he said. "Get out of my bed. Go sleep in the other room. Here, I'll call housekeeping and have the couch made up for you."

With all the dignity she could muster, Aria rose from his bed. "No, Lieutenant Montgomery, I will manage on my own." She did not want another woman to know she had been rejected on her wedding night. She walked into the living room. Behind her, he closed the door loudly with a muttered, "Damn!"

Aria sat on the couch for the rest of the night. She did not close her eyes once. She kept thinking of all the things she should have done, should have said, but what she remembered most clearly was how much trouble she had gone to to please him and he had rejected her.

She hated him.

She wasn't well acquainted with the emotion but she certainly recognized it. Several of her ancestors had made marriages, for political reasons, with husbands or wives they hated. In the eighteenth century one couple had not spoken for over twenty years. Of course the woman had three children during that time, all of them looking like her husband the king, Aria thought.

She sat rigidly on the couch waiting for daylight. She would learn what he had to teach her so that she could get her country back, but all hope of anything else between them was gone. Perhaps her sister could produce an heir to the throne.

Aria did not cry—and holding the tears back now was much more difficult than when she had broken her arm.

* * *

J.T. woke slowly, his mouth tasting foul, his eyes heavy, and a pain in his back. He lifted himself and removed his twisted belt from where it was gouging in his kidney. He still wore his uniform and his shirt was twisted tightly about his body.

He knew without looking that the princess wasn't in bed beside him and he also somehow knew that she was in the living room of the suite. Probably sulking, he thought with a grimace. Probably hating him even more because he wasn't doing what she thought he should.

He closed his eyes a moment and thought of the past events. She had been impossible since the day he had rescued her. She had been demanding, overbearing, autocratic, always wanting more from him. No matter how much he gave, she expected more. He handed her an enormous amount of money—his money, which he had been saving for a new boat—and she never so much as said thank you.

He had never been so glad to get rid of anyone in his life as when he put her on that train and sent her to Washington. He sincerely hoped he would never have to see her again.

But he had not been so privileged. A few days later, by order of the president, J.T. was "requested" to go to D.C. They did everything but put a gun to his head in order to enforce their "request."

No one would tell him what was wanted of him but he knew it had something to do with Her Royal Pain in the Neckship. Repeatedly, he cursed having met the woman.

Almost as soon as the army plane landed, they started on him. They wanted him to *marry* that bitch. At first he had merely laughed at them but he couldn't laugh for long. They denied him food, drink, and sleep. They pounded at him hour after hour, preying on everything he held sacred. They talked about how he was betraying his country, how he was betraying his family's name. They said they would give him a dishonorable discharge and send him home to live with the disgrace. They sent a woman in to talk to him. She purred at him, said the marriage would only be temporary and America needed him so badly.

He had agreed at long last because he realized they were telling him the truth. America did need someone to help the princess, and her country's mineral deposits and strategic location were important to the war effort.

He was exhausted by the time he entered the conference room where some of the biggest brass of both army and navy were waiting for him. Someone had pity on him and gave him a chair and he immediately put his head down and was nearly asleep when he was woken by the princess giving him orders as if he were her lackey.

He would have liked to wring her little neck. He had agreed to help her get her country back—this was something *she* wanted—yet she had the audacity to belittle him.

All through the short service she stood like a martyr readying herself for sacrifice. J.T. saw the other people giving him hostile looks, as if he were doing something vile to this lovely woman. *Lovely, ha!* he wanted to yell. He had already saved her life, spent two years' savings on her, put up with one nasty remark after another from her, yet *he* was being cast as the villain.

Even the WACs were giving him hostile looks, and that was something else that was further angering J.T. He had never had trouble with girls before. At home his family was the richest in town, he and his brothers weren't bad to look at, and he had always liked girls. It had, until now, seemed to be a devastating combination. But since he had met the princess, every woman seemed to look at him as if he were the devil incarnate. Yet as far as he could tell, he had done nothing wrong. He had saved her from drowning and he had even agreed to marry her—but everyone seemed to think he had done something horribly wrong.

After the ceremony, all he had wanted to do was sleep. It had been an ordeal getting the princess back to the hotel. She didn't lead and she refused to follow. Every two minutes he had to turn around to see if she was still with him—which she usually wasn't—then he had to go back and get her. He barely made it to the bed before he was asleep.

When the telephone rang and the man said she had been arrested for shoplifting, it seemed a perfect end to a hideous week. He dragged himself to the police station and there she sat with that haughty look on her face, as if she expected someone to save her.

Of course she didn't say one word of thanks to him for once again saving her ass. She just sat there as if expecting a red carpet to be rolled out for her to walk on.

At the hotel *he* had almost apologized to *her*. He had tried to explain how tired he was, how hungry, but it didn't affect her. She could have been carved out of marble. Her perfect little face was set into a cold, perfect little mask.

He ordered food, then had to show her how to work the bathtub. He planned to nip this trend in the bud right away or she would have him playing her maid.

He was glad to get rid of her when room service knocked. She stayed in the tub the entire time he was eating. He was a little chagrined at himself for having eaten all four dinners and he meant to tell her to order herself something else, but the bed seemed to be calling him. He fell asleep before she left the bathroom.

The next thing he knew someone was yelling "Ready!" in his ear. He came awake suddenly, sitting upright and thinking there was another ammo fire. It took him a moment to get his bearings.

The princess was lying beside him, wearing some frilly pink thing, her fists clenched at her side, her legs stiff—in fact her whole body was so rigid she could have been made out of steel. It took him a minute to understand that she expected him to ravish her. He had never seen anything as undesirable in his life as this cold, unfeeling woman.

He didn't know whether to laugh or rage at her. It made him angry that she seemed to have successfully reduced him to her idea of a primitive male who wouldn't be able to control himself at the sight of a beautiful female in his bed wearing a low-cut, gossamer-thin nightgown that clung to and outlined every one of her not-inconsiderable curves.

The next thing he knew he was yelling at her.

Her expression didn't change—after all marble didn't move. She got up from the bed and left the room.

Immediately, he had felt guilty, as if *he* had done something wrong. He turned on his stomach and punched his pillow with his fist. If she would just smile at him, just show him that she *could* be human. *If* she could be human, that is. It took him awhile before he could go back to sleep.

Now, he looked at the clock and knew it was time to get up. Maybe he had dreamed the whole thing. Maybe he wasn't married to the haughty princess after all. Maybe he was just plain Lieutenant Montgomery and not Public Enemy Number One.

At nine the next morning Aria looked up as Lieutenant Montgomery emerged from the bedroom, still wearing his rumpled uniform, his jaw now black with whiskers. He looked like a pirate.

"It's true then," he mumbled, looking at her with eyelids still heavy with sleep. "I thought maybe I dreamed all of it."

She rose from the couch, not letting him see her stiffness.

"About last night . . ." he began.

She started past him toward the bathroom.

He caught her arm and pulled her around to face him. "Maybe last night I was a little too harsh. The brass kept me awake for hours, then when I finally got to sleep I get a call saying you're in jail."

She looked at him with cold eyes.

"Is that what you stole?" he asked, his voice lowering, one hand moving to touch her shoulder. "It's nice."

"It is a—as I believe you called it—'silly' garment." She moved away from him but he grabbed the long, flowing skirt of her negligée.

"I'm trying to tell you that I'm sorry about last night. You could have been Rita Hayworth and I wouldn't have touched you. I didn't mean to hurt your feelings."

"You did not," she lied, chin up. "I merely misunderstood the situation. If you will release me and allow me to dress, we can get started on my learning to be an American."

"Sure," he said with anger. "The sooner we get this done, the sooner you can get your kingdom and I can go back to controlling my own life."

She did not slam the bathroom door; she was able to control herself that much. She looked at herself in the mirror. Was she so unattractive? Perhaps her nighttime braid was too tight, perhaps she didn't look so young and carefree as the pretty American girls she saw, but was she really so undesirable?

She dressed in a simple little Mainbocher suit: slim skirt, padded shoulders, a little veiled hat perched over her left eye. She had a devil of a time with the seams in the hose but she managed at last.

Lieutenant Montgomery was lounging in a chair when she emerged. "Finally," he muttered, barely looking at her before entering the bathroom.

He emerged shaved and showered, a towel around his waist. Aria left the room.

He started lecturing her the moment they left the suite. He showed her how to use the room key, and the elevator. He lectured her about menus and American waiters. They ate breakfast and he said nothing to her that wasn't a criticism: she was holding her fork in the wrong hand, she was to use her hands to eat her bread and not cut it with a knife and fork, she was not allowed to return her eggs, which she had ordered soft-boiled and received scrambled. And in between his corrections he handed her change and told her how to count it, laying little piles of coins on the tablecloth and making her total the amounts in her head between bites. He was ready to leave when she was only half finished.

"We haven't got all day," he said, pulling back her chair. "Every American should know about the nation's capital."

He made a telephone call then half pulled her along to a waiting military car.

All day they went sightseeing. He dragged her through one building after another, lectured her on the history of the place, then impatiently waited while she got back into the car and they were off again. When they were in the car, he told her about glorious American women who had died for their country, women who were afraid of nothing, women who lived for their men. He seemed especially taken with someone named Dolley Madison.

"What's that?" Aria asked just as he was shoving her back into the car after seeing a statue of someone named Lincoln.

"It's a drugstore. Come on, let's go. We still got the Smithsonian to go to and the Library of Congress."

"What are they drinking?"

"Cokes. We don't have time for lollygagging, let's go."

Aria watched the drugstore until it was out of sight. How she would like to do something pleasant.

At the Smithsonian, they met Heather. She was a plump little blonde who came hurrying around a corner and nearly ran into them.

"Excuse me," she said, then the next moment she squealed and said, "J.T.!" She dropped the leather portfolio she was carrying, threw her arms around J.T., and kissed him passionately.

Aria stood by and watched without much interest except to note that Americans acted this way on public streets.

"J.T., honey, I've missed you so much. How long are you in town? Let's do the town tonight. Then later we can go back to my place. My roommates can leave us alone for a few hours. What do you say?"

"Baby, there's nothing I'd like better. You don't know how good it is to see a woman smile at me. The last few days of my life have been sheer hell."

Aria walked away at that. She didn't halt when J.T. yelled, "Wait a minute!"

He caught up with her, holding Aria's arm with one hand and the blonde's with the other.

"J.T., who is this?" the blonde demanded.

"This is Prin . . . I mean—" He looked at Aria. "What *is* your name?"

"Victoria Jura Aria Cilean Xenita."

After a moment's pause, J.T. said, "Yeah, that's right. Vicky. And this is Heather Addison."

"Aria," she corrected. "My family calls me Aria."

Heather looked at J.T. suspiciously. "And what do *you* call her?"

Aria smiled sweetly. "Wife," she said.

Heather gave J.T.'s cheek a resounding slap then turned on her heel and walked away.

"Stay here," he ordered Aria, and took off after Heather.

Aria smiled to herself and felt good for the first time in days. It had been very nice to see that man slapped. Across the street was one of those drugstores. She waited for the light just as J.T. had instructed her then crossed the street and went into the store. Several people, young men in uniform and girls in thick socks and brown and white shoes, were sitting on red stools.

Aria sat on an empty one.

"What'll you have?" asked an older man in a white apron.

She searched her memory for the word. "A coat?"

"What?"

A handsome young man in a blue uniform moved down to the stool beside her. "I think she means a Coke."

"Yes," Aria said, smiling. "A Coke."

"Cherry?" the man asked.

"Yes," she answered promptly.

"You live around here?" the soldier asked.

"I live—I am staying at the Waverly Hotel."

115

"Plush. Listen, I got a few friends in town and tonight we're going out to do the town."

"Do the town," she murmured, just what Miss Addison had said. The man served her a Coke in a strange glass that was metal with a paper cone in it. There was a straw in it. She glanced at the teenage girls and mimicked them. Her first sip nearly choked her, but when her mouth and throat adjusted to the bubbles, she found the drink delicious.

"What do you say?" the soldier beside her asked.

Another soldier walked up behind her. "A babe like this to go out with scum like you? Listen, honey, I know a couple of nightspots where we can dance 'till dawn then—"

A third soldier moved behind her. "Don't listen to them. Neither one of them knows how to treat a *real* lady. Now, I know a place over on G Street that—"

He broke off as J.T. shoved his way between them.

"Take your turn, buddy, we saw her first."

"You want to *eat* all those teeth of yours? I married the woman yesterday."

"Don't look to me like you're taking very good care of her."

Aria kept her head bent over her Coke but she was smiling. Oh how she was smiling. She glanced down the bar toward the teenage girls who were also smiling. One of them winked at her and Aria decided that this was a part of America she rather liked.

"Come on," J.T. said angrily, grabbing her arm. "Let's get out of here."

"Wait! I have to pay for my Coke." After her bout with the police, she knew she had to pay for everything.

"That's all right, I'll do it," the soldiers said in unison.

"No, no, I must learn your money." Deftly, she

moved out of J.T.'s grip and made her way through the hovering soldiers. She asked the man behind the bar how much the Coke was then took her time opening her handbag and her change purse. "A nickel is this one, isn't it?" she said, holding up a quarter.

The men fell all over themselves helping her find the correct coin.

"You're French, aren't you? I knew it the moment I saw you."

"Oui, I speak a little French."

J.T. pulled her out of the crowd and out of the store. He didn't say a word until they were in the car.

"You just can't obey, can you? I'm doing my best to teach you how to be American and what do you do but run off and display yourself like a common tramp."

"Not like Heather," she said under her breath, not meaning for him to hear.

But he did hear. "Leave my friends out of this. In fact, leave *me* out of this. I *am* an American. *You* are an American *wife.* You are not some French floozy who sits in drugstores and lets men ogle her. You conduct yourself in a proper manner. You'd think that being a princess you'd have some idea of decent conduct, but it's obvious you don't. The American wife is a lady. She is respectful to her husband, she obeys him—which you wouldn't even do in our phony marriage ceremony. And she—"

"You remember that but you do not remember my name?"

He ignored her. "The American wife helps her husband in every way that she can. She listens to him; she learns from him; she—"

He lectured her every minute during their sightseeing excursion until Aria began to feel that her brief adventure in the drugstore had branded her as a cross between Nell Gwyn and Moll Flanders. She tried her best to pay attention to the American pictures in the National Gallery but she saw other couples holding hands, the men sneaking kisses, the women giggling. "I don't guess they're married, are they?" she asked J.T. "Or else they wouldn't be acting like that. The women would be doing something dutiful."

He didn't answer but read aloud another paragraph from the guidebook.

Waiting in their hotel room was a three-foot stack of history books.

"I had them sent," J.T. said, "and they're all textbooks with questions at the end. You're to read a chapter then I'll quiz you on it. Get started while I take a shower."

"Get started while I take a shower," Aria mocked, and held up a book to throw at the closed bathroom door but then she saw a newspaper on the bureau and above one column the words LANCONIA'S PRINCESS TO VISIT NEW YORK MONDAY.

"Lanconia," she said to herself. "Lanconia. I must learn to be an American so their government will help me get my kingdom back." She opened the first textbook and began to read.

J.T. came out of the bathroom, wearing only his trousers, just as the telephone rang. He listened to the person on the other end. "No, baby, I'm not mad at you," he said in a tone she had never heard him use before.

Aria looked up from her history book. His bare back was to her and she found the sight not unpleasant. Muscles moved about as he talked. There were scars on one side of him, more healed than they were on the island, but she did not find them unattractive.

"Yeah, I might be able to get away. After the work I've done today, I need a break." Abruptly, he turned to look at Aria, who looked back at her book. "No, no problem at all. I'll see you here in half an hour."

Aria didn't say a word when he hung up the telephone nor did she say anything when he emerged from the bedroom in a dark blue uniform, clean shaven, and she could smell the fresh scent of lotion across the room.

"Look, I'm going out for a while. You have enough to do that you don't need me. Call room service and order yourself dinner. I might be late." He didn't say another word but left the room.

Aria's mother had explained about men's infidelities and said that they were something a wife had to bear, but she had not described how they made a woman feel. Aria went to the window and looked down at the street. J.T. was leaving the hotel, his arm around the plump Heather, and as Aria watched, he kissed her.

Aria turned around, her fists clenched to her side. *"Kneq la ea execat!"* she muttered, then put her hand to her mouth at her use of such language.

She called room service and ordered caviar, pâté de foie gras, champagne, and oysters. She glanced at the stack of history books. "And send me a selection of your American magazines."

"You want movie mags, confessions, or what?" the bored woman on the other end asked.

"Yes, anything. And I'd like a Coke, no, two Cokes and . . . and a whiskey."

There was a pause on the other end of the phone. "How'd you like a couple of rum and Cokes?"

"Yes, that will do fine." She dropped the telephone.

The meal arrived with a stack of the oddest magazines Aria had ever seen, all about people she had never heard of with the most intimate stories told about them. She read while she ate, while she bathed, and after she climbed into bed wearing a sedate white nightgown. She thought that Lieutenant Montgomery could sleep on the couch. The thought of him made her bury her nose deeper in the magazines. MY HUSBAND BETRAYED ME WITH ANOTHER WOMAN. She read that story avidly.

Chapter Eight

T HE next morning an awful sound woke Aria and she opened her eyes to see Lieutenant Montgomery lying beside her, on top of the covers, snoring loudly. She hadn't been aware of when he had returned to the room.

The telephone rang, and as it was on his side of the bed, she wasn't going to lean across him to answer it. He picked it up on the sixth ring.

"Yeah, this is Montgomery." He listened for a moment then turned and looked at Aria. "Yeah, she's right here with me. Yeah, in the same bed, not that it's any of your business." He moved the phone away from his mouth. "How soon can you be ready to fly to Key West?"

"As soon as someone packs my—"

"An hour," J.T. interrupted. "Pick us up in an hour."

He dropped the telephone then sat up. "An American wife packs her own bags and her husband's. Oh

121

damn, my head. You can get started while I take a shower."

Aria had no intention of obeying him. She called room service and ordered herself breakfast then picked up a magazine that carried photographs of Mr. Gary Cooper.

Minutes later, J.T. snatched the magazine from her hand. "What is this trash? Where did you get this and why aren't you dressed yet? You ought to have half the bags packed. Listen, Princess, if you want to be an American, you better make an effort to learn. How many of the history books did you read last night?"

"The same number that you did. If you think that I am going to pack your suitcases—"

She was interrupted by a loud knock and a call of "Room service."

When he saw that she had ordered only one breakfast, he was furious. He said she had no idea what it meant to be a wife and she pointed out that she couldn't order for him as she had no idea what he liked to eat. He said it was obvious to him that she wasn't really interested in being an American or in helping her country.

That made Aria stop arguing. Very calmly, she went to the telephone and ordered a second breakfast, the particulars of which he dictated to her with an air of smugness that she hated.

She kept trying to remember how she had come to be under this detestable man's rule and how important Lanconia was to her, but it was difficult. He sat at the table and ate while she tried to pack all their clothes, eating her eggs while packing. He ate; she worked. He read the newspaper; she worked.

"Why do American women *do* this?" she muttered. "Why don't they revolt?"

"Are you ready yet?" he asked impatiently. "Why does it always take women so long to dress?"

She looked at the back of him and imagined hitting him with a suitcase. Her mother's lessons in princess-like behavior had not prepared her for this.

The telephone rang and it was a soldier saying their transportation was downstairs.

"Does an American wife also *carry* the luggage?" she asked innocently.

"If her man wants her to, she does," he answered. He called the bellhop and they brought a cart for Aria's many bags.

They were given transport on an army carrier, but this time there was no attempt to make the interior luxurious. J.T. dozed in his seat, opening his eyes only now and then to make sure Aria was reading the history book he had brought with him. He quizzed her on Christopher Columbus and then on the Pilgrims. She answered all his questions correctly but he didn't give her one word of praise.

When she started on the third chapter, he fell asleep, so Aria removed one of her movie magazines from her purse and placed it in front of the history book. She might have succeeded if she hadn't leaned her head back and also fallen asleep. The book fell open on her lap.

"What is this?" J.T. demanded, startling her awake.

"It's swell, isn't it?" she asked, half awake.

To her surprise, she saw J.T. almost smile but he seemed to catch himself. "You're supposed to be reading about Colonial America," he said softly. The noise of the plane enclosed them and their heads were close together.

He was quite good-looking from this distance. "Isn't there more to America than history?"

"Of course. There's entertainment." He nodded to her movie magazine. "But you've seen that. And there's family. Maybe I can explain how the American family works."

"Yes, I would like to hear something besides history."

He thought for a moment. "Everything in the American family is absolutely equal, divided fifty/ fifty. The man earns the money; the woman takes care of the house. No, wait, it's not really fifty/fifty, it's more sixty/forty or perhaps seventy/thirty since the man's duties carry a backbreaking responsibility with them. He's the one who always has to provide for his wife and children. Whatever they need, it is his duty to give it to them, to make sure they want for nothing. He works day after day at his job, always giving, always there with that check, asking little in return but giving much. He . . ." J.T. stopped and straightened in his seat. "Well, you get the picture. We men do very well at holding up our end, even while you ladies spend your afternoons drinking tea." He sighed. "And war is our duty too."

"I see," Aria said when he had finished, but she didn't see at all. "By 'take care of the house' do you mean that if the roof leaks she fixes it?"

"No, of course not. She calls a roofer. I mean she cleans the thing, washes the windows and such. Cooks. Of course she doesn't fix the roof."

"She washes windows? What about floors?"

"She cleans *all* of it. It's not such a big deal. After all, it's only housework. Anybody can do it, even a royal princess."

"You say she cooks. Does she also plan menus? Clean the dishes?"

"Of course. The American housewife is very versatile, and self-reliant."

"What if there are guests? Does she cook for them? She doesn't *serve,* does she?"

"I told you that she takes care of the house and whatever's in it. That includes guests."

"Does she take care of clothes?"

"Yes."

"Children?"

"Certainly."

"Who helps her with correspondence?"

"The man usually turns his paycheck over to his wife and she pays the bills, buys the groceries and whatever the kids need."

"I see. And she drives a car?"

"How else can she get to the grocery?"

"Amazing."

"What's amazing?"

"As far as I can tell, the American housewife is a secretary, bookkeeper, chambermaid, chauffeur, caterer, butler, maid, chef, treasurer, lady-in-waiting, and nursemaid. Tell me, does she garden also?"

"She takes care of the yard if that's what you mean, although, if he has time, the man may help on that."

"One woman is lord chamberlain, lord steward, and master of the horse all in one. And yet she has time to spend her afternoons drinking tea. Utterly amazing."

"Could we drop this?" His earlier softness was gone. "It's not like you make it sound."

"Of course men did start the war, didn't they? I don't remember any woman wanting to bomb another woman's children. But then she may have been too busy drinking tea or clipping the hedges or washing the dishes or—"

"I'm going to the can."

Aria picked up her history book but she didn't read

it. Perhaps being an American was going to be more difficult than she thought.

When the plane landed in Key West, there was transportation waiting for them and the driver took them through narrow streets overhung with bright flowers to a two-story house next to a large cemetery. The houses next to it were very close.

J.T. opened the wooden gate with its peeling paint as the car drove off. "I don't know how the navy got us a house. There's a year-long waiting list."

Aria had a hideous vision of standing in line for a full year.

The house was tiny to Aria. The lower floor consisted of one room that was living–dining room, then a half partition hid some of the kitchen. There was a bathroom containing a large white machine also on the first floor. Up steep, narrow stairs was a long room, a double bed at one end, a single bed concealed behind the bathroom wall. The house was filled with wicker furniture and painted in pale blues and pinks.

J.T. hauled all of Aria's luggage upstairs. "I'm going to the base. Unpack our clothes and hang them up. The army said they'd furnish the place so I hope that means food. When you get done, hit those books again." He paused a moment at the head of the stairs, seemed about to say something, then turned and left the house.

There was a balcony leading off the upstairs and Aria went outside to look at the narrow street below and across to the cemetery.

"Hey! Is anybody home?" she heard a man's voice from downstairs.

"J.T.?" she heard a woman call.

How odd, Aria thought. Did people always walk into one another's houses in America? She walked to the head of the stairs. Below her, coming in the door, were three couples.

"Wow!" said one of the men looking up at her. "Are you J.T.'s heartbreaker?"

They all stopped to stare up at her. Aria might not know how to dress herself or how to count money but she was quite confident of herself as a hostess. "How do you do?" she said regally, descending the staircase as if she were floating.

"Princess!" came another voice as Bill Frazier entered the door, a pretty blonde behind him. "I mean . . ." He trailed off, embarrassed.

"I am—" Aria began.

"Princess will do," one man said, laughing. "It suits you. Princess, let me introduce this clan. We came to welcome the new bride." He introduced Carl and Patty, Floyd and Gail, Larry and Bonnie. Bill introduced his lovely wife Dolly to her. There was another guest, a bachelor named Mitch.

Mitch took her arm. "J.T.'s a fool to leave a beauty like you alone."

"*Where* did you get that dress?" Patty asked. They had each brought casseroles and grocery bags of food.

"Is that *silk?*" Bonnie asked. "*Real* silk?"

"I thought you two just flew in today. If I had on a dress like that, it'd be a mass of wrinkles!"

"I think I'd die for a dress like that."

Aria desperately wanted these American women to like her. They wore pretty, flowered cotton sundresses and cool-looking sandals. Each had short hair that looked so young and carefree, and they wore dark red lipstick. Standing before them in her silk suit, her long hair drawn severely back, she felt old-fashioned—and very foreign. They were looking at her expectantly and she searched her mind for something that would please them.

"Lieutenant Montgomery bought me several dresses that are still packed. Perhaps you'd like to see them."

One minute Aria was standing in the living room and the next she was being pushed up the stairs before a herd of stampeding women.

"What about dinner?" a husband called, but no woman answered him.

Ten minutes later the upstairs was a flurry with women pulling clothes from Aria's many suitcases. She began to smile and in another ten minutes she was having *fun!* For the first time in America, she was enjoying herself. She asked if Bonnie would like to try on a Schiaparelli and the next minute the four women were in their underwear.

"I have to show Larry this," Bonnie said, wearing a gorgeous red Worth evening gown.

"In those shoes?" Aria said softly. "With socks? Perhaps these would be better."

She held up a pair of silk stockings.

Bonnie looked as if she were going to cry and reached for them.

Aria held them back. "There's a price."

The woman hesitated. There was something a little daunting about Aria.

"Will you find me a hairdresser who can cut my hair like yours?" Aria asked. "And a place where I can buy cosmetics?"

The evening turned into a fashion show, with the women modeling Aria's gowns, suits, and dresses for their husbands. Dolly was a little too plump for the suits, but what she did for one strapless dress was a sight to behold. The women laughed at the men who started cheering when Dolly descended the stairs.

"Bill was horribly jealous," Dolly said triumphantly.

The smell of roasting meat drifted upward from the tiny backyard.

"J.T. better get back soon or he'll miss the hamburgers," Gail said. "Where is he anyway?"

The women paused, their hands on the clothes.

"He went to his job," Aria said. "Do you think I look all right in this lipstick?"

The women were obviously very curious about her marriage. J.T. went away to rest after his hospital stay, came back exhausted, snapping at everyone, and a few days later a black limo pulled up on the dock, J.T. got in, and then he was gone for days. When he did return, he had a wife.

"I think you look swell," Dolly said, smoothing over the awkward moment. "Let's get this cleaned up and get downstairs. There won't be anything left to eat by the time we get there."

Aria was in her element as hostess. She quietly made sure everyone had enough to eat and that no one's glass was ever empty. It was a little difficult coping without servants but she managed. She caught Dolly watching her a few times and smiled.

J.T. arrived for dessert.

"Here's the bridegroom," Gail called. "Move over, Mitch, and let J.T. sit by his bride."

"This is fine," J.T. said, moving toward Bill and Dolly. "Anything left to eat?"

"No more meat but there's coleslaw, potato salad, shrimp salad, whatever, over there. Help yourself."

J.T. gave Aria a hard look. "My wife will fix me a plate."

For a moment the group was silent, then Aria put her plate aside and stood. "Larry, would you like more apple pie?"

"No thanks, Princess, I've had more than enough."

"Princess?" J.T. asked.

129

"It's my nickname for her," Bill said pointedly.

Aria took a plate and began filling it with food.

J.T. moved to stand across the table from her. "American women wait on their men. They are also good hostesses. Did you make demands that everyone serve you? You didn't use a knife and fork on your hamburger, did you?"

"Lay off her," Bill hissed. "She's doin' just great. Real nice party, Princess."

"Does this please you, master?" Aria asked, handing J.T. a plate heaped with food.

"Don't get smart with me, I'm—Oh, hello, Dolly." He took his plate and left.

Dolly stood for a moment watching Aria, then took her arm. "Let's you and me get together Monday and have a nice long girl talk."

At that moment, someone put on a Glenn Miller record inside the house and Bill asked Dolly to dance. One by one the couples went inside and began to dance in the living room. Only Mitch, J.T., and Aria were left outside.

"Mrs. Montgomery, may I have this dance?" Mitch asked. J.T. never looked up from his plate of food as Mitch escorted Aria inside the house.

Her first encounter with American dancing was shocking to Aria. Even the man to whom she had been engaged had never held her this close.

"Come on, honey, loosen up," Mitch said, holding Aria's stiff body.

"Are American wives, as you say, loose?"

"Where are you from?"

"Paris," Aria answered quickly.

"Ah," he said, and tried to pull her closer but she wouldn't bend. "If you're French, you ought to know a little about love."

"Absolutely nothing," she said quite seriously.

Mitch laughed aloud at that and hugged Aria. "I've always wondered about ol' J.T."

Dolly pulled Bill to dance by Mitch and Aria. "You'd better behave yourself," Dolly said to Mitch, nodding her head toward the back door where J.T. was entering.

The other couples held their breaths as J.T. strode purposely toward Mitch and Aria. But he walked past them as if he didn't see them. "Bill, you got a minute? I want to talk to you about installing the radar."

"Now? This is Saturday night."

"Yeah, well, a war doesn't have weekends. You want to go to the base tomorrow and look at it again?"

"On Sunday?"

J.T. rubbed his jaw. "It's the first radar we've installed and I'm concerned about it, that's all. The damned thing is from Britain and I don't know if it's going to fit our American ships. Probably make the ship sail on the wrong side of the ocean."

Bill smiled but Dolly didn't. "I still think you should spend the day with your wife."

"I got more important things to do. Doll, did you bring any of your chocolate cake?"

"Yes. Can you cut it yourself or should I get your big strong wife to do it for you?" Dolly turned on her heel and left them.

"Is she mad about something? You do something to tee her off?"

"It's not *me,* buddy," Bill said. "How are you and the princess getting along?"

J.T. yawned. "As well as can be expected. She's pretty well useless. I had to teach her how to turn on the bathtub."

"Mitch doesn't seem to think she's useless."

"That's thanks to my teaching. A week ago she'd have been demanding he serve her oysters on a gold platter."

Bill shook his head. He knew the story of why J.T. had married Aria. "She must really want that country of hers. When I met her she wouldn't let anyone touch her and now she doesn't seem to mind Mitch's hands all over her." He looked up at J.T. but J.T. didn't react.

"Is everything about ready for the conversion of the distillation ship?"

"Yeah," Bill said, and there was disgust in his voice. "I think I'll get another beer."

J.T. walked toward Aria and again everyone held his breath as Mitch removed his hands from J.T.'s wife. "I've got some work to do upstairs," J.T. said. "You take care of everybody. And I mean that. Get them whatever they need." J.T. looked at the group of people who were standing quietly. "Stay as long as you want. Have a good time. Good night."

They watched as he mounted the stairs.

"Talk about a wet blanket," Gail muttered.

"What happened to the J.T. I used to know?" Larry asked.

All eyes turned toward Aria as if expecting an answer.

Dolly stepped forward. "How about if we all meet at the ice cream parlor on Flagler tomorrow at eleven?"

"I think J.T.'s going to work," Bill said.

"Well then we'll have to do without him, won't we? We'll pick you up at ten-forty-five . . . Princess," Dolly said, smiling.

It took them only minutes to clean up and get ready to leave. Mitch kissed Aria's hand. "Until tomorrow, Princess," he said.

Aria stood at the door and said good night. She heard Dolly say, "You're going to tell me what's going on, Bill Frazier, if you stay up all night doing it."

Upstairs, J.T. was ensconced in the big bed, a sheet covering the lower half of him, the upper half bare. Papers were all around him.

"I guess the little bed is mine," she said.

"Mmm," was all J.T. answered.

Aria wrinkled her nose at him, but he didn't look up. She opened a chest of drawers and looked at her pile of nightgowns. On impulse she removed the pink silk one she had bought for her wedding night—a wedding night that had never come.

In the bathroom she began humming one of the tunes she had heard that night and remembered being in Mitch's arms. Of course it had been very awkward, and by Lanconian standards, it was very improper, but all in all it had been rather pleasant.

After her bath she brushed her hair loose, letting it flow over her shoulders and down her back. She was still humming and smiling when she left the bathroom and took her clothes to hang them in the closet across from J.T.'s bed. She was getting quite used to taking care of her own wardrobe and was beginning to feel some pride at seeing her clothes neatly hung.

"Who is this Mitch?" she asked J.T. behind her.

"What? Oh, he runs the optical shop."

"Optical? He makes eyeglasses?"

J.T. put down his papers. "His department repairs chronometers and ship watches."

"Then he's an important person?"

"Everyone's needed in the war effort."

"Yes, but how does he rank? Is he your superior?" She sat down on the edge of his bed.

"Oh, I see, you want to know if he's a duke or a prince. Sorry, Princess, but he's not my superior. I have only one boss and he's the industrial manager. I'm Mitch's boss—and Bill's boss and Carl and Floyd and Larry's boss. What's that smell?"

"Perfume from the saleswoman in Miami. He seems very nice."

"You always wear perfume at night?"

"Yes, of course. The others were very nice too. America seems so free and there don't seem to be many rules governing conduct."

"Get off of my bed and go to your own. And don't wear that nightgown again and put your hair in a pigtail. Now get out of here and leave me alone. And take that history book with you. You'll have a test over chapters seven through twelve tomorrow."

"Not if I'm eating ice cream all day," Aria whispered defiantly as she left him. In bed she looked at pictures in the movie magazines and tried to decide how she wanted her hair cut.

"Well, I'll be damned," Dolly Frazier said, leaning against the headboard of the bed.

"Dolly, I don't like my wife using such language." Bill stayed snuggled under the covers, refusing to sit up.

"And I don't like my husband keeping such secrets from me."

Bill turned over to face her. "I thought the whole thing was J.T.'s business. Heaven help the married man who thinks he can keep a secret."

"A princess. A *real* princess right here in Key West and I met her. Do you realize that someday she'll be a *queen?* And if J.T. stays married to her, maybe he'll be king. I would know a king *and* a queen."

Bill turned back again. "J.T. doesn't *want* to be king. You know his background. He's got more money than ninety percent of the kings of this world. He married the princess to give her a cover and to teach her to be an American. As soon as everything is set up in Lanconia, he takes her back there and the marriage is annulled."

"Teaching her to be an American, ha! Did you see that stack of history books? And the way he made her wait on him! I think the two of them didn't get along too well on that island and J.T.'s still mad at her."

"He says she's a nuisance, that she's been waited on all her life and expects everything to be done for her. She'd never even dressed herself and he says she expects him to walk two paces behind her."

"I didn't see anything like that."

"She was arrested for shoplifting in D.C. Didn't know she had to pay for things, and he says she hands out hundred-dollar bills to porters."

"So what did he do, make her learn to count money?"

"Of course," Bill said, bewildered. "What else was he supposed to do?"

"Take her shopping. That's the only way to learn about money."

"He took her shopping in Miami. Spent a bundle. Dolly, baby, could we get some sleep now?"

"Sure. I was just thinking, though. What if J.T. fell in love with her? Then he wouldn't want to leave her and he'd stay and be king."

"I'm not sure an American can be king."

"Of course he can. If he's married to the queen, then he's king. I wonder if Ethel would open her beauty parlor on Sunday? I think I'll call right now and ask her."

"Dolly, it's two o'clock in the morning," Bill said, but Dolly was already out of bed.

"She won't mind. We'll make the princess so beautiful J.T. won't be able to resist her. By the time they get to Lanconia he'll face a firing squad before giving her up."

Bill groaned and pulled the pillow over his head. "What have I done?"

Chapter Nine

G ET up," J.T. said. "This morning you're going to learn to cook my breakfast."

Reluctantly, Aria opened her eyes. J.T., fully dressed in his tan uniform, was standing on the far side of the room and yelling at her as if she were in the next state. She stretched. "What time is it?"

"Breakfast time. Now get up."

"Are you always so loud this early?" She lay back against the pillows. "At home my maid brought a pot of tea to me every morning in bed. It was always served in the Lily set of china. Such a peaceful way to start the day."

J.T. didn't say a word, so Aria turned to look at him. He was watching her with a strange expression on his face and she began to blush as her eyes met his.

"Get up," he repeated, then turned on his heel and went down the stairs.

Smiling to herself, Aria took her time dressing in a silk shantung suit, hoping it was all right for an ice cream parlor visit.

J.T. was sitting in the living room reading a newspaper. "You took long enough." He stood and went into the kitchen.

"This is a skillet. These are eggs. This is butter—or it's what we have instead of butter during a war. Put the butter in the skillet, drop in the eggs. Damn! I forgot the bacon. Get it out of the fridge."

"Fridge?"

He pushed past her and opened the refrigerator. "This is bacon. You'll have to learn to cook it, and before long you'll have to learn to go to the grocery and buy it. Get another skillet out of the bottom of the stove and put the bacon in it."

Aria opened a door and a drawer before finding a second pan like the egg pan but there was nowhere to set it. The top of the stove was covered with an egg carton, a loaf of bread, a pan from last night, eggshells, and odd-looking shiny metal utensils. She thought she could make room by moving the handle of the egg pan.

The hot handle seared her palm and she moved away quickly but she didn't say a word.

"Have you got that bacon in there yet?"

She tried using only her left hand to remove the bacon but it was difficult. Pain was shooting through her body.

"Can't stand to touch it?" J.T. asked angrily. "Here, use both hands."

He grabbed her right hand and Aria gave a slight intake of breath that made J.T. stop and look at her white face. He turned her hand over to look at it. The skin was beginning to blister. He slapped margarine onto her palm.

"You burned yourself that bad and didn't say a word?"

138

She didn't answer but was grateful for the cooling relief of the grease.

"Hell," he said in exasperation. "Stand over there and watch." He finished cooking his breakfast while muttering things about Aria being useless. Then, as he put his food on the table, he again cursed because he realized Aria had no breakfast. While his grew cold, he cooked her bacon and eggs.

At last, they both sat down to eat in absolute silence.

How unpleasant this place is, Aria thought. How different from breakfast at home with her grandfather and sister. She smiled as she thought of how she would entertain them with stories from last night. Her grandfather would laugh loudly at the absurdity of the Americans.

"Care to share that with me?" J.T. asked.

"I beg your pardon."

"You were smiling and I wondered why. I need something to cheer me up."

"Actually, I was thinking of how I'd describe last night to my grandfather."

"And?"

She looked at her breakfast, a bit repulsed by the greasiness of it. "I don't think you'd like it. They are your friends."

J.T.'s eyes narrowed. "I want to know how you'd describe my friends to your royal family."

He said the words with such a sneer that Aria didn't care what he thought. Her grandfather often said that commoners had no sense of humor, that they took themselves very seriously and were always concerned about their dignity.

Aria's face immediately changed expression as she opened her mouth a bit, shifted her head to one side, and began to look somewhat dazed. "Bonnie, where's the ketchup?" she said in a deep voice that conveyed the idea of a little boy lost. "Bonnie, I need some tomato. Bonnie, where's the mayonnaise? Bonnie, didn't you bring an apple pie? You know how I like apple pie."

J.T.'s eyes widened. "That's Larry. Dolly said he'd starve to death if Bonnie weren't around."

Aria's face changed again; this time she made her eyelashes flutter rapidly. "I just loved that red dress. Here you are, honey. Of course red isn't usually my color. It's right there, honey. But I did wear red as a child. You don't think my hair's grown too dark for red? To your right, honey. But maybe I'm getting too fat for red. Here it is, honey. I have put on some weight since I got married. You want a slice of onion, honey?"

J.T. began to smile. "Larry's wife, Bonnie."

Aria smiled and resumed eating.

"What about Patty?" J.T. asked after a moment.

Aria's eyes sparkled as she put down her fork. She stood, turned her back to J.T., then perfectly imitated Patty's walk, an odd walk with her knees together, her feet flat, not bending, and her arms bent at the elbow, her hands stuck out like chicken wings. "Carl, I do believe I shall have a lamp like this," Aria said in a high, singsong voice. "It gives out the most wondrous color. So good for one's skin."

Aria stopped and looked back at J.T. He was beginning to laugh, and Aria thought how good it was to have an audience again. She had always been able to mimic people and her grandfather and sister had begged her for her performances after every official engagement. Of course she had only performed for her closest relatives.

She performed for J.T. with all the gusto she had

used at home. She went over each of their visitors of the night before and ended with a full parody of all of them talking at once. According to Aria's portrayal, the men were lazy, a little dumb, and as helpless as infants. The women handed them food and utensils, catered to them and pacified them as if they were large children, all the while talking a mile a minute about clothes, money, hairdos, money, cooking, money, and money. Yet her portrayals were never spiteful, and somehow made the people seem quite lovable.

J.T. was laughing hard when she finished.

Who would have thought, she wondered, that the American male had a sense of humor?

"We're that bad?" he asked, smiling at her.

"Mmm," was all Aria answered.

He was still smiling. "Come on and I'll show you how to wash dishes. You're going to love this little task."

For the first time ever he didn't snip at her as he showed her how to fill the sink with water and add the liquid soap. "Now you stick your hands inside and start washing."

Aria started to obey but he caught her wrists.

"I forgot about your burned hand." He held her wrists and looked at her for quite some time before releasing her. "I'll wash, you dry. Tell me something about your country," he said as he handed her the first clean dish.

Aria began to enjoy the task as she told him about her country, about the mountains and the cool night air.

"A lot different from Key West, isn't it?"

"From what I've seen, yes," she said. "But the flowers here are very pretty."

"Maybe we can go sightseeing."

The word made Aria shudder. Sightseeing was what

they had done in Washington, D.C.—that day he had pulled her in and out of a car, the day he had screamed at her for drinking a Coke.

J.T. saw her shudder and looked back at the sink full of dishes. "Maybe it could be a bit more pleasant this time. Look, I need to go to the base. You have anything to read today?"

"I have the history books."

"Yeah, well . . ." he stammered.

"Dolly said she was taking me to an ice cream parlor at eleven."

"Good, then you won't be here alone." He let the water out and dried his hands. "I better go." He went upstairs and returned a moment later with a handful of papers. "Have you seen my briefcase?"

"Here it is, honey," she said, mocking Bonnie's answers to Larry.

J.T. laughed as he walked forward to take it from her. "See you tonight, baby," he said, then caught himself. He smiled. "I mean, Your Royal Highness." He left the house.

Aria leaned against the door and smiled. "I think I like 'baby' better," she said.

Dolly arrived exactly at eleven. "Is that what you wear to an ice cream parlor? You look like Merle Oberon."

"I have nothing else. It isn't suitable?"

"If you were meeting a grand duke, it would be great." Dolly was watching Aria's eyes. "Come on, we'll go to Gail's first and see what we can scare up for you to wear. J.T. already go to the base?"

"Yes."

"Well, maybe we can fix that. I have a surprise for you today. The others aren't meeting us until three."

Aria had no idea what Dolly had planned but she followed her out the door.

J.T. looked at the stack of papers on his desk. There were new plans for changing a ship into a water distillation plant, other plans for installing English radar in an American ship, and other plans for something else under those. He rubbed his eyes. He hadn't slept well last night, not after Her Royal Highness had sat down on the edge of his bed wearing some exotic scent and two thin layers of silk. And this morning he had watched her awhile before waking her.

He had a job to do, he told himself. He was to teach her to be an American and then get rid of her. That meant no involvement with her personally—and definitely not physically. But there were times when all he could remember was the time on the island when he had stepped around the path and seen her standing nude in the pool. She wasn't built bad for a princess. Hell! Who was he kidding, she wasn't built bad for Miss America.

But staying away from her had been easy so far. She was so damned haughty, so cold and inhuman. But this morning she had thawed a little. He smiled at the memory of her imitation of Patty's walk.

What a strange person she was, he thought. So helpless but at the same time so fearless. Why hadn't she said a word when she had burned her hand? And the eggs he had cooked! He seemed to remember now that eggs didn't take as long as bacon to cook but he had put the eggs on, then the bacon, and taken them out at the same time. They were awful but she had eaten them just the same.

"J.T., you still here?"

J.T. was on his feet instantly and saluting smartly to Commander Davis. "Yes sir, I'm still here."

"I heard you just got married."

"Yes sir, three days ago."

"Then why are you here now? Why aren't you home with your new bride?"

"I wanted to go over the radar plans and the—"

The commander waved his hand. "I'm glad you're so conscientious but there are other aspects of life besides work—even in wartime. Now this is an order, Lieutenant: go home and spend the rest of the day with your new wife."

J.T. began to smile. "Yes sir, I'll obey that order immediately."

Aria looked at her reflection in the mirror as if she were hypnotized. She didn't know the young woman who looked back at her. She put her hand to her hair, now a shoulder-length bob that felt so light and cool. Instead of a somber silk suit she wore a yellow-and-white-print cotton sundress that exposed her arms and shoulders and neck.

"Well?" Dolly asked. "You like it?"

"Very much," Aria said breathlessly, then held out her skirt and turned about. "It feels so free, so . . . so . . ."

"American?" Dolly prompted.

"Exactly. Do I look American? As American as Dolley Madison?"

"Dolley Madison?" Gail laughed. "You look as American as Coca-Cola. You're one hundred percent red, white, and blue."

"Do you think Mitch will think so?" Aria asked, still looking at herself in the mirror.

"Mitch?" Bonnie gasped. "But J.T.—"

Aria caught herself. "Of course I meant my husband. It's just that Mitch laughs. I mean, I'm sure that Lieutenant Montgomery does too. I've even seen him laugh. But as a general rule . . ." She trailed off as the four women watched her with interest.

Dolly broke the silence. "J.T.'s a barrel of laughs. A regular riot. He's just had a lot to think about lately what with this new radar and all. He'll cheer up as soon as he's sure everything's gonna work. You'll see. Hey! It's quarter after three. We better get going. The guys'll be waiting."

Bonnie, Gail, and Patty left through the front door of Gail's house while Dolly caught Aria's arm. "J.T.'s a really great guy. He's had every single woman and half the married women on the island after him since he arrived."

Aria was incredulous. "Really? Perhaps there is a shortage of single men."

"In a navy town during a war?" Dolly gave Aria a long look. "J.T. hasn't been very good to you, has he?"

"He is my husband." Aria realized that these American women had a way of making her forget herself. "He has been very kind to me."

"Bill starts being 'kind' to me and I'll think there's another woman. Come on, let's go get some ice cream."

The husbands, except for J.T., were there, and Mitch was waiting for them. The way Mitch looked at Aria made her lower her head and blush. Involuntarily, she wished the army had chosen someone like this man for her husband.

"You are gorgeous," he said, taking her arm and leading her to a chair.

It never occurred to Aria to tell this man he wasn't allowed to touch her. The other couples, all newly married, were wrapped around each other, acting as if they hadn't seen one another for months. Aria, with her new haircut and her borrowed sundress, felt almost as if she were one of them instead of a foreign princess. It seemed natural when Mitch moved his chair very close to hers and put his arm around the back of her chair.

"I can't get over how different you look," he said softly. "You were beautiful before but now you could stop traffic. Maybe later we could get together for a moonlight drive."

Aria looked at her hands. This man was making her feel heavenly, as if she were enormously desirable, so very different from the way she had been feeling since she had arrived in America. "My husband," she murmured.

Mitch moved a little closer to her. "It's obvious that J.T. doesn't appreciate a dish like you. Princess, I'm serious about you. I like the way you look, the way you move. I've never met a girl like you. You and J.T. don't seem to be exactly in love. There must be some other reason why you married him. A baby on the way?"

"Certainly not," Aria said, but gently.

Mitch's hand moved to her shoulder, his fingers caressing her skin, and his touch felt delicious. No man had ever touched her skin like this before.

She looked up into his eyes, their noses almost touching.

"Let's get out of here," Mitch whispered.

She was on the verge of agreeing when all hell broke loose—the hell being in the form of Lieutenant J. T. Montgomery.

"Jesus H. Christ!" he bellowed. "What have you done to your goddamned hair?"

In an instant, Aria went from being an American wife to being a royal princess. She was on her feet.

"How dare you use such language in my presence!" she yelled back at him. "You are dismissed! Go! Leave my chamber."

The crowd in the ice cream parlor had come to a halt at J.T.'s first shout. Some of them had smiled at his words. But Aria's command left them stunned.

Dolly recovered first and, at the moment, she feared J.T. less than she did the autocratic Aria. "J.T., honey, sit down and stop glaring so. Waitress, bring this man a root beer float." She turned to Aria, her voice automatically lowering. "Your Royal—I mean, Princess, please have a seat."

Aria was recovering and she realized how she had called attention to herself and how she had reestablished herself as a foreigner. She felt Mitch take her hand and give a gentle tug. She sat, J.T. still standing, still hovering, still frowning.

"Sit down, J.T.," Dolly commanded, her voice filled with disgust. "Newlyweds," she said loudly to the watching crowd, and gradually they turned back around, although one ensign muttered, "Who's married to who?" as he nodded from J.T. to Aria to Mitch.

J.T. sat down at last and fastened his glare on his root beer float.

Gail patted Aria's hand. "I think you were right, Princess. Never let a man use the Lord's name in vain. Once he starts, he'll never stop."

Aria looked at the strawberry sundae someone had ordered for her and wished the floor would open up and swallow her. Mitch still had his arm around the back of her chair but it was different now. He was no longer leaning toward her but, instead, leaning a little back.

Once again she was a freak. Just as she had been the day they had arrested her. They had put her in a glass-walled cage and stared at her and laughed at her. Everything she did seemed to amuse them. And the only person she had known in America—Lieutenant Montgomery—had treated her the worst of all. Yet she had tried so very hard to please these new people. She had tried so hard to fit in.

"Let's go to the beach," Dolly said cheerfully. "We'll get our suits and go swimming at sunset, and J.T., you can catch us some lobsters and we'll grill them."

"I have work to do," J.T. muttered, moving his straw up and down in his untouched drink.

Dolly leaned forward. "Then maybe you'd be so kind as to drive your *wife*"—she emphasized the word—"to my house so I can loan her a bathing suit."

"Sure," J.T. said, fumbling for his keys. "You want to go now?"

Dolly stood. "On second thought, why don't you and I go and we'll all meet at Larry and Bonnie's apartment in an hour? Take care of our princess," she told Bill, then had J.T.'s arm and was leading him out the door.

"You bastard," Dolly said as soon as they were in the military car that was at J.T.'s constant disposal. "Bill told me everything and I think you're being a bastard."

"I've had all the abuse from women today that I can take. Don't you start on me."

"Someone should. The way you're treating that lovely girl is disgraceful."

"Lovely? Lovely girls don't allow men who aren't their husbands to drape themselves all over them."

"Hallelujah! You noticed," Dolly said sarcastically. "Mitch likes her, as we all do except you." Suddenly, she softened. "J.T., I've seen you charm lady sergeants, tough old broads who terrified every other man, but you had them eating from your hands. So why aren't you using some of your charm on your wife?"

J.T. turned a sharp right. "Maybe it's because she hates me, or maybe it's because she looks down her nose at me. She thinks I'm a commoner. Or maybe because she can't do anything useful. My job is to teach her to be an American and I'm doing that."

There was something in his tone that made Dolly change hers. "She's pretty, isn't she?"

"She's all right if you like the overbred type."

"I see," Dolly said.

"You see what?" he snapped.

"You're afraid of her."

"What?" he yelled, and slammed on the brakes at a stop sign.

"You're afraid that if you unbend a bit, you'll find she's quite courageous and rather likable. I'd never be able to do as well as she has. Bill said she couldn't even dress herself when she came to America but now she's cooking your breakfast."

"Sort of. She burned herself."

"Yes, but she's trying. Did you ever think how lonely she must be? She's in a strange country married to a man who despises her, but she's made the best of it. In spite of you, she's surviving."

"In *spite* of me? *Because* of me she's surviving."

They were silent for a while then J.T. spoke quietly. "I don't want to get involved with her. As soon as the army takes the imposter princess, she goes back to her throne. Then, no doubt, she'll hold out her hand for me to kiss and say 'so long, sucker.' Or maybe she'll give me a medal on a ribbon and she'll hang it around my neck."

"You didn't mind getting 'involved' with Heather Addison, or Debbie Longley or Karen Filleson or—what was the redhead's name?"

J.T. smiled. "Point taken. Aria's different, as you well know. You can't very well have a one-night stand with a royal princess. She doesn't dream of cottages with white picket fences, she dreams of castles and land management and lifelong servitude. Kings have no privacy or freedom."

"So you'll be mean to her instead."

"I'm not mean exactly, I just keep my distance. As that Mitch goddamn well better do. Oh, sorry."

Dolly turned away to hide a smile. Her Royal Highness had made her point about cursing. "I think she may be falling in love with Mitch."

"What!" J.T. slammed on the brakes again as the car skidded into the parking lot of the Marina Hotel.

"I don't blame either one of them. She needs a little kindness and every woman needs a man to tell her she's beautiful. She looked great today, didn't you think so?"

J.T. seemed to be deep in thought as he got out of the car and started toward the hotel, leaving Dolly sitting. She smiled as she got out of the car and went after him. At least she had made him think.

The hotel had once been a resort for the rich but the war had changed that and it was now used as temporary quarters for married officers. But the magnificent old lobby was the same and there was still a gift shop off to the side.

"Wait!" J.T. said as they walked past the window.

"Think she'd like that?" He pointed to a Catalina swimsuit, straight cut legs, a deep, square neckline.

"Sure," Dolly said, following J.T. into the store. She helped him choose a beach cover, a straw hat, "to protect her white skin," he explained, and a big matching straw beach bag.

"What else does she need?"

Love, Dolly almost said, but didn't because she didn't want to push too hard too fast. "Something to take her mind off Mitch."

J.T.'s smile left at that. "You have any jewelry?" he asked the saleswoman. "Any diamonds? Emeralds maybe."

She swallowed. "No sir, but we do have a rather fine selection of French perfumes."

"Good. I'll take a quart of whatever you've got. No, make that a half gallon."

"It's sold by the ounce," the woman said meekly.

"Then add up the ounces," he said impatiently. "You ready to go?" he asked Dolly.

"As soon as I go upstairs and get my suit."

J.T. smiled at her. "Need a new one?"

Never pass up a gift from a handsome gentleman, Dolly's mother used to say, and worry about the price later. "I would love a new suit."

Chapter Ten

ARIA was quiet during the drive to Larry and Bonnie's apartment. The others tried hard to lighten the atmosphere but she kept thinking that they were watching her and that they somehow knew she was different from them.

And it was Lieutenant Montgomery's fault. That awful, dreadful man had been the cause of everything bad that had happened to her in America—except the kidnapping, of course. He had saved her life then. At this moment she wished he had let her drown.

She was standing in Bonnie's tiny living room when the door opened and in walked J.T. and Dolly. Immediately, Aria went to the kitchen and J.T. followed.

"I brought you something," J.T. said softly from behind her.

She turned. "A biography of George Washington including ten essay questions at the end?"

He gave a little laugh then held out a paper sack.

Tentatively she took it and withdrew the dark blue swimsuit. She gave him a skeptical look.

"I picked it out myself. And there's a hat and purse and a little robe in here. And I got a sack of perfume in the car." His eyes sparkled. "And not one history book."

Aria didn't smile.

"What did you get?" Gail squealed from the doorway.

Aria held out the bag and Gail took it and rummaged inside.

"Not a bad apology, J.T.," Gail said. "You might make a good husband yet. Well?" she said, looking at Aria.

Aria realized Gail was expecting something from her but she didn't know what.

"When a husband apologizes, you kiss him and make up. Now get to it. I'll give you two minutes, then it's upstairs to change and we go to the beach. I'm hungry." She left them alone in the room.

"I . . . ah, I guess it is a peace offering," J.T. began. "I guess I shouldn't have said what I did. It was just such a shock seeing you look so different."

"I guess so," Aria said. "I wanted to look American and the long hair was so old-fashioned."

"I liked it."

"Did you?" she asked, surprised. "I never knew. I mean, you never said one way or the other."

He took a step closer to her. "Well, I did like it. It suited you."

"This feels so nice," she said, touching her hair.

"Does it?" He put his hand up and wrapped a fat curl around his fingers. "It does at that."

"I meant—"

"Time's up," Gail called. "Let's go."

Confusion showing in her eyes, Aria stepped past

him and left the kitchen. Upstairs she forgot about the curious incident when she found that the bedroom was to be a communal dressing room. It was one thing to be nude before your ladies-in-waiting, but before *strangers!* Besides, it took her forever to get in and out of clothes and this swimsuit had a zipper down the back.

But Dolly didn't give Aria time to think. She unbuttoned the back of Aria's sundress and began to help her out of it. "Now me," she said when Aria was wearing only a borrowed rayon teddy.

Thanks to Dolly, the disrobing was easier than Aria expected, and when she pulled on the boned, stiff swimsuit, she felt as if she had accomplished something grand.

She was smiling when she went downstairs. And there stood two men, the handsome, smiling Mitch and her husband. But this husband was someone she had never seen before. He was lazily leaning against the staircase and laughing at something Bonnie was saying. Now what does he plan? Aria thought. Is this some special American torture he had planned for her?

"Princess?" Mitch said, holding out his arm for her. Smiling, she took it.

J.T. pushed his way between them. "I think I'll escort my wife myself."

"It's about time," Mitch muttered, and after one sad look at Aria, he excused himself from the night's revelries.

They all piled into J.T.'s car, the women sitting on the men's laps except that J.T. drove and Aria sat beside him. He kept smiling at her, and the more he smiled, the more suspicious she grew. What terrible thing was he planning now?

At the beach the men stepped into the darkness to

don swim trunks while the women gathered drift-wood for a fire.

Dolly whistled when J.T. came into the light wearing nothing but the black trunks.

He winked at her then turned toward the ocean waves. "Want to swim, Princess?" he called back.

"Not at night in that water," she answered.

J.T. did what he was supposed to and returned with a dozen lobsters, which the group dispatched in a hurry. After dinner, with the fire nearly out, the couples entangled themselves about each other and began kissing.

Aria looked away in embarrassment.

"J.T.," Dolly called when she came up for air, "why don't you introduce your princess to the good old American custom of necking?"

"I think I will," he answered, then picked up Aria's hand.

Before he could get it to his lips, she pulled away. "You cannot possibly consider doing to me—in public—what they are doing," she hissed at him.

"Is everyone in your country frigid?"

"I live in a warm country," she said, confused. "We have winters but they are mild."

"You want to be an American or not?" he snapped.

"I am trying to learn."

He calmed himself. "Yes, and you're doing a fine job of it. Look at them." He gestured to the other couples. "They wouldn't be aware of a German invasion right now so they won't notice us. What they're doing is called, among other things, necking, and it's what newlywed couples are supposed to do."

"All right," she said, leaning away from him and holding out her hand. "You may kiss my hand if you do not twist my arm or pull it or do any of the other painful things you are inclined toward."

"Listen, lady—"

"It's Your—"

He slipped his hand behind her head and kissed her before she could say another word.

Only twice before had she been kissed on the lips, once when Count Julian asked her to marry him and once by Lieutenant Montgomery on the island. Neither time had prepared her for this.

First one of his hands and then the other enveloped her head in a gentle, protective gesture and his lips played on hers softly. Aria kept her eyes open and her hands moved as if to push him away, but then she began to feel quite different. Her hands moved to his shoulders and she liked the feel of his bare skin under her palms. Gently, he moved her head to one side and his kiss deepened.

Aria closed her eyes and leaned forward ever so slightly.

When he moved away from her she stayed where she was, eyes still closed. *"Lantabeal,"* she murmured. Then slowly her eyes fluttered open. He still had his hands on the side of her face.

"That's one of our American customs. You don't have that in Lanconia?"

She knew he was teasing her, but she didn't care.

"And how does my kiss compare to Mitch's?" he asked.

She straightened at that, and before he knew what hit him, she gave him a resounding slap. "I learned *that* American custom from your friend in Washington." She stood. "Someone may take me home now."

"Listen," J.T. said, standing in front of her, "we aren't your servants. You *ask* for things here, you don't command them."

"Then I *ask* to leave this place."

"*I'll* take you. I'm your husband, remember? Although a fat lot of good it does me." He turned to Dolly. All the couples were gathering their gear. "I tried. I bloody well tried. Come on, Your Royal Highness, I'll take you home."

The trip around town to let the other couples off was made in silence. Aria's heart was still pounding. She knew she had made too big a fuss over something that wasn't such a terrible thing to say— in fact she rather liked her husband's display of jealousy—but what had prompted her attack was fear.

From the time she could walk, decorum and self-discipline had been drilled into her. At all times she was to control her emotions. She had attended the funerals of her beloved parents and never shed a tear in public. She had suffered a couple of physical injuries and never cried. She had been through two kidnappings and never lost her wits. She had *always* controlled herself.

Yet, tonight she had come closer to losing control than she ever had before. What that man's kiss had made her feel!

She wished she could talk to her grandfather about this. Was this right? Count Julian had never made her feel like this. But then she had never lived with him, slept in the same bed with him, had never even dined alone with him. Maybe this feeling would have come if she had married the count.

Right now she could feel Lieutenant Montgomery's side pressed against hers and he touched her knee every time he shifted gears. It made her heart beat harder.

When they were alone in the car, she wanted to apologize to him, but he said, "Over there. I want you to move to the far end of the seat. As far away from me as possible."

Aria did as he bid and they didn't speak again.

The next two days were miserable. She went shopping with Bonnie and Dolly, had her hair done, went swimming, but it wasn't the same. J.T. returned to his old, cool self, no more laughing and asking where his briefcase was, and he lost patience with trying to show her how to cook and do laundry.

"But I washed dishes yesterday," Aria said.

"Yes and they have to be done again today. They have to be done three times a day, seven days a week."

"You are making a joke, aren't you? If I wash dishes every day, dust the furniture every day, wash the clothes, cook the food, buy the groceries, when do I get to read a book? When do I get to shop with Dolly and Bonnie? When do I get to be Aria and not Mrs. Montgomery? When do I get to think about something besides which dishwashing detergent to buy?"

"I have to go to work."

Later that morning a Mrs. Humphreys, hired by J.T., showed up to clean the house and bake a casserole for dinner.

That night Aria set the table with candles and made the room as attractive as she could with the little the navy had used to furnish the house.

J.T. turned on every light and blew out the candles.

She knew he was very angry with her and she wanted to make him smile at her again. He thought their marriage was temporary but she knew better. She no longer hated him but he was still a stranger to her.

She served Mrs. Humphreys's cold lobster salad, then on impulse, she arched her back, thrust her chest forward, and said in a southern drawl, "Would you rather have that little ol' lobster or little ol' me?"

Her excellent imitation of Dolly made him smile.

She sat down across from him. "What do American couples do when they're alone?"

"Outside of bed I have no idea."

She blinked a few times at that. "Don't American women find this life somewhat boring? Do they *really* enjoy cleaning even if it is for their families?"

J.T. smiled again. "Maybe 'enjoy' isn't the right word. What did you do as a princess?"

"I always got a great deal of exercise. My sister and I rode horses, fenced, had dancing classes."

"That's why you look—" He broke off.

"I look what?"

He grinned. "Look so good in a bathing suit."

"Thank you," she said.

"The first time I've heard those words."

"The first time you've deserved them," she shot back.

"Oh? Saving your life didn't rate a thank-you?"

"For all I knew you were worse than the kidnappers. 'Breathe for Daddy Montgomery,'" she mocked.

He started to say something then stopped. "Maybe you'd like to see the blueprints for the new distillation ship. Maybe that'll help relieve the boredom."

"Yes, please," she said.

It was very pleasant sitting on the couch together leaning over the blueprints. The war needed ships that could distill fresh water from seawater and deliver it to troops. J.T. was in charge of converting the first of these ships.

Her mind was hungry for something of interest, something of the present instead of the past.

"Could a plant like this be made on land?" she asked.

"It would be easier on land than on a ship. Why?"

"At home in Lanconia our major crop is grapes for wine, but in the last five years we've had a drought. We are losing our grapes. But seeing this I wonder if such a plant could be made and we could irrigate the grapes. The young people are leaving my country because we are losing a major source of income."

"You'd have to have some engineers look at it but I imagine something could be done."

"You'd look at it? I mean, when we go home, you'd help my country?"

"I don't know what I can do but I'll try."

She smiled at him. "It would mean a great deal to my people if you did. Dolly says you know as much about shipbuilding as anyone alive today."

J.T. laughed. "Not by a long shot, but my family knows a lot." He looked at his watch. "You ready to go to bed, baby?" He caught himself. "I mean—"

She smiled at him. "I'm beginning to like the 'honeys' and 'babies,' although I'm not sure about 'Princess.'"

"It fits you," he said, yawning. "Cool, stiff, unbending, not quite human. The name means someone untouchable and that's what you are."

"Oh," she said softly, and turned away. "Someone not quite human." She went upstairs, and as she was creaming her face and putting a net over her hair she thought about his words. Was she like he described? Two nights ago he had kissed her and she had felt such passion that she had been afraid. Hadn't he felt anything? Maybe when he kissed Heather she was warmer. Maybe Heather knew a great deal about kissing.

Aria went to her narrow bed on the other side of the partition from J.T. and lay awake. It was hot, as always, and she wore a thin peach-colored nylon nightgown, more a slip than a gown. "Rita Hayworth style," Dolly had said when they bought it.

It began to storm around midnight and the wind lashed at the thin-walled little house. The thunder cracked and the lightning lit the room. Aria threw off the covers, the nightgown feeling heavy and confining. It grew hotter and closer in the room and she began to perspire.

Another crack of thunder made the windows pop. Aria tried to get comfortable but she couldn't. Images floated through her mind: J.T. on the island standing over her, his big body nearly nude; J.T. in his swim trunks. She remembered the look in his eyes as he had entered the clearing and seen her bathing in the pool. She remembered his two kisses.

She started and pulled the sheet over her body as she heard the floor creak behind her. In the dim light she saw J.T. walk past her bed and close a window.

He turned back, glanced at her, then stopped. "Are you awake?" he whispered.

She nodded.

He came closer to the bed. "The storm wake you?"

She shook her head.

Frowning, he sat down on the edge of the bed. "Are you all right?" He put his hand on her forehead.

Aria caught his hand and held it in both of hers.

"What's wrong, baby, have a bad dream?" He pulled her into his arms as if she were a child who needed comforting.

But what Aria needed wasn't comfort. She held on to him, pressed her body against his, feeling her breasts against his bare chest.

J.T. understood instantly. "I am lost," he murmured in the tone of a man going down for the third time, then he pulled her face to his and began to kiss her hungrily. "Oh, baby," he said, "my sweet beautiful princess. You're mine, you know that?" He was kissing her neck as a man who was dying of hunger. "I saved your life and you're mine. You wouldn't be alive now if it weren't for me."

"Yes," she gasped. "Yes. Make me alive. Make me glad to be alive." She said more but it was in Lanconian and J.T. didn't understand her, but words weren't needed.

He hadn't realized how much he had been wanting her. Ever since he had seen her nude on the island, her big-breasted, slim-hipped body had haunted him. And seeing her every day, her back straight, her chest thrust forward, made him sweat.

He tore the nightgown off of her, hungry to get at those breasts he had dreamed of so many times. He buried his face in them, made them cover his ears while his hands held them.

Aria groaned, her head back.

J.T. tried to tell himself to go slowly, that she was a virgin and probably frightened, but he couldn't control himself any more than he could have stopped a freight train.

He began kissing her body, her arms, her breasts, her shoulders, back up again to her neck, briefly touching her lips, then down again. It was as if in the past few weeks he had memorized her skin. There was a mole on her collarbone and he kissed it.

His head moved downward, kissing whatever he came in contact with: her hips, her belly, her thighs. She made not a sound but her skin grew hotter and hotter as if her temperature were rising by degrees.

"Jarl," she whispered.

"Right here, baby," he answered, and climbed on top of her.

He had to guide her since she had no idea what to do, but she was a quick learner. Oh, heavens yes, she was quick. And after his first slow entry, he was beginning to believe she was possessed of a very natural talent.

He kissed her lips and he kissed her breasts as he made long, slow strokes. She was right: she had exercised a great deal in her life and her body was strong and agile and she followed his lead easily. Once he even had to hold her back, but then he could no longer hold himself back.

He finished in a satisfying explosion that shuddered through his body and he collapsed on her, pulling her into a tight little roll in the tangle of his arms and legs.

It took him quite a while to recover. "Are you okay?"

He felt her nod under his chest and he smiled. "Can you breathe?"

She shook her head and he chuckled, then moved just a bit so she could get some air. He held their sweaty bodies close together as outside the rain began to fall.

"Did I hurt you?" he asked softly.

"A little sore," she said, "but not terribly. I . . . I liked that."

He had been a little afraid to look at her, afraid of what would be in her eyes, but now he pulled back to see her face. She was more beautiful than he remembered. Her hair was soft about her head, with sweaty tendrils clinging to her cheeks. Softly, he kissed her mouth.

"How about a bath?" he asked. "Together. The two of us in a tub."

She opened her eyes wide. "Is that . . . done? Do men and women do that?"

"This man and woman are about to." He stood and she turned away modestly from his nudity. She searched for her nightgown while holding a sheet over her breasts.

J.T. pulled her out of bed. "No coverings. I want to *look* at you."

"Oh," she said, blushing, eyes downcast.

He stepped back, still holding her hand, and gave a low whistle. "You, lady, are a sight to behold. No, not lady, I mean, Your Royal—"

She stepped forward so the tips of her breasts were touching his chest and put her finger to his lips. "You may call me baby or honey or lady or whatever you want tonight."

"Keep talking to me like that and we'll never get bathed. Come on, sweetheart, let me wash you."

Chapter Eleven

W ELL, you've done it now," Bill Frazier said. He and J.T. were sitting in one of the many sleazy beer joints on Duval Street, working their way through their fourth beer. "How are you going to hand her over to her prince?"

"He's not a prince, merely a count, and he doesn't have any money, and he also happens to be shorter than she is."

"I can tell you weren't interested enough to do any research on the man."

J.T. downed the beer and held up his hand to the waitress for a fifth one.

"The SPs will have your hide if you're drunk."

"I'm not drunk," J.T. snapped. "Although I'd like to *get* drunk. How could I possibly involve myself with an overbearing woman who keeps ordering me from her presence?"

"You get those circles under your eyes from her being overbearing last night?"

J.T. smiled. "She isn't useless after all." He stopped

smiling. "That isn't the problem. Look, she's been raised to marry somebody she's never met, so she'll do fine with her Count Julie. Besides, I hear that all those royals take lovers."

"So stay around and be her lover."

J.T. slammed the beer mug down so hard half of it sloshed onto the table. "Like hell I will. *She* may regard this marriage as a lark but it's not that way to an American."

"That's not what you said when you called from Washington. You said you were marrying her to help America and you'd be glad to get rid of her when the time came. You said no man could love such an idiot of a dame. You said—"

"What are you? A wire recorder? I know what I said. Now the problem is, this marriage is getting a little too intimate. I'm sure this would have happened with *any* woman. You can't put two young healthy people together like the army's done to us and not expect something to happen. I just need some perspective, that's all. I've been around her so much I'm beginning to *like* her."

"Not difficult to do."

"Yes it is," J.T. said. "You don't know her like I do. She argues about *everything*. Acts like housework is a death sentence. And she spends money like there's no tomorrow. Do you have any idea what last week's bill from Ethel's Beauty Parlor was?"

"I bet it wasn't any more than Dolly's and your wife sounds just like mine."

"That's just it—she's not my wife. I guess it's like the difference between borrowing a car and owning one. It's not the same. You can use the borrowed car but someday you have to give it back."

"You sure borrowed one hell of a car in that little lady."

J.T. finished his beer. "Yeah, I borrowed a Rolls, but, unfortunately, I'll have to spend my life with some Buick."

Bill laughed. "So what do you do now? You got another week before she goes back, right?"

"One more week and then I take her to her country, slip her back into her castle, and turn her over to her scrawny little count. They deserve each other."

Bill looked at his watch. "We better go. Dolly said to meet her at the pool at seven and it's quarter after now."

They walked from Duval Street to the swimming pool opened by the navy for the officers.

"You two smell like a brewery," Dolly said. "J.T., what did you do to Aria? She looks positively radiant."

Before J.T. could answer he saw Aria, wearing only her swimsuit, walking away from the concession stand beside Mitch, who was in uniform, both of them laughing. J.T. didn't think; he just acted. He strode the few steps around the edge of the pool, grabbed the smaller Mitch by the back of his collar and the seat of his pants, and threw him into the water.

"Stay away from my wife, you understand me?" he yelled down when Mitch came up for air.

"Of all the primitive displays I have seen, this is the worst," Aria said, then bent to offer her hand to Mitch.

J.T. grabbed her shoulders and pulled her around so that Mitch fell back into the water. "We're going home."

Their little house wasn't too far away, and when Aria was dressed, he started walking home, Aria barely able to keep up with him. She didn't say a word to him on the way because she didn't want a public scene but she meant to speak to him once they were home.

How could he be so disagreeable after last night? She could still feel his soapy hands on her body, still feel his lips on her skin. They had bathed each other last night, except that she had been too shy to fully explore his body. He had laughed and said, "There's time for that." After their bath he had dried her then carried her to his bed and made love to her again. She had felt no pain the second time and they had fallen asleep in each other's arms.

When she woke, it was morning and he was gone. There was no note, no message left for her. All day she had hoped the phone would ring but it hadn't. At two she made an emergency trip to Ethel's to have her hair done so it would look nice when he got home. She again set the table with candles.

At 5:30 Dolly had come by and told her they were to meet the boys at the officers' swimming pool. She was surprised J.T. hadn't told Aria.

The next thing she knew J.T. was throwing Mitch in the pool.

When they arrived at the house, he unlocked the door for her but he didn't enter. "I got to go somewhere," he muttered, and turned toward the gate.

She ran after him and put her hand on his arm. "Jarl, is something wrong? Did something bad happen today?"

He moved his arm from her touch. "No one calls me Jarl except my mother and she's not borrowed. It's J.T. Got that?"

She stepped back. "Certainly, Lieutenant Montgomery. I will not make that error again. Should I keep supper warm for you? I believe that is an American wifely custom."

"I'll get something somewhere else. And sleep in your own bed tonight."

She schooled her face not to betray her feelings. "Yes, Your Sublime Highness. Will there be anything else you desire of this poor concubine?"

He glared at her then slammed out the gate.

"I will not cry," Aria whispered. "He will not make me cry."

J.T. buried himself in his work. He felt as if he were fighting for his life, that he was the one drowning—but there was no one to save him. She was getting under his skin like no one ever had before. Every day she changed dramatically. She laughed; she danced; she made jokes. He had shown her plans for the ships and she had understood everything he told her. She was smart and sexy and funny. And she was *not his*. He tried to remember that but then he would make a fool of himself when another man so much as looked at her.

He just wanted to stay away from her and try to get her out of his mind, so he stayed at work and slept on the ratty couch outside the officers' mess. But it didn't help much. He dreamed about her.

As if he didn't have enough trouble in life, he received a telegram saying his mother was coming to visit. J.T. knew Amanda Montgomery had hundreds of friends, and no doubt she had heard of her son's marriage from one of them. It was not going to be pleasant because he knew she was going to tell her son what she thought of his marrying and not telling his family.

"Women!" J.T. muttered. He wished he could row out to an island and spend some time alone. He groaned at that thought when he remembered his last time "alone" on an island.

He braced himself before he went to see Aria to tell her about his mother. Aria was wearing a sundress with little bows on her shoulders, her neck and arms bare, and she was as delicious looking as a peach. He tried to explain to her that he would like her to not request his mother to kiss her royal hand, but Aria stuck her nose in the air in that way that only she could do, and it made him so mad he ended up slamming from the house.

Aria hadn't counted on two whole days of J.T.'s absence. He didn't come home at all that first night and the next night he stayed less than an hour—only long enough to lecture her.

"My mother sent me a telegram and she'll be here Saturday. She'll come to the house first, then the three of us will attend the Commander's Ball. Do you have anything proper to wear? Do you know how to ballroom-dance? Do you know the proper forms of address to navy officers?"

Aria was too astonished to answer. She was a royal princess and he was treating her as if she had just come in from the fields. "I believe I can manage to not disgrace myself," she murmured. But her sarcasm didn't reach him.

He went on to tell her about his mother, this woman who was a cross between Attila the Hun and Florence Nightingale. She was a Daughter of the American Revolution and a Daughter of the May- flower.

"And she married a Montgomery," J.T. said as if that explained everything else.

"Perhaps we should send her my family tree for approval. I am descended from every royal house in Europe thanks to the English Queen Victoria. Or do foreign kings not matter when pitted against your American heroines?"

J.T. glared at her then left the house.

He came back the next morning to change clothes, barely said anything to her except to remind her that his mother was arriving and he wanted the house spotlessly clean, then left for work.

Dolly came over at one o'clock, just after Mrs. Humphreys left. "What's going on?" she asked by way of greeting.

Aria had always lived surrounded by servants and she knew that the only people in whom one could confide were blood relatives. "I was about to have luncheon. Will you join me?"

"I'm not interested in food. Floyd told Gail who told Bill that J.T. was out all night last night. You two have a fight?"

"There is a lovely shrimp salad and cold tomatoes."

"Honey," Dolly said, putting her hands on Aria's shoulders. "I know everything. I know you're a princess and I know you want to get back to your country and I know how this marriage came about. But I also know something bad has happened, and I want you to talk to me."

Perhaps Aria was more American than she thought. In the last few days she had sat by quietly while the other women talked and revealed the most intimate secrets about themselves.

To Aria's disbelief, she burst into tears. Dolly's arms about her felt good and Dolly led her to the couch.

After Aria had regained some control, Dolly urged her to talk.

"He . . . he made love to me." Aria sniffed, part of her mind not believing what she was revealing. Royalty could never trust anyone not royal, as outsiders tended to write books—one couldn't even trust the aristocracy. "But then he hated me. I don't understand. What did I do wrong?"

"Absolutely nothing. Bill and I fought about it but he finally told me some of what J.T. said. Who is Count Julie?"

"That is Lieutenant Montgomery's name for the man I was engaged to marry." She blew her nose.

"Did you know J.T. thinks you're still going to marry this count?"

Aria didn't answer.

Dolly leaned forward. "*Why* does J.T. think that?"

"He wouldn't marry me unless he believed our marriage was temporary. Of course I cannot get a divorce, it isn't thinkable."

Dolly leaned back. "Then J.T. *will* be king."

"Prince consort." Aria waved her hand. "But I don't understand why he's so angry with me now."

"Easy. Of course he never admitted it to Bill, but he's afraid he's falling in love with you. He thinks he has to turn you over to someone else and he doesn't want it to hurt so much."

"Perhaps I should tell him the marriage is permanent."

Dolly's mouth dropped open. "Tell a red-blooded American male that he's been snookered? Bamboozled? Taken for a ride?"

"Not the done thing?"

Dolly laughed. "I think you ought to make him finish falling in love with you."

"Wear low-cut dresses, feed him strawberries and wine?" Aria said, having no idea how to make a man fall in love with her.

"First you have to get his attention. You can wear a sexy dress to the Commander's Ball."

"For his mother," Aria muttered.

Dolly laughed. "I heard she might be here. She's some bigwig, isn't she?"

"Enough that the manners of a royal princess are considered to need work to meet her."

Dolly put her hand on Aria's arm. "*Every* man is that way about his mother. Bill told me so many glowing stories about his mother that I was ready to worship at her feet. He constantly bragged about her cooking and he insisted that I beg and plead if necessary to get her fabulous recipes. So when we went to visit the first time I took along a pad and pencil to take notes. Some cook she was! You know how she made spaghetti sauce? Two cans of tomato soup and one can of tomato paste. It was ghastly. Her 'famous' turkey dressing consisted of nine slices of bread cut into cubes, a half cup of water, and an eighth of a teaspoon of sage. No onion, celery, or anything else. She stuffed it into the turkey and cooked the bird until it was so dry you could have used slices of the breast for powder puffs. Then the old biddy had the gall to ask me if I thought I was a good enough cook for her little boy."

Aria's eyes twinkled. "Count Julian's mother curtsies to me and addresses me as Your Royal Highness."

Dolly laughed. "A dream come true. I'd like to see Bill's fat ol' mother curtsy to me. Does she kiss your ring?"

"She touches her forehead to the back of my extended hand," Aria said airily.

"*That* I'd like to see."

"If I ever get home, you have an invitation."

"Deal. Hey! How'd you like to go to a movie? There's a matinee on today."

"I would love it."

The women had heaping plates full of shrimp salad

175

for lunch and they drank most of a bottle of wine. They were laughing as they set off to walk to the movie theater.

Aria was smiling and laughing when she heard Dolly gasp. When she turned to look, Dolly placed herself in front of Aria. "Let's go this way," Dolly said. "The cannonball tree is in bloom. I hear it's the only one on the island. It's really very beautiful and—"

Aria stepped around Dolly to look across the street. J.T. sat at a tiny table at a cafe, a pretty redhead across from him. While she watched, he lifted the woman's hand and kissed it.

"Yes, let's see the cannonball tree," Aria said, starting to walk briskly.

Dolly ran after her. "So what are you going to do?"

"A wife ignores her husband's infidelities."

"What!" Dolly grabbed Aria's arm and halted her. "That may be the way in *your* country but that's not American. You should have gone over there and snatched that floozy bald."

"The woman? But what has she done? She merely accepted his invitation. Perhaps she doesn't know that he's married. It is Lieutenant Montgomery who has committed the wrong."

"I never saw it like that, but I guess you're right. So, anyway, what are you going to do to get him back?"

"A royal princess is above revenge," she said, her nose in the air.

"There's the difference between you and me. I'd *do* something."

They were silent the rest of the way to the theater. The movie was *Springtime in the Rockies* and one of the players was an outrageously dressed woman named Carmen Miranda. To Aria, she was a carica-ture of what Americans seemed to think all foreigners were like. Dolly kept laughing at the woman's eye rolling and mispronunciations but Aria did not find the performance amusing.

That's what Jarl thinks the people of my country are like, she thought. He's not sure but what I won't show up at his American ball with a dozen bananas on top of my head. He worries that I'll embarrass his pedigreed mother when the truth is my ladies-in-waiting have more exalted family trees than she does. *He* worries about *my* conduct while he publicly consorts with a redheaded harlot—a *fake* redhead, at that.

Dolly's words—*What are you going to do to get him back?*—echoed in her head.

Maybe she was becoming an American, maybe the short hair and the flowered cotton dresses were making her an American, because she didn't feel like ignoring Jarl's (*Only my mother calls me Jarl*, she thought with disgust; one's initials were what was embroidered on one's linens) infidelity.

She looked up at the movie. Carmen Miranda was wearing a purple and white frothy concoction now.

Aria began to fantasize about meeting her illustrious mother-in-law with her belly bare, a slit up her skirt, and an eighteen-inch headdress weaving about on her head.

"Something that sparkles," she whispered.

"What's that?" Dolly asked.

"Has this woman recorded any of her songs?"

"Carmen Miranda? Sure. She has lots of records out."

Aria smiled and began studying the woman's movements. She was so exaggerated that she would be easy to imitate.

After the movie Dolly saw by Aria's eyes that she was happier than she had been. "Cheer you up?"

"I am going to be just what my husband thinks I

THE PRINCESS

am. I am going to the Commander's Ball dressed as
Carmen Miranda. I am going to meet Lieutenant
Montgomery's mother and pinch her on the cheek
and say, 'Chica, Chica.'"

"I . . . I don't think you should do that. I mean, the
Commander's Ball is the biggest event of the year and
it's very formal—only the top brass. Bill and I aren't
invited. J.T. is because his mother's coming. And,
Aria, you *have* to be nice to your mother-in-law. I
think it's a law somewhere. She can treat you like dirt
but you're always supposed to be nice to her. Believe
me, an angry mother-in-law can make your life hell."

"More hell than it is now? I don't have a country;
my husband spends his time with another woman and
treats me as if I am nothing. He said I was cold and
inhuman. I shall show him that I am not."

"J.T. said that? You definitely should get him back
but there has to be a better way. I'd rather face a firing
squad than anger my mother-in-law."

"Who can we get to make the dress? I think I'll have
it made in red and white and we shall use the very
cheapest fabrics. What is the sparkling powder?"

"Glitter. Aria, really, I don't think the Commander's Ball is the place—"

Aria stopped walking. "If you help me with this,
when I get back to my country, you can come for a
month-long visit and I will let you try on every crown
I own. There's twenty-some of them."

Dolly swallowed, her eyes wide. "We could put red
Christmas balls in your hair and Bonnie's landlady
has the biggest, ugliest pair of seashell earrings from
Cuba that you've ever seen. They're red and white
polka dot."

"Perfect," Aria said, smiling. "Now let's go buy
some records. I plan to sing while I dance. I shall get
Jarl Tynan Montgomery's attention all right."

"I hope you can handle it. His mother is going to hate you." Dolly brightened. "But men do like women with spunk. They don't like cowards. You know, this might work."

"He'll look at me and not that redhead."

"I can guarantee that. It's just how he's going to look at you that worries me."

Chapter Twelve

W<small>E</small> made it," Dolly said, leaning against the rest-room door. "Did J.T. believe your reason about why you couldn't attend the ball?"

"I gave him something to think about. I said I was suffering from morning sickness."

"You didn't," Dolly said, giggling. "I almost feel sorry for him. Here, let's get you dressed. I gave the maid five dollars to keep people out for fifteen minutes, so let's get to work."

Aria removed her long raincoat, then untied her skirt so it fell to the floor. It was made of cheap white satin, tight across her hips and slit from her hip to the floor. The slit and the hem were covered with three layers of one-foot-wide gathered nylon that was sprinkled with dots of red and white glitter. The white satin halter top left her stomach bare. Red satin ribbon trimmed the waist and halter. The sleeves were three layers of nylon dotted with more glitter.

On her arms were gaudy red bracelets that reached from wrist to halfway up her forearm. Around her neck she wore fourteen strings of cut-glass beads that hung almost to her waist.

But the *pièce de résistance* was the headdress of five seven-inch-wide nylon flowers and a half-moon piece of cardboard covered in glitter set on top of a white satin turban. The earrings were sewn to the turban.

"Now, if we can get this thing on," Dolly said, holding the headdress aloft. She halted when, behind them, a toilet flushed. "I didn't check," Dolly whispered miserably.

Out of the stall came a pretty woman, tall, slim, with dark chestnut hair and wearing a stunning draped, black Molyneux. She had beautiful skin that refused to tell her age.

Both Dolly and Aria stood frozen, Dolly with the turban held above Aria's head.

"Is there to be a show tonight?" the woman asked.

"An impromptu one," Aria answered.

"Oh. May I help with that?" she asked Dolly, referring to the turban.

"Sure."

The woman adjusted Aria's hair in the back and pulled the turban in place. "Is it heavy?"

"Not bad," Aria said. "I guess I'm ready."

"Oh no, my dear," the woman said. "Your makeup isn't nearly enough; your face is lost against the glitter. I have a few cosmetics with me. May I assist?"

Obediently Aria sat down in front of the mirror and the woman went to work.

"I didn't mean to eavesdrop but I take it this has to do with a man."

Aria didn't say a word but Dolly let go. "It's her husband. He's been . . . well, the SOB has been seeing another woman and Aria and I decided to pay him and his mother back."

"His mother?" the woman asked.

"She's some Yankee snob, came down here to give her daughter-in-law the once-over, and J.T. acts like Aria hasn't got sense enough to pour—"

"Dolly," Aria cautioned.

"I see," the woman said, standing back to look at Aria's face. "I think that's much better. Now, why don't I give the maid another five, then I'll persuade the band to play a little calypso and you can make an entrance?"

"This is awfully kind of you," Aria said.

"I've had a mother-in-law and I have a husband. Don't *ever* consider allowing a man to get away with infidelity. I hope he's *very* embarrassed and you teach him a good lesson. I have a feeling he'll not be so neglectful in the future. Oh, what shall I have the band play?"

"I know the words to 'Chica Chica Boom Chic,' 'Tico-Tico,' and 'I, Yi, Yi, Yi, Yi, I Like You Very Much.'"

"All of my favorites," the woman said, and they all laughed. "Wait until you hear the music."

Aria let the calypso music play for a couple of minutes before she burst from the rest room. She had been practicing for days and had seen Carmen's movie four times, so by the time she entered the ballroom with its sedate lighting, its conservatively dressed matrons, its hushed music and conversation, its polite and genteel laughter, she *was* Carmen Miranda.

She had a thick Spanish accent and an exaggerated wiggle as she made her way through the astonished crowd.

"You are so cute," she said to one admiral as she pinched his cheek. "It is so many stars on his shoulder, no?" she said to the admiral's wife.

One by one the crowd stopped and watched her.

She plopped down on a lieutenant commander's lap and moved her bottom back and forth. "You want we should chica-chica-boom-boom?"

"Young lady!" the man said, astonished. "Were you invited to this?"

"Oooh yes," she squealed. "I am zee wife of a very powerful man."

"Who?" the man bellowed. He was trying to get her off his lap.

"Zere he is."

J.T. had been watching this with amusement, having no idea who the woman was.

"Oh my God," he said when he realized it was Aria. He bounded across the room and pulled her off the lieutenant commander's lap.

"I'm *very* sorry for this, sir," J.T. said. "I had no idea she . . . I mean, sir . . ."

"You seem to like women in red," Aria said so only he could hear, "so I wore red. Maybe this red is dyed with the same dye she uses on her hair." She turned to the crowd. "He ees so forceful, no? So . . ." She rolled her eyes then stuck her rear end out, baring one leg to her hip, and moved her bottom down J.T.'s leg. "Ooooh," she squealed.

"Lieutenant Montgomery!" an admiral shouted.

"Yes sir," J.T. said weakly.

"Oh, but I want so bad to meet hees mother," Aria said petulantly. She broke away from J.T. and undulated over to a captain. "Men can be so cruel, do you not think?"

"I am Jarl's mother," said someone behind her.

Aria turned and her face fell. It was the woman from the rest room. "Oh my God," she said, for the first time in her life using the Lord's name in vain. "I . . . I . . ." she sputtered. I want to die, she thought. Please, God, strike me dead now.

Mrs. Montgomery leaned forward to kiss Aria's cheek. "Don't give up now," she whispered. She turned to the others. "My daughter-in-law and I are going to sing you a song. Jarl, loan me your pocket knife."

"Mother, I'm going to take the two of you home."

"Yes, Lieutenant, I think that would be wise, and tomorrow morning I want you in my office," said an admiral.

"Yes sir." J.T. saluted smartly and took Aria's arm firmly.

"Coward!" said Mrs. Montgomery to Aria as she was pulled past.

Aria jerked away from J.T. "He is a tyrant, no?" she said loudly. "He makes me to clean the dishes, to scrub the floors, to wash his back, but he never lets me to sing."

Several people laughed.

"Let her sing," called someone from the back.

"Yes, do let her sing," said the admiral's wife.

"Your knife, Jarl," said Mrs. Montgomery. She took his knife and slit the skirt of that divinely beautiful and very expensive dress to above her knee, exposing a shapely leg. She took three huge red hibiscus from a table decoration and tucked them in her hair.

"Tell the band to play 'Tico-Tico,'" she told J.T.

Aria and her mother-in-law put on an extraordinarily good performance in spite of the fact that they had never rehearsed. They played well off one another because neither was afraid of an audience. Aria had a repertoire of sexy moves she had seen Carmen Miranda do, but Mrs. Montgomery had the lifelong experience of being a sexy woman. They began to play a game of who-can-top-this? If Aria moved one way, Mrs. Montgomery moved another. They passed the song back and forth, moving their shapely bodies to the music. The band began to participate with drum rolls and long instrumental sections. All Aria's years of dancing lessons paid off.

When at last the song ended with the two women with their arms around each other, the applause was thunderous and many flashbulbs went off. After many bows they made their way to the rest room.

"Can you ever forgive me?" Aria said to Mrs. Montgomery as soon as the door closed. Dolly was waiting for them. "I had no idea you were . . . Lieutenant Montgomery said you were . . . Oh, I am so sorry."

"I haven't had so much fun in years."

"You'll come home with us now?"

Mrs. Montgomery laughed. "You, my dear new daughter, are going to have to face your husband alone. Just remember that the Montgomery bark is worse than the bite. Stand up to him. Give him a good long hard fight, then another good long time in bed, and you'll be fine."

Aria blushed.

"I have to go now. I have my own husband waiting for me in Maine. I hope the two of you come to visit very soon. Oh, by the way, were you actually suffering from morning sickness?"

"No," Aria said, smiling. "But give me time."

"The first one will probably be here before the year is out if I know my son. He's always liked girls." She kissed Aria's cheek. "Now I really must go. Come see me soon." She left the rest room.

"She's not like *my* mother-in-law at all," Dolly whispered. "*That* woman would never pour tomato soup over spaghetti."

Aria looked toward the door. "Your American men do not deserve the women."

"Uh-oh," Dolly said, and ran to lean against the door as the first people reached it and began trying to enter.

"Grab your raincoat and climb out the window. I'll hold them off. And you're right about the women," she called as Aria's foot disappeared out the window.

J.T. was waiting for her.

"Of course," he said before she was halfway out the window, "where else would I find my royal wife but climbing out the bathroom window?" He took her about the waist and helped her down. "You go shopping and you get arrested for shoplifting. Of course you've more than conquered that problem. All the shop owners in town now genuflect at the sight of you. You go to a ball and you humiliate me. You have my own *mother* prancing about half dressed."

He led her to his car, opened the door for her, and she climbed in. As she waited for him to walk around the car, she stuck her hands in the pocket of her raincoat and found his pocket knife. Mrs. Montgomery must have put it there.

"This is not the way an American wife acts," J.T. said as he opened the car door and got inside. "Nor is this the way a royal princess acts. *Nobody* acts as you did tonight."

"You are right," she said contritely. "This is a terrible dress for anyone to wear." Very solemnly, she took the knife and cut the inch of ribbon that connected the two cups of the halter top, and exposed her breasts to the dark interior of the car. "And the skirt must go too," she said, holding the knife at the slit and moving so her leg was exposed from hip on down.

J.T. started to speak, then he glanced out the back window. He was on her instantly, covering her body with his.

"I want to see you in the morning, Lieutenant Montgomery" came a man's voice from outside.

"Yes sir!" J.T. replied, still covering Aria.

The admiral looked embarrassed at the intimate scene and walked away.

J.T. and Aria looked at each other then burst out laughing.

He kissed her passionately, his hand fumbling under her coat and searching for her breast. "You were great, baby, absolutely great."

She kissed him back, moving her hands to the buttons on his dress uniform. "Was I? Better than your redhead?"

"She's my secretary, that's all."

She pushed at him. "You kiss your secretary's hand?" She was getting out of breath. He was tearing at her skirt.

"When she stays up all night typing a report for me, I do. What did you sew this with? Fishing tackle?"

His elbow hit the horn, making them both come to their senses. He looked at her, his eyes hot and hooded, then he rolled off of her and started the car.

Using the same techniques she had used to free herself from her kidnappers' ropes, Aria wriggled out of the remnants of the Carmen Miranda dress so that she was nude under the raincoat.

J.T. drove too fast to reach their house and he must have cooled off some too because he started lecturing her again as soon as they were inside. "You don't want to draw attention to yourself, yet you display yourself like tonight. This was *not* American behavior. This was not the behavior of *my* wife."

She dropped the raincoat and stood nude before him. "Is *this* American? Is *this* the behavior of your wife?" she asked innocently.

He blinked a couple of times. "Not exactly, but it'll

do for the moment." A split second later he was on top of her, knocking her to the floor. "I'm tired of fighting," he whispered. "I'm going to enjoy what time we have together."

They made love on the living-room floor, then J.T. carried her to the stairs and, in a contortionist's nightmare, made love to her with her back against a stair tread. She began backing up the stairs and he followed. They finished on the floor at the head of the stairs, both of them out of breath, sweating, and limp with exhaustion.

"What do I get if I dress as Jean Harlow?" Aria whispered, her body feeling like rubber.

"Not more of the same because I'm done for."

"Oh?" she said, wiggling under him, but it was a halfhearted motion.

"You are definitely a quick learner. Now go take a bath."

"You'll wash my back?"

"Maybe, but not your front. Your front gets me in trouble."

She laughed at that.

He sat in the bathroom while she bathed and she asked him questions about his mother. He was still in a state of shock over his mother's performance, saying that the woman he knew was quite a bit different from the high-stepper of that night. He remembered milk and cookies.

"And your father remembers begetting you," Aria said, smiling, and she smiled broader when she thought she saw him blush.

"You want your back washed or not?"

"*Sí*, meester, I do," she said in her Carmen Miranda accent.

J.T. groaned but when he washed her back he kissed her neck.

He bathed next and she washed his back. Aria put on a lilac spaghetti-strap nightgown and stood quietly outside the bathroom.

"What are you waiting for?" J.T. asked.

"I wondered which bed was to be mine tonight," she said shyly.

He pulled her into his bed. "With me, of course." He cuddled her to him and went to sleep right away.

"I got his attention," she murmured.

"What, honeybunch?" J.T. muttered.

"A new name," Aria said happily, and snuggled closer to him and went to sleep.

The next morning she woke slowly, smiling at the sunlight coming into the room. It was already growing hot but she didn't mind. Her body felt heavenly. She moved a bit to see J.T. lying beside her. Last night had been a dream come true. No pain, no discomfort at all, just pure sensual happiness.

She eased onto her elbow to look at him. My, but he was good-looking. Wasn't it odd how the more time they spent making love, the more handsome he became? He was much better-looking than Count Julian. In fact, right now she thought he was better-looking than any other man on earth.

How would it be, she wondered, if he opened his eyes and whispered, "I love you"? How would it feel to have a man say those words to you? Of course Count Julian had said them to her but they both knew he had only wanted her kingdom. This man didn't want her kingdom. In fact, all he wanted from her was her body.

She smiled at that. On the island she had been a princess and he hadn't obeyed her, hadn't done anything she had wanted, but when she acted as a woman acts . . . *then* he did anything she desired.

She realized that she wanted to please him. She had been taught to believe that the only persons she had to please were those of higher rank than she. But here in America she had wanted to please the wives of the other officers, she had wanted to please her mother-in-law (she swallowed at that memory), and now she wondered what it would be like to please her husband.

She knew he wanted her to learn to be an American and she vowed to try even harder to be as American as she could be. Maybe she would barbecue hamburgers for him; American men seemed to love big pieces of meat.

He stirred in his sleep, opened his eyes, and looked at her. "Good morning," he murmured as he pulled her to him and cuddled her against his big, hairy body.

"What is that American bear the children hold?" she asked.

"A teddy bear?"

"Yes. That's the one. You make me feel like your teddy bear."

"You don't feel like any kind of bear to me," he said softly, running his leg up hers. "You're too thin and not enough hair."

"Too thin?" she said in alarm, turning toward him.

"Too thin to be a teddy bear."

"Oh." She slipped her leg between his. "But not too thin otherwise? Not, oh, what did you say? 'A skinny ass'?"

"I think it would be better if we both forgot what was said on the island," he said before he kissed her.

"It is . . . all right to make love during the day-light?"

"I don't know. Let's try it and see. If the earth opens up and the devil takes us, at least we'll go happy."

Aria made a sound remarkably like a giggle just before J.T. began to kiss her neck.

He took his time caressing her body and she, for the first time, began to touch him too. How different his body felt from hers, no softness, just angles and planes and hard muscle. His skin was different too, coarser feeling, and his hairiness was a delight.

"Happy?" he asked, looking at her, smiling.

"Yes," she whispered.

"Perhaps I can make you happier."

He did.

Later, they lay together, sweaty but holding each other close, both of them content.

"I have to get up," Aria said. "I have to wash my hair and Ethel showed me how to set it in pin curls. It has to dry before this evening."

"Pin curls? Not those awful bobby pins that poke a man's eye out?"

She twisted away from him. "What do you know about women's pin curls?"

"Less than you know about Count Julian's mustache."

"How did you know he has a mustache?"

"A guess," J.T. said, but Aria smiled, knowing he was lying. She hummed in the bathroom while she washed her hair.

She managed with washing and rinsing her hair but the curling was beyond her.

J.T. had stayed in bed, half dozing, half smiling at the sound of her in the bathroom.

"Lieutenant Montgomery," she called. "I need your help."

Stubborn wench, he thought. He had told her not to call him Jarl and for some reason she refused to call him J.T., so she insisted on Lieutenant Montgomery.

Fifteen minutes later, to his utter disbelief, he was

wrapping her hair about his fingers and fastening it with bobby pins. "I cannot believe I am helping you deceive me," he muttered, making Aria laugh.

But later, as he was getting dressed, Aria ran past, gave him a quick kiss, and said she was going to cook him lunch. He leaned back and smiled. There were redeeming features to this marriage: lovemaking for breakfast and home cooking for lunch.

Later J.T. was just coming down the stairs when there was a loud knock at the door. Before he could answer it, the door burst open and General Brooks barged in. J.T. stopped on the third step, came to attention, and saluted.

"What is this?" General Brooks roared as he shoved the door shut in the face of his adjutant. He was holding aloft a copy of the *Key West Citizen* and pointing at the front-page photo of Aria dressed as Carmen Miranda arm in arm with Amanda, both women doing a high kick. "Is this Her Royal Highness?" he bellowed. "Is this Princess Aria?"

"Yes sir!" J.T. said smartly, eyes straight ahead.

General Brooks began to pace, punching the newspaper as he walked. "Do you know what you've done? You've exposed our plan to the world, that's what. Or you will have if anyone from Lanconia sees this."

"I don't think anyone will recognize her, sir."

"Don't get smart with me, young man. This is *your* fault. The army gave you a solemn responsibility and you have failed. What coercion did you use to get that poor young woman to do this? You were to teach her to be an *American*, not some South American hootch dancer."

"Sir! The idea was hers alone. It was a surprise to me." J.T. was still standing on the stairs, still at attention.

"Who's playing that confounded radio?"

"It's—" J.T. began.

"*Her* idea? You expect me to believe that? For God's sake, man, the woman is a royal princess. She's been raised in style and elegance, yet here she is wearing"—he held the paper up—"wearing platform shoes."

"Again, sir, it was not my idea."

General Brooks sat down on a wicker chair, the stiff straw creaking under his weight. "Well then, maybe you should have allowed her a little freedom. Sometimes women are like wild ponies: you can't keep them locked up all the time, sometimes you have to let them run a little free or else they break the traces altogether." He ran his hand over his face. "I've been married thirty-two years and I'm no closer to understanding my wife today than I ever was. What a day this has been! I've been on that plane for hours. You have any bourbon?"

"Yes sir," J.T. answered, but didn't move.

"Then get it!" General Brooks snapped.

J.T. went to the kitchen while the general continued talking.

"To pull this off, the princess has to act like an American. American women don't dress up in bare-legged skirts and dance at a Commander's Ball. It seems like a simple thing to ask that you could explain that to her. Did she think it was one of her blueblood masquerades? And who is that harlot with her?"

"My mother, sir," J.T. said, handing the general his drink.

"Lord," General Brooks gasped, and downed the drink. "I thought they checked you out. Look, Lieutenant, this is an order, you take control of the princess or I'll give you a desk job under the stupidest officer in the navy. You understand me? What the princess did was obviously a reaction against too tight a rein. My wife once reacted like that when we were first married." He waved his hand. "That's neither here nor there. Let the princess have a little fun now and then and maybe she'll learn to be an American. Time is running out. She'll never fool the Lanconian kidnappers this way. Damnation, but that radio is loud! Tell whoever is playing it to turn it off."

"Sir," J.T. said, "perhaps I could show you something."

The general looked tired and greatly put out but he heaved himself up from the chair and followed J.T. to the kitchen window.

In the backyard was a smoking barbecue grill and a cord stretched through an open window leading to a radio blaring "Don't Sit Under the Apple Tree with Anyone Else But Me." Aria was wearing baggy jeans rolled up to her knees, triple-rolled bobby socks, brown and white saddle oxfords, a plaid shirt of J.T.'s, and her hair was in pin curls with a polka-dot scarf tied over her head. She was chewing gum to the tune of the music while slapping hamburger patties between her hands.

"*That* is Her Royal Highness?" General Brooks gasped.

"She does look like an American housewife, sir."

"She looks *too much* like an American housewife." He turned to glare at J.T. "There is such a thing as going too far in the opposite direction." His expression changed and he put his hand on J.T.'s shoulder. "You want to talk about it, son? I mean, this isn't exactly the usual wartime assignment. Has it been very difficult?"

J.T., seeming to forget the general's rank, poured out two glasses of bourbon and took a healthy drink of his. "I can't make her out at all. One minute she's stretching out her hand to me like I'm one of her damned subjects and the next she's embarrassing me in front of hundreds of people and the next she's—" He broke off. "Let's just say that she's not shy when we're alone." His eyes narrowed. "And she refuses to do what I tell her to do. I explained to her about ironing and she laughed at me."

"My wife refuses to iron too," General Brooks said sadly. "Always has."

"I guess I don't know much about wives, sir, only women, and this woman doesn't fit into either category."

"You like her, do you?"

J.T. grinned. "I'm beginning to, but I sure as hell don't want to. I plan to fight it. I'm going to turn her over to her fiancé count with a clear conscience."

A look of guilt crossed General Brooks's face but he didn't say anything. "It looks to me like she's got your lunch ready and I better go. Don't tell her I was here. Tomorrow someone will come and tell you the details of returning to Lanconia. Do me a favor and don't let her pack her Carmen Miranda dress when she goes. Who knows what she'll do."

"No, sir, I won't," J.T. said, smiling as he walked the general to the door. He stood for a moment, thinking that the Carmen Miranda dress was in shreds, still lying on the floor of his car.

Aria called that the hamburgers were almost ready and, still smiling, he went outside.

The radio was blaring "Shorty George" and Aria took his hand. "Let's dance."

"Wait until something slower is on. I'm not good at this dancing."

"Okay," she said, turning back toward the hamburgers. "I'll ask Mitch the next time I see him. He's a great jitterbugger."

J.T. grabbed her hand, spun her around, and began a wild jitterbug with her. He had been rowing since he was a boy and his arms were very strong. He tossed her over his head, slid her beneath his legs, then whirled her out at arm's length.

She was breathless when the song finished.

"I told you I wasn't any good," he said smugly, making Aria laugh.

Companionably, they sat down to eat their lunch and J.T. watched Aria. Her hair in pin curls, her chewing gum stuck on the side of the plate, her fingers tapping to the music, eating a hamburger with her hands and drinking beer from a bottle, she was a different person from the princess on the island.

He began to realize that the general's visit had upset him because it made him aware that soon he would have to return his borrowed princess.

Since the war, it seemed that every man he knew was getting married, but J.T. had thought he was too wise to get trapped by a woman. More than once, he had seen a man marry some beautiful dish then two weeks later she would look like Aria looked now. J.T. had been disgusted. He liked his women combed and powdered and perfumed. But right now, looking at Aria, he wouldn't trade her for a beauty queen.

"Where did you get that shirt?" he asked over the radio, referring to the oversize, beat-up plaid she wore.

She gave him a level look over her beer. "From a box in your closet."

"The box way in the back? The one that is—was—taped and tied and has 'private' written in three-inch-tall letters on all six sides?"

"That sounds like the one," she said, watching him.

J.T. grunted and she smiled at him. He had always

heard men complaining about the lack of privacy in marriage and he had always thought that if he had a wife she would never invade *his* privacy. But now he found it didn't matter at all. In fact, he rather liked that she had been curious enough to search his belongings. It made it seem as if they really were married.

He looked back at her. He was going to have to turn her over to another man.

Right then he made a vow that he would be like a man falling off a horse—he would get right back on. As soon as he gave her to her short, old, effeminate count, he would get himself another wife. He liked having someone to come home to. He liked sitting in the backyard on a Saturday afternoon and eating hamburgers. He even liked the intimacy of rolling a woman's hair.

Of course he wondered if he would be able to find another wife as interesting as Aria. He smiled at the memory of last night. Most young officers' wives were terrified of any man with a star on his shoulder, but Aria hadn't cared one way or the other. And maybe he *had* been a little overbearing about his mother's visit—of course who knew that one's mother would act as his had?

He leaned his chair back and turned down the radio. "Yesterday you said you were suffering from morning sickness. Was that true or did you just want to get rid of me?"

"It wasn't true," she answered.

"What would happen if you were going to have my kid? Would your blueblood count still accept you?"

"I would still be queen, and as he wants to marry a queen, I don't believe it would interfere in any way."

"And what about the kid?"

"If he were a boy, as the oldest, he'd someday be king. If the child were a girl and I had no male issue, she would become queen."

J.T. took a deep drink of his beer. "I see. No objection from your short husband?"

Aria coughed to cover a laugh. "I will be queen and the decision about the child would be mine."

"Ol' Julian would be a father to someone else's kid?"

"He wouldn't be involved much in the upbringing even if the child were his. Royal children are reared by governesses and tutors. My father died when I was quite young and until I reached womanhood at fourteen, I only saw my mother from six to six-thirty each evening."

"And that's how your children would be raised?"

"I know of no other way."

"In America we do things differently. If we had a kid right now, he'd be here with us. You'd be feeding him and I'd be tossing him a ball."

"Another example of American equality," she said. "The woman does the work and the man gets to play."

J.T. looked like he might get angry but then he laughed. "It beats giving the kid to strangers. If you fell and cut yourself, who hugged you?"

Aria looked puzzled. "A doctor would be called. But a royal princess is too well guarded to get hurt very often, although I have injured myself falling from a horse."

"Guarded? When I was ten I rowed myself out to an island and camped for two nights alone."

"Royal children are never alone. Even at night someone sleeps in their room. At fourteen I was given my own room but a maid slept in an adjoining chamber."

199

"I see," J.T. said, taking a big bite of his hamburger. "And our kid—I mean, if we made one—would be raised like that?"

"It is tradition." She was quiet a moment. "But you could visit him whenever you wished."

"No," J.T. said slowly. "I'm not sure I could do that." He leaned back, turned the radio back up, and fell silent.

Chapter Thirteen

O<small>N</small> Monday morning J.T. received a telegram from General Brooks saying that all was arranged and the two of them would be shipped out to Lanconia on Tuesday.

"The beginning of the end," he murmured as Bill entered his office.

"Something bothering you?" Bill asked.

"The princess and I leave for Lanconia tomorrow."

"I'm going to miss her, and Dolly's not going to be fit to live with. Those two have become as thick as thieves. And the merchants around town are going to cry too."

J.T. crumbled the telegram in his hand. "I better call her so she can pack," he said solemnly.

"And I'll call Dolly so she can help."

Later that day Dolly called J.T. and said she was inviting everyone to a cookout on the beach. "A farewell party for her," Dolly said, and there was a catch in her voice.

You aren't going to miss her more than I will, J.T. thought.

It was a subdued Aria who met him at the beach. He took her hand in his. "Cheer up, baby, you're going home."

"I shall miss America," she said softly. "I shall miss its freedom and its music and its feeling of progression."

Not to mention missing me, he thought with some anger. "I guess I'm to catch the lobsters."

"Yes," she said disinterestedly. "Probably."

Aria couldn't cheer up, no matter how hard she tried. And Dolly was as bad as she was. A princess never shows her emotions in public, Aria chanted.

J.T. brought back lobsters and the men put them on the grill.

"Oh no," Dolly said. "Look what the cat dragged in."

Aria looked up to see a plump Heather Addison on the arm of Mitch. "Good evening, everybody," Mitch called, then looked at Aria. "You look lovely, as usual. J.T. taking better care of you?"

"I take *great* care of her," J.T. said, holding a barbecue fork as if it were a weapon.

Heather gave a contemptuous look at Aria then wiggled over to J.T. She took his arm and snuggled her breasts into his side. "J.T., honey, I haven't seen you since Washington. Remember the night we did the town? The day after you got married?" she added loudly.

"Just what we need—fireworks," Gail groaned. "J.T., let's make this evening pleasant, okay?"

Mitch went to sit by Aria. "I hear you're shipping out tomorrow. We're going to miss you. J.T. going too?"

J.T. turned around. "She's going with *me*, not the

other way around. This country of Lanconia needs some shipbuilding advice, and I'm giving it. My *wife* goes with me."

Mitch moved closer to Aria. "I hear Lanconia is very pretty with long, cool nights, nothing but cowbells ringing."

"True," Aria said sadly. "No McGuire Sisters, no garbage trucks at three A.M., no honkytonks, no beach parties."

"You've been there?"

"No," J.T. and Aria said in unison. "We've just been reading about it," J.T. added.

"J.T., honey, I left my wrap in the car. Would you get it for me?" Heather asked.

"Somebody watch the grill," J.T. called, and stepped away from the light of the fire and into the darkness.

Heather lost no time in following him. "J.T.," she called, "wait for me."

He halted. "You shouldn't have come."

"Don't give me that," she said. "I know what's going on. I had to pay three lipsticks and four pair of nylons to get the information about you and that . . . that princess. If she's royalty, I'll eat my bathing suit."

"You better start chewing." J.T. turned away.

Heather hurried after him. "I also know the marriage is temporary and that she's going to dump you as soon as you two get to her country. I hear she's going to throw you over for a skinny little duke with blue blood."

"Heather, you have a big mouth." He stopped at Mitch's car, opened the door, grabbed her beach cover-up, and shoved it at her.

"You used to like my mouth," she said, leaning into his chest. "Honey, I'm only concerned about you. What are you gonna do when she ditches you? You aren't fool enough to end up with a broken heart, are you?"

The words hit too close to home. "Let's go back," he said, but there was no conviction in his voice.

"I'll be here, sweetie. When you come back here all alone, I'll be waiting."

He looked at her a moment. "I might take you up on that offer," he said.

They walked back to the firelight together.

"Are you going to stand for that?" Dolly asked, looking up at Heather and J.T. bending over the grill.

"That's a nice suit," Aria said absently. "Do you think she bought it here?"

Dolly rolled her eyes then got up and pushed herself between J.T. and Heather. "Your *date* is over there," she said pointedly to Heather.

"My date for tonight," Heather said smugly.

The evening grew worse. Aria and Dolly were depressed and Heather was angry at J.T. for having married someone other than herself, Mitch kept making hints to Aria about having a night of farewell, and the rest of the group wished they hadn't come.

Aria watched J.T. and Heather and saw that J.T. was making no effort to keep Heather's hands off his body. In fact, he kept looking at Aria as if he expected something from her. But the more Heather oozed over J.T., the straighter Aria's back became. She felt closer to being a royal princess tonight than she had in weeks.

By the time the group said good night, Aria's manners were very formal. "So good of you to have invited me," she said, and held out her hand to shake—not a hearty American shake but the fingers-only type royalty used to save their hands from hundreds of handshakes in a few hours.

"I'll see you off tomorrow," Dolly said softly, a little intimidated by Aria's manner.

"Thank you very much," she said to J.T. when he opened the car door for her. "A most pleasant party," she said as he drove away.

"What, no mimicking of Heather?"

"She is a lovely young woman," Aria said. "Such lovely hair."

"It's not a natural color."

"Oh? One would never have guessed." They were both quiet the rest of the way home.

"You must pardon me," Aria said when they were home. "I am most tired and think I'll go to bed. I wish you a pleasant good night."

"Damn!" J.T. said when she was upstairs. Did the woman have no feelings? How many times had he made a fool of himself out of jealousy over her? But tonight he had allowed Heather to make the most outrageous remarks and Aria had said nothing. He went into the backyard to smoke a cigarette and drink a strong gin and tonic. Perhaps she was looking forward to getting rid of him. Perhaps she was too cold-blooded to feel such an emotion as jealousy.

As usual in Key West, it was starting to rain. He crushed his cigarette out and downed his drink as he glanced up and saw the light go out in the window above. It looked like she was sleeping in her single bed tonight. Good, he thought, it was better to start breaking apart now.

The upstairs was dark and he made no effort to be quiet as he stumbled about and undressed.

He went to Aria's end of the room to close the windows. A bolt of lightning showed her to be lying with her face buried in the pillow.

"Damn," he said under his breath, and went to

stand over her bed. "Look, it's almost over. You'll be home soon. You'll be back in your castle and you'll never have to wash a dish again and you'll never have to look at my ugly mug again."

"Or see Dolly," she said into the pillow.

"Are you okay?" He sat down on the bed. "You and Dolly get into it?"

She whirled around like a tornado and came up with fists clenched, pummeling at his bare chest and arms. "You humiliated me," she yelled. "You embarrassed me before people who have become my friends."

He grabbed her fists. "Look who's talking! You with your 'Chica Chica' in front of my commanding officers."

"But you deserved that! You insinuated that I wasn't good enough for your mother."

"I never did such a thing in my life." He was aghast.

"Then what was that 'Do you know how to act at a formal ball?' 'My mother hates chewing gum so don't blow bubbles in her face.' 'You are to be courteous and respectful to my mother. Treat her as if she were a queen so don't go telling her she does or does not have permission to speak.' 'And she can sit wherever she wants'? What was all that?"

J.T. grinned in the darkness. "Maybe I did go a little overboard."

"You deserved 'Chica Chica.' I did *not* deserve Heather. I've been very good the last few days."

J.T. moved his hands to her back. "You sure have, honey," he said, leaning forward to kiss her.

She drew back. "How can you have the audacity to touch me? Get away from me."

J.T. stopped abruptly. "Sure. Fine. I'll leave you alone. You can lie there and dream about the time when you never have to see me again."

He went to his own bed but he was too angry to sleep. He kept thinking of the injustice of it all, how he had saved her life and married her and taught her to be an American, and she screamed at him and told him to leave her alone. He flopped about in the bed and the sheets began to stick to him. He punched the pillow but sleep wasn't anywhere near.

Maybe he shouldn't have let Heather act like that. She always was a bit of a pest. She had wanted to get married and he acted as if he had no idea what she had in mind, but all along he had suspected that Heather wanted Warbrooke Shipping more than she wanted him.

Cursing women, cursing the army for marrying them, cursing his love of seafood that had made him want to go to that island where he had first met her, J.T. got out of bed and went to her end of the room. She still had her face buried in the pillow. He sat down on the edge of the bed.

"Look, maybe I shouldn't have behaved like I did. I know Heather can be a little cat and I'm sorry I embarrassed you."

She didn't say a word.

"You hear me?" He held out his hand to touch her temple. "You're crying," he said as if he didn't believe it. He pulled her into his arms. "Oh, sweetheart, I'm sorry. I didn't mean to make you cry. I didn't even know you *could* cry."

"Of course I can cry," she said angrily, sniffing. "A princess just doesn't cry in public, that's all."

"I'm not public," he said, sounding hurt. "I'm your husband."

"You didn't act like it tonight. You acted as if Heather were your wife."

"Well, maybe she will be."

"What?" Aria gasped.

"Well, honey, I have to think of the future. You're going to stay in Lanconia with your scrawny count and I find I'm growing rather fond of marriage."

"Oh? How so?" she asked, snuggling against him.

"I don't know. It's sure not the peace and quiet it's added to my life."

"I wonder, Lieutenant Montgomery, maybe you could stay in Lanconia and remain as my husband. My country could benefit from some of your knowledge."

"And be king? I'd just as soon be put in a zoo. No thank you. *No* woman is worth that. Hey, where you going?" he asked.

"As you say, to the can."

"Now what did I do wrong?" he muttered.

Dolly and Bill came to the plane to say good-bye and it felt natural to Aria when Dolly hugged her in public.

Dolly held out a package. "It's just a little something to help you remember America." There were tears in her eyes.

J.T. shook hands with Bill. "I'll be back as soon as . . . as soon as this is done." He was hovering over Aria as if he thought she might fly away.

"Good-bye," they called as Aria and J.T. boarded the airplane.

It was to be a long flight because they had to go north over Russia instead of risking being shot down over Germany.

Aria leaned back in the hard leather seat and looked out the window at Dolly and Bill on the ground.

"Cheer up," J.T. said. "You're going home. What did Dolly give you?"

Aria blinked away tears and opened the package. The box was filled with chewing gum. She laughed.

"I'll get her back," J.T. groaned. "A princess who likes bubble gum."

When they were in the air, the copilot brought J.T. a fat package. "It's our orders," J.T. said. "By the time we get to Lanconia you're to have memorized a new background and assumed a new identity. Look at this!" he said, scanning the cover letter. "General Brooks recommended that you come from Warbrooke, Maine, and that you and I have known each other all our lives. That way I can tell you about my hometown. And your name is Kathleen Farnsworth Montgomery. Okay, Kathy, let's get to work."

Aria couldn't help contrasting this trip to their earlier flight from Washington to Key West. J.T. didn't doze while she studied; instead, he told her about his hometown and the people who lived there. He told her about his father, who was now single-handedly running what J.T. described as the family's modest shipping business. He told her about his three older brothers, about the rowing races they used to have.

"I always won," he said smugly. "I was the smallest and strong for my size."

She looked at the length and breadth of him sprawled in the airplane seat. "You're not *still* the smallest, are you?" she asked, and her voice conveyed her fear of a family of giants.

"Of course not," he said, eyes twinkling, and leaned over to kiss her, then he shoved the papers off his lap and gave all his attention to kissing her.

"Not now!" she hissed at him, and he withdrew, grinning at her flushed face.

"Where were we?" he asked. "Oh yes, Warbrooke." He continued to tell about his town and his family until she began to feel she knew the place.

The plane landed in London for refueling and for

hurried dashes to the rest room for the two passengers. When they reboarded, they started again with the study. This time J.T. asked her questions about her upbringing in America and about her own vital statistics.

They fell asleep against each other somewhere over Russia and didn't wake until they landed in Escalon, the capital city of Lanconia.

J.T. looked out the window and saw blue-green, snow-topped mountains in the distance.

"Most of Lanconia is very high. We're about seven thousand feet elevation now, so the air is thin."

He kissed her. "You know *nothing* about this place, remember? Neither of us has been here before."

"Okay, babe," she said, snapping her gum.

"That's better—sort of. Do you have to chew that stuff?"

"It's very American, and besides, I'll have to give it up soon enough. Crowns and bubble gum don't go together. Hurry up and get off, I want to make sure no one hurts the box of records I brought my sister."

"*Kathy* has no sister, remember?"

He was looking at her very sternly, so she crossed her eyes and blew a bubble at him.

"Go!" he said, laughing.

The air was cool and fresh and sharp as only mountain air can be; even the fumes of the planes couldn't override the cleanness of it.

It was a small airport, and with the war there was very little traffic through it. A car was waiting for J.T. and Aria.

"Lieutenant," said a man who was wearing a dark suit and carrying a briefcase, "everything is ready for you. Good morning, Your Roy—"

"Good to meet ya!" Aria said, grabbing the man's hand and pumping it. "It always this cold in this

210

place? It looks pretty dead around here. What's to do?"

The man's eyes sparkled. "Good morning, Mrs. Montgomery."

"Just call me Kathy, ever'body does. 'Cept him. Sometimes he calls me other things." Chomping away on her gum, she hugged J.T.'s arm and gave him an adoring look.

"Well, yes," the man said uncomfortably. "Shall we go to your hotel?"

"Who're you playing?" J.T. asked when he opened the car door for her.

"Every Lanconian's image of an American."

The man who drove them was James Sanderson and he was assistant to the American ambassador to Lanconia and only he and the ambassador knew the truth behind the imposter princess.

"Otherwise, your story is well covered," Mr. Sanderson said. "Tomorrow, Lieutenant, you will be escorted to the local water plant. You are supposedly an expert on distillation plants."

"Then someone is starting to work on the grapes?" Aria asked.

"We are working with the king every day," Mr. Sanderson answered.

"How is he?"

"Aging," Mr. Sanderson answered, but said no more.

Aria looked out the window. Lanconia looked the same as it had for centuries and she could feel the place creeping into her bones. The streets had been made for goatherders and for walking, so they were much too narrow for the long, wide American car. The cobblestones were hard on the tires and made for a rough ride.

The houses were plastered and whitewashed and

211

everywhere were the distinctive blue-gray roof tiles that Lanconia manufactured. In the twenties Lanconia had briefly become a fashionable resort and the people who were in the know took crates of the tiles home and had little Lanconian playhouses built. But the fashion hadn't lasted long and the factory was left with thousands of surplus tiles.

The people in the streets were on foot or on bicycles and there were a few horse-drawn carts, but no automobiles. Their clothes were simple, in a style that hadn't changed in centuries: long, dark skirts, white blouses, and pretty, embroidered belts. For a while, those belts had been fashionable too. The men wore heavy shoes, thick wool socks to their knees, and wool knickers. Their white shirts were covered by a sleeveless embroidered vest. The women were proud of their skill with a needle and showed off on their own belts and their husbands' vests. The children wore smaller versions of their parents' clothes, without the belts and vests, but with finely smocked shirts.

J.T. and Mr. Sanderson had stopped talking. "It's like going back in time," J.T. said softly.

"More than you know," Aria replied.

"Here we are," Mr. Sanderson said, pulling the car into the circular drive of the three-story white hotel. He leaned forward to look at Aria. "I don't think anyone will recognize you, but you should be prepared if they do. You want to be seen as much as possible, so when the imposter is taken—it's planned for tomorrow, by the way—they will have an idea of where to look for a replacement."

"No idea yet who 'they' are?" J.T. asked. "No idea who tried to murder the princess?"

"We have suspicions but nothing concrete yet. Okay, here's the bellboy, let's go."

"Wait," Aria said, her hand on J.T.'s arm. "I know

him." The bell "boy" was actually a man nearing
seventy. "He was our third gardener. His wife used to
bake me cookies. This isn't going to be easy."

"We've come too far to blow it now. You've never
been here before and never seen this man before."

"Okay," she said, taking a deep breath.

She stood on the bricked entryway while Mr. Sanderson went inside and J.T. helped load the luggage
on a cart.

The old man nearly dropped two bags when he saw
Aria.

She smacked gum out of the side of her mouth.
"Seen a ghost, honey?" she asked the old man. He just
stood and gaped so Aria leaned over and pulled her
skirt halfway up her thigh and adjusted her nylons.
The man was still staring. "Seen all you want?" she
said rather nastily.

J.T. grabbed her arm and pulled her inside the
hotel. "You're going to lower America's reputation
into the gutter. Use a little subtlety."

"Sure, ducky," she answered. "Anything you say,
sugar."

J.T. gave her a warning look.

The inside of the hotel looked like a Russian czar's
hunting lodge: log ceiling, plaster walls, big pine
furniture scattered about. Above the desk was a flag of
Lanconia: a red ground with a stag, a goat, and a
bunch of grapes on it.

"Quaint," J.T. said under his breath. "Do they have
bathrooms in this joint?"

"Remember America's reputation," she reminded
him.

While J.T. signed the register, the hotel clerk looked
up and did a double-take on Aria. He stared at her
until she winked at him. He looked down at the book.

"Excuse me, Lieutenant Montgomery, I must get

213

something," the clerk said, and disappeared through a door behind the desk.

J.T. looked questioningly to Mr. Sanderson, who shrugged.

The clerk reappeared with what looked to be his entire family: a fat wife and two plump teenage girls. They all stood and stared at Aria.

Aria walked to the desk. "You got any postcards in this burg? Nobody back home will believe this place is for real."

No one moved; they just stared at Aria.

She leaned across the desk and into the manager's face. "What's the matter with you people?" she asked belligerently. "How come ever'body's starin' at me? You people don't like Americans? We're not good enough for you? You think—"

J.T. caught her arm and pulled her back. "Kathy, be quiet."

The manager began to recover himself. "Pardon our rudeness. We did not mean to stare. It's just that you look like our crown princess."

Aria's jaw dropped down. "You hear that, honey?" she said, punching J.T. in the ribs. "They think *I* look like a princess."

The manager's fat wife reached under the desk and withdrew a postcard and held it at arm's length to Aria.

She took it and studied the official photograph of Her Royal Highness, Princess Aria. Aria's face showed her disappointment. "Nice rocks but I've seen better-lookin' women. In fact Ellie down at the diner is better-lookin', ain't she, honey? Hey! Wait a minute! You sayin' I look like this stuck-up blueblood? I'll have you know I was Miss Submarine Romance of 1941. I was voted, by two hundred and sixteen sailors, mind you, the girl they most wanted to submerge with." She looked up at J.T. "I don't look like her, do I, honey? She looks like somethin' out of a silent movie."

He put his arm around her, took the postcard, and angrily slapped it on the desk as he glared at the clerk and his family. "My wife is much prettier than that woman. Come on, honey, we'll go upstairs and you can rest and try to forget about this insult." He led her away with her head buried in his chest.

When they reached the room, the three didn't speak until the bellboy had left.

Mr. Sanderson looked at Aria in amazement.

"Congratulations, Mrs. Montgomery, you are the *most* obnoxious American I have ever had the misfortune to meet."

She snapped her gum, grinned, and winked at him at the same time. "Thanks, toots."

Chapter Fourteen

M~R.~ Sanderson stayed in their room for three hours as he talked about the seriousness of the coming venture and how important Aria's return to the throne was. He talked about America's need for the vanadium and how much America needed to have military bases in Lanconia.

"Our plan is this," Mr. Sanderson said. "We will take the imposter princess and her aunt, Lady Emere, tomorrow just as they return from America, before anyone of her family in Lanconia sees Princess Maude, and I imagine the brigands who put her in Princess Aria's place will contact Her Royal Highness immediately. For them to be aware of your presence, you two will have to be seen as often as possible within the next twenty-four hours. Once Her Highness is taken, Lieutenant, your services will no longer be needed. She cannot reenter the palace with an American husband at her side. The ambassador and I have arranged for you to be returned to America as soon as contact is made."

"But—" Aria began, wanting to tell the man that Lieutenant Montgomery was to remain as her husband.

J.T. put his hand on her arm. "So we have a couple of days," he said softly.

"Yes," Mr. Sanderson said, looking from one to the other, taking note of their closeness.

"I am concerned for her safety," J.T. said. "I don't want her alone among her enemies. Someone tried to kill her before."

"Yes, but now whoever tried to kill her will think she is an American. I'm sure the murderers believe the actual princess to have been drowned in Florida. We plan to negotiate for the imposter princess's return with whoever contacts Her Royal Highness. Princess Aria—they think—will be discharged once the imposter is returned. Someone believes the real princess is dead, but it may not be the same person who contacts Kathy Montgomery."

J.T. stood, pacing and frowning. "I don't believe whoever planned this is as stupid as you seem to think. She's bound to give herself away. I think I—"

"Lieutenant," Mr. Sanderson said sharply, "your services will no longer be needed. We can protect Her Royal Highness."

Aria was trying to control her emotions but she was very pleased that the lieutenant wanted to protect her, that he was so concerned about her safety. Perhaps it was a camouflage of the truth. Maybe he wanted to remain with her forever.

J.T. turned his back to the two of them and looked out the window.

"We, the ambassador and I," Mr. Sanderson said, "thought perhaps that the two of you might give some evidence of not being a happily married couple; then, when Her Royal Highness is contacted, it will seem natural that she is willing to participate in this farce without her husband."

J.T. didn't turn around but continued staring out of the window. "Yes, that makes sense," he murmured. He turned back. "Shall we go to dinner? It's been a long flight for both of us and we'd like to get to bed early."

Mr. Sanderson cleared his throat. "Tonight, if possible, we thought perhaps you two could stage an argument at dinner, a loud, public argument, and Her Royal Highness could run to the embassy in anger and spend the night there. We need the time to brief her and we need to establish her contact with our embassy. There are many details to work out yet."

"So, I'm no longer needed," J.T. said, his eyes dark. He didn't look at Aria. "I'm going to take a shower— if I can find a bathroom in this place—then we can go to dinner and start our fight. That should be easy." He grabbed clean underwear from a suitcase, a towel from a rack, and left the room.

"No, no, no," Aria said to Mr. Sanderson the minute J.T. was out of the room. "You have everything wrong. We are not to be separated. The American government would not help me unless I agreed to put an American on the throne beside me. We are to remain married and it is better that he stay beside me." She felt a bit of panic. America was still in her veins and she didn't want to let it slip away. And she didn't want to lose this man who made her feel so lovely.

Mr. Sanderson gave her his best diplomatic look. "Of course we were informed of this aspect of your agreement, Your Royal Highness, but that was a military agreement, not a diplomatic or political one. You could not possibly consider putting an American on the Lanconian throne. He knows nothing of the duties of being prince consort, nor does he know about Lanconia. And from what I hear, he has no desire to become prince consort. He could not do a good job even if, by some freak chance, the Lanconian people would accept an American commoner as their queen's husband. You must think of Lanconia and not your, ah . . . personal feelings."

Aria could feel Lanconia seeping into her, rather like someone opening a window and letting a room gradually grow colder.

"But royalty does not divorce," she said softly.

"Your marriage will be annulled," Mr. Sanderson said. "It was made under duress and the Lanconian High Council will agree to it, as will the American government. We are trusting that you can persuade the king to award the vanadium to America and that, as a result of the help we have given you, in the future we may station American troops in your country."

"Yes," she said. "America has helped me and I will show my gratitude."

Mr. Sanderson's face changed. "I am sorry to cause you any unpleasantness. I had no idea the two of you had become fond of one another in so short a time. I was given to understand that you'd welcome an annulment."

"At one time," she murmured. Her head came up. "Let us have this time together, to say good-bye. We can part in anger when I am contacted. He can say that no wife of his will do such a thing and I can go against his orders. Later I can say that I like being a princess better than being a wife. The marriage can be dissolved when I am restored to my rightful place."

"Yes, but—"

"You may leave me now." As soon as Aria said it she realized how long it had been since she had given a regal order.

"Yes, Your Highness," Mr. Sanderson said, then stood and gave a little bow as he left the room.

Aria walked to the window and looked down at the narrow street, at the people walking there. They seemed so old. There was no spring to their step. There were no children in sight. Every year more young people took their children and left the country. There was no industry for them, no jobs, no modern entertainment.

As she watched, she became even more aware of how these people were her responsibility. The High Council passed laws, worked on the trial system, but it was up to the royal family to create interest in the country. In the last century she and her family had become a tourist attraction.

She glanced down at her dress, the easiness of it, such a simple dark brown thing with no diamonds, no royal insignia, and she began to remember how she had to dress as a princess. It took three women two hours each morning to dress her and to arrange her long hair. All day long she changed clothes. There were morning clothes, afternoon clothes, reception clothes, tea clothes, and long, formal dinner gowns.

She thought of her social calendar: every minute of every day was filled with engagements. From ten A.M. until six P.M. she was on public display. She inspected factories, listened to people's complaints, shook thousands of hands, sidestepped personal questions. Then there were the trips around Lanconia, for several days in a row when she did nothing but visit one hospital after another, comfort one dying child and his parents after another. Then at night she was escorted to some long, tiring ball where people talked to her with quaking voices.

Before she had gone to America, she hadn't minded her duties so much. They had been what she had done since she left the schoolroom and she had been trained for them. But now . . . now she had been able to shop in stores, she had gossiped with other women, she had jitterbugged in public. She had been able to be a normal ordinary person who wasn't watched and judged every minute.

She remembered once, when she was eighteen, that she had worn a dress with a low neckline to an afternoon garden party. At the party, a man had suddenly fainted at her feet. When she bent to help him, he whipped out his camera, snapped her picture, then scampered away. The next day every paper in the free world carried a photograph of the semiexposed bosom of Princess Aria of Lanconia.

That was her life. She lived in a glass box, her every movement scrutinized and examined then exposed to the world.

Yet she had considered asking this American husband of hers to share that life. How would he be as king? Would he toss reporters into swimming pools? Would he call people like Julian "Count Julie" to their faces? Would he dine with common-looking women in public places? Would he show up at dinner wearing his undershirt?

And how would the people of Lanconia react to him? Would he be contemptuous of the goatherders? Of the grape pickers?

All Americans seemed to think their country was the only one on earth. Could Lieutenant Montgomery give up his American citizenship to become a Lanconian? Would he bother to learn the language?

He was so quick-tempered, so impatient, so intolerant. She remembered their time on the island. She understood now some of his intolerance, some of his anger, but if he remained in Lanconia, he would be consorting daily with people whose lineage could be traced to generations of kings. Their snobbery made Aria's seem like that of a peasant. How would they treat this American commoner? How would he react to their treatment of him? She had a vision of Lieutenant Montgomery wrapping Cousin Freddie's pearls about his thin neck the first time Freddie looked down his nose at the American.

And then there was the fact that the lieutenant didn't *want* to be prince consort. She didn't think he could do a good job at best, but if he was reluctant, he would be like a large, spoiled two-year-old.

She took a deep breath and turned away from the window. Mr. Sanderson was right: it was over.

Her easy, happy American interlude was over. It was time now to return to her destiny. She had been born to be queen and now she must continue preparing for that duty—no, the honor of being queen, she corrected herself.

She was able to smile when J.T. reentered the room. He frowned. "I guess you're glad to be home."

"Yes and no. America will always be a fond memory to me. Dolly said she will visit me, so I don't plan to lose all contact with your country. Perhaps you will visit—"

"No," he said sharply. "Can we get this over? I mean our public argument?"

"It has been postponed." She was studying his face. Until today she had thought they were always to be married but now she knew these were their last few hours together. "We dine together and . . . and spend the night, then tomorrow or the next day I'll be contacted, I'm sure. Tomorrow we must be seen as often as possible by as many people as possible."

He wore only a towel about his middle and was

rubbing his wet hair with another towel. He looked so good her fingers ached to touch him.

"I wish you hadn't," he said. "I need to get back to the base as soon as possible and the sooner . . ." He trailed off.

She stiffened. "The sooner you get rid of me the better."

He looked at her for a long moment. "It'll be better for me to get this over with."

Dinner was one of the most difficult meals she had ever experienced. She felt like a fool because the idea of not seeing him again was making her very sad but he couldn't wait to get rid of her. He was cool and remote to her.

Aria had to hide her feelings and play the despicable American when any Lanconian was near.

"You think we want a table out in the middle?" she demanded. "J.T., honey, they want to stare at me. They want to point at me and say I look like their plain-faced princess. Do we have to stay in this town? I don't know if I'm gonna be able to stand it."

"This way, madame," said the haughty waiter, and led them to a secluded table in the corner.

"What will you do when you get back?" Aria asked when they were alone.

"Look at Buicks," he said, then glowered at her. "Work. Do what I can to help in the war."

"Will they let you keep our little house?"

"I don't want it."

Aria smiled at that. Perhaps he too was upset at their parting. "I shall miss America and I shall miss you," she whispered.

He looked down at his empty plate. "It'll be nice to have my time be my own again. I've been neglecting my work."

She didn't say anything in reply to him. Their food came and still she said nothing.

"Will you see Heather again?" she asked at last.

"I'm going to go out with every woman in the southeastern U.S. And you? You going to marry your little count?"

"Really!" she said, her eyes glaring into his. "Sometimes you can be most infantile. Count Julian is a perfectly suitable man and he will make an excellent prince consort. Better than you could do."

"Better than *I* could do? Let me tell you, baby, what this backward place of yours needs is a shot of new blood. You'd be lucky if I stayed with you, but I wouldn't have this place on a platinum platter. There's a war going on out there, but these people are so wrapped up in their own petty problems that they don't even see anyone else's."

"We are not involved in a *war* and that is what is *wrong* with us?" she seethed. "You aggressive, angry Americans could learn a lot from our peaceful country. We don't destroy ourselves and other countries with our war machines."

"Because you don't fight *for* anything. You just let the outside world take care of you. You're willing to profit from the war by selling the vanadium but you aren't willing to sacrifice your men for soldiers."

"Are you calling us cowards? Our country was founded by the greatest warriors in the world. In 874 A.D. we—"

"What the hell do I care about your history? *Now* you're a bundle of lily-livered extortionists with a petticoat ruler."

At that she rose and slapped him hard before storming out of the dining room. She ran out of the hotel and into the street, into the cool night air, past people who looked as if they were seeing a ghost, down one street after another. She had no idea where she was going. Her experience of the streets of Escalon was limited to rides in ceremonial carriages. When she was a little girl, she thought the driver merely followed the trail of rose petals to get where he was going.

How could she have considered that man as prince consort? How could she have allowed bed pleasure to influence her rational thinking? He was the pigheaded, intolerant bigot she had first thought he was. She was quite willing to learn American ways and to see thoughts and ideas through American eyes, but he could see no other way than his own. His country was very young, with an adolescent's energies. America wanted power and was willing to kill for it. Her country was old and had learned the power of peace. At one point her ancestors had ruled a big portion of Europe and Russia. In fact, the reason her family was in power was because they had bred the largest, strongest warriors.

Yet this American had called them cowards! Extortionists!

She walked for a long time, not seeing where she was going, just walking and cursing herself for being such a fool.

She halted when she ran into someone. "Excuse me," she said, still using the American expression. She looked into the eyes of her Lord High Chamberlain. He was an arrogant man who expected the streets to clear when he walked them. Intelligence burned in his black eyes.

Aria wanted him to see her and to remember her. "Path not wide enough for you, bub?" she said. "You knock ladies into the street here?"

He drew back from her as if she were a bit of fungus.

Aria leaned forward and put her hands on his badge of office. "Hey! Are you royalty or somethin'? What's that say on there? Is that Latin? We have Latin in America. Do you know the princess? People here say I look like her, but I don't think I do, but I was thinkin' maybe I could borrow a crown of hers and have my picture taken. It'll be real funny back home. How much do you think she'd charge to rent one of her crowns? Or maybe she'd just loan it bein' as we look alike an' all. What d'ya think, buster?"

The Lord High Chamberlain flared his nostrils at her and moved away.

"That's no way to treat an American citizen," she yelled after him, disturbing the tranquil street. "We own your country, you know. You ought to be nice to us."

People looked out of their doors and windows at her.

"I'm gonna report you to the American ambassador," she said loudly, then turned to an openmouthed bystander and demanded directions to the embassy.

It was after midnight when she arrived and she was surprised to see every light in the building on. Someone must have been watching the entrance because the door opened before she reached it.

A large, matronly woman who was desperately trying to hold on to her figure via the use of rigid corsets swooped into the room like a decorated snow shovel and ushered Aria up the stairs.

"Oh my dear," the woman said. "I mean, Your Royal Highness, it has been dreadful here. How could the American government do such a thing to you? You poor, poor darling."

227

"What has happened?" Aria asked, standing in the big bedroom, surrounded by sumptuous blue silk wall coverings and darker blue silk bed hangings. The Americans didn't skimp on their embassies.

"My goodness," the woman gushed. *"Everything* has happened. We didn't have much notice that you were coming, and with the war and all it was difficult to get what we needed. But I did manage a nightgown for you. It's made by French nuns and the sewing is exquisite. I do hope you like it, although I am sure it's not the quality you're used to."

"What has happened?" Aria insisted.

"That man was here, that awful man my own government married you to."

"Lieutenant Montgomery? Is he here now?"

"Oh no, although it wasn't easy to get rid of him. My husband the ambassador got rid of him but only after what could only be described as a brawl in the foyer. He had a fistfight with four armed guards."

Aria sat down on the edge of the bed. "Why was he here?"

"He said he wanted to see you and didn't believe anyone when we told him you weren't here. We have been so dreadfully worried about you. My husband insisted he leave but he refused, thus the brawl."

"Was he injured?"

"No, a bruise or two, no more. My husband finally had to tell him that he was not going to be king no matter what. That news made him calm down and they went to my husband's study. I just hope the guards didn't understand what my husband meant. It has been so difficult keeping all this a secret. I am to treat you as a niece, not as Your Royal Highness. I do hope you can forgive me. We have tried so hard to make everything comfortable for you but we were given such short notice that—"

"What did your husband say to Lieutenant Montgomery?" Aria asked.

"He explained that the bargain you'd made with the army could not possibly be kept and that no matter how hard he fought he'd never be allowed to be king."

Aria looked away from the woman. "So he's been told," she murmured.

"My husband told him in no uncertain terms. The very idea of an American as king. I mean, it is my own country, but an American—especially one such as him—as king! The idea! Such a crude young man. Fisticuffs in the foyer!"

"You may leave me now," Aria said.

Startled, the woman stopped speaking abruptly. "Yes, Your Royal Highness. Will you need help dressing?"

"No, just leave me." She waved her hand at the woman.

Once she was alone, Aria took her time undressing and putting on the long, high-necked nightgown. It was indeed like she had worn all her life—no more Rita Hayworth style, she thought with regret. It seemed that minute by minute she was losing America and returning to Lanconia. Already she was dismissing people from her presence.

She climbed into the empty bed and thought about her husband. He must be very angry about what he had heard tonight.

She drifted off to sleep wondering why he had come to the embassy in the first place.

J.T. looked out the car window in silence. He had been told that he was to lunch with his wife, then he was to be taken on a token tour of Escalon then put on a plane and shipped out. After his initial rage, he was glad that that had been changed and it was at last over, that he could return to America and get back to work on something of importance.

Last night he had felt guilty about their argument—not that every word he had spoken hadn't been true—but because, after all, it was her country and no one wanted to hear the bad things about his country. So he had gone to the embassy to talk to her. He had been attacked as soon as the door opened.

He had barely got himself out of that mess when he was informed he couldn't be king no matter how much he tried to blackmail himself into the position. He listened to the pompous little ambassador for twenty minutes, somehow managing to keep his blood from boiling over.

While the man postured and lectured and talked to J.T. as if he were semiretarded, J.T. was able to piece the story together. Aria had told the army she would put her American husband on the throne if America would help her. Now she was reneging on her word.

J.T.'s anger was quiet, running through his body like poison. He had been used, duped into something that he stupidly had believed on a surface level. He had been told he was to marry her to teach her to be an American, but now he realized that a gaggle of women could have done that.

As he watched the ambassador pose and strut as he lectured, J.T. thought of the *real* reason he had been married to Her Royal Highness. No doubt Warbrooke Shipping had something to do with it. Then there were the lumber mills and steel mills owned by the Montgomery family. How useful all that would be to this poor, desolate country.

Wonder what she demanded, he thought. The richest American available? What a fool he had been. He had thought he was chosen because he saved her scrawny neck. He was angry at her, sure, but part of him had been flattered that he was chosen. Yet she had just wanted his money. No wonder she agreed to put him on the throne beside her. Montgomery money was needed in this poor country.

He had stood. "I'll be going now and I won't bother you again," he told the ambassador. "I'll find my own transportation back to America. Tell the princess so long for me and I'll arrange the divorce or annulment —whatever is needed." He turned to go.

The ambassador began sputtering and said that J.T. *had* to help them. He had to continue in his role as husband until the imposter princess was taken and Aria was once again princess.

J.T. said he had had enough games and lies to last him a lifetime and he just wanted to get out of the country.

The ambassador changed his tune after that. He began to ask rather nicely that J.T. remain as long as Lanconia and America needed him.

"You are to be seen together today, at luncheon, then you will have another spat and separate. Her Royal Highness will take a walk by herself into the hills. We think she will be contacted there. At dinner a waiter will drop soup on you, and the two of you will be so angered, you will pack and leave Lanconia. Her Royal Highness will be taken off the plane a hundred miles south of here. You will return to America."

"You seem awfully sure they will contact her," J.T. said.

"The American government has said that if the papers giving the vanadium to us are not signed within eight days, America will consider Lanconia an enemy. The papers will not be delivered until after the princess is taken and I'm sure the king's advisers will do anything to prevent the king from finding out that his granddaughter has been kidnapped, or he might be too upset to sign the papers. Or worse, it might give him another heart attack."

"Then the Lanconian government would have to sign the papers."

"The vanadium is on land personally owned by the king's family."

J.T. was torn. He wanted to help his country and make sure it got the vanadium but he wanted to get away from the intrigue. Most of all, he wanted to get away from Aria, the woman who had made such a fool of him. Everything she had done in America, the lovemaking on the stairs, the grilled hamburgers, the being nice to his friends, it had all been to get his money for her country. All of it had been false.

"I will stay in this country for twenty-four hours more and that's all."

The ambassador gave a weak smile and held out his hand to J.T. but J.T. ignored it.

Chapter Fifteen

$\mathcal{D}$

At eight A.M. tea had been brought to Aria's room on a tray, served in a Lily set of Limoges china. All morning, as close as possible, her life in the palace had been duplicated. She could feel herself slipping back into the former pattern of her life. She allowed the ambassador's wife to help her dress; she sent the strawberries back to the kitchen; she complained because her shoes had not been polished during the night; she berated the maid for not putting toothpaste on her brush. Part of her didn't like what she was doing but another part of her seemed to have no control.

At twelve forty-five she hurried down the stairs, eager to greet Lieutenant Montgomery. When she saw him, she could feel her petulance falling away, and she began to think of beach cookouts and Tommy Dorsey's band.

But J.T.'s expression was one of controlled rage. He pulled her into a reception room. "So," he said, his eyes black with fury, "you double-crossed me. You never meant for there to be an end to our marriage."

There was no need to ask what he was talking about. "It's the only way your government would help me. I had to agree to make my American husband prince consort."

"King," he snapped.

She looked at him.

"So, you lied to me and lied to them as well. I've always viewed this marriage as temporary."

She didn't answer him.

"When did you plan to tell me about this? Some night when we were in bed, you'd say, 'By the way, you have to live in this godforsaken country the rest of your life'? 'You have to give up your family, the sea, ships, and everything in America so you can ride around in a broken-down horse and buggy and wave at a bunch of people who'll hate you because you're an American'? Is that what you expected of me?"

"I never considered you at all. I thought only of my country."

"You thought only of what *you* wanted. Let me tell you that I'm an American and I plan to stay one. I don't want to live here and I sure as hell don't want to be a wind-up toy king. I'm not trading my freedom to live in a cage. I'm leaving for home today. The army's deal was with you, not me. I'll have our marriage annulled as soon as I return. It'll be like it never existed and you'll be free to once again dupe some other sucker into being a half-king." He grabbed her arm. "Now let's get this over with."

Aria's body was so rigid, it's a wonder she didn't snap in half. She relied completely on her royal training to get her through that long, silent walk back to the hotel and into the dining room. "I believe we are to argue," he said coolly as soon as they were seated.

"I do not feel like arguing," she answered haughtily.

"So, the princess has returned. I guess you got tired of pretending to be an American. You've returned to being the spoiled brat I met on the island. Am I supposed to bow to you? Kiss your hand? Lady, you should be given an Academy Award for your performance in Key West. You'll have some great laughs when this is all over. Will you tell your royal relatives what fools we were, how we believed your act? Will you do your imitations of Dolly and Bill and the rest of us for your bluebloods? Will you tell your new husband of the sexual acts you had to perform with me in order to get your country back?"

Aria went from stunned to hurt to a feeling of wanting to protect herself all in a few seconds. "I love my country as much as you do yours and one does what one must."

He glared at her. "Well, you lost out on this one. I'm returning to America tonight and I'll have the marriage annulled immediately. You'll never touch Warbrooke Shipping."

She had no idea what he was talking about but she wasn't going to let him know that. "I can do without it."

"You'll have to, baby."

"It is Your Royal Highness," she said, looking down her nose at him.

He started to say something else but the waiter arrived and J.T. didn't speak.

Aria began to chew as if she had gum in her mouth. "So! You'd rather have fat little Heather Addison than me," she said loudly for the waiter's benefit.

"I'd rather have *anybody* than you," he said, his

eyes deadly serious. "You are a liar, a money-grubbing little bitch, and besides that you're the worst in bed I've ever had."

There was no need for Aria to fake the tears in her eyes. "Really?" she whispered.

"Really."

Slowly, she rose from the table and left the dining room. Her mother had been right: one cannot trust people not of one's class. Right now she greatly regretted how much she had relaxed in his presence. She had let him see her as no one else ever had. She had even let him see her cry.

The ambassador had shown her on a map where she was to walk, the place where she would be most visible to the townspeople. As a side street curved around, there was a dirt goat path winding up around the mountain.

Her shoes weren't made for climbing but the exercise felt good and she began to walk faster.

She was startled when a man jumped from behind a bush at her. In her bewilderment, she almost greeted him by name. He was the king's third secretary, a mild, quiet man one rarely noticed and certainly never thought of as a villain.

"Mrs. Montgomery, would you come with me?"

"Not on your life, buster," she said, and turned to go back down the hill.

Another man blocked her path. He was the Master of Plate's assistant. "This is more than a request." He took her arm and led her away as she yelled in protest, but they were too far away from town for anyone to hear her.

She was taken to a goatherder's hut and sitting inside was the Lord High Chamberlain. Aria had to conceal her anger. This was a man her grandfather had always trusted.

He didn't conceal his contempt for her. "Mrs. Montgomery, I have a proposition for you."

Twenty minutes later, Aria leaned back in her chair. "Let me get this straight. You want *me* to be your princess?"

"For a short time only. We fear that the news of his granddaughter's kidnapping will kill the king. He is old and his heart is bad and this news could be too much for him. You won't have to do anything but stay in Her Highness's apartments and be seen from a distance now and then. We shall say that you have an illness and cannot leave your room. Now and then someone will look in on you and you will have to play the invalid in bed, but for the most part you will be free to read or listen to records or whatever you Americans do." There was a sneer in his voice.

"So I'm to be a prisoner in a couple of rooms. I see what you get out of this but what's in it for me?"

The Lord High Chamberlain stiffened. "You will be helping an old man who is near death, and our country needs you."

"That's just what I said: what's in it for me?"

The man's eyes blazed. "We are not a rich country."

"Well, maybe you can pay me some other way. How about a title? I'd like to be a duchess maybe."

The man's face showed his revulsion. "Duchess is a hereditary title. Perhaps a directorship. You would be addressed as Mistress."

"Mistress!" she gasped. "That's what my husband's got. I'll not be called a mistress."

"It does not mean the same thing in our country. It is a title of great honor."

She stood. "Look, I gotta go. It's been real nice meetin' you, but no go. I don't wanna sit in some rooms for a couple of weeks and pretend I'm sick."

"All right then, what can I offer you?"

Aria thought a minute then sat back down. "Me and my husband ain't been gettin' along so well. I'd like to *be* this princess for a while, know what I mean? You teach me how to talk like her and act like her and maybe I can get somethin' on with one of your dukes or somethin'. Then when your real princess gets back maybe I can stay and be married to a duke. Or maybe a prince. A prince would be nice."

The Lord High Chamberlain could not conceal his horror.

"Take it or leave it, buddy," Aria said, rising. "And who knows about what you're tryin' to do? This sick ol' king know about this? The American ambassador? Are you sure this is on the up and up?"

The Lord High Chamberlain left the room and a second later returned with Princess Aria's lady-in-waiting, Lady Werta.

"Can it be done? Can she be trained not only to meet Princess Aria's family but also to carry out her rigorous schedule?" he asked.

Lady Werta gave Aria a condescending look. "Stand," she ordered. "And walk."

It was on the tip of Aria's tongue to tell the woman to mind her manners, but she did as she was told. She slouched across the room, putting lots of wiggle in her hips.

"Impossible," Lady Werta said. "Totally impossible."

"Oh yeah?" Aria said. "Watch this, honey." She strode across the little room until she was inches from Lady Werta's face. "You will address me as Her Royal Highness and nothing else. And I will not tolerate such insolence of manner again. And you"—she whirled to face the Lord High Chamberlain—"how dare you sit in my presence? Now bring me my tea."

"Yes, Your Highness," they said in unison, then looked in shock at Aria as she grinned and blew a bubble.

"I used to be an actress. I can play a part real good."

"Humph!" Lady Werta sniffed. "Perhaps she is trainable after all." She left the hut.

"Old biddy," Aria said under her breath. "Well, I got the part or not?"

"We will give you two days of instruction and we shall see at the end of that time."

"You'll be amazed at how fast a learner I am."

"Mrs. Montgomery, I am beginning to believe you cannot further amaze me. Now, shall we discuss details?"

Aria sat in her hotel room, sitting utterly still, and waited for J.T. It had been a hideous afternoon. Her instruction in being Princess Aria had begun immediately and it had been as if she were training for prison. Her few short weeks in America had made her forget the loneliness and isolation, the rigidity of being a princess. Rules, rules, and more rules. Lady Werta had spit out one rule after another, all the things a princess was not to do. With each word the haughty old woman spoke, Aria could feel herself getting closer to being the crown princess than to being Mrs. Montgomery.

Tomorrow Lady Werta said she would bring corsets and see if they could fit Aria's expanded body—too much good American food—into them.

Right now, more than anything, Aria wished she could return to America and go with Dolly to Ethel's Beauty Parlor and cook J.T. some spaghetti for supper.

The thought of J.T. made her stiffen. She didn't like

to think how much his words hurt her. She had grown fond of him while all she had been to him was a pain—no, a *royal* pain—in the neck from beginning to end.

When the door opened and he entered the room, she was sitting as she had been taught to sit for hours at a time: back utterly rigid, seated away from the back of the chair. "Good evening," she said formally.

"It's Her Royal Highness," he said sarcastically, then pulled his suitcase from out of the closet and opened it. "You pack this?"

"Yes," she said softly. "Wives pack for their husbands. You taught me that."

He didn't turn around and his shoulders were hunched as if in protest of something. "Let's go down and get this over with. I'd like to go home."

She rose stiffly and formally.

"Did they contact you today?" J.T. asked on the way down the stairs.

"Yes."

He took her arm and halted her. "Look, I feel some responsibility toward you. I'm worried they'll find out you're the real princess. Somebody tried to kill you before, they may try to again."

"There will be people there to save me. People who will not be so burdened with my presence as you have been."

He looked at her for a long while and Aria held her breath because he looked as if he might kiss her. "Sure. You'll be fine. You'll have your country and you'll get to sit on your gold throne—I assume you have a gold throne."

"It's only gold leaf."

"Such hardship. Come on, baby, let's go have our last meal together."

Aria had a great deal of difficulty trying to maintain her guise of obnoxious American. They were to wait for the waiter to spill soup on one of them before leaving in anger.

"The embassy was to take you on a tour of Escalon today," Aria said. "Did you see anything of interest?"

"I saw a country living in the nineteenth century. No, maybe it was closer to the eighteenth. As far as I can tell, the newest car in town, not owned by an American, is a twenty-nine Studebaker. People don't even have wells, they carry water from the rivers. I can understand this in some poor, uneducated country, but you have schools and you have access to modern communication."

"But we have no money. We are a poor country with no resources except the vanadium, and when the world isn't at war, there is the tourist trade."

"You have the grapes. The only thing wrong with them is lack of water because of the drought."

"Yes, we pray for rain but—"

"In the meantime, have you people ever heard of irrigation, of dams, of wells?"

"I told you that we cannot afford such—"

"Afford, hell! Two-thirds of your men sit on their duffs in cafes and drink bad wine and eat goat cheese all day. If they got up and did some work, maybe they could help this country."

"You have called us cowards and now we are also *lazy?*" she hissed at him.

"If the shoe fits, baby."

"And I guess your country is so much better. Your people have the energy to create bombs."

"Your country is so peaceful that they kidnap their own princess then try to shoot her."

"You shot your Abraham Lincoln."

241

"That was generations ago. Look, let's not talk about this. I'd like to eat one meal in this town and not get indigestion."

They began to eat in silence but they had taken no more than a few bites when the waiter spilled soup on J.T.

J.T.'s exclamation was one of genuine anger. "I've had it," he yelled. "I've had it with you and this country. There's a troop ship coming through here to refuel tonight and we're going to be on it." He grabbed Aria's arm and pulled her up the stairs.

"That was foolish," she said once they reached their room. "Lanconia cannot refuel military planes from any army. We cannot take sides in this war."

He didn't say anything but grabbed their two suitcases and started out of the room. At the desk he plunked down a hundred-dollar bill and left. A taxi was waiting nearby and jumped at J.T.'s whistle. J.T. slammed the luggage into the trunk. "To the airport," he said, nearly pushing Aria into the back seat.

"You should have changed your uniform," she said softly. "You have soup all over you." He didn't answer as he looked out the window and Aria wondered what he was thinking.

For her, she knew he was her last connection to the freedom she had enjoyed in America. She tried to control herself and remember that all this was for her country. In another couple of weeks she would barely be able to remember this man, and if she did remember him it would be as someone who was rude and boorish. She would remember that dreadful week on the island when he had thrown fish in her lap. She would *not* remember the way he held her at night or the afternoon when they had grilled hamburgers in the backyard or dancing with his mother.

"We're here. You getting out?"

Aria boarded the plane silently. On board was Mr. Sanderson with a lapful of papers. The plane took off and he started talking. The plane was to develop engine trouble a hundred miles south of Escalon and at that time J.T. and Aria were to separate, with her remaining in Lanconia and traveling back to the capital city in a goatherder's cart. She could keep her early morning meeting with the Lord High Chamberlain.

"We have no idea if he is the man who ordered Princess Aria's execution," Mr. Sanderson said. "The Lord High Chamberlain may just be reacting to the kidnapping of the woman he believes to be the actual princess. Lady Werta must know something. She's too close to the princess not to know."

The plane had barely taken off before it was landing again.

Mr. Sanderson looked out the window. "The goatherder is waiting for you. He's one of our men and he'll make the journey as pleasant as possible. There has been a bed made in the back of the wagon. I hope you can sleep."

Mr. Sanderson was waiting for her at the door, but J.T. sat in his seat looking out the window.

She held out her hand to J.T. "Thank you so much for your help, Lieutenant Montgomery. Thank you for saving my life and I apologize for the inconvenience I have caused you. Please tell Dolly I will write her as soon as possible."

J.T. seemed to move in one lightning-swift motion. He pulled her into his arms and onto his lap and kissed her with passion.

She clung to him and part of her wanted to beg him not to leave her.

"Good-bye, Princess," he whispered. "Good luck."

"Yes," she said, realizing that he didn't feel the way she did.

"Your Royal Highness," Mr. Sanderson said impatiently. "We must go."

She rose from J.T.'s lap. "I wish you the best of luck also," she said formally, and left the plane.

Minutes later she was hidden in the back of a smelly goat cart, its jarring making it impossible to sleep. It was over, she told herself, and from now on she must only look ahead. She would try her best to forget America and her American husband. From now on she must think only of her country.

Perhaps she should marry Julian right away. He had been trained to be a king. Even though the monarchy had been abolished in his country in 1921, Julian's father had reared his son to rule, and it was one reason her grandfather had chosen Julian for her husband.

She snuggled deeper in the straw. Yes, Julian was the man she should look to. He was handsome, knew what the word "duty" meant, and had been trained for the monarchy. *He* understood protocol. *He* knew to walk two paces behind his queen-wife.

For a moment Aria had a vision of J.T. as prince consort. The two of them would be mounting the stairs into the High Council building wearing the twelve-foot trains of state when J.T. would suddenly become impatient because their sons were playing in Little League—which he coached—that afternoon and he would grab Aria's arm and pull her into the building.

It wouldn't do at all, she thought, but she smiled at the thought of their sons.

Absolutely not! She was to be a queen, not an American housewife, and she couldn't have a husband who knew nothing of duty and responsibility. She *had* to concentrate on Count Julian. She remembered their single kiss and wondered if Julian were capable of more. Before she went to America, she had no idea she was capable of passion, so how could she judge Julian? She would have to find out about him, not just as a prince consort but as a husband.

Toward dawn she began to grow sleepy. How did one build a dam? she wondered. How could one irrigate crops growing on the sides of mountains? Perhaps Julian would know. Or perhaps she could hire an American engineer to help her.

She slept.

"Lieutenant," the pilot said. "It looks like we *do* have engine problems. It's going to be a while before we take off, so if you want to get out and stretch your legs, we'll have a few minutes."

"Sure," J.T. mumbled, and left the airplane.

It was dark out but the moon was bright and he walked to the far side of the runway, looking out at the short, sparse mountain vegetation. He lit a cigarette and drew deeply on it, wanting something to calm him.

He had never wanted anything as badly as he wanted to get out of this country. He wanted to put as many miles as possible between himself and his princess.

"Not *my* princess," he muttered as he threw the cigarette down and crushed it.

"You will come with me," said a voice behind him.

J.T. turned and saw an armed man. He hadn't heard him approach. Behind them, the airplane started its engine.

"You will come with me, Lieutenant Montgomery," the man repeated.

"I've got to get on that plane." J.T. started to push past the guard but three more men slipped out of the darkness, guns in their hands.

"You are to accompany us."

J.T. knew when it was senseless to fight. Two men were in front of him, two in back; he followed them to a black car hidden in the darkness. From the car window, he watched the plane take off. "Damn her!" he muttered because he knew that what was going to happen now directly resulted from his having met Princess Aria.

They drove for forty-five minutes until they came to a large stone house surrounded by towering trees.

"This way," one of the guards said.

Inside, the house was lit by hundreds of candles in old silver candelabra. There were flags hanging from the ceilings and old, dusty tapestries on the walls.

One of the guards opened a door and motioned J.T. inside, then shut the door. It took a moment for his eyes to adjust. The stone-walled room was dark except for its far end.

A big, gray-haired man sat at the middle of a table covered with silver platters of food. Behind his high-backed, tapestry-covered chair stood a tall, gaunt man.

"Come in and sit down," called the gray-haired man. "Have you eaten?"

"I don't like being ordered about at gunpoint," J.T. said, not moving from where he stood.

"Very few people do, but one has to tolerate such indignities during a war. I have venison, hare, game pie, and some of your American beef. There's also quail that I shot myself. I don't believe you've had dinner."

J.T. moved closer to the table. The man looked to be in his fifties but with the strength and constitution of a younger man. He was strongly built and J.T. was tempted to ask if he had wrestled the steer to death.

"Ned," the man said, "pour our American some wine."

J.T. gave a shrug and took the seat across from the man and began to fill his plate. "What's so important that you made me miss my plane?"

"Your president and I have a favor to ask of you."

J.T. paused with a piece of venison on his fork. "Roosevelt?" He gave the man a hard look. "Who are you?"

"I'm the king of this country, such as it is."

J.T. looked at the man awhile longer than began to eat. "I heard you were on your deathbed. You don't look very sick to me."

"You will address His Majesty properly," snapped the gaunt man behind the king.

"Ned is very protective of me," the king said, smiling. "But I don't think we're going to teach an American to be subservient. I assume my grand-daughter is safely on her way to Escalon to take her rightful place."

J.T. didn't answer. He had heard the king didn't know what was going on with his granddaughter, but he obviously knew something. J.T. wasn't going to play his hand and tell the king more than he already knew. "Why don't you tell me," he said at last.

"All right," the king said. "I believe it started right after my granddaughter began her tour of America. She was kidnapped, probably by someone from Lan-conia, then she was to be shot. I believe you, at the risk of your own life, saved her. I will be eternally grateful."

"You're welcome."

"With your help, she went to the American government to ask for help in reinstating her to her throne.

Your army insisted she marry an American and put him on the throne beside her. I believe their objective is military bases in my country."

"Among other things."

"Ah yes," the king said. "The vanadium. But then Aria had already agreed to give that to America. Am I correct so far?"

"I'm not bored yet."

The king smiled. "You were chosen to be the husband and I must say, after looking at your family tree, for an American, your ancestry is quite good."

J.T. didn't reply to that but kept eating.

"The two of you lived in Key West, where you were stationed and where my granddaughter learned to be an American. You must tell me about the photograph that appeared in the *Key West Citizen* of Aria and your mother. Mrs. Montgomery looks to be a delightful woman."

"She's married. Could you get on with this? I'd like to find another plane leaving this country and get home. I have war work to do there and I can't afford to be gone any longer."

"Ah, your war job. More wine, Lieutenant?" the king asked, and motioned to Ned to refill the glass. "Now my granddaughter has returned and she has, with the help of that bumbling American ambassador, gotten herself reinstated as Princess Aria. And she has once again put her life in danger."

J.T. stopped eating. "I was told she'd be protected."

"Who can I trust? Ned here is the only person I know to be clear of this plot and he stays with me. I cannot trust Aria's advisers, her relatives, even her ladies-in-waiting."

"Can you find out who put the imposter princess on the throne? That woman has been kidnapped; maybe you can find out something from her."

"I sent her to America," the king answered. "When your president radioed me that my granddaughter had been taken while on American soil, I saw right away the hazards. It could have forced Lanconia into the war. I sent Ned south to get Aria's cousin, who, except for fifty pounds or so, looks like Aria. She was sent to America immediately to pose as Aria."

"Aria said that if you found out she was taken, it would kill you."

The king looked at his wineglass. "I am harder to kill than that. Duty and country come first, before personal involvement."

"She is just like you."

The king smiled. "Your spats are well known, both in America and Lanconia. She is a very good mime, isn't she?"

"What do you want from me?" J.T. asked.

"I want you to remain in Lanconia."

"Not on your life," J.T. said, rising. "I want out of this place. My country is at war and I am needed."

"You have already been replaced."

"There aren't many people who know as much about ships as I do," J.T. said. "I'm not easy to replace."

"How about Jason Montgomery? He took over two days ago. Think he'll be able to do the job?"

J.T. sat back down. His Uncle Jason was his father's youngest brother and J.T. hoped that someday he would know as much about ships as his uncle did. "He'll do quite well. Who is helping my father run Warbrooke Shipping?"

"Your mother and one of your brothers who was wounded. He prefers to convalesce behind a desk in the shipping office instead of in an army hospital."

"You seem to know a damned lot," J.T. said angrily.

The king put up his hand to halt Ned. "I have become very interested in you and your family in the last few weeks. I wanted to make sure I could trust you."

"I wouldn't trust anybody if I were you. I never saw a place so riddled with intrigue."

"I agree, which is why I want someone who I know is not involved to be near my granddaughter to protect her."

J.T. took a deep drink of wine. "Would you mind telling me why anyone would want this backward country? Is vanadium that valuable?"

"No, but uranium is," the king said mildly. "Just after the war broke out, Lanconia was found to have several deposits of uranium. I realized right away that if this were made public knowledge we would be part of the war because countries would want control of the uranium. I did my best to keep it secret, but obviously someone knows and someone wants control of the country. Whoever it is must know that Aria is not someone easily controlled so he or she tried to get rid of her."

"Then who is left? I don't imagine you'd go down without a fight."

"I was probably next on the list. My granddaughter Eugenia, Aria's younger sister, would be queen, and she could be controlled rather easily, I'm sorry to say."

"You have no idea who wants Aria dead?"

"It could be anyone or a group of people. I want you to stay and find out, or if not that, stay and protect her."

"She's too hardheaded for anyone to protect. Look, this isn't my fight. My own country is at war, and if I'm not needed in Key West, I can tote a rifle as well as any man."

"But this is something not any man can do. I have told your president that if he releases you to me, I will sell the uranium to America." The king handed J.T. a sealed envelope stamped TOP SECRET.

J.T. opened it reluctantly because he knew what it contained. It was a letter from President Franklin Roosevelt asking him to remain in Lanconia and help with this difficult matter. He said J.T. could help his country more in Lanconia than he could in America.

"Why couldn't he ask me to go to the front line?" J.T. mumbled, folding the letter away.

The king began eating grapes. "May I ask why such an assignment is so repugnant to you? You will be living in a palace surrounded by great beauty; the most strenuous task you will have is to accompany my granddaughter on her morning ride. You will have the finest food. Why would you rather be shot at?"

"Because I don't want to see your granddaughter again, that's why. She is a spoiled brat who uses people and I've had enough of her."

"I see. So it is personal. So Americans put personal relationships before duty to their country."

"No we don't. It's just that—" J.T. stopped talking. "My country means more to me. I want to help however I can."

"Then please stay and protect my granddaughter," the king said. "I'm not used to begging but now I am. She may be a problem to you but she is the comfort of my life. She is kind and warm and loving and she is the future hope of our country. I am sorry you do not see her as I do."

"She can be all right," J.T. said reluctantly, toying with his fork. He did not want to return to seeing Aria every day. "How would I do this?" he asked. "I mean, if I agreed, how would I be introduced into her circle?"

"As yourself. I would say I had met you when your plane stopped near here for repairs, liked you, and hired you as a technical adviser. Or we could say that your president ordered you here to take charge of the vanadium. Your wife, of course, returned to the United States. You would not have any duties either way except to protect my granddaughter. You would be given every courtesy and every comfort."

"What about the people who think Aria is Kathy Montgomery?"

"They will curse the luck of having a meddling old king."

J.T. sat silently for a moment, playing with one of the five forks to the left of his plate. "I can't do nothing but follow your granddaughter around. I want to make some changes in this country."

The king's face changed from that of a sweet old man to one of a man descended from centuries of warriors. "What changes did you have in mind?"

"Irrigation. Dams. I'd like to bring some of the twentieth century to this place."

The king's face showed amazement. "You know of such things? How utterly splendid. Of course you may help the peasants in any way you want."

"Peasants? No one has freed them?" J.T. asked sarcastically.

"Of course they are free. It is just an expression." The king paused. "Lieutenant Montgomery, there is something I want to ask you. There was a General Brooks who reported directly to your president. His description of my granddaughter, of what he saw at your little house in Key West, was it correct?"

J.T. smiled and let himself remember that afternoon. He seemed able to hear the blaring radio. "Pin-curled hair, blue jeans, my shirt, radio blasting away, slapping hamburgers, and dancing?" he asked.

"Yes." The king sounded incredulous. "I have never seen her like that. Her mother, my son's wife, was very aware that Aria would someday be queen and she raised Aria to have no emotions, or at least never to display them. Tell me, have you ever seen her cry?"

"Only once."

The king contemplated J.T. for a moment. "She allowed you to see that? I had no idea you were so close."

"There's two Arias. There's Aria, my wife, who can be . . ." J.T. smiled. "Who can be all right. Then there's Princess Aria, the little prig. *That* Aria I can't stand, and with every minute in this country she becomes more like the bitch I met on the island."

The king studied his wineglass. "Perhaps you could teach her to be less of a—what is that word? Prig."

"Not me," J.T. said, pushing back his chair. "I'm staying here to protect her and to help with this country. For my sake she can remain a prig. I'm safer that way. I'm not likely to get involved with her when she's like that."

"You worry about becoming involved with her?" the king asked quietly.

"Yeah, I do. It was hard enough saying good-bye to her once, and when I have to do it again, it'll be worse."

"Yes, I see," the king said. "Of course you'll have to say good-bye again. Your government should have researched our laws. No American commoner can be married legally to the queen. She would have to abdicate. Unless, of course, the people of Lanconia asked for you, which I doubt would happen."

"She won't abdicate, and even if she wanted to, I wouldn't let her. And it's good to hear I can't be king but I wouldn't accept the position if offered. Now, can somebody point me to a bedroom, or am I to spend the night in the dungeon with the other prisoners?"

The king nodded to Ned, who pulled a cord on the wall. Immediately, the door opened and the four guards entered.

"Take Lieutenant Montgomery to the red bedroom," the king said.

When J.T. was gone, Ned spoke. "An insolent man. He isn't worthy of touching Her Royal Highness's gown."

The king leaned back in his chair and smiled. "He is more than I hoped for. You'd better be nice to him, Ned, because if I have my way, that man is going to be the next king of Lanconia." He laughed at Ned's sputters.

Chapter Sixteen

No, no, no, no!" Lady Werta screeched. "He is your *seventh* cousin and twenty-eighth in line for succession."

Aria placed the side of her tongue between her back teeth, hoping the pain would remind her to be quiet. She had been awake all night in the goatherder's cart and they had started her training lesson at six A.M. It was now four P.M. and she was past exhaustion. This morning she had been made to walk for hours. At first Aria had pretended to be a clumsy American trying to walk like a princess, but she was tired and she wanted to be allowed to sit down, so she started walking as she had walked when she was a crown princess.

It wasn't good enough for Lady Werta. She said it wasn't nearly right, that Princess Aria's walk was much more royal and that this American was never going to be able to carry off the impersonation.

It was Aria's first encounter with prejudice. From then on she didn't try to be anyone but herself—yet, in Lady Werta's eyes, she was a failure. The lady-in-waiting showed her photographs of people she had not seen since she was a child, quickly told her who they were, shuffled the cards, and expected Aria to have memorized them. And Lady Werta lectured her endlessly on the most trivial matters, such as how to get around the fact that she supposedly did not understand or speak Lanconian.

The Lord High Chamberlain came into the room at noon. "How does it go?" he asked in Lanconian.

"She is all right but she doesn't have Princess Aria's personality. I hand her a cup of tea and she says 'thank you'! I think if I served her in a tin mug, she would say 'thank you.' No one will believe this person is Princess Aria. She is so *nice*."

Aria was jolted by this information. Had she always been a pain in the neck to everyone?

She didn't change her act for several hours but at tea break she was very tired and she let everyone know it.

"What are these dishes?" she asked. "What are these flowers on them?"

"I believe they are sweetpeas," Lady Werta said haughtily. "Hurry and finish so we can continue our lessons."

They were in the Lord High Chamberlain's country house, a place of such spaciousness and grandiosity that Aria vowed to look into the minister's finances. "I want roses on my tea dishes. Didn't you say Princess Aria always has roses on her dishes at tea? Then if I am to be her I want *roses*. And I want fresh cakes. Some of these look like they were left over from the servants' meal. Do you understand me? I want roses and fresh cakes and then I want a nap. I am tired and I must rest."

"Yes, Your Royal Highness," Lady Werta said, backing out of the room.

Aria smiled to herself. It had been a while since ill temper had got her what she wanted.

She made up for lost time. For the next twenty-four hours she ran Lady Werta's legs off. There was *nothing* she didn't complain of. If it was food, it was too hot or too cold or she didn't like it. Clothes had to be remade. The Lord High Chamberlain lit a cigarette in her presence and she sent him away with his ears ringing.

"She's doing better, isn't she?" the Lord High Chamberlain said in Lanconian.

"In a manner of speaking," Lady Werta said, pushing a stray tendril of hair out of her eyes. "She is almost as arrogant as the real princess."

"Shall we introduce her into the family?"

"Tonight. People are beginning to ask me where she is. Have you heard anything about the ransom?"

"They want millions," the Lord High Chamberlain said. "I do not know how we can raise it."

"Is His Majesty well? No one has told him yet of the kidnapping?"

"He's at his hunting lodge. As innocent as a child, although it's been difficult to keep the secret from him. He's demanding to see his granddaughter. Princess Eugenia is with him now."

Lady Werta sighed. "We'll have to ready her. The king is getting old. I hope he won't see through the farce. We should be grateful Princess Aria is such a cold woman. No one will miss her lack of warmth."

Aria listened to this stiffly. She hadn't been cold in America. "You are very rude to speak a language in front of me that I do not understand," she said angrily. "Now come and show me these photographs again. Who is at the palace now?"

* * *

The oldest part of the Lanconian palace had been built in the thirteenth century by Rowan the Bold. It was a magnificent structure of massive stone blocks, a fortress as strong as the ruler who built it, situated on land that fell away on three sides, the fourth side a gentle slope that in the fourteenth century was used for Hager the Hated's many public executions. A small river flowed at the bottom of the southeast slope and ran down to the town that the palace overlooked —and dominated.

In 1664 Anwen, the great lover of art, covered the old stone walls, enlarged the palace, and made it look like a very long, very large six-story Italian villa. The old castle was the east wing, with a new, larger central block and a new, matching west wing. At an expense that depleted the Lanconian treasuries, he imported a rare yellow sandstone from Italy for the facade.

In 1760, Princess Bansada, the wife of the king's fourth son, decided to do something with the grounds after overhearing a derogatory remark by an English duchess. She managed to put the kingdom in debt once again, but she made a splendid garden. There were a dozen hothouses that kept the palace supplied with fresh flowers at all seasons. There were formal gardens at the ends of the east and west wings, a twenty-acre wild garden, a rose garden, a man-made lake with a bridge across it that led to a ladies' outdoor sitting room. There were three gazebos: one Chinese, one Gothic, and one made to look like a medieval ruin. There were statues everywhere, mostly of handsome young men. Someone unkindly said they were Princess Bansada's lovers and that when her voracious appetite wore them out, she had them dipped in plaster. When Aria was an adult, she realized the statues were marble and therefore the story could not be true.

When the Lord High Chamberlain rode with Aria to the palace, it was done in great secrecy. She was veiled and swathed in heavy black cloth so that no one would recognize her. She sat in the back of the black limousine and didn't say a word. With every turn of the wheels, she came closer to the palace and she could feel the pull of the place. It was as if her ancestors were calling her home.

The palace, so remote to some, was home to her and her eyes teared at the beauty of it, the way the sunlight lit the yellow facade, the way the mountains rose behind it. She was glad the veil hid her face and she was glad for the training she had received that kept her from showing her feelings.

The Lord High Chamberlain, who had not deigned to speak to her for the entire trip, now spoke and his tone carried contempt in it, as if he refused to believe she had any intelligence. "You must remember *at all times* that you are a crown princess. You are to exercise the most rigid control. You must not relax for a second, not even when you think you are alone. For a princess is *never* alone. A princess is protected and watched and cared for."

He had not turned to look at her. "You are not to indulge in that despicable American custom of finding amusement in everything."

Aria opened her mouth to speak but closed it again. Her life could benefit from a little humor. She smiled at the thought of having a jitterbug contest in the Grand Salon. Perhaps she could introduce some of the more lighthearted and frivolous American customs to her relatives who lived in the palace.

She and Julian, that is, she amended. She wondered if Julian would like to grill hamburgers by the river. She would have barbecue grills made, and instead of dressing in a long gown for dinner, they would wear blue jeans. She smiled as she thought of trying to persuade Great-Aunt Sophie to wear jeans.

"You are not listening to me!" the Lord High Chamberlain snapped.

Again, Aria bit back what she wanted to say. While she was princess, he had been the epitome of fatherly gentleness to her and all her royal family. She had, of course, heard rumors that he was not well liked by the people, but she had dismissed the complaints. He was such a sweet old gentleman that Aria couldn't believe anyone disliked him. He had even generously refused to live in the house provided for his office. Aria had been touched, but now she had seen his country house and she understood he had other reasons for his magnanimous gesture. She vowed to look into her people's complaints more thoroughly.

He was droning on about her deportment, her duties, her responsibilities, telling how she was to be a machine, an automaton who did nothing but sign papers and dedicate factories.

"Don't this princess have no fun?" she asked loudly, enjoying his wince at her bad grammar. "I mean, she has a boyfriend, don't she? When do they get together and have a giggle? You know?"

"Count Julian does not"—he almost gagged—"giggle. He is the perfect choice of a husband for Her Royal Highness. When you are with him, you will not be alone—you are *never* to be alone together—so your conduct must be beyond reproach."

Aria kept looking out the window. Part of her was beginning to feel sorry for Princess Aria, who never got to play. But now she was a new Princess Aria. Her experiences in America had changed her—and she meant to change the life in her palace.

Lady Werta had shown Aria a floor plan of the palace but she had been told that the Lord High

Chamberlain would show her as many rooms as possible before taking her to her own chambers. Even with her heavy veil he predicted that many of the retainers would recognize her. The story they had spread was that, after her American tour, she had been felled with a particularly nasty strain of flu and had been taken to a private clinic in Austria until she recovered. No one knew when Aria was to return, and there were rumors that she had died.

The Lord High Chamberlain started to lead her into the palace, but Aria stood where she was, refusing to let him precede her. He gave her a look of hatred then stepped behind her.

The grand entrance hall was designed to impress people. Scrolled plaster work made panels on the walls and ceiling. The panels on the ceiling were filled with paintings depicting Rowan the Magnificent's exploits. The wall held carved oak medallions of the coats of arms of every monarch and his queen. Aria's arms were on the east wall, with a space below for the arms of her husband. For a moment she wondered what Lieutenant Montgomery would have put in that place. An UNCLE SAM WANTS YOU poster?

The Lord High Chamberlain cleared his throat behind her and she walked through the big doorway into the war trophy room—another room made to impress. One wall held a twenty-foot-square portrait of Rowan on a rearing horse. Since Rowan had left behind no likenesses of himself, it was an artist's conception of a magnificent warrior. Aria's grandfather said Rowan probably looked a good deal more tired and dirty and wore quite a bit less gold braid than the artist depicted.

Aria smiled at the memory and then remembered how Lieutenant Montgomery had said the people of Lanconia were now cowards.

She sniffed and walked ahead toward the grand staircase, a staircase that a six-horse carriage could be driven up—Hager the Hated had proved that. Of course the driver of the carriage's life depended on his winning his king's wager. He had succeeded but the deepest nicks in the marble stairs had never been smoothed out.

Behind her, the Lord High Chamberlain was whispering directions but she ignored him. At specific intervals along the stairs and outside the rooms stood the Royal Guard. They stood, with only one break, for eight hours at a time. Aria had never given them a thought before but now she knew a little more about waiting. Later, when this problem of her identity was solved, she might do something about these Royal Guards.

The Lord High Chamberlain's whispering became frantic with insistence as Aria approached her apartment, but she continued to ignore him. In the hall portraits of her ancestors looked down at her, their eyes solemn, as if they knew she was harboring unroyal thoughts. She could almost feel her mother's horror: shall we supply the guards with chairs? Perhaps Rowan would have won his battles sooner if he had fought with his men in lounge chairs.

Aria braced her shoulders and entered her bedchamber as the two guards opened the doors. Behind her the Lord High Chamberlain's voice died away as the doors shut.

On their knees in a deep curtsy before her were her four ladies-in-waiting and two dressers. They were all older women, all chosen by her mother, and Aria's first impulse was to tell them to get off their knees.

"Welcome, Your Royal Highness," they chorused.

She nodded to them but made no answer to their

welcome. She really knew very little about these women as her mother had trained her not to be intimate with her attendants.

"Leave me," Aria said. "I want to be alone."

The women looked at one another in question.

Lady Werta stepped forward. "Perhaps Her Royal Highness would like a bath drawn."

Aria gave the woman a look that sent her retreating. "Must I repeat myself?"

The women left and Aria breathed a sigh of relief. She lifted her heavy veil and looked about the room. This was *her* room, a room where she had spent many hours, a room she had had done, against her mother's wishes, in yellow. The walls were silk moiré with the same draperies surrounding her many tall windows that looked out onto the wild wood.

There were eleven tables in the big room, all of them with delicate legs, all of them in some way unique and precious. One was a gift from a sultan, inlaid with tiny bits of precious stones. Another had an enamel portrait of Aria, her parents, and sister, each holding a musical instrument. Several of the tables were covered with family photographs in silver frames.

There was a seating arrangement of a tiny couch and three chairs, each covered with yellow and white silk. On the floor was an enormous blue, white, and gold Aubusson carpet. A year after her mother's death, Aria had walked about the palace and chosen all the portraits and miniatures of the most beautiful women and had them moved to the walls of her rooms.

Her desk was here, a small, exquisite ormolu and mahogany creation. Each instrument—letter opener, fountain pen, stationery holder—was a work of art, none of it chosen by her but given to her as her right. "Rather like Julian," she whispered, but corrected herself immediately.

Through the sitting room was her bedroom, done in the palest of sea green, the walls painted over a hundred years ago for another queen with fantasy scenes set in an imaginary forest peopled with unicorns and wood sprites. Her bed had been made for Queen Marie-August in the seventeenth century and had taken six men two years to carve the delicate tendrils and leaves and vines winding their way up the four posts. It was said that Queen Marie-August's husband never saw the bed—nor did any man for that matter.

One wall of the bedroom was a series of semihidden doors that led into her four closets. Each closet was actually the size of the bedroom she had had in Key West.

The first closet contained her daily clothes, hundreds of silk blouses, many hand embroidered by the women of Lanconia. There were rows of tailored skirts and a wall-length rod hung with her silk dresses.

She took one off the rod and looked with dismay at the buckram in the waist. "No more loose-fitting little rayon numbers." She sighed, but then the feel of the silk made her smile.

The second closet contained her ballgowns and ceremonial garments, each in a specially made cotton sack with a transparent voile shoulder so one could see the dress. Even under the voile, the gold work, the sequins, the tiny diamonds, even the pearls, glowed and made the pale pink of the walls look like a sunset.

The third closet contained her accessories: hats, gloves, rows of handmade, hand-fitted shoes, purses, boots, scarves. One wall was lined with drawers filled with handmade underwear: slips, underpants, night-gowns. And the heavy, elastic Merry Widow foundations. She grimaced at those and shut the drawer.

The fourth closet contained her furs, her winter suits, and, behind a mirror, the safe for her jewels. She tripped the three latches to the mirror, swung it back, then turned the combination to her safe. Two six-foot-tall rows of velvet-covered drawers greeted her. Red velvet meant sets: necklace, bracelet, earrings. Black velvet was for rings, yellow for earrings, blue for watches, green for brooches, and white was for her tiaras: pearl tiaras, diamond tiaras, rubies, emeralds. Each piece was in its own fitted compartment.

Aria smiled as she opened drawer after drawer. Each jewel had a history; each had belonged to someone else. Aria had never purchased a jewel nor had she been given one that had not belonged to generations of royalty before her.

Frowning, she shut the drawers and mirror abruptly since she heard someone in the outer chamber. On walking out of the closet, she saw Lady Werta standing there.

"Very good. You are examining the princess's belongings."

Aria was not going to allow this woman to think she could rule her. "How dare you enter my room without permission," she said, all her anger showing.

Lady Werta looked surprised for a moment then recovered. "You can stop the act with me. I *know* you, remember? We have to talk about tonight. Count Julian is here."

"I'll discuss nothing with you." Aria started toward the door leading to the hall.

"Wait a minute," Lady Werta said, grabbing Aria's arm.

Aria was actually horrified at the woman's touch. She wasn't the new American Aria pretending to be the princess. She *was* the princess.

Lady Werta stepped back. "We have to talk," she said, but there was no strength in her voice.

"Call my ladies," Aria said, turning away. "I must dress for dinner."

Aria wore a long white gown that was embroidered with thousands of seed pearls to dinner. It was high-necked, long-sleeved, very prim, very proper—sexless. The diamonds she wore in her ears Lady Werta had fetched for her, not showing her where the major jewel chest was hidden, probably for fear the American would steal the contents. Instead, she had selected three pair of insignificant earrings and presented them to Aria. "This is all?" Aria had complained so only Lady Werta heard.

"We are a poor country," Lady Werta sniffed, her eyes showing she was angry.

"We are glad to see that you have fully recovered from your American illness, Your Highness," her three other ladies-in-waiting said as they moved about the room, waiting to obey Aria's merest whim.

One of her dressers looked her over critically. "You are thinner than you were in America."

Aria gave the woman a withering look. "You will keep your personal remarks to yourself. Now dress me."

It was difficult not to be impatient with the women because she knew she could have dressed herself in half the time. The long foundation garment felt familiar and strange at the same time, and she felt as if the last vestiges of the American Aria disappeared when her dresser pulled her much shorter hair back into a tight chignon. Her secretary sat in a chair behind a screen, the princess's social calendar in her hand.

"Tomorrow at nine A.M. is riding; at ten-thirty, you will visit the new children's hospital. At one you lunch with three members of the council to discuss the American vanadium contract. At two you will hand out gold watches to four railroad employees. At four you have tea with council wives. At five-thirty the Scientific Academy is giving a speech on the insect life of the northeastern Balean Mountains. At seven you return to ready for dinner at eight-thirty. And at ten—"

"There is a jitterbug contest in the ballroom," Aria said, making everyone in the room stop.

Lady Werta gave her a quelling look. "It is from Her Royal Highness's visit to America. She makes a joke."

Politely, the women laughed, but they looked at her oddly, as if her making a joke was a very, very strange thing to do.

"Don't do that again," Lady Werta warned under her breath.

Later, when Aria walked into the dining room, everyone came to a halt. They stared at her, waiting for some signal from her as to how to act. When the king was away, the crown princess set the tone.

Aria took a deep breath. "Well, Freddie," Aria said to her second cousin, Prince Ferdinand, "I can see you still have no manners. Do I deserve no greeting?"

He came to her and bowed over her extended hand. "We have been worried about you," he said in Lanconian.

For a moment, Aria hesitated. This man was her cousin, they had spent a great deal of time together, yet he greeted her after a long absence as if she were a slight acquaintance. "In English please. If we are to deal with these Americans, we must be able to understand them. They do not learn other people's languages." She looked at him as if she had never seen him before. Freddie was a small man, a few inches shorter than Aria and quite thin. He slouched when he walked. Aria had always ignored Freddie—as everyone did—but now she thought she saw anger burning in his dark eyes. He was third in line for the throne after Aria and her sister. Could he want the throne enough to kill for it?

"You look good, Aria," her Great-Aunt Sophie shouted. The old woman was nearly deaf and compensated by shouting at everyone. She was dressed as only Aunt Sophie dressed, in layer upon layer of baby-blue chiffon, big blue silk roses around the indecently low neckline that exposed her wrinkly bosom. What was that American saying? Mutton dressed as lamb. Her grandfather said Sophie had always had hopes of snagging a husband but so far no man had been so stupid as to ask.

"Well enough, I guess, after having nearly died," Aria shouted back, making everyone in the room look at her in surprise. Princess Aria did not shout.

"Good!" Great-Aunt Sophie shouted back, and turned away to yell at a waiter that she wanted more brandy.

"I am glad too that you are well" came a suave voice, and she was face-to-face with Count Julian.

Lieutenant Montgomery had always referred to the man as Count Julie and had always insinuated that he was effeminate. But Aria saw virility in the man's eyes. He wasn't big and strong like Lieutenant Montgomery, but a woman could do worse. He was quite handsome, about the same height as she was, with the erect, straight carriage of a military man. Her grandfather said Julian had been forced to wear a steel back brace from the time he was four until he was sixteen.

"Welcome home," Count Julian said, taking her

hand and lightly kissing the back of it. "Would you like something before dinner? A sherry perhaps."

"Yes, please," she answered. She watched him walk away. What would he be like as a husband? Once the bedroom doors were closed, did he become a tiger? She smiled at him when he returned from the sideboard with her sherry. He stood silently by her and Aria realized how very little they had ever actually talked.

She looked at the other dinner guests. There were her cousins Nickie and Toby, her Aunt Bradley, and her young, beautiful cousin Barbara, who was seventh in line for the throne.

"Where are Cissy and Gena?" Aria asked Julian, referring to Freddie's sister and her own sister, knowing that Cissy was in the custody of the American government.

"Both are with His Majesty at his hunting lodge," he answered.

The meal was deadly boring. The men could talk of nothing but the number of animals they had killed in the last week—since blood sports were their only occupation, there was nothing else they knew about. Great-Aunt Sophie bellowed at the people around her, trying to carry on a conversation but not able to keep up with anyone's replies. Freddie, Nickie, and Toby's affectations made Aria want to shout at them. Barbara flirted with each man, batting her eyelashes and leaning forward to show her décolletage.

"I think a husband should be found for Cousin Barbara," Aria said under her breath.

Julian looked at her in surprise but made no comment.

Wouldn't they be surprised, Aria thought, if she began to flirt? She looked at Julian, so properly eating

269

his sturgeon in dill sauce, and she wondered if he would be very shocked if she batted her lashes at him.

With her heart pounding, and quickly, before she lost her nerve, she reached out and touched Julian's hand. "Will you meet me in the King's Garden after dinner?"

He nodded once, but she could see the slight frown between his brows as he moved his hand away. She had just done something a crown princess did not do.

She turned away to answer a question Great-Aunt Sophie was bellowing her way.

After dinner she had to work to escape Lady Werta, whose face showed she believed the end of the world to be at hand. Aria slipped through the Green Waiting Room, through the Mars Room, ran past the Gallery of Kings, then out into the White Horse Courtyard, past the Greek Orangery, and finally reached the King's Garden. The garden was so named because it was believed to have a masculine air with its tall pine trees and secret, twisting paths. It was said that Rowan once had a camp in this place.

Julian was waiting for her, a slight frown on his face.

He was sixteen years older than she was and she had always been a little in awe of him. After all, now she realized that theirs wasn't to be an ordinary marriage. Their marriage was arranged for political and diplomatic reasons; theirs was a marriage of state.

"You wanted to speak to me, Your Royal Highness," Julian said politely, but there was disapproval in his voice.

She wished there was something snappy she could say, or something wise. "You are angry with me," she said in a little-girl voice, and cursed herself for doing so.

She thought she saw a hint of a smile on his lips. He

was actually very handsome—in spite of what Lieutenant Montgomery said—and the moonlight made him more so.

"I think only of your reputation. It would not do for us to be seen alone together."

Aria turned away. On their wedding night he was going to find out that she was not a virgin. She looked back at him and took a deep breath. "For an engaged couple, we have spent very little time together, alone or with others. Since we are planning to spend our lives together, I thought we should talk and get to know each other better."

He looked at her for a while before responding. "And what did you want to discuss? The coming elections? I am sure our current Lord High Chamberlain will remain in office. In fact I think he may pass on the office to his descendants."

"No," she said. "I mean, yes, I do want to discuss the council and its officers but I thought perhaps . . ." Her voice trailed off.

"Your trip to America?"

He was standing absolutely rigid, shoulders back, every hair, every medal in place, no flaw anywhere. Aria remembered Jarl coming home from work, his uniform dark with sweat, pulling it off as soon as he entered the door and saying, "Get me a beer, honey."

"Do you drink beer?" Aria blurted.

Julian looked startled for a second then seemed to be trying to control a smile. "Yes, I drink beer."

"I didn't know that. I know so very little about you and sometimes I wonder if we'll be . . . compatible. I mean, we are to live together, and marriage is, I mean, I have heard, that marriage is so very intimate and . . ." She trailed off again, feeling a bit silly and childish because Julian was still standing so stiff and rigid.

"I see," he said.

Aria didn't like his smug tone or maybe she didn't like the way she was feeling. "I am sorry to have imposed upon you with this trivial matter," she said royally, and turned away.

"Aria," he said in a voice that made her halt. He stepped in front of her. "Your questions are quite valid. Before I submitted my proposal of marriage to the king, I gave a great deal of thought to the matter. Marriage is indeed a serious undertaking, but I have every reason to believe we will be most compatible. We have been reared in the same way, I to be a king and you to be a queen. We know the same people; we know the protocol of the monarchy. I think we shall make an admirable marriage."

Aria's shoulders drooped. "I see. Yes, I think we will make an admirable royal couple." She looked down at her hands.

"Is there something else?"

He was standing very close to her but he made no effort to touch her.

There was no way to say it but to blurt it out. "But what about *us?* What about me as a woman? Do you feel anything for me besides as a *queen?*"

Julian's expression didn't change, but he reached out and put his hand to the back of her head and drew her to him, then kissed her with what could only be expressed as long-repressed desire. When he pulled away, Aria still had her eyes closed and her mouth open.

"I look forward to the wedding night with *great* anticipation," he whispered, and she could feel his breath on her face.

Aria opened her eyes and straightened her body. "I did wonder," she managed to say at last.

At that Julian smiled at her, and he smiled with

great warmth. "You are a beautiful, desirable young woman. How could you have doubted that I am longing to make love to you?"

"I . . . I guess I never thought about it." Once again he was standing away from her, looking at her.

"Has something happened?" he asked softly. "Tonight at dinner you seemed different, as if you were worried about something."

The thought that he had noticed made her smile. She had agreed to their marriage without giving the marriage much thought. She had been much more interested in his ancestors and his training than she was in Julian as a man. But now it was different. Now she understood more of what went on between a husband and wife.

"In America," she said, beginning slowly, "in America I saw young lovers holding hands, walking together, and kissing on park benches."

"I had envisioned America to be like that," Julian said with disapproval.

"America is a *wonderful* place," Aria snapped. "There is a feeling there of moving forward. Nothing remains the same. They are not burdened with hundreds of years of tradition; they accept what is new. In fact, they *seek* the new."

"Lovers in a park is not new," Julian said, amused and smiling. "I forget how young you are. You have never seemed to want courting. You accepted my marriage proposal without seeming to want more than a handshake and a ring. Was I wrong?"

"No, but things happened in America . . ."

"The sight of the lovers made you wonder what it would be like if you had your own lover?"

"Something of that sort," she murmured, then looked straight at him. "Julian, I want our marriage to work. I *need* for it to work. It has to be more than a marriage for Lanconia. I am a woman and I want to be loved for myself and not just for my crown."

Julian looked even more amused. "No one has ever asked something easier of me. Shall I court you?" He took her hand in his and kissed her palm. "Shall I show up at your door carrying a bouquet of wildflowers? Shall I sing love songs under your window? Shall I whisper love words into your pretty ear?"

"That will do for a start," she said, watching him kiss her hand.

"I will meet you at dawn and we will ride."

"At dawn? But I am scheduled to ride at nine."

"Break it," he said commandingly. "I will come for you at dawn, but now I must escort you back to the White Horse Courtyard. We will be seen by fewer people if we enter there."

He turned around and motioned for her to lead, as was her right, but then he smiled and pulled her arm through his.

At the edge of the courtyard she turned to him. "Will you kiss me again?" He glanced at the windows of the palace and seemed to hesitate. "Please, Julian. I need to know that our marriage will be good. I need to forget—"

He put two fingers over her lips. "We all have things we wish to forget. I will kiss you until you can bear no more, my darling." Slowly, he drew her into his arms and kissed her as if she were Rita Hayworth and Betty Grable rolled into one.

He released her. "Now go!" he ordered, smiling. "I will see you in the morning."

She started to move away but he caught her hand.

"If it takes kissing to make you forget, you will have amnesia by noon tomorrow." He released her and she ran inside the palace.

Lady Werta was waiting for her. "What did he say?

Did he guess? He was close to Princess Aria so he might know that you weren't she. They may have shared lovers' jokes."

The woman was beginning to bore Aria. "Go to your bed. I have no more need of you tonight."

"But I—"

"Go!" Aria snapped.

"Yes, Your Royal Highness," Lady Werta said, and retreated backward.

Upstairs Aria stood still as her dressers removed her gown and put on her nightgown. She didn't speak to them as they worked, and when they turned out the light and bid her good night, she still didn't speak.

She settled down to sleep and she felt good for the first time in days. Perhaps her life was not going to come apart because she no longer lived with Lieutenant Jarl Montgomery. Perhaps she could forget him and make a life of her own.

Tomorrow she planned to give all of her attention to Count Julian. He was the man Lanconia needed and he was the perfect husband for her. All she had to do was make herself fall in love with him—and judging by his kisses, that wouldn't be overly difficult.

As she went to sleep, though, her self-control faded and she began to remember Jarl sitting in the bathtub, Jarl tasting her fried chicken and telling her she should have been a chef, Jarl touching her breasts.

Chapter Seventeen

SHE had just fallen asleep when the door burst open and the light was turned on. In a flurry of silk petticoats, blond hair, and layers of diamonds, Princess Eugenia jumped into Aria's bed.

"I've missed you," Gena said, throwing her arms about her sister's neck. "Please don't tell me to behave myself and please don't tell me to leave. I've just ridden all night with the most divine man to get here as soon as I heard you were well enough to receive visitors." She hugged Aria tighter. "Aria, they said you nearly died. I couldn't have borne to have to be queen."

Aria, smiling, held her sixteen-year-old sister at arm's length. "I wouldn't like for you to be queen either."

"Are you going to send me away? Tell me so I won't get comfortable."

"No," Aria said, "I'm not going to send you away. Tell me what has happened while I've been away."

Gena stretched out on the bed. She was very pretty, and pretty in a modern sort of way, Aria thought jealously. Put her in a bathing suit and she would win any beauty contest in America. Too bad she had cotton for a brain.

"The same as usual." Gena sighed. "Nothing ever happens here. But *you* went to America. Was it *filled* with soldiers? Were they all as divinely handsome as *my* American soldier?"

"What is this about?" Aria asked sharply. "Have you fallen in love again?"

"Don't scold me, Aria, please don't. Grans has hired him for something or other—something to do with the peasants—but my soldier allowed me to ride around the countryside with him. He even let me sit in the front seat beside him. He acted as if he were reluctant to have me, but I won him over. He is a most handsome man and he's smart—Grans says so. Oh, Aria, you're going to adore him, at least I hope you do, because Grans sent him here to work with you."

"With me? Doing what?"

"I don't know, but I think he may be coming here to put all of us in order. I've never seen Grans like anybody so much. They sat up late and drank and told each other vulgar stories. Ned nearly died, but Grans looked the best he has in years."

Aria sat up straighter in bed. "I wish you'd stick to the story. *What* is this American to do here? Has he come about the vanadium?"

Gena's eyes were beginning to close. "Aria, may I sleep here with you? It's so far to my chamber. Call someone to undress me and fetch my nightgown."

"Here," Aria said impatiently. "I'll help you undress and you can wear one of my nightgowns."

Gena's eyes flew open. "Wear someone else's nightgown?"

"Don't be a prude. *I* have slept on sheets slept on by other people."

"No," Gena gasped, stunned into speechlessness.

Aria pulled her sister out of bed then began to remove Gena's clothes.

"Are you sure you know how to do this?" Gena asked.

"It would help if you weren't an inert weight. Lift your arms. Now tell me what Grans has hired this American for."

"Something about dams, I believe. He is *so* handsome. Ouch! I think I should call my dresser."

"Gena," Aria said softly. "What is this man's name?"

"Lieutenant Jarl Montgomery. He is *so* nice and—Aria! Where are you going? You can't leave me here in my underwear."

"Gena, look in the closet and find a nightgown and put it on yourself. It's very easy. Where is Lieutenant Montgomery staying?"

"The State Bedroom—Rowan's room—so you know Grans thinks he's important. But I'm sure he's in bed by now. Aria! Don't leave me," Gena called, but Aria was already out of the room.

Aria knew the palace well and she was able to make her way down twisting corridors, through state rooms where no guards stood, down a very narrow spiral staircase, where she hid in the shadows as two laughing guards walked past.

She threw open the door to the State Bedroom. It was the room reserved for Lanconia's most honored guests. Its big, old, carved four-poster was draped in specially woven red Italian brocade, the walls covered in a matching red silk. No one was sure but it was rumored that Rowan had used this room when this part of the palace was a stone castle.

J.T. was wearing only a towel about his middle, his hair wet. "What are you doing here?" she asked, leaning against the closed door.

"Her Royal Highness herself. Now this is a welcome. I was just wondering if I pulled one of these cords on the wall, would one of those pretty maids wearing a short skirt and black stockings come and warm my bed. Instead, I get the princess. Come on, honey, get your clothes off and let's get to it. I'm ready."

"Lieutenant Montgomery," she said through her teeth. "What are you doing in Lanconia?"

J.T. continued drying his hair. "I'm not here because I want to be. My president and your king have requested my services. Contrary to what I've been told, they think your life is still in danger. I'm to protect you and do what I can with your . . . ah, peasants."

"But my grandfather knows nothing."

"He's heard enough to know there could be some trouble," J.T. answered quickly.

"You cannot stay. It is not possible. I will arrange for your transportation back to America tomorrow. Good night, Lieutenant."

J.T. caught her as she was leaving and pulled her back into the room. His towel slipped and he grabbed it with one hand while leaning his other hand on the wall behind her head. "I told you: this is not up to me, but my war assignment is to guard your life. Roosevelt seems to think I'm of more value here trailing after you and picking up your hankies than I would be in a fighting zone. So I'm staying."

She ducked from under his arm and walked to the other side of the room. "How long must you remain?"

"Until I know you're safe or until your grandfather says I can go."

"There will have to be rules. You cannot treat me with the insolence that is your normal manner. You will have to use the proper forms of address." She turned back toward him and saw how he narrowed his eyes at her. "The time in America was not something that can be repeated. Here I am not your wife."

J.T. didn't speak for a moment. "I married you to help my country and I'm staying here for my country. No other reason. As far as I'm concerned, our marriage is over."

"Does that include your jealousy?" she asked, one eyebrow arched. "Count Julian and I will be planning our wedding. His family is a very old one and the marriage is advantageous to my family. I cannot have you throwing him in a swimming pool."

"You don't have to worry about me," he said, anger in his eyes. "I might be jealous of my wife, but Her Royal Highness stirs no such feelings." He looked her up and down, standing there in her prim, high-necked nightgown and heavy brocaded robe that looked as impenetrable as armor.

She turned away again because the sight of him in just his towel was beginning to make her remember their nights together. "How are you to be introduced?" she asked.

"Supposedly I have been sent here by my government to buy the vanadium, but I am also to discuss military bases here. The king wants you to show me Escalon and the outlying country because, the story is, America is considering buying your country."

"Doing what?" She whirled on him. "America is to *buy* my country?"

"That's the story I hear. Actually, from what I've seen, we wouldn't have the place. We're just getting over one depression and this place might send us into another one. But the story gives us a reason to spend time together. You're to show me the household accounts. You're to teach me about your country and, in general, be very nice to me. You're to—dare I use the word—seduce me into liking your country."

"I . . . I don't think this is possible. Of course my grandfather knows nothing of what has actually occurred between us, but he cannot ask this of me."

"He knows enough to know that your life may be in danger. Look, are you sure it's good for you to be in here with me? People must have seen you enter."

Aria blinked a couple of times. She knew no one had seen her enter but the sight of Jarl and his bed was making her forget her newfound promise of happiness with Julian. "I must go." She started toward the door.

"Not that way," he said, clutching her arm. He went to his duffel bag lying on the floor and withdrew a sheaf of papers. "Your grandfather gave me some maps of underground passages in this place."

"He did what?"

"He said that each monarch inherited these maps at the reading of the will but he thought this was a time for extreme measures. Here we are," he said, looking at one of the maps. "This room is called the State Bedroom, right? I knew he had a reason for putting me in this room. He seemed to think it was special." He began running his hands along the oak paneling. "Here it is." He pushed a button but nothing moved. "I imagine the door needs oiling." There was a letter opener on the desk and he pried open the door until he could get his fingers into the opening then pulled the door open. A musty smell filled the room and they could hear the movement of wings.

"If you think I'm going down that, you are wrong," Aria said.

J.T. got a flashlight from his duffel bag. "If you leave this room dressed like that, you will have the whole place gossiping. Your Count Julian won't marry you because your reputation will be ruined and they'll probably hang me, a commoner, for daring to look upon the royal nightgown. Come on. How bad can it be?"

It was awful. It looked like no one had been inside the passage for centuries and cobwebs and bat droppings covered the damp stone steps that led downward. It was very dark and her slippered feet kept sliding.

"Why do I not know of this place?" she whispered.

"It seems that one of your past kings had everyone who knew about the tunnels put to death. He wanted only the king himself to know of them."

Aria put up her hand to protect herself from a hanging web. Her slippers were so filthy they would have to be discarded. "That would have been Hager the Hated in the fourteenth century. He used any excuse to put people to death."

"Fine relative to claim. Who built this place?"

"Rowan," Aria said, and something in the way she said it made him look at her.

"I take it he was a good guy."

"The best. Where does this lead?"

"Here," J.T. said, stopping at a rusty, iron-clad door. "Let's just hope we can get it open." He handed her the flashlight.

"Where does that lead?" she asked, pointing the light toward a corridor heading toward the left.

"Down to your dungeons then underground to somewhere in the town. Your grandfather said the way out was probably blocked now since a house was built over the old exit. I got it open! Turn off the light."

Aria looked at the cylinder. "How?"

He took the flashlight from her and turned it off.

"According to the map we're at the north end of the King's Garden. Do you know where that is and how to get back to your room?"

"Of course." She walked out into the cool night air.

"Wait a minute, Princess, you haven't told me where you'll be in the morning. I don't plan to let you out of my sight."

Aria wasn't about to tell him she was riding with Count Julian in the morning. "My calendar has my first engagement for nine A.M.," she said truthfully. "I will go riding."

"Stay in your room, I'll meet you."

"But I'm not supposed to know you. We'll have to arrange a formal introduction first."

"You can say your grandfather telephoned you—if this falling-down pile of stones *has* telephones."

"We are more modern than you believe," she said, her chin up. "Good night, Lieutenant Montgomery." She turned away.

"Wait," he said, putting his hand on her arm. He looked at her in the moonlight for a long moment. "Go on, get out of here."

She nearly ran from him, hurrying down the paths she knew so well, then through a servant's door, up the stairs, and into the newer wing where her rooms were.

"I am going to love Julian," she whispered to herself. She was going to compel herself to love Julian and she was going to forget about the crude, insolent American who was temporarily her husband. He had told her that he thought she was cool and remote, not quite human. She was going to show him how haughty a royal princess could be. No matter how much time they spent together, she was going to treat him as the lowliest commoner.

There was no one in the hallway except for the

guard who stood outside her door. She had to get past the man and into her room and be there when her dressers arrived in the morning. If there was gossip that she had left her room wearing her bedclothes late at night, her dressers would say it was impossible since she was there in the morning and no one had seen her reenter.

American movies had taught her a great deal. She picked up a valuable egg-shaped piece of malachite from its stand on a table and sent it rolling down the hall at the feet of the guard. He watched it for a moment, then, as she had hoped, he went after it. Aria slipped into her room as fast as possible. Her heart was pounding as she leaned against the closed door.

Of course, she had to change her clothes and she was glad she knew how to dress herself. She was also glad she knew how to take a sponge and get most of the cobwebs from her dressing gown. The slippers were beyond hope, so, to keep her dressers from finding them, she stuffed each into a sleeve of a ceremonial gown.

It was late when she was able to slide into bed beside a warm, sleeping Gena. For a moment, Aria thought she was with J.T. and snuggled against her. Then she caught herself. She was *not* going to let that man back into her life. There were more important things to life than what one did in bed.

Tomorrow she would have time alone with Julian and she would allow him to help her forget.

"Your Highness!"

Aria woke slowly to her dresser's voice.

"Count Julian is waiting for you." The woman smiled smugly. "He seems most impatient to see you."

Sleepily, Aria pulled herself out of bed and made

her way to the bathroom. Slowly, she began to waken and remember the events of last night. This morning she meant to begin forgetting her American husband. She would have hours alone with Julian—alone in the dim early morning light in the mountain forest.

She was impatient with her dressers but she couldn't dress herself and make them wonder where she had learned how.

Once in her riding habit, she hurried out of the room. She stole a glance at the guard outside her room but he had his eyes straight ahead. She must remember his face because if there were rumors that she had not been in her room last night, he would have spread them.

"Good morning, Your Highness." Julian greeted her at the door to the stables, then, as the groom walked inside, he leaned forward and planted a kiss just below her ear. "Or should I say 'my darling'? You look ravishing."

Aria blushed prettily. "You may call me what you wish in private," she said demurely.

"Then I would like most to call you wife," he said seductively. "Shall we go? In an hour we can be deep within the forest. Just the two of us alone. We don't have to be back for hours."

Aria continued blushing.

"Well, Count, that being alone part isn't exactly right." J.T. lazily moved out of the shadows of the stable door.

"You!" Aria gasped.

"Do you know this man?" Julian asked, looking from one to the other.

She squinted her eyes at J.T. "I had the misfortune of meeting him in America. We had business dealings there."

J.T. smiled. "I'm in charge of buying the vanadium from Lanconia."

Julian stepped forward and took Aria's arm. "Her Royal Highness will see you when she returns from her ride."

"No," J.T. said, placing himself between them and the horses, "that's not the way it is. You see, there was a little trouble in America and we   "

"Trouble?" Julian asked seriously. "What does he mean?"

"Nothing big," J.T. said before Aria could speak. "Just some people who seemed to want to cause the princess a little discomfort. So, to protect its own interests, America sent a couple of us soldiers over here to make sure there was no more funny business. One guy stays with the king and I'm to stay with the princess here."

Julian kept a tight grip on Aria's arm. "I'm sure that is very thoughtful of your government, but I can assure you that when Her Royal Highness is with me, there will be no need for your protection."

He moved toward the horses but J.T. intercepted.

They were contrasting men: J.T. dark, tall, his skin weathered from a life spent outdoors, while Julian was the product of centuries of careful breeding: his skin cared for, his hands manicured, his short, trim body held rigidly.

"Sorry, Count," J.T. said. "I go with her or she stays here."

Impatiently, Julian snapped his riding crop against his tall, polished boots. "I will not tolerate—"

"What's a matter, Count?" J.T. said jovially. "'Fraid I'll interfere in your time with the lady? I'll stay way back and you two can moon all you want." He winked at Count Julian, whose face was beginning to turn purple with rage. J.T. smiled. "Of course, you have to understand that if I don't go with the princess, then the deal with America is off. We won't buy the vanadium from a country that's hostile to us, and if we don't buy it, we'll sure as hell not let anybody else buy it, which means we may have to do something warlike to keep you from selling it. Then you'd be king of a country that's maybe been bombed and has no money since you can't sell the vanadium. That's up to you." J.T. turned and started to walk away.

Aria rolled her eyes skyward. "He doesn't mean a word of it," she said to Julian.

"You are risking war and poverty," Julian snapped at her. "I am surprised at you. Does your country mean so little to you?" He went after J.T.

Aria gritted her teeth and wondered which one Julian was most concerned with, war or poverty? He wouldn't like to marry the queen of a war-bombed country.

She chastised herself for her thoughts and allowed Julian to help her onto her horse.

"He will stay well back and we will be almost as if we were alone," Julian said as if in apology, and kissed her gloved hand.

She jerked away from him, then made herself smile at Julian. Lieutenant Montgomery was *not* going to ruin her outing. Perhaps she would give the American something to see. She wondered if he could ride a horse.

"We'll take the north path, to Rowan's Peak."

"Aria!" Julian gasped. "Are you sure? You haven't been on a horse for a while."

She leaned toward Julian. "Perhaps we can lose our escort and be alone," she said, looking at him through her eyelashes.

"I will follow you to the ends of the earth, my darling," he said under his breath.

J.T.'s horse plunged between them, breaking them apart and making Aria's mare dance on the cobble-stoned yard. "Sorry," he said. "I sure wish they'd put a steering wheel on this thing. If you two don't mind, could we go on an easy path? I'm not used to horses." His horse was prancing about and turning sideways, making the distance between Aria and Julian even wider. "Where's the brakes on this thing?"

"Pull back on the reins," Julian called. "Damned Americans," he muttered. "Why did the English fight for the place? Aria, what is his name?"

"Lieutenant Montgomery," she called over her shoulder as she cantered out of the stableyard and headed for the mountain trail.

Julian followed her, J.T. still in the courtyard, his horse wildly turning around in a circle.

Aria knew that her only chance of escaping Lieutenant Montgomery was to outrun him or to lose him on the twisting path that branched off in many directions. Her horse was rested and needed the exercise, and she gave it, urging the animal higher and higher into the mountains.

The air was cool and dry, and as she went up the rocky dirt path, the air got thinner. Around her were tall pine trees, closing off the rays of the morning sun. Huge gray boulders sometimes made the path very narrow and a couple of times her horse's hooves slipped, but she kept going.

She was perspiring from the effort, and at a bend in the trail she paused to see Julian not far behind her. She smiled when there was no sign of Lieutenant Montgomery. She motioned to the right to show Julian which path she was taking. There was a mountain spring a few miles down the trail and she thought they would stop there and rest—or whatever.

She brushed branches from her face, buried her face in her horse's mane to keep from getting struck, and kept riding. By the time she reached the spring, she was exhilarated with the exercise. She dismounted and breathed deeply of the clean mountain air. How she had missed her country.

Julian arrived, his face damp and wearing an angry expression. "Aria, I must protest. A lady should never ride such a strenuous path. It is much too much for someone of your delicate nature."

"Are you going to sit up there and scold me or are you going to get down and kiss me?"

His face registered momentary shock, then he dismounted rapidly and took her in his arms. "You *have* changed," he murmured before kissing her. "Let's set a date, my darling," he whispered, clutching her to him. "I don't know how much longer I can wait for you. I think your subjects would frown on our first child being born an inadequate length of time after our marriage."

Aria moved her head back so he could kiss her throat. He felt so very good.

"Whoa there, ol' Dan Tucker. Whoa!" J.T. burst into the little clearing like a rocket, and making about as much noise. Aria had tied her horse but Julian had not and at J.T.'s noise the horse jumped and went trotting further down the narrow path.

"You will fetch my horse," Julian ordered J.T., his face red with suppressed rage.

J.T. looked the soul of contrition. "I'm real sorry, Count, but I can't leave the princess. I guess you'll have to run after him yourself. Or you can take my horse. Brother! What a climb that was. About twenty times I thought I was gonna fall off and now I'm plumb tuckered out." He dismounted.

Aria glared at him. He was obviously lying because he didn't look in the least tired. In fact, he looked ready for some "real" exercise.

"You okay, Princess?" he asked.

"I am Your Royal Highness, to you," she said, then turned to Julian. "I will walk with you to find your horse. *You,*" she said to J.T., "will stay here."

J.T. lowered his eyes. "I wish I could do that, Your Royal Mightiness, but—"

"Your Royal *High*ness," Julian snapped. "Aria, I refuse to spend another moment with this provincial idiot. I shall cable the American government as soon as I return to the palace and protest. Come, Aria. *You* remain here."

Julian took Aria's arm and they started walking.

"Darling, I am sorry," Aria said. "As soon as the vanadium is sold and we once again have some capital in the treasuries, I shall send him packing."

"I do not think I can bear him until then. He is an uneducated, boorish lout. He is stupider than most of the peasants."

"Not all of them are stupid," she said. "In America I met some who were quite intelligent."

"How did you get away from your protectors to meet American peasants? Is that how you got into 'trouble,' as this idiot American so eloquently puts it?" He was looking at her speculatively.

"Well, no, I . . . I mean I . . ."

"Lookee here," J.T. shouted. "Hey, Count, I found your horse for you." Like a knight's lackey, he ran up the path holding the reins to the stallion. "Black brute," J.T. said fearfully. "I'm glad I don't have to ride him. Here you go, Count." He handed the smaller man the reins. "Hey! I brought some whiskey with me. You two wanna share it?"

"*Share* whiskey?" Julian asked, sneering. "Aria, we must return so that I may send a telegram. No, I will radio that American—what is his name? Roosevelt. I will radio him and protest this intolerable position he has put us in."

"You can radio President Roosevelt?" J.T. asked, eyes wide in wonder. "You must be a real powerful man. That oughtta help make up for your size."

Aria stepped between the men just as Julian raised his riding crop. "Julian, please. It would be like striking the American government. Let me speak to him. Please?" She asked the last very sweetly.

Julian turned on his heel and went back to the spring.

"You are making a fool of yourself," she spat at J.T. when they were alone. "And where did you learn to ride so well?"

He smiled at her. "In Colorado on the back of the meanest broncos my Taggert cousins could find."

"Your country bumpkin act is bad enough but your jealousy is intolerable."

He lost his smile instantly. "Jealousy, hell! How do you know it isn't your little count who wants you dead? Maybe he arranged the kidnapping in Key West. Maybe he wants you out of the way so he can marry that featherbrained little sister of yours."

"You leave my sister out of this!" She stopped. "And by the way, just what did the two of you do when you were at my grandfather's? All she could talk about was you when she returned last night."

"Yeah?" J.T. grinned. "Luscious little piece, that."

"How dare you," she said, doubling up her fists.

"Better not get too familiar, Princess, here comes your little stud. You better warn him that if he hits me with his little whip, I may wrap it around his throat. Probably go around about four times," he added, smiling.

"Leave us alone," she hissed as Julian approached. "Just leave us alone."

"Not until I know he can be trusted. Howdy, Count," he said loudly. "The princess here has given me a talkin' to set my ears ringin'. I'm sorry if I don't know how to treat royalty. We Americans ain't used to kings and dukes and counts and such. You two go on ahead. I'll be as quiet as a mouse and stay way back here."

Count Julian had been surrounded by servants all his life—servants who were respectful and knew their place in life. He imagined that this American had at last recognized his place. He turned back to Aria. "Shall we walk, darling? Perhaps we should discuss our wedding preparations. I think we should be married within three months at the most. It will be autumn then and we shall honeymoon in that mountain retreat of the king's."

"I don't know, there is a world war going on."

"And there are many marriages being performed. People need a little happiness now."

"I agree, Princess," J.T. said from behind them as he moved forward. "You two make a fine-lookin' couple and you ought to share your future with the world. The princess could wear a long white dress, symbol of her purity, and one of those diamond crowns—but not too tall 'cause of his royal countship here. I can see it now."

Count Julian raised his riding crop.

"Of course," J.T. continued, "America will pay for the wedding—sort of an appreciation gift for selling us the vanadium."

The crop lowered.

"We will return to the palace," Julian said, taking Aria's arm and leading her away.

She was angry herself, and as they returned to the horses, she vowed she was going to elude Lieutenant Montgomery and spend some time alone with Julian.

Julian's face was a mask as he helped Aria mount then mounted himself. The three of them started down the mountainside.

"Was it something I said?" J.T. asked, eyes bright as he reined his horse next to Aria's.

She kicked her horse forward and reached for Julian's hand. "Tonight I will meet you alone, at nine-thirty in the Queen's Garden under the gingko tree," she whispered.

He gave a curt nod but kept looking straight ahead.

They rode halfway down the mountain without speaking, J.T. staying just inches away from the back of Aria's horse. She glanced back a few times but he was always looking at the scenery with an intent expression. When they were back at the palace, she meant to talk to him about what she would and would not tolerate. And interfering with her growing relationship with Count Julian was one thing she would not abide. Another was his seeming interest in Gena. Gena was very young and frivolous and Aria could not allow her to spend time with an older, experienced man like Lieutenant Montgomery.

J.T. made no sound before he leaped. One second he was on his horse and the next he was sailing through the air, leaping toward Aria. She heard a sound behind her and saw this enormous man flying toward her. Only half of her scream escaped.

The shot missed her by inches. She was tumbling down the side of the horse, J.T. clutching her when the bullet whizzed over their heads.

Julian's horse reared, he lost the reins, and the

horse tore down the mountainside, Julian barely hanging on. The other two horses, now riderless, followed Julian's.

J.T. twisted his body so that he landed first on the rocky ground, Aria on top, then he moved so that they rolled off the path and into a little gully hidden by bushes and tall undergrowth. He covered her body with his, completely protecting her as he lifted his head slightly to look at the steep mountainside facing them.

"Was it a shot?" Aria whispered, looking up at his face.

"Something big, is my guess, maybe a sporting rifle because it had a shiny barrel. I saw it glint in the sun."

"Perhaps it was a hunter."

He looked down at her. "And they thought our horses were bighorn sheep?" He looked back at the mountainside. "They were shooting at you, Princess."

"Oh," she said, and her arms came up to wrap around him. "You saved my life."

"Again." He looked back at her. "I think I like this time better."

He looked as if he were going to kiss her but he pulled away. "We have to get you home. We can't take the path, we'd be too exposed. We're going through the forest and we're going to stop and listen often. No talking. Where's the nearest point of civilization? I guess it would be too much to hope for a car, but maybe there's a telephone. We need to call your army and get some protection on the trip down."

"There is a hunting lodge up the mountain," she said. "There are caretakers there who can take a message down but there are no telephone lines on the mountain. The nearest telephone is at the bottom. But Julian will bring help."

"Don't count on it, baby. He didn't look like he'd

stop running for miles, and if he gets back to the palace, he'll probably hide under the covers."

"I resent your saying that. Julian is not a coward."

"There was a rifle shot and all I've seen is the back of him. He should have returned with the horses by now. How far is this lodge?"

"It's not far if we don't use the road, but it's straight up."

J.T. groaned.

"It is a difficult climb, I admit, but—"

"We'll be exposed on the side of the mountain. Stay down and keep in the scrub oak as much as possible. Try to keep something between you and the sight of the rifleman."

"Perhaps he has gone."

"And miss an opportunity to pick you off? Come on, get up and let's go."

Aria had never made the climb before and she only knew about it because the son of one of her ladies-in-waiting had been lost from the lodge. During the three-day search she had heard much about the surrounding terrain.

The climb was strenuous and made worse because J.T. insisted they take the most difficult way. But he helped her over rocks, through groves of five-foot-tall oak trees struggling to survive, and under brush too thick to navigate except at a crawl.

It was noon when they reached the hunting lodge. J.T. pushed Aria into some shrubbery then began pounding on the door. A frightened-looking older woman opened it.

"Sir, you cannot—"

J.T. pushed past her and pulled Aria inside.

"Your Royal Highness," the older woman said, bobbing a curtsy.

"It's all right, Brownie," Aria said. "This is Lieutenant Montgomery, an American," she said, as if that explained his manners. "Could we have some lunch?"

"No one told us of your coming. We aren't prepared." The woman looked as if she were about to cry as she stood there fiddling with her apron.

J.T. moved away from the window he was looking out. "What are you having for lunch?"

Brownie gave him a quick look up and down as if to determine what his status was. "A humble shepherd pie with a potato crust. It's not fit for a princess."

"Sounds great to me," J.T. said. "How about you, honey?"

Brownie's face showed her shock.

"He is an American," Aria reemphasized. "The pie sounds excellent. May we have one?"

"Yes, my lady." Brownie disappeared into another room.

"Stop calling me honey!" Aria said the minute they were alone.

"Is 'darling' the name royalty use?" He was looking out the window again.

"Do you see Julian yet?"

"No sign of the front or back of him." He turned toward her. "You seem to be taking this well. But then you always recover from assassination attempts rather quickly. They only seem to make you hungry."

"It is part of my training. Since the beginning of time, people have wanted to kill royalty, either for the attention it brought them, for personal grievances, or for political ideals."

"Who taught you to spout out that answer?"

"My mother," Aria said before she thought.

He looked at her awhile. "You know something? I think I'm beginning to get to know you. How about a double whiskey?"

"Please," she said gratefully, and he smiled.

She was doing her best to remain the princess, to keep her head high, but inside she was shaking. Someone here in Lanconia was trying to *kill* her. One of her own people wanted her dead. She was almost grateful when J.T. pulled her from the foyer into the parlor hung with medieval tapestries and filled with chairs covered in dark, threadbare needlepoint.

"Sit down," he ordered as he went to a sideboard and poured a Waterford glass three-quarters full of whiskey.

She gulped a third of it. Her eyes watered but she needed the whiskey's warmth.

"I know about the time on the island and now this. Have there been any other attempts on your life? Maybe some 'accidents'?"

"I tripped over something on the stairs a week before I left for America. Lady Werta was behind me and caught my dress or I would have fallen."

"What else?"

Aria looked away. "Someone killed one of my dogs," she said softly. "I felt it was perhaps a warning to me."

"Who did you tell about these things?"

"No one. There was no one I could tell. My grandfather is too ill—"

"He's as much ill from pampering as anything else," J.T. said as he poured himself a whiskey. "I'm going to stay by you every moment. You're not getting out of my sight. You're to go nowhere without me."

"But I cannot possibly do that. I have many responsibilities. My grandfather has never believed in a monarch who dies one day and leaves the country to an untrained person. I am always in the public eye. It is the price I pay for the privilege of being a princess."

"So far I can't see that it's much of a privilege."

"And I have a duty to my fiancé," she said, draining her glass. "Julian is right: a royal wedding would help our country."

"Luncheon is served, Your Royal Highness," Brownie said at the doorway.

J.T. drank the rest of his whiskey. "Great. Send me an invitation. I'll do everything I can to help just as soon as I'm convinced he's not involved in this. Let's eat."

Chapter Eighteen

TWENTY minutes later Count Julian arrived with what indeed looked to be an army. They were planning to use the hunting lodge for their headquarters while searching for the princess and her attacker, but Julian strode into the dining room to see Her Royal Highness sitting at a table with a commoner and sharing a disgustingly coarse meal.

"Good to see you, Count," the American called. "Thought we'd seen the last of your back."

"Seize him!" Count Julian ordered one of the four guardsmen behind him.

Aria stood. "No," she said to the guard. "He saved my life and he is not to be harmed. Leave us."

With a court bow, the guard and his men left the room.

"Julian," Aria said firmly. "The guard and you will escort me home. I have engagements this afternoon."

J.T. stood and walked back toward them. "You can't go into the public."

301

"What am I to do? Lock myself in a tower? Should I find a food taster to check for poison? Am I to incarcerate myself?" She turned to Julian. "To explain the appointments I missed this morning, we will say that I fell from my horse and had to walk down the mountain. It will be better to be laughed at than to frighten people." She walked ahead of him out the door.

J.T. stopped Julian. "We can't let her do this. It's too dangerous for her."

Julian somehow managed to look down his nose at the taller J.T. "You cannot possibly understand. She is a crown princess; she will be queen."

"I understand that you're supposed to love her," J.T. said.

"What has that to do with it?"

"Her life is in danger, you little—" J.T. stopped. "Or would you like to see her out of the way?"

"If this were another era and you were a gentleman, I'd call you out for that." He stepped around J.T. and left the room.

"I'm ready when you are," J.T. called after him.

For J.T. the rest of the day was a nightmare. He stayed as near as possible to Aria but too many people pushed them apart. They were eager people with their hands outstretched, people with tears in their eyes who wanted to see their princess. She had been away for so long and they desperately wanted to see that she was well and not as ill as had been rumored.

As an American, it was difficult for J.T. to understand what she meant to these people. An ancient man in a wheelchair burst into tears when Aria held his hands in hers. "I have not lived in vain," he croaked out. "My life has some meaning now."

J.T. tried to envision the Americans' reaction to

seeing the president. Probably half of them would use the opportunity to tell him what he was doing wrong. Also, there was always the feeling of impermanence. Four years and he was out.

But Aria was a princess for life—however long that would be, J.T. thought with a jolt.

These people lined the street as she walked wherever she could. At the Scientific Academy he stood against the wall and listened to an incredibly boring speech about bugs. He let out a loud yawn that made that lipless Lady Werta turn and glare at him.

At 6:45 Aria was ushered into an ancient, highly polished Rolls to be driven back to the palace. J.T. pushed his way through the crowd, opened the opposite door, and climbed in with Lady Werta and Aria.

"Get out!" Lady Werta shouted. "Stop the car," she screeched to the driver.

"It's all right," Aria said.

"No, it is not all right," Lady Werta sniffed. "You cannot be seen with him. You are going to make people suspicious and then we will never get the real princess back. We will never see her again."

Aria started to pat Lady Werta's hand but J.T. shook his head. "What do you want?" she asked angrily, playing Kathy Montgomery, but it wasn't easy for her. "I told you I never wanted to see you again."

"Yeah, well, the old king hired me to protect the princess and I can't do that if you're out in the middle of all these people."

"She *must* do her duties," Lady Werta said haughtily.

J.T. started to say more but he stopped. Didn't any of these people have a bit of sense? They adored their princess, but if they didn't *protect* her she wasn't going to exist anymore.

It was only with reluctance that J.T. left Aria once they were back at the palace. His rooms were far away from hers and he knew he couldn't get to her quickly enough should she need help.

There was a small man wearing what seemed to be the household colors of gray and gold standing in his room.

"What are you doing here?" J.T. asked suspiciously.

"His Majesty has asked that I take care of you during your stay in Lanconia. My name is Walters and I will dress you, deliver messages, whatever you need. His Majesty has instructed me to be perfectly discreet. Your bath is waiting and your dress uniform is pressed."

"I don't need anyone," J.T. began, but then he thought that perhaps Walters might be useful.

"Here is a letter from His Majesty," Walters said.

The letter, on thick cream-colored paper and sealed with red wax impressed with a coat of arms, told J.T. that he might trust Walters with his life, that he had been told everything, and that he was excellent at hearing things.

J.T. began to undress, brushing Walters's hands away when the older man started to unbutton his uniform shirt.

"Did you hear what happened today?" he asked Walters.

"It was put about that Her Highness had an accident."

J.T. gave Walters a sharp look. "Was that all you heard?"

"Count Julian said she'd lost her way, but I managed to overhear him telling Lady Bradley that someone shot at her. The count seemed to think it was a

304

hunting accident." Walters turned his head away as J.T. finished undressing and stepped into the bathtub.

"What do you think?" J.T. asked.

"I buried her little dog, sir. Someone killed it with a knife, but it had been cut open from neck to tail then put under her bed while she slept. She saw its tail sticking out between her slippers. She called me to take it away before anyone else saw it."

J.T. leaned back in the old-fashioned, short, deep, recessed tub. All the bathrooms in the palace had been added about the turn of the century and were sumptuously done in squares of marble, with heavy porcelain fixtures and taps in the shapes of swans or porpoises. There was hot water but it took an eternity to get it up from the bowels of the palace. J.T. remembered Aria saying she had told no one of her "accidents," yet this servant, Walters, had taken her murdered dog away. How many other "no ones" knew nothing of what was happening?

"Walters," J.T. said, "tell me who lives in this place."

Walters recited a list of people and their lineages and titles that sounded like something from a fairy tale. There were three young princes, all direct descendants from a male monarch. There was Aria's Aunt Bradley, the Duchess of Daren, a woman who was directly related to nearly every royal house in the world. "Except the Asians, of course," Walters added. Her Royal Highness Sophie was the king's sister, and Barbara—"a mere child," Walters said—who was Aria's deceased father's deceased brother's only child.

"How did Aria's parents die?" J.T. asked suspiciously.

"Her father caught a cold but would not postpone or cancel a scheduled three-day trip to the southern part of the country. It rained and he stood in the rain to take the bows and curtsies of his subjects. He died two weeks later of pneumonia."

"And her mother?"

"Cancer. It might have been operable but Her Royal Highness told no one until she could no longer stand."

J.T. digested the information. No wonder Aria was the way she was. It was bred in her.

After he was shaved and dressed, J.T. followed Walters down to the Green Dining Room. This was supposed to be the dining room for intimate dinners but it was larger than a basketball court.

Walters pulled his watch from his vest. "We are a little early, sir. Royalty is always punctual. One could set one's watch by royalty."

"I'll have to remember that," J.T. said, one eyebrow raised.

J.T. wanted a cigarette but, somehow, the portraits of stern ancestors that lined the hallways seemed to frown on anything so modern. In the twenty or so hours that he had been in the palace, he had begun to conjure up a picture of the life of royalty: all duty and no laughter. He tried to remember his best table manners as his mother had taught him. If nothing else, he didn't want to embarrass Aria or have Julian laugh at him. At the moment he desperately wished he could remember the name of that ancestor of his who had been an English earl. Maybe he could just drop the name when Lady or Lord So-and-so was speaking of their relationship to Rowan the Twelfth or whoever.

"It's time," Walters said, and led J.T. to the door of a drawing room where everyone met before dinner. "Good luck, sir," he said as J.T. entered the room.

Aria handed her drink to a liveried servant, who

seemed to be waiting for the honor, and made her way to J.T. "Come, I will introduce you. Wait," she said, stopping and lowering her voice. "I cannot introduce you as . . . as . . ."

It took him a moment to understand. "As J.T.? What is it you have against my name?" he asked angrily.

"Initials are put on one's underclothes," she snapped. "It is an absurd American custom of abbreviating a name. I can only introduce you as Lieutenant Jarl Montgomery—that is, if you can part with your mother's hold on that name."

J.T. laughed, causing the others to turn and stare. "Honey, you can call me what you want." He reached out to touch her bare upper arm but she froze him with a look. "Okay, Princess, start the introductions."

The first person in line was a beautiful woman, about forty, but with skin like cream and a cleavage that made J.T. blink a couple of times. She held his hand just a second too long, and when she left, J.T.'s eyes followed her.

"Are you planning a liaison with my aunt?" Aria asked under her breath. "She is *much* older than you are, you know."

"So are all the best wines."

Next came a voluptuous little nymphet named Barbara. "But Aria, he is utterly divine. It is so kind of His Majesty to send us something like him." She clutched J.T.'s arm and started to lead him away.

But the door opened and in ran Gena, looking exquisite, her face flushed from a run down the stairs. "Sorry, Aria," she said quickly, then grabbed J.T.'s other arm. "He's mine, Barbara, and if you touch him, you'll draw back a bloody nub."

J.T. smiled from one young lady to the other. "I'm willing to share," he said pleasantly.

Aria started to separate the trio but Julian caught her arm. "Dinner is served and I think we ought to go inside."

The two young ladies led J.T. into the dining room, where he found place cards showing he was to sit between Lady Bradley and Princess Gena. Lady Barbara was across from him.

The meal was not what he expected. If he had ever thought about it—which he hadn't—he would have thought the best table manners in the world belonged to royalty, but that was not the case. They were a motley group, reminding J.T. of a group of spoiled children who had always been given their own way. Each person at the table, ten in all, had his own servant, and J.T. thought perhaps there should be two per person as each servant was kept busy with demands: one person liked cold wine, another warm wine; one person would not eat carrots, another ate an entirely different meal than what was served. One of the cousins, Nickie, ate with his mouth open while punching the air with his fingers to tell about his latest animal kill. And not one of them touched food with his hands. It was as if a curse had been placed on the food, that whoever touched it would die. The entire group came to an abrupt halt when J.T. reached for a roll on his bread plate. Defiantly, he picked it up in his hands, and after a moment they returned to eating and J.T. returned to his observations.

He looked at Great-Aunt Sophie, a loud, rude woman who did her best to dominate the table—while everyone else did his best to ignore her. Barbara and Gena seemed interested only in sex, and tonight he was their object of desire. Lady Bradley hardly spoke but gave him long looks over her wineglass.

As J.T. watched the people, he realized that the only one to interest him was Aria. She sat at the head of the table, ate with impeccable manners, and didn't shout or make demands.

"How you are observing us," Lady Bradley said softly. "Like animals in a cage."

He smiled at her. "As an American I'm not used to formal dinners. I'm used to hot dogs cooked on the beach."

She smiled in a knowing way. "There is breeding somewhere in you. I can sense it. Are you one of those very wealthy Americans?"

"I was hired to do a job, that's all." His eyes were on Aria.

"Mmm," Lady Bradley said. "You do not answer." She glanced at Aria. "Are you in love with her?"

J.T. told himself he would have to be more careful of what he revealed about himself. "She is different, that's all."

Lady Bradley's laugh rang out. "Aria has to behave herself. She has all the responsibility while the rest of us have the luxury. She does the work while we share in the rewards." She laughed at his expression. "The others will give you a long list of what they do to earn their keep, but the truth is, Aria supports us. She will make an excellent queen."

Barbara began demanding his attention and J.T. had to turn away from Lady Bradley, but the thought of Aria as queen brought him back to the present problem. Someone was trying to kill her and it was quite likely that that someone was sitting at this table. Maybe what Lady Bradley had said meant something. Aria supported them all. Perhaps someone wanted more than just room and board. Tomorrow he thought he would look into the household accounts and find out who needed money.

He looked at Gena, laughing at something the effeminate Freddie was saying, and J.T. knew that if

Gena were queen and personally owned the fortune that uranium would bring her, she would give it to whoever asked for it. She would probably go through the money and the resource in five years. And whoever had Gena would share the money. All that was needed was to get rid of Aria and the king and Gena would inherit.

The meal was long and tedious with course after course served on a different pattern of china. The royal family did not eat much, but seemed to drink a great deal.

"Why doesn't the king live in the palace?" J.T. asked Lady Bradley.

"He says the air near his hunting lodge is better for his health, but the truth is, he doesn't like us. Oh, he likes Aria and Gena all right, but no one else. In the fall we move to a much smaller palace south of here, then His Majesty moves into this palace. When we return, he leaves. It is most convenient for everyone, even Aria, because she is, in essence, queen while her grandfather is away."

J.T. thought he didn't blame the king one bit.

All through the long meal, which seemed to consist mainly of overcooked food laden with thick, rich sauces that after a while began to taste the same, J.T. watched Aria. She and Julian had their heads close together several times and once something Julian said made her blush.

J.T. began to remember their time in Key West. He remembered her laughter, how she had discussed the distilling plant with him, how she had danced at the ball with his mother. He remembered holding her, waking up with her, making love with her.

The wineglass stem snapped between his fingers.

Only Lady Bradley noticed as a servant covered the

stained tablecloth with a white brocade napkin and replaced his glass within seconds.

Aria lifted her eyes, met his, seemed to not like what she saw, then frowned and looked back at Julian.

You can't have her, J.T. told himself. She belongs here and you belong in America. You have to keep yourself remote from her. Guard her, protect her, but for your own sanity, don't fall in love with her. And, also for your own mental health, let Julian have her. He wants to be king and he may make a good one.

After dinner the men and women separated, the men going to a room to smoke cigars and drink brandy. Freddie, Nickie, and Toby were still talking about the number of animals they had managed to slaughter in their lifetimes and Julian refused to speak to J.T., so J.T. was not included in the group.

He gave a yawn, downed his brandy, and announced he was going to bed.

This effectively stopped everyone and he knew he had committed some great *faux pas.*

"You may not leave until Her Royal Highness has bid us good evening," Julian said, and his tone implied that any slug would know this.

"Tell her I hope she sleeps well," J.T. said with a wink. "See you around." He nodded toward the three princes.

"I'll be damned," he heard one prince gasp in disbelief before he got out of the room.

J.T.'s plan was to get Walters to show him where Aria's room was and somehow figure out how to guard her at night.

Walters was waiting for him with pajamas and robe—silk pajamas and a cashmere robe.

"I have to find a way to guard the princess at night," J.T. said, eschewing the nightwear.

"She is meeting the count in the Queen's Garden immediately after dinner," Walters said.

J.T. told himself he didn't care, told himself it would be better to allow them to meet alone. "Where is the Queen's Garden?" he asked after a moment.

"Over the bridge, go right, and follow the path. It's just past the tall hedges, a very secret place, sir. It was named so because it is a traditional assignation place for queens and their lovers."

J.T. left before he changed his mind.

The gardens around the palace consisted of acres of carefully tended grounds, some of which he had seen from his window. One part of it, about half an acre, was laid out with the Lanconian flag in five-inch-tall shrubbery, the insides filled with different-colored flowers: the grapes were green, the goat white, and there were bands of gray and gold.

Beyond the coat of arms he could see trees and brilliant patches of flowers and occasionally pieces of white that looked to be marble.

The path to the bridge was well tended and bordered on each side with drooping willow trees. He turned right past the bridge and the plantings became denser. The trees blocked the moonlight until it was so dark he could barely see the path.

"Julian?" he heard Aria whisper.

He stopped where he was, listened, then made a leap in her direction, catching her about the waist.

She opened her mouth to scream, so he did what came natural to him: he kissed her.

He missed her more than he thought possible. He held her so tightly he thought he might break her body in half—half for him and half for Lanconia. He drank of her lips and it felt very good when her arms went around his neck and she tried to pull him closer.

"Oh, baby," he whispered, kissing her neck and

burying his fingers in her hair. Her hair fell about her shoulders, soft and loose the way it was supposed to be, the way *his* Aria wore her hair.

It was a while before he realized she was struggling to get away from him. He was feeling a little dazed but he released her.

"Why are you doing this to me?" she gasped as if she were out of breath. "Why did you follow me? Can't you understand that I don't *want* to see you again? I didn't want you on the mountain and I don't want you now."

J.T.'s brain was beginning to clear of the fog that had invaded it when he was touching her. "I came to protect you," he said, but his voice had an unusual thickness to it, as if his tongue were swollen. He cleared his throat. "I just wanted to demonstrate how unsafe it is for you to be here alone. I could have been your attacker."

"You *did* attack me," she said. "Now will you please leave me alone? I am here to meet my husband-to-be."

"He's supposed to protect you? That little—"

"Stop it!" she said, and there were tears in her voice. "He's not big like you. He's not, as Gena says, divinely handsome, but he is suitable. Can't I make you understand that I have more to think about in a marriage than bed pleasure? You can*not* be my husband so please stop . . . stop touching me. I am going to love Count Julian. Do you understand that? I do not *want* you to protect me or even be near me. Now, would you please return so I can meet my lover in private?"

J.T. was glad the darkness hid his face and she didn't see him wince at her use of the word "lover." "You are right," he said at last. "But I do have a job to do." His voice was formal to the point of coolness.

"My president has asked me to guard you and I plan to do so. I am not sure that your little count isn't part of the conspiracy to harm you, so I plan to stay near you while he's here."

"What does Julian have to gain by my death?" she asked, exasperation in her voice. "He gains by my being alive."

"Does he?" J.T. asked softly. "He will marry a hardheaded, stubborn wench of a queen who will make him walk two paces behind her, and he will never be more than a prince. Knowing you, you would never allow him any control of the country. This morning he gave an order to a soldier and you countermanded the order—and the soldier obeyed *you*. I don't think a banty rooster like your count is going to like a lifetime of that."

Aria was silent for a moment. "And if I am dead?" she whispered.

"Your little sister will inherit. Whoever marries her will rule the country. He'd have to since Gena is incapable of governing anything."

"But Lanconia is so poor. Why would anyone *want* control of it?" she asked.

"It's not as poor as you think. Listen! Someone is coming." He leaned closer to her. "I'm not leaving you alone. I'm going to hide but I'll be near. And fasten your hair back up," he snapped before disappearing into the shadows.

Aria tried to pull her hair back but she had no pins to hold it. Her hands were shaking too badly to do much anyway. Until Jarl's words, she had made excuses for the attempts on her life because she hadn't been able to see any advantage to her death, but she knew what he said was right. What did he mean that Lanconia wasn't as poor as she thought?

"Aria, my darling," Julian said, pulling her into his

arms. "Alone with you. I never thought it would happen." He began kissing her face. "Your hair is down. How very *intime.*"

Aria was intensely aware that Jarl was near them and listening. She pushed Julian away but still held his hands. "It is good to see you alone at last. Come and sit down and talk."

"Talk in the moonlight? Oh, my darling, no. Let us make love."

"Julian, please," she said firmly, and drew him to a curved marble bench. "I think we need to talk. We have never talked about our future together."

He kissed her hands, first the backs then the palms. "I thought I was marrying a country but I find I am marrying a woman."

"After we are married, what do you plan to do? I mean in Lanconia. Do you plan to adopt charities? What form of sports do you play? I really know very little about you."

"How delightful that you are interested," he said, leaning forward to kiss her lips, but she drew back. He sighed. "I have never been interested in sports. Other than riding a bit, that is. I was trained to run estates. I believe my father hoped he could make back some of the wealth my grandfather frittered away. But he could not. Everything was lost." There was bitterness in his voice. "All I have left is my lineage and my knowledge. I came to Lanconia because I heard there was a crown princess to be had but I . . ." His voice softened. "I had not heard she was so beautiful. Aria, our marriage will be very happy."

"Yes, perhaps," she said, "but what do you plan to *do* after our marriage?"

"Be a king, of course," he said as if she were an idiot.

"I see."

He began kissing her hands. "Yes, my darling, you will be a beautiful hostess. I shall buy you Paris gowns once this foul war is ended and we will entertain nobility from all over the world. We will produce lovely children and I shall teach our son how to be a king."

"How will Lanconia pay for these gowns and entertainments? Shall we tax the peasants?" There was an edge to her voice. "Shall we take a third of their crops and leave them with hungry children?"

He dropped her hands and sat up straight. "You shall leave payment to me. I will manage everything. You have merely to plan the menus."

Aria was shaking, both with anger and fear. Here was a reason this man could want her dead. And if a man who was supposed to love her could want her death, what about the unknown people?

She put her hands over her face. "Oh, Julian, you don't know how heavenly that sounds. To not have to wake up every morning worried about making decisions! I should love to fly to Paris twice a year for the new collections. And I'd love to have children. I would spend a great deal of time with them if I didn't have to worry about . . . about serious, government problems."

In the darkness, J.T. nearly burst out laughing. It was a perfect imitation of Dolly, minus the southern accent. How many times had he seen Dolly pretend to be helpless then end up managing everyone? J.T. almost felt like warning Julian.

Julian took Aria's hands from her face. "My darling, I've never been sure how you felt. You are making me the most happy of men. Tomorrow I will begin work. I must look at Lanconia's revenues and we can begin planning our wedding."

"But the king—" Aria began.

"Bah! He is an old man. He knows nothing of what is going on. I must prepare for when I am king. Come, let us return to the palace."

"Do I get no more kisses?"

"Of course, darling." Quickly, he kissed her lips. "This cool air is not good for you. We must return."

"No," she said. "I will stay here awhile longer. A girl needs time alone to contemplate her marriage," she said flirtatiously.

"I don't like it, but all right." He kissed her hands again and turned swiftly down the path.

Aria stayed sitting on the bench for a moment until she heard J.T. move behind her. She fought back tears. Was it not possible for someone to love her for herself and not for her kingdom?

She stood quickly, hands clenched at her sides. "Are you happy now?" she spat at J.T. as he emerged from the darkness. "Did you enjoy finding out that you were right? Julian wants Lanconia, not me. He plans to become king and relegate me to the nursery. An American housewife has more power than I am to have. Why aren't you laughing?"

He pulled her into his arms, holding her hands down as she flailed against his chest. "I'm sorry, baby," he said, stroking her hair.

Much to her shame, Aria began to cry. "I used to know he only wanted to marry me for my country, but I seem to have forgotten. I thought maybe he did love me. I'm a fool! Is it not possible for someone to want *me*? Just me—without Lanconia."

J.T. turned her chin up to face him. "Baby, if you didn't have this damned country tied around your neck like it was the *Titanic* on its way down, I'd take you and run."

"Would you? You'd want me as a woman?"

"I'd want you home with me throwing your red

blouses in with my white T-shirts, telling me that you will not iron, and making me crazy by dancing in a skirt cut up to your hip." He moved his hands to her face. "Honey, I'd want you there to wash my back. I'd want you in my arms when I woke up in the morning."

He brought his mouth to hers and began to kiss her with all the lonesome hunger he felt for her. "Stay with me tonight. Don't let me wake up alone again."

"Yes," she whispered. She forgot where she was. She was once again Mrs. Montgomery and she was free to laugh, free to dress in an absurd costume and not worry that she was letting people down. She was free to eat with her hands, free to choose friends, not restricted to people who might not write stories about the intimate details of her life.

She clung to him, remembering and savoring those few glorious, heavenly weeks.

Then a bird called, giving its long sweet song to the night air. It was a rare bird, found only in the mountains of Lanconia and therefore treasured, protected, and honored as its national bird.

It made Aria remember where she was.

Violently, she pushed away from J.T. "No, no, no," she screeched. "You are the devil tempting me. I am *not* an American housewife. I am a princess—a *crown* princess—and my life belongs to my country. I *do* have Lanconia tied to me—no, we are part of each other. We are not separate. Do not touch me again, do not try to make me leave my country. If I did not love Lanconia so much, I would never have met you. Oh, how I wish I had never met you. I was content before. I didn't even know there was a life other than mine. You have made me very unhappy. I wish I had never seen you! I hate you!"

Still crying, she began to run down the path toward the palace.

J.T. followed at a discreet distance, making sure she was safe. He was torn between feeling miserable and elated. She *had* missed him. Underneath the princess was the woman.

But what she had said was true. Was he selfish to want to make her say that she wanted him and not some little blueblood? He was here to do a job and that job did not include making Her Royal Highness cry.

Love didn't matter; desire didn't matter. They could never be together except temporarily and she knew that even if he seemed to forget. From now on he swore he was going to keep his hands off of her. In fact, he was going to help her find someone to marry. Someone who would stay out of the way. Someone not overly ambitious. Someone who liked her as much as he did.

Someone impotent, so he wouldn't touch what belonged to J. T. Montgomery.

J.T. corrected himself, followed Aria until she went past her guard and into her room, then, sighing, he made the long trek to his own empty bedroom.

servers that were warmed by a candle underneath.

Chapter Nineteen

J. T. was waiting for Aria the next morning outside her bedroom door and started walking with her down to breakfast.

"You cannot do this," she hissed at him.

He paid as much attention to her protests as he usually did. "I want to have a look at the books of this place."

She smiled. "Our library is excellent. We have a few manuscripts from Rowan's time, even a map belonging to him."

"I want the books telling how much it costs to run this place. The ledgers. Accounts. Understand?"

"Like the household budget you put me on?"

"The one you overran every week," he said.

J.T. stepped back and allowed her to enter the dining room first and she was glad he did not embarrass her in front of her relatives, who were already eating. She took a plate from the end of a long sideboard and began to fill it from the many silver servers that were warmed by a candle underneath.

"This is a lot of food for so few people, isn't it?" J.T. grumbled as he filled his own plate.

He didn't say much during breakfast and Aria saw him watching the people at the table. She knew what he was thinking. Just what did these people *do* all day? Aria realized she had no idea. She saw Freddie snub J.T., looking at the American's plain uniform with no medals, no stars on his shoulders. Of course Freddie's uniforms were laden with gold braid and many medals but he had never done anything to earn them.

"Ready?" J.T. asked, standing behind Aria's chair, waiting to pull it out for her. "We have work to do."

He seemed oblivious to the open mouths around them, but Aria knew she had to obey him or he might cause a scene. Once they were out of the dining room, she let him have it. "You can*not* treat me this way. I am a royal princess. You are supposed to be a guest in my house. People are going to say—"

"I hope people will say, 'You'd better stay away from the princess, or that American will flatten you.' I want people to realize that if they get near you, they have to deal with me. Now, let's go look at the ledgers."

"I will take you to my treasurer and you two can look at the accounts. I have engagements today."

They were at the door to her bedroom. "Let's see your schedule."

"I do *not* have to get your approval."

"You bring it out here or I go in there. How do you think your old, little count will like my being in your bedroom?"

She returned with her secretary holding the big maroon leather-bound book that was her schedule. "The Royal Society of Entomology wants—" the secretary began before J.T. took the book from her.

He scanned the page. "There's nothing here but

more bug lectures and some ladies' societies doings. No sick kids or old people." He shoved the book back at the skinny little secretary. "Tell everybody Her Royal Highness is still weak from her illness and cannot attend. And from now on don't accept every invitation sent to her. She needs a little time to"—he looked at Aria—"to jitterbug. Come on, baby, let's go find your treasurer." He took her arm and started pulling her.

Aria knew she would die of embarrassment if she looked back at her secretary. "You cannot touch me," she said in exasperation.

J.T. dropped her arm. "Okay, so I forgot. So shoot me."

"And the names are intolerable. And you cannot cancel my schedule without my permission. You can't seem to remember that *I* am in control in Lanconia." He was walking so fast she had trouble keeping up with him.

"Uh-huh. You're so much in control that someone wants you dead."

"Here!" she said, stopping at a pair of carved walnut doors. There were two Royal Guardsmen standing on either side of the doors, their backs rigid, their eyes straight ahead. With a precise movement, they opened the doors and Aria sailed through without missing a step. J.T. looked at the two guards for a moment. "Thanks," he said, and went into the office.

Four men were on their feet instantly and it was easy to see that they were unaccustomed to visits from Her Royal Highness. They mumbled greetings and tried to hide dirty coffee cups.

J.T. stepped forward. He was going to drown in all the "Your Highnesses" going around the room. "I have been hired by the king to look at the economy of Lanconia and I'm starting with the palace accounts."

The four men of the treasury dropped their jaws. The oldest man's eyes bugged.

Aria stepped forward and said in a cajoling voice, "He is an American and he has been sent here by the king. Perhaps you could show us the household accounts and leave us."

The men didn't say a word as they put the books on one of the four desks in the room then left.

"You aren't helping America's image," Aria spat at J.T.

"I want to have the reputation of being an SOB. Maybe it'll put a little fear in somebody."

"All right, you have your books so I'll go now. Julian and I—"

"You are staying with me. You're not leaving my sight."

"But Julian and I—"

"You'd be *dead* now if you'd gone out alone with him yesterday. Now sit there and be quiet."

Aria sat down on the edge of a hard chair, her body as rigid as flesh and muscle could be. Lieutenant Montgomery was ruining her present life and her future life. She wouldn't blame Julian if he left her, but then she remembered his words of last night and she wondered if she cared if he left. Of course, she wasn't going to delude herself that she could get anyone better for a husband. A princess's choices were severely limited.

"What is this?" J.T. asked loudly, making her jump. "Is this an entry for *snow*?"

"It's probably for Freddie's snow cream." Perhaps she could put an ad in a paper seeking some royally connected man who didn't want to be a king.

"Snow cream?" J.T. asked, interrupting her thoughts.

On the other hand, maybe she could rule alone, a

virgin queen like England's Queen Elizabeth, but then it was a little late for the virgin part and she would rather like to have children.

"Aria!" J.T. snapped. "Answer me. What is this bill for snow?"

She sighed. Sometimes he could be so common. "Freddie loves snow cream so snow is brought down from the mountains for him."

"He eats this stuff every day?"

"Of course not. He only has it four or five times a year, but of course the snow must be ready for him should he decide he wants some."

"How stupid of me not to realize that," J.T. said quietly. "And are these other expenses for other necessities of life? Here are imported blueberries."

"For Great-Aunt Sophie." She was beginning to understand what he was saying. "These people are of the royal family, they are entitled to a few luxuries."

"Fresh salmon from Scotland?" J.T. questioned.

"For Aunt Bradley."

"How do you get these things during a war?"

Aria kept her face motionless. "My Aunt Bradley seems to have an 'arrangement' with a few pilots. I have never been inclined to look into the exact details of how she procures the supplies."

"I can imagine," J.T. said. " 'Procure' might be the correct word. The Lanconian government pays for this and your Aunt Bradley—"

"Stop," Aria warned.

J.T. looked over the ledger at her. Minute by minute she was becoming more princesslike, more like the prig he had first met. "You've got your underwear back on, haven't you?" He was pleased to see her blush but she didn't relax her rigid posture. "Here," he said, holding out a stick of Juicy Fruit gum.

"Ooooh," she said with great pleasure in her voice.

"*I* never got that reaction for anything I ever did."

She started chewing, the gum snapping. "You did, only you were making too much noise to hear me."

He looked at her with lowered lashes. "You'd better behave or I'll give you what you're asking for. Why don't you find something to do and stop sitting on the edge of your chair? You're giving me the heebie-jeebies."

"Sure thing, baby," she said, and got up.

He could hear her muttering "heebie-jeebies" under her breath, practicing the new word. It was difficult for him to concentrate on the books. The gum seemed to have transformed her back into *his* princess, the one who wore sundresses and pin-curled hair.

He forced himself to look back at the ledgers. As far as he could tell, the Lanconian royal family consisted of a bunch of parasites who had no idea they lived in a poor country that was surrounded by other countries at war. They were a large group of spoiled children who had never been made to grow up. If he had any control over the group, he would parcel out Aria's duties among them. That young Barbara would probably love getting out into the public and Gena could review troops. He didn't know what use Freddie, Nickie, and Toby could be but they could damn well sit through bug lectures. Great-Aunt Sophie could go to whatever ceremonies they had where cannons were shot off. At least she would be able to hear what was going on.

"What's that little smile for?" Aria asked.

J.T. leaned back in the chair. "I was thinking about your family."

"A bit of a mess, aren't they?" she said with some apology in her voice.

326

"Is that Princess Aria talking or Mrs. Montgomery?"

"American Aria," she said, slumping into a chair. "Freddie's snow cream seemed perfectly reasonable before, but it costs money, doesn't it? A lot of money."

"Too much."

"So what do we do?"

J.T. turned his head away from her for a moment. What do *we* do? He should have punched the king in the nose and hitchhiked out of the country before seeing her again. He was tempted to say, "Let's ask Count Julie," but he didn't.

Instead, he turned back to her and told her how he thought her work load could be shared by her relatives.

Aria was thoughtful. "They won't like it. Gena would enjoy looking at the young men of the Royal Guard—they're the only troops we have—and Aunt Sophie will *love* the cannons, but the others will protest."

"Then I'll have to persuade them. I mean, your husband will have to persuade them."

"My . . ." Aria said. "Oh yes, whoever I eventually marry."

There was a quick knock on the door and the doors were opened. "Your Royal Highness, Count Julian," said the guardsman.

Julian strode in, obviously already angry. "Aria, what are you doing in here alone with this man?"

Aria jumped out of her slouch and came to attention so quickly she swallowed her gum. "We are looking at accounts." Her eyes were wide.

"It won't hurt you," J.T. said under his breath. "Every kid in America would be dead if it did." He turned to Julian. "We were looking into Lanconia's debts and the princess is here so I can see that she's safe."

Julian looked at Aria as a father looks at a wayward child. "Aria, it is time for our ride."

Before Aria could reply, J.T. stepped in front of her. "The princess is busy. You got that, buster? *Busy.* Now skedaddle."

Julian gave J.T. a look of fury then turned on his heel and left. A guardsman closed the door behind him and J.T. thought he saw a glint of approval in the guard's eyes.

"Oh no," groaned Aria, sinking back into the chair. "Now you've done it. He'll never marry me now."

"Good!" J.T. said. "You deserve better than him."

"Where am I going to *find* better than him?"

"On any street corner in America."

"You really don't understand, do you? I have to marry someone with royal blood, someone who understands the monarchy, someone who—"

"Tell me about this Royal Guard of yours," he said, cutting her off. "Is it my imagination or do they all look alike?"

"They are matched."

"You mean like dishes?"

"Something like that. Their size is based on what is traditionally thought to be Rowan's size. They are from six foot one to two, have forty-eight-inch chests and thirty-two-inch waists. They cannot be larger or smaller. It is the greatest honor a Lanconian male can achieve to be a Royal Guard—but he must fit the uniform."

J.T. was thoughtful. "Forty-eight-inch chests don't grow, they have to be built. Do these guys have a training place?"

"Rowan's Field."

"Rowan again," J.T. groaned. "I think I've seen enough of these books for a while. We're going out to see the countryside. I want to see the grapes and I want you to tell me about this guard. Can they do more than open and close doors? And don't give me that princess look. Here, have some more gum," he said, leading her out the door.

Aria's dressers were horrified when she insisted on wearing a simple wool challis skirt and blouse and heavy-soled, short-heeled walking shoes when she planned to leave the palace grounds.

"But, Your Highness, please think of your responsibility to the people. They will expect to see a princess."

"And they'll see a human," Aria snapped. Lady Werta looked as if she were about to faint. "No, I don't want gloves and I'm going to let my hair hang." Aria swept from the room before they made her feel too guilty and so change her mind.

J.T. was outside her bedroom talking to one of the guardsmen, but he turned toward her when her door was opened. "You look great," he said, grinning, and Aria felt as if she had lost twenty pounds; her feet didn't quite touch the ground.

He led her down the stairs, quite improperly holding her arm, but she didn't reprimand him, not even after Aunt Bradley saw them and lifted her eyebrows. She led him to the garages at the back of the west wing and stood back and looked at the mountains while J.T. argued with a chauffeur about who was going to drive one of the cars. Just as she knew he would, J.T. won.

He backed out of the garage driving a cream-colored front-wheel-drive Cord, a low, sexy, gorgeous vehicle. "This is Aunt Bradley's car," Aria breathed, feeling very risqué as J.T. leaned across the seat and pushed the passenger door open to her. She could feel her chauffeur's horror at the gesture.

Aria rolled down the window and let her hair get mussed. She felt extraordinarily free and happy. She had a day of no duties, she was alone in a car with a handsome, sexy man, and she had left her heavy corset at home.

J.T. kept glancing at her until he could stand it no more. In a practiced American gesture, he put out his right hand, caught her by the back of the head, and pulled her over to kiss him while keeping his eyes on the road. "Good to see you again, baby," he said, releasing her.

She settled back in her seat, smiling. "Where are you taking me?"

"First we're going to your Royal Guard's training grounds. Ever been there?"

Aria laughed. "When I was fifteen I sneaked away one afternoon and hid in the bushes and watched the men train. They are all quite beautiful."

J.T. laughed. "They'll take away your princess badge if they find out."

She laughed again, feeling very unprincesslike.

The guards' training ground was nearly a mile from the palace on a broad plain that had always been free of trees and was traditionally used as the site of tournaments and trials by combat. Around the edge of the two-acre plain was a long, low open-front stone building.

When they were within sight of the men, J.T. stopped the car and looked. There were about a hundred and fifty men, all rather eerily the same size, all of them wearing nothing but a white garment that could only be described as a loincloth. Their nearly nude bodies rippled with muscles under sun-bronzed skin covered with sweat. They were involved in a great variety of sports: wrestling, archery, fighting with long thick sticks, sword fights with broadswords, hand-to-hand combat. Here and there was a gray-haired man wearing a red armband who now and then shouted at the combatants. Their gray hair did not lessen the magnificence of their bodies.

J.T. felt as if he had stepped into a time warp. This scene, these men with their old-fashioned weapons, their primitive garments, the stone shed in back, was something from long ago. "Straight out of your thirteenth-century Rowan, isn't it?" J.T. said softly, his voice filled with awe. Suddenly he realized he would like to train with these men. If there had to be fighting between men, it should be like this, not the dropping of bombs on anonymous thousands.

"Uh-oh, they've seen us," Aria said.

A moment later, one of the gray-haired men blew a whistle and the guardsmen disappeared from the field, returning in seconds wearing long gray robes and standing at attention in a perfect line. They were an impressive sight.

J.T. eased the car forward.

"They won't like that I'm here," Aria said.

"You're their princess, don't forget that."

"But they are very private people. Grans says—"

"Stick by me, honey, I'll protect you."

"Ha! They are *my* guard, *my* men, *my* . . ." She trailed off and smiled as the gray-haired man, now wearing a long, black robe, came forward to open her door.

"Your Highness," he said formally, "welcome."

J.T. and the captain of the guard looked one another over and judged each other quickly. "I need your help," J.T. said.

"You have it," the captain answered without question.

Medieval-looking wooden chairs were brought and J.T. and the captain were seated under one end of the stone building while Aria was given a chair several feet away. Contrary to Aria's belief that she would not be welcomed by the men, they made her a little *too* welcome for J.T.'s taste. One man brought out a fat-bellied guitar that J.T. supposed was a lute and began to strum it, another man offered her cakes from a plate, two other men held out silver goblets of drink. And whatever they were saying was putting an enormous smile on Aria's face. She looked like a princess of old surrounded by her handsome courtiers whose heavy, muscular legs stuck out bare beneath their scanty clothes.

The captain looked from Aria to J.T.'s frowning face and smiled. "We do not get many visitors to our training ground and our princess has never been here." He chuckled. "Except once when we were not supposed to know she was here."

J.T. smiled. "How much do you know about what is going on?"

"Someone shot at Her Royal Highness," the captain said, his mouth set in a grim line.

"It has been more than that." J.T. knew that he could trust this man. Perhaps because they were descended from the same warrior stock, but J.T. knew he could trust this man with his life. He told him that someone had tried to kill Aria in America. He told of the other attempts on her life and J.T. could feel the captain's growing anger.

"We have been told nothing of this," the older man seethed. "In the past hundred years we have been relegated to doing nothing but opening and closing doors. Our king may have forgotten our true use, but

332

we have not. We are ready to lay down our lives for our king and his two granddaughters."

"And the rest of them be hanged," J.T. said. "I agree with you. I want her watched every minute of every day. I wish there were women who could stay with her in her bedroom. I don't trust any of those women with her now."

"Perhaps there is someone. Come with me."

J.T. was reluctant to leave Aria alone with those half-naked men but he followed the captain.

"There was a time," the captain said as they walked, "when Lanconian warriors were the finest in the world. Over the centuries most of the people have turned to farming but a few of us have kept the tradition of training. We are not as much in favor now since Lanconia has been declared a neutral country."

They turned a curve in the path and rounded a grove of trees. Opening before them was a small clearing and here ten women wearing white, draped garments that reached only to the tops of their magnificent legs were participating in games like the men's.

"My God," J.T. said with sharp intake of breath.

The captain smiled. "Centuries ago, the women were trained beside the men. Beautiful, aren't they?"

J.T. couldn't close his mouth as he looked at the six-foot-tall, bronzed goddesses wrestling and fighting. A whistle blew and the women lined up, and a dark-haired woman wearing a longer red garment started walking toward them.

The captain turned his back to her for a moment. "Jarnel trains the women. She is also my wife."

J.T.'s eyes were on the woman. "No wonder you stay so fit."

J.T. and the captain talked to Jarnel and it was agreed that, somehow, one of the guardswomen would be substituted for one of Aria's ladies-in-waiting.

Later, as he and the captain were walking back to the men's training ground, J.T. said, "Tell me, do the guardswomen welcome men like your men welcome the princess?"

"No," the captain answered. "Lanconian women are pursued. They do nothing to win a man; he must go to them. Of course there have been exceptions. In Rowan's day sometimes the women fought each other for a man. In fact, that was the case with Rowan himself."

"You mean this Rowan I keep hearing about was the prize in a contest? Some muscular broad *won* him?" J.T. laughed.

"I imagine the warriors looked somewhat like our guardswomen," the captain said mildly.

J.T. remembered the ten tall, beautiful women in the field behind him, their skin gleaming with sweat, and he stopped laughing.

It was nearly noon by the time Aria and J.T. drove off in the Cord, three carloads of guardsmen behind them in old but perfectly kept black Fords. J.T. wanted to see a vineyard. He followed the directions the captain had given him and arrived just as the workers were sitting down to their midday meal.

Aria often saw the city dwellers but these country people had too much work to do to stand in line to gawk at a pretty princess. They were stunned into speechlessness at the sight of her looking a great deal like their own daughters and sweethearts.

"Your . . . Your Highness," one woman stuttered while the others stood quietly, their lunches forgotten at their feet.

"May we join you?" J.T. asked. "We brought our own food."

334

The people nodded hesitantly.

Aria followed J.T. to the trunk of the car. "We did bring food? Are you sure this is all right? They don't seem very friendly."

"They're scared to death of Her Royal Highness but I bet they'll like Mrs. Montgomery."

He was right. It took Aria awhile to forget that she was a princess and the people a little longer to lose their awe of her, but it did happen. They ate and talked, Aria telling them about the wonders of America and the people answering J.T.'s questions about the drought and the state of the grapes.

The Lanconians were a tall, good-looking people, both men and women slim and muscular from years of going up and down steep hills carrying big baskets of produce. They planted on top of the hills and lived below in tiny villages.

Everyone worked, from toddler to ancient. Young women strapped babies to their backs and went up the hills. Quite often the men took care of the younger children and it wasn't unusual to see a fifty-year-old man trailed by three four-year-olds.

J.T. realized that he was looking at what had once been a great society but now he knew it was dying. There were so very few children in Lanconia. Here, sitting at lunch with twenty-seven people, he guessed the average age to be fifty-two. There were only four children under sixteen when there should have been a dozen or more. He knew that too often the young people left home at an early age, prowled the streets and cafes of Escalon for a while, then left the country altogether.

At three o'clock he realized the people were impatient with politeness and wanted to get back to work. He asked if they could see the vineyard.

He had been given a tour before but then he had

looked at the place with disgust. Now he wondered if there was something he could do to help the economy of the country.

Aria seemed to be happy, walking up the mountain with three women, one of whom had a baby that Aria seemed fascinated with, four guardsmen surrounding her about twenty feet away and watching the area with hawklike gazes.

The women started picking grapes and Aria, without thinking, joined them. He smiled at the looks on the faces of the Lanconian women but they recovered quickly and picked alongside their princess. Aria passed out sticks of Juicy Fruit and moments later he heard laughter.

He left her with the women and guards as he went back down the mountains to the old winery that was dug into the side of the hill. This year's grape crop was the best in four years, but it still wasn't enough to make a profit. The wine had to age for three years, so even if this year had been magnificent, it would be three years before the wine could be sold. And in three years' time hundreds more Lanconians would be forced to leave the country.

J.T. stood outside in the sunshine and held a bunch of ripe green grapes and watched the people carrying basket loads of grapes down the mountainside. If only there was a quick cash crop for grapes.

Raisins, he thought. Men at war living on canned field rations might welcome the freshness of raisins. Maybe he could persuade the U.S. government to buy raisins along with the vanadium. Maybe his majesty the king would refuse to allow American bases in Lanconia if America didn't buy raisins.

As J.T. thought, he wondered how the Lanconians would take to the idea of raisins. They were a proud people and they might refuse to have anything to do with something as lowly as a raisin.

"Have you ever thought of doing something with the grapes besides making wine?" he began, talking to the four older Lanconian men near him.

J.T. needn't have worried. Lanconians were proud but not stupidly so. They were willing to try anything to help their impoverished country. Their only concern was that if they used the grapes now for raisins, three years from now they would have no wine.

"Next year we irrigate and we have a bumper crop." The words weren't out of his mouth before he realized he wouldn't be there next year.

It was six before he got Aria back into the car and they headed back to the palace. She was sunburned, windblown, and tired—and he had never wanted anything so much in his life as he wanted to make love to her.

"Have a good time?" he asked in a voice that was little more than a whisper.

"Oh yes, a lovely time. You seemed to enjoy it too."

"I did," he said, somewhat surprised.

At the palace they were whisked back into the present. Lady Werta was there, angry beyond words at Aria. Julian was livid and wanted to discuss her behavior. J.T. thought a couple of her retainers were going to choke when Aria thanked her guardsmen for watching over her.

J.T. put his hands in his pockets and went off whistling.

He felt more secure now that the guardsmen were watching her. The day had been a good one and he didn't even mind the way Walters fussed over him. J.T. let the little man tell him all the gossip Aria's unusual day had caused. There were stories of the crown princess drinking alone with goatherders, of Her Royal Highness working as a field hand. And some people were beginning to hate Lieutenant Montgomery, who was trying to make a monarchist country into a socialist one.

J.T. sat in the tub and smiled.

He didn't think he could face dinner with Aria's disapproving relatives and he was pleased with the palace system when he realized he could order dinner to be taken wherever he wanted. Walters told him how to get to the library and J.T. went there to eat and be alone and think.

Aria left the drawing room as soon as she could get away. It had been a heavenly day of laughter and then she had returned to the palace to find everyone treating her as if she were a traitor to her country. Julian was angry because she had been alone with "that despicable American." The Lord High Chamberlain had berated her because he thought she was actually Kathy Montgomery and had been out with her husband and because her behavior was very common.

But no matter what anyone said, Aria was deliciously happy. Maybe she had been so demanding all her life because, in her heart, she felt herself to be useless. Today she got some idea of how important her role was to her country.

And how important Jarl Montgomery was to her life.

It seemed that the happiest times in her life had been spent with him: cooking out on the beach, making love on the stairs, even crying in his arms had been a pleasure.

She had been very disappointed when he had not

come to dinner. She walked down the hall and saw one of the Royal Guardsmen standing as if he were a statue instead of a man. A few days ago she would never have considered speaking to a guard.

"Excuse me," she said politely, "do you know where Lieutenant Montgomery is?"

"In the library, Your Highness," he answered.

"Thank you."

"You are most welcome."

She saw the briefest hint of a smile on his handsome face. Please and thank you, she thought. Magic words.

She found her husband in the big library bent over one of the four long walnut tables, books scattered around him, the green shaded lamp on while he sketched on a pad of paper.

"Hello," she said when he didn't look up. "Did you have dinner? What are you doing?"

He rubbed his eyes and smiled at her. "Come here, honey, and look at this."

He showed her a drawing of gears and pulleys that meant nothing to her. She moved closer to him as he began to explain his ideas for bringing the grapes down from the hills via a motorized pulley system. He planned to use the motors of the derelict cars rusting in the fields of Lanconia to run the pulleys. "That'll free more people to dry the grapes," he explained.

"Dried grapes?" she asked.

As he explained about the raisins, she looked at him—and realized that she loved him. This was where she wanted to be more than anywhere else in the world: sitting here at night close to him and talking about future plans. She wished she were wearing a nightgown and they were in their little Key West home.

J.T. was asking her a question. "What?" she asked.

"Your little count mentioned a radio. Is there a two-way radio around here that I can use to call the States?"

"I guess so. Who are you going to call?"

J.T. pushed his chair back and stood, and when she stayed seated he took her hand and pulled her up. "Come on, let's go find the radio. I'm going to call my father and see if he can get Frank out here." Before she asked, he explained. "Frank is my seventeen-year-old Taggert cousin—knows more about cars than anybody else alive." He was holding Aria's hand as he strode down the long library then out into the corridor. "Last I heard Frank was mad because his father refused to let him join up. Frank in a good mood is difficult enough but Frank in a bad mood is not something I'd like to see."

"And you're going to invite him here?"

"We need him. If you had ships, I'd be able to help, but cars I don't know too much about." He stopped and asked one of the guardsmen where the radio was. Of course the guardsman knew and Aria led J.T. down to the northeast chamber of the vaulted cellars.

Chapter Twenty

ARIA came awake slowly, rubbing her eyes and yawning. She had been up late last night with J.T. and the man who she found out was the Royal Herald. His predecessors had cried the news throughout the towns but now he radioed his news. It was the first Aria had heard of him.

It took two hours to get through to Maine in the U.S., then they had to wait while someone drove to J.T.'s father's house and got him. Aria got to speak to Mr. Montgomery for a moment to ask him to say hello to Mrs. Montgomery.

Later, J.T. had mumbled something about his parents making his life miserable when this was over.

Mr. Montgomery said he would send young Frank out as soon as possible.

It was midnight before J.T. walked Aria to her bedroom. He glanced at the two guards flanking the doors and abruptly left her standing alone.

Now she stretched and wondered what he had

planned for today. She knew that at ten A.M. she had to be sixty miles south of Escalon at a vineyard for the blessing of the harvest. She wondered what J.T. would do and say today, how he would make the day interesting.

Her dressers drew her hair back into a perfectly neat and tight chignon. They snapped the steel fasteners of the long Merry Widow and dressed her in a somber black suit with a big diamond brooch on the left shoulder. For a moment, Aria considered exchanging the brooch for the gaudy enameled parrot she had bought in Key West on a shopping spree with Dolly, but she didn't have enough courage to carry out her idea.

Outside her room, J.T. was not waiting for her and he wasn't in the dining room. She was beginning to learn to ask a guardsmen if she wanted to know anything. J.T. had left the palace before six A.M. and had given no hint as to when he would return.

She waited until the last minute but she had to reach the Blessing Festival on time. She tried not to let her face fall when she saw Count Julian standing by the car door. His expression was stern.

"I thought perhaps you were going to discard your obligations again today," he said in reproach.

She didn't answer him because she felt too guilty about yesterday. She had had a good time yesterday. But princesses weren't supposed to have fun. They were to fulfill obligations, not play with the peasants' babies and exchange gossip about American movie stars.

"Aria, people are beginning to talk," Julian began once they were in the long black car. A Royal Guardsman sat beside the chauffeur behind the glass partition, and a carful of guardsmen followed them. "The king is too ill to take the firm hand with you that he should so I am left with the duty. You are behaving like a . . . a woman of the streets with that crude, vulgar American. You spent every waking moment with him yesterday and it is all anyone could speak of this morning. If you care nothing for your own family, think of what the servants say. They do not want a princess who is one of them—they want a *princess*. I hear you even dared to invade the Royal Guard's training ground. Have you no respect for the privacy of those men?"

Aria sat in the seat, her hands tightly clasped in her lap, feeling more awful with his every word. Then, to her utter astonishment, the guardsman in the front seat turned and *winked* at her! She came very close to giggling. What especially surprised her was that he had obviously heard every word Julian had said—and she had always believed the partition to be sound-proof.

Julian kept fussing and Aria kept listening, but she wasn't worried any longer. Maybe her family was ashamed of her, but it didn't look as if her people were.

Meeting the people today was very different from yesterday. The people were in their Sunday best and were using their best formal manners. They smiled at her, but no one laughed and they just asked her questions. It was really quite tedious for her.

The people seemed pleased to see Count Julian and repeatedly asked when the wedding was going to be. "But I'm already married," she wanted to tell them.

It was one o'clock before they were on their way back to the car and over the heads of the people Aria could smell food. There was a break in the crowd, and some distance away, at the side of a tiny house, a woman was ladling something into a piece of bread and handing it to a little boy. Aria knew what it was; she'd had one as a child. A piece of thick Lanconian bread, still warm from the oven, with a thick, chewy crust, was split and inside was ladled a generous scoop of spicy chicken stew made with grapes. Fresh goat cheese was sprinkled on top.

Aria wasn't even aware of what she was doing, but she turned away from where Julian waited by the open car door, started saying, "Excuse me," and made her way through the crowd to the woman's house. "May I have one?" she asked the astonished woman.

The old woman just stood there and stared.

"Gramma!" the little boy said loudly, bringing the woman to her senses. She spooned stew into the bread, sprinkled it with cheese, and held it out to Aria.

"Thank you very much," Aria said, biting into it. She suddenly became aware of the silent crowd behind her. She turned, a bit of sauce on her upper lip. "It's delicious," she said, and the crowd cheered.

A guardsman handed her a clean handkerchief to use as a napkin and she saw that there were four guardsmen near her. They had followed her as she went through the crowd.

"Princess," she heard, and looked down to see the little boy holding out a rough stoneware mug to her. "It's buttermilk."

Aria smiled and took the mug. "Thank you," she said.

The little boy grinned. "You're not like a real princess at all."

"Thank you again," she said, making the crowd laugh. The guardsmen parted the crowd as she made her way back to the car.

Julian was fuming. He lectured her all the way back to the palace as she greedily ate her sandwich and drank her buttermilk. He wanted to throw the mug out the window but she wouldn't let him.

When they arrived at the palace, the guardsman who had sat in the front seat opened the door for her and she handed him the mug. "I would like to thank that woman for her food. Would you please find out what she needs?"

"I saw an empty chicken coop," the guardsman said softly.

"Fill it," Aria said before Julian gave her a sharp look. "Do you know where Lieutenant Montgomery is?" she whispered.

"With the guards, Your Highness."

Aria turned her head so Julian wouldn't see her talking. "Would you please see that my horse is ready in twenty minutes?"

The guardsman merely nodded as they rounded the car and she was within earshot of Count Julian.

Aria had some difficulty escaping Julian and she saw a few other members of her family looking askance at her as she ran across the courtyard and made her way to the stables. Her horse was saddled and waiting for her and four Royal Guardsmen were ready to ride with her.

It was a matter of minutes before she reached the guardsmen's training field then halted her horse to watch the men. J.T. was with the guardsmen, wearing the white loincloth and battling with a stick against a guardsman. J.T. was as tall as the guardsmen but paler skinned and not as heavy. He wasn't very good with the stick either and the guardsman he was sparring with seemed to be toying with him.

"He will learn," said the guard beside Aria. "In another year or so he will be the best fighter in Lanconia."

Aria smiled at that, but then she remembered that in a year J.T. would probably be back in America and she would be married to Julian.

At that moment J.T. glanced at her, she waved, and the next moment J.T. was sent sprawling on the ground.

"Keep your mind on what you are doing," the guardsman standing over J.T. yelled.

Aria went running to J.T. "Are you hurt?" she asked as she knelt beside him. She glared up at the guardsman. "I'll have your head if you've hurt him."

J.T. smiled at her as he rubbed his bruised shoulder. "I may die of embarrassment but nothing else. Tell Rax you didn't mean what you said."

Aria was aware that many of the guardsmen were now watching them with curiosity. She genuinely wished she had not made such a fool of herself, but before she could say a word, Gena came running across the field. She was wearing practically nothing: a short-skirted, one-shoulder dress, a heavy gold bracelet on her right upper arm.

"J.T. darling," Gena said, falling to her knees by his side. "Are you all right? Have you been injured?"

Aria didn't speak but slowly rose with great dignity and walked away. She reached her horse before J.T. caught up with her. He grabbed her arm and pulled her into the trees. Aria squirmed to get away from him.

"Come on, baby, don't be mad," he coaxed, running his hands up her arms.

His bare skin was hot and sweaty and her face was inches from his chest.

346

"I had to do something with her. She was following me everywhere, so I gave her to the women to train. It's keeping her out of trouble."

"And *you* enjoy her. No doubt the sight of her in that little skirt—" She broke off as he kissed her.

She was breathless when he finished and she clung to him, her cheek against his damp chest.

"We shouldn't do this," he said after a long while. "This kind of thing will make our parting harder. Tell me what you did this morning."

"Gena is so pretty," Aria said, holding on to him.

He pushed her away just enough to look at her. "Not as pretty as you. Not as smart as you. Not as much woman as you."

"Really?" she asked, beginning to smile.

"Really." He kissed her again, but lightly. "Now tell me what you did. Did the guard protect you? Were you safe? Come back to the field with me and I'll give you some beer and we can talk."

Aria ended by spending the afternoon at the guards' training ground. For the first time she met the guardswomen and she saw Gena trying to learn to wrestle. The men were watching the event as if it were very serious, but Aria saw the light in their eyes. She was sorry she had been jealous of her little sister when she saw the way Gena looked up at her with such adoration in her eyes.

Aria leaned toward J.T. "This Frank who is to come, what is he like?" she asked.

J.T. looked at Gena and began to smile. "He may be exactly right for her, although I don't think he'll want to stay here. He won't fit any more than I do."

Aria felt like laughing because if anyone fit it was Jarl. He was dressed in a white robe, his big legs bare, sitting on one of the wooden chairs, drinking beer. He could have been one of the guardsmen. The captain of the guard caught her eye and smiled as if he knew what she was thinking.

Five minutes later all hell broke loose because Julian arrived in a long black limousine. He was horrified by Aria's common behavior and told her she was late for tea with the Ladies' Historical Guild.

Aria left with him, surrounded by guardsmen, before he saw Gena in her skimpy dress.

For four days Aria tried to behave herself. She rode with Julian and six guardsmen in the morning, then answered requests from people until midmorning, and at ten she left the palace to attend one function after another. She did not see Jarl. He did not come to dinner nor did he attend one evening's festivities when the Lanconian Opera Company performed. The soprano was not very good and the tenor kept stepping in front of her so the audience could not see her—which made the soprano angry and her singing worse. Aria was afraid she might nod off.

On the fifth morning, she was having breakfast when J.T. strode into the room. He looked tired. "Frank's plane is about to land. You coming?"

Aria gulped a cup of tea and left with him to the astonishment of her relatives at the table. He didn't speak until they were in the backseat of the car and on their way to the airport. He turned to her and his eyes seemed to eat her.

"I've missed you," he whispered, then took her hand in his and held it tightly. They were silent for a moment, then both began to speak at once.

J.T. told her how he had been working eighteen-hour days, traveling all over Lanconia, trying to educate the farmers about selling their grapes as raisins. He had twice been in radio contact with

President Roosevelt and it looked like America was going to buy raisins. "But not very many," J.T. said. "America has California with millions of raisins." He sighed. "There has to be something else we can do to help this country stand on its own feet."

"We," Aria whispered. "We."

The two American airplanes were just landing when they arrived at the airport. Out of the first plane came several older American men then a hundred soldiers. These were the men to mine the vanadium.

Off the second plane came a six-foot-tall man who could have been twenty or forty-five. He had dark hair, dark eyes, and a big, thick body that looked like it could carry a great deal more weight than it did and a handsome face set in a scowl.

"There's Frank," J.T. said, taking her hand and pulling her behind him.

"*He* is seventeen years old? Why is he angry?"

"He was born angry but don't let him scare you. He's a good kid."

Aria stood back while J.T. and Frank shook hands. "This is Her Royal Highness, Princess Aria," J.T. said.

"Pleased," the boy said, holding out his hand to shake hers, and Aria accepted it. He seemed to dismiss her as he looked back at J.T. "When do we get to work? I brought crates of tools and I'm ready as soon as they unload them."

Aria looked back at the plane in time to see three children being helped down the stairs. She touched J.T.'s arm. "Who are they?"

J.T. looked at one of the pilots near him. "Who are the kids?"

"Orphans. Their relatives were killed in France and a couple of guys smuggled them on board. We're stuck with them until we get home where we hope we can get somebody to take them."

Aria had no idea she was speaking; the words might have been someone else's. "I'll take them," she said.

"But Your Highness . . ." Lady Werta had followed Aria and J.T. as soon as possible to the airport and now she was giving warning looks to Aria.

Aria looked at the pilot, her chin up, her voice clear and loud. "I will take these children and Lanconia will take all the orphaned children you can find."

The pilot smiled indulgently. "Lady, there's a war going on and there are thousands of orphans out there. This place doesn't look like it could feed them."

At that J.T. stepped forward. "If Her Royal Highness says she wants children, then she's gonna get them. We'll take any children of any country and don't worry about food, we'll feed them."

The pilot obviously didn't like J.T.'s attitude. "Okay, buddy, you're on. If it's kids you want, it's kids you'll get."

Feeling very pleased with herself and with her husband, Aria went to the frightened French children and began to talk to them. Lady Werta didn't want her to touch the dirty children but Aria waved her away.

In the car on the way back to the palace, Aria held the two-year-old on her lap, while the three- and four-year-olds sat on either side of her. J.T. and Frank talked about making pulleys for getting the grapes off the hills.

At the palace, Gena came running to greet them, as usual, a little late and more than a little flushed after her run down the stairs. Her cheeks were pink, a curl had escaped her careful coiffure—and she looked divine.

Aria turned to greet her sister but then Gena's eyes widened and she came to an abrupt halt. A second later she moved past Aria as if in a dream and stopped in front of Frank Taggert and just stood there staring. Frank's angry look left his face as he gaped at Gena, his lower jaw slightly dropped.

"I think they want an introduction," J.T. said, smiling. He lifted a hand of each teenager and put them together. "Gena, Frank. Frank, Gena. Now, Gena, take Frank outside to play."

As if sleepwalking, the two teenagers started down the hall.

"I'm not sure . . ." Aria began. "I mean, Gena is . . . And Frank is . . ."

"Young. Both of them are young. Come on, let's get something to eat. I bet these kids are starving."

With one more glance at the backs of Gena and Frank, Aria followed J.T. toward the dining room.

That night Aria bathed the children and had beds put in her bedroom. The next morning four couples begged to see her, said they had heard of the children, and asked to be allowed to raise them as their own.

Aria didn't want to part with the children, but she turned them over to the couple that spoke French.

Forty-eight hours later an American plane landed and it was filled with one hundred and seventeen children, mostly French but some Italian. They arrived just as the entire royal family was assembled to watch a ceremonial parade celebrating the defeat of the northern tribes in 1084 A.D.

The Royal Guard brought the children to the capital city on horseback, in jeeps, on motorcycles, and in goat carts. The parade came to a halt. J.T. began thrusting children into the arms of the royal family.

After some initial protests from the family mem-

bers, the dirty, tired, scared children were taken back
to the palace, where tub after tub was filled with hot
water and the scrubbing began.

Freddie, Nickie, and Toby found they had a new
audience for their stories of their bravery against
ferocious fawns and demented doves. Lady Barbara
chose three pretty little Italian girls and washed them
herself. Great-Aunt Sophie bellowed orders to two big
boys who had fought all the way on the plane and they
obeyed her meekly. Aunt Bradley chose two handsome boys of about fourteen.

Aria and J.T. parceled out the other children to
various retainers until everyone was scrubbing behind
ears.

"That's it," J.T. said. He and Aria had personally
bathed fourteen kids and sent them off with the
ladies-in-waiting to be fed and dressed in whatever
could be found for them.

They were sitting on the damp marble floor of her
bathroom, alone in the suite.

"Why are you looking at me like that?" she asked.

"I was remembering the woman on the island who
demanded everything. You wouldn't even let a commoner sit with you and now you wash these very
common children."

"Lanconia needs children. Whatever I have done, I
have done for my country."

"Have you?" His eyes were beginning to grow hot.
"Has everything been for your country?"

He was on her in seconds and their hands tore at
each other's wet, soapy clothes, their hunger making
them urgent.

"Baby, oh baby, I've missed you," J.T. kept saying
as his hands grabbed her breasts.

They made love on the cold marble floor, then J.T.
lifted her and set her on the side of the tub and

attacked her with a renewed, driving force until she fell backward into the dirty water. He didn't even pause but grabbed the plug chain and kept up his long, deep strokes as the water drained.

They finished together, wrapped inside the marble of the sunken tub.

J.T. was the first to move. Quite suddenly, he looked at her as if she were something horrible and got out of the tub. "I have to go. I have to get out of here," he mumbled as he began pulling on his uniform. He had to get out, had to get away from her as quickly as possible. He murmured good-bye to her then fled the room as if a thousand demons were on his heels.

He ignored the guardsmen standing at the door as he hurried down the corridor, down the stairs and out into the garden. He made it to the King's Garden before stopping. As he lit a cigarette, his hands were shaking.

Seduction, he thought. Everything about the country was seductive.

Whenever he wanted food, it was there waiting for him. He dropped his clothes wherever they fell and minutes later they were gone. There were always silent people standing nearby waiting to obey his merest wish. If he wanted a car, he merely had to ask and it was readied for him.

And the choices he had! He could drive or be driven. He could get up early or sleep late. He could do nothing or work twenty hours a day. He could swim, ride a horse, climb a mountain, train with athletes, walk through acres of beautiful gardens. The freedom of so many choices was intoxicating.

J.T. leaned against a tree and inhaled on the cigarette.

And there was Aria—the most seductive of all. He

had looked at her tonight, her dress damp from the children's bathwater, and he had remembered her on the island. The king had said she was a warm and kind person but J.T. hadn't believed it. She was, but she had covered it with her haughtiness, and her rules to live by.

He understood better now, understood how she had been trained to believe that the world was her servant. He wondered what he would be like if he had been raised like she had. Would he be like Toby and pout because there was a tiny bit of green on one of his strawberries? Would he get so used to cashmere sweaters that he would toss them on the floor like Gena did? Would he become so used to the servants that he would walk in and out of rooms and not see them? Would he believe he was someone else's superior by divine right?

He knew how bad the atmosphere of this place was, but he was also feeling seduced by it, sucked into the vortex of it. Ever since he was a child he had loved hot chocolate. He had never mentioned it because he knew that people—these unbelievably well-trained servants—watched what he ate and drank and made sure that what he liked was always near. Now Walters brought him a pot of hot chocolate as soon as J.T. woke and pulled the bell by his bed.

For the last several days, ever since he had felt confident that the Royal Guard could protect Aria, he had worked long hard hours. He had enlisted a couple of Aria's secretaries, both intelligent men who generally had too little to do, to help him find out who needed money or who would most benefit from Aria's death. Aria walked about the countryside as if there had never been an attempt on her life, but he never forgot for a moment. He had spent hours with the kitchen staff, much to the chagrin of Aria's butler, who considered J.T. part of the royal family, trying to find out what gossip he could. But as far as he could tell, no one knew anything.

He was no closer to finding who had tried to murder Aria than he ever was.

He had tried his best to treat his time in Lanconia as a job and nothing else, but he wasn't succeeding. When he and Aria had parted the first time, he had been so angry he was almost glad to get rid of her. He still remembered his fury when he had found out that she had tricked him and he was to remain in Lanconia forever. At the time all he could think of was that he was a sailor and she was asking him to live inland. He had also been enraged that he had been tricked so easily. His temper hadn't been helped by her grandfather ordering him to remain in Lanconia.

But now, a few weeks later, he understood more of what it meant to be part of the royal family. He saw how much Aria meant to the people. He had been among them and heard the special tone of reverence they used when referring to her.

He finished his cigarette, crushed it under his foot, and smiled as he remembered the day they had gone to see the vineyard. She hadn't been a princess then, she had just been his girl, and he had been proud of her. He had watched the faces of the people, seen how wary they had been of Aria, then he had seen how much they had *liked* her. Ol'-fashioned *liked* her, not because they were supposed to, but because she was pleasant and amusing and interested in them.

It had been so very, very difficult to leave her that night. It would have been perfectly natural to climb into bed with her, just as every husband had a right to do. But he knew better than to touch her because he knew she was borrowed and he had to give her back.

He had stayed away from her after that day, deliberately trying to forget her and hoping that she would forget him. He had felt his chest tighten every time he saw her with her little count, but he had not interfered. Of course he had to admit, though, that some of the gossip had given him great pleasure. Aria had pushed through the crowds and eaten a sandwich made by a peasant woman—and later she had sent the woman a flock of chickens in gratitude. He doubted if she had any idea how such actions pleased the people of Lanconia.

So far, J.T. had been able to force himself to stay away from her but sometimes he couldn't control himself. When she had shown up at the guards' training ground and threatened a guard's life as if she were a warrior queen of old, he had been very pleased. And then her jealousy attack over Gena later! It had been a woman, not a crown princess, who had stormed off that field. Then he had had to sit back and watch her ushered away by that pompous little count. The twerp didn't understand that what Aria did outside her official duties was more important than having tea with a bunch of fat, pedigreed women.

The captain of the guard had put his hand on J.T.'s arm just as J.T. was about to nail the little overbearing fop.

So now, J.T. had done the worst thing he could have: he'd made love to her again. Not really the long, slow all-night lovemaking that he dreamed of at night, but he had attacked her with all the pent-up passion that he felt every time he saw her. And she had responded in just the way he remembered.

He had to stop! He had to keep his hands off of her and his mind on the work that needed doing. He had asked the guardsmen to be especially vigilant in the coming days because he felt that another attempt would soon be made on Aria's life. This time he was sure the murderer would be caught, and as soon as he was, J.T. meant to return to America.

He closed his eyes, smelled the pine trees and the soft mountain air blowing across the acres of flowers that were planted everywhere, and tried to remember the sea. He would marry some pretty little woman who liked the sea and after the war he would settle in Warbrooke, work in the family's shipyard, and raise a few kids. He wanted only the average things in life, nothing special. No kingdom to rule. No gold-plated throne to sit on. No crown to wear. No pretty princess to make him laugh.

"Damn!" he cursed aloud. Maybe he'd go wake up Frank and they could work on some more plans, or better yet, they could start rebuilding a few car engines. He had never seen people who knew as little about machine maintenance as these Lanconians. What they needed were a few good vocational schools to teach the young people how to maintain equipment. And why wasn't there a good agricultural college here? And why weren't the girls learning to be nurses and secretaries?

He stopped and took a deep breath. Lanconia wasn't his responsibility. In another few weeks he would be gone and what King Julian and Queen Aria did was their business.

As he passed the garage, he saw that all the lights were on and he heard Frank Taggert's deep, angry voice. "A *crescent* wrench, not a ratchet wrench."

"How am I supposed to know which is which?" J.T. heard Gena say with just as much anger. "I'm a princess, not an auto mechanic."

"You have yet to prove to me you're worth anything. *This* is a crescent wrench. Oh, honey, don't cry."

J.T. laughed in the darkness and thought it would

be better not to disturb the two of them. It looked like Gena wouldn't be following him anymore. Probably tomorrow she would be wondering what she ever saw in somebody as old as him.

Smiling, he went up to his lonely, empty bedroom. At least somebody somewhere was happy.

Chapter Twenty-one

SLOWLY, Aria got out of the car at her grandfather's hunting lodge. It was dusk and she was tired after a long day of meetings with the Americans, but she so badly wanted to talk to her grandfather. It had been a harrowing day trying to bargain with the Americans over the price of the vanadium. Julian had insisted that she sit back and allow him to handle the negotiations but Aria soon realized he knew no more about bargaining than she did. Unwisely, she suggested they ask Lieutenant Montgomery to attend the meeting. Julian turned furious eyes on her until she was quiet.

After two hours, Julian seemed satisfied but Aria was not. She sent for Lieutenant Montgomery. He arrived wearing a sweat-stained undershirt, and when he saw the contract the Americans were offering, he laughed. Thirty minutes later he had sold half as much of the vanadium for twice as much money. "We'll negotiate for the rest of it later," he said. To Aria's disbelief all the Americans seemed happy with the deal and very pleased with J.T., yet they gave looks of contempt to Julian. Aria didn't understand at all because she would have thought the Americans would have liked Julian better.

After the meeting she wanted to talk to J.T. but he brushed her aside, saying he had to get back to the engines. She had felt rejected, and worst of all, she felt lonely. The rest of the day she had performed her duties but her heart hadn't been in them. At four P.M. she told her secretary to call her grandfather and tell him she was coming to visit him.

Lady Werta had nearly died when she heard of Aria's planned visit but Aria was getting good at ignoring the woman.

And now she was here and Ned was opening the front door to her. "He is in the garden, Your Highness," Ned said, bowing to her. "I have presumed to prepare a supper for you and set it in the garden. His Majesty said you wanted to be alone."

"Yes," she said as she hurried forward. Now that she was this near, she desperately wanted to see her grandfather. He was standing under a big elm tree and waiting for her with open arms. To the world he was a king but to her he was her grandfather, someone who had held her on his lap and read her fairy tales. With her mother and the rest of the world she had had to be a princess but with her grandfather she could be a little girl.

He held her close, his big, heavy body enveloping her, and she felt safe and protected for the first time in a long while. She could feel tears gathering in her eyes. She who a few months ago never cried seemed to always be crying now.

Her grandfather held her at arm's length and studied her. "Sit down here and eat," he said gruffly.

"Ned's given us enough to feed Rowan's army. It's about time you came to see me."

Aria took a seat and gave him a guilty little smile. She could feel herself becoming a little girl again, especially when she saw a dishful of the tiny chocolate cakes Ned had made for her, just as he had done all her life. But she had no appetite.

"What's on your mind?" the king asked.

Aria hesitated. How could she burden her grandfather with her problems? He was an old man and not well. She took a seat across the table from him.

The king raised one eyebrow at her. "Turning coward on me, are you? Has someone shot at you again? Or tried to drown you? And how's that American husband of yours doing with the car engines?"

Aria choked, and while her eyes watered and she gulped hot tea, her grandfather smiled at her.

"Why is it that young people think age brings stupidity? We're smart enough to raise children and run our lives for fifty-odd years but when we turn sixty, young people assume we're senile. Aria, I know *everything.* I know you were kidnapped in America and I was told you were dead. I knew there would be a scandal if you were killed on American soil, so I sent Cissy in your place."

"But I thought—"

"That Cissy wanted to be queen? She's got too much sense for that."

Aria was silent for a moment. "I see."

Her grandfather reached across the table to take her hand. "No you don't see at all. You aren't easily replaced if that's what you're thinking. I went through hell when I thought you were dead." He squeezed her hand. "You can't imagine my joy when the American president radioed me that you were safe and well. Of

361

course by that time you were already married. He apologized for that and offered to have the marriage annulled and you returned to me."

Aria's head came up. "But you didn't."

"For all I knew, it was a love match. After all, he had rescued you from being killed. I was very grateful to the man."

Aria was pushing a bit of thinly sliced beef about on her plate. "So you let me stay with the man and fall in love with him." There was bitterness in her voice.

The king speared a turkey leg. "Why don't you tell me about that place where you stayed? Awfully hot, wasn't it? And whatever was that photo in the newspaper? Was that actually your lieutenant's mother? Good-looking woman she looked to be. My sources said you cooked dinner *and* did the laundry. Not possible, Aria, really not possible."

Aria gave her grandfather one of her American grins and started talking. As much as listening to her, the king watched her, saw the way she relaxed her body when she talked about America and the friends she had made there. He laughed with her when she told of learning to dress herself, of getting the money confused and tipping taxi drivers hundred-dollar bills. She laughed at how obnoxious she was on the island and told how she had started to eat the shrimp raw. She talked of the glorious freedom of going shopping, then went into a ten-minute tirade about the monotony of doing housework.

And every other word was "Jarl." It was how Jarl reacted to everything, whether an action made him angry or happy, how astonished he had been when she had dressed as Carmen Miranda (Aria stood and did a quick rendition of "Chica Chica"), how furious he had been when he had found out he was supposed to remain married to her. She told how proud he had been of her when she took the orphaned children. She talked of how magnificent he was when he had saved her from being shot.

She spent thirty minutes telling of all the things Jarl had done in Lanconia. "He has sold the grapes to America and he's bringing them down from the mountains with engines. This morning at breakfast he talked of schools to teach the young people how to do things so they won't leave Lanconia. He says the country could move into the twentieth century with a lot of work. Jarl said that Lanconia has a great deal of potential, that all it takes is know-what—no, I mean, know-how. American slang is so difficult to remember. And Jarl dealt with the Americans for the vanadium. He only sold them the rights to mine one site because he said it might be worth more later. The Americans said he was a fool but I don't think so, and they didn't really look as if they thought so either. And this morning Freddie got very angry because there was no snow for his snow cream. The Exchequer says Jarl has cut fifteen percent off the palace's budget. And the Royal Guardsmen adore him. He wrestles with them and he says it's a shame that over the centuries they've been relegated to door openers." Suddenly she stopped, out of breath and a bit embarrassed. She took a deep drink of her tea.

"And how is Count Julian?" the king asked, looking at her over his beer mug.

To her disbelief, Aria put her face in her hands and burst into tears. "Oh, Grans, I love Jarl so much. Why doesn't he love me in return? He is so very, very good for Lanconia. We need him so much. What can I do to make him stay? How can I bear to give him up?"

The king was big and Aria was thin and light, so he had no trouble pulling her into his lap and holding her as he did when she was a little girl. "You are asking him to give up his country. You want to keep what you have, yet you ask that he make many sacrifices."

"But it's not the same," she sniffed. "He is merely one person in his country. He is not a king or a prince. His father has other sons to run his business. If I were not a crown princess, I would go with him to his country. I would follow him anywhere. I would give up . . . I would give up Lanconia for him."

The king was quiet for a moment. "Thinking of abdicating, are you?" he asked softly. "Then Gena would rule Lanconia. Perhaps she could bring Lanconia into the twentieth century."

"Gena will do only what she is told," Aria said in disgust. "If I were to abdicate, Julian would no doubt ask for her hand in marriage—or rather ask for her throne in marriage," she said bitterly.

"Ah," the king said. "Tell me about Julian. I thought his father trained him to be a king."

Aria sat up in her grandfather's lap, pulled a handkerchief from his shirt pocket, and blew her nose loudly. "He was trained to be what kings *used* to be. He stays in the palace all day, doing heaven knows what, while the people of Lanconia are leaving by the truck load because there are no jobs. He gets angry with me because I eat a peasant's meal—a meal prepared by one of my own people! He told me he desperately wanted to marry me, that he . . ."

"Desired you?" the king supplied.

"Yes, he said that but it was a lie. He will do anything to get my throne. But all he wants from Lanconia is the prestige of being a prince consort and the luxury of the palace. He is terrified of being poor. But poverty isn't so bad. I know."

The king's voice was very quiet. "Aria, do you think he would kill you if he thought he couldn't marry you?"

"Perhaps, but then the first attempt was when we were firmly engaged."

"Firmly? And you aren't now?"

Tears formed in her eyes again. "I am Mrs. Jarl Montgomery for as long as I can be. He may not want me, but I want him for as long as I can have him."

The king hugged her. "I doubt if he doesn't want you. In fact, my guess is that he is going through hell right now."

She pulled away from him and smiled. "Do you think so? Do you really think so?"

The king smiled back at her. "Agony. Torture. Excruciating pain."

Aria's smile broadened. "What can I do to make his pain worse? How can I make him love me so much that he will never leave me?"

The king took her chin in his hand. "I asked him to stay to protect you. Now he has the guard protecting you, so why is he still here? Why didn't he go home last week?"

Aria's eyes widened as she thought about this. "I think I'm hungry. I think I'll eat that whole plate of chocolates and do you think Ned could open a bottle of champagne? *Lanconian* champagne?"

The king laughed. "Go tell Ned to open two bottles and get off my leg before it dies and get me a clean handkerchief, you've soaked this one. Really, Aria, didn't anyone ever teach you any manners?"

She laughed as she got up. "I guess they didn't take." She turned and started running across the lawn toward the house.

The king crossed his hands on his belly and smiled contentedly.

J.T. woke instantly, at the first sound coming from behind the panel that led down to the concealed staircase. Silently, he left the bed and made his way toward the panel. His service revolver was in the drawer by the bed and he got it as he moved.

With the revolver held ready, he waited for the door to open. It creaked on its hinges, then whoever was opening it stopped until it was silent again and pushed the door further open.

"Freeze," J.T. said, lowering the pistol.

His answer was a hiccup.

"Gena?" he asked.

"Gena!" Aria said, her voice just a bit slurred. "Gena!"

J.T. backed away from her as if she were diseased and turned on a floor lamp. Aria was clutching a bottle of champagne and wearing a thin, clinging bathrobe that looked as if she wore nothing underneath. "Get out of here," he said under his breath.

She took a step forward. "But, Jarl, aren't you glad to see me?"

"Aria, are you drunk?"

"I believe I am, but since I have never been drunk before, I'm not sure if I am. How does one know?"

J.T. backed away from her until he was against the wardrobe. "Why did you come here? Someone might have seen you."

Aria advanced until she was just a few steps away from him. "I came to spend the night with you," she whispered.

He started to say something in protest but then Aria dropped her robe. She was not wearing anything underneath and the sight of her nude body made him forget his protests. He was wearing only his pajama bottoms and he opened his arms to her, feeling her bare breasts against his chest.

He kissed her neck and cheeks and lips hungrily. "You shouldn't be here," he said, his lips trailing hot kisses up and down her neck and shoulders. "You have a reputation to uphold. A royal princess cannot—"

She put her mouth on his. "I am your wife tonight, not Her Royal Highness."

He pulled back and looked at her. "I like that," he whispered. "I like that very much."

Bending, he picked her up in his arms and carried her to the big bed, laying her across the sheets and looking at her for a long while before touching her, and Aria thought he was looking at her as if he planned to remember her for always.

"What is it you Americans say? 'Aren't you going to offer a lady a drink?'" Aria said, holding up the bottle of champagne she still held.

J.T. was still looking at her, sitting on the edge of the bed and lightly running his fingers over her breasts and her ribs, down her arms.

Aria used her thumbs to open the champagne bottle and the cork flew out. The champagne spewed over her belly and down J.T.'s back. She laughed and started to brush the flood of liquid away but J.T. caught her hands and begin to drink it off her body, his head moving upward until his mouth settled on her breasts.

She was intoxicated, feeling wonderfully free, able to do anything. With a quick, strong move, she pulled J.T. to the bed then wriggled out from under him and began to drink the champagne droplets from his bare back. She straddled his legs, loving the feel of his strong, heavy thighs between her own as she ran her tongue up his spine, then began making nippling little kisses down his back. He lay absolutely still under her, as if, were he to move, she might stop. Her breasts against his skin felt so good that she raked the tips of them across his back, her stomach touching his buttocks. She stretched out on him, her legs straddling his, moving her body along his, savoring the sensation of his skin against hers. She rubbed her hair and face on his back again and again, feeling him, tasting him, smelling him.

She moved downward and began to kiss his buttocks, his legs, the backs of his knees, his calves, his feet. She pressed the soles of his feet to her face, breathed deeply, then moved upward again.

When she reached his neck, she took her kisses across his cheek to his lips, and when she kissed his mouth, he turned over. His eyes were on fire and his stillness was gone. His hands were rough and quick on her body as he picked her up and set her down on his manhood.

She gave a delighted scream of surprise then began to move with all the abandonment she felt, her legs strong and moving with hard strength until they tightened and began to ache. J.T. turned her over and slammed into her with a few deep, hard thrusts until they came together in one blinding explosion.

He held on to her tightly, holding her against his chest, her legs wrapped around him.

"I love you," she whispered. "And I want you to stay with me."

He was still for a moment, then he rolled off of her to sit on the side of the bed and pull on his pajama bottoms. "Is that what this is about? You climb into bed with me and then demand payment? We have a name for women like you." He moved across the room and picked up her fallen robe. He didn't look at her as he tossed it to her. "Get out of here."

Aria tried to react with dignity, but she was a little too drunk on champagne and lovemaking to be perfectly lucid. She got out of bed, tripping on her robe, and made her way to the panel door he held open for her. He kept his head turned away as he held out a flashlight to her and she went down the stairs. The sound of the door closing behind her was horrible.

She was halfway down the stairs when a hand closed over her mouth and a gun was stuck in her ribs.

She struggled against the person holding her.

"So this is how you move about in this moldering old castle" came a familiar voice. "Keep that flashlight still."

She scratched at the hand on her mouth. "Freddie!" she gasped.

"You say one more word and I'll break your neck here and now, Aria. Everyone I've sent has failed at the job of killing you, so I might as well do it myself." He was dragging her down the dark corridor away from the door leading to the garden. "They'll find your body in a few days, and when they do, I plan to make myself king. All I have to do is get rid of Gena and I figure the old king will die of grief. I am next in line to the throne."

She managed to move her head enough to speak. "Why do you want to be king?" she gasped out.

"Dear, stupid Aria. You only looked at the peasants, nothing else. This is a dying country. Better to sell it to the Germans than to try to keep its independence. Uranium, my dear. The country is riddled with it. I shall sell the whole place to the highest bidder and live in France. Damn, but you have been hard to kill, Aria."

"And she's going to be harder" came a voice from the darkness.

Aria had seen several American movies and she imitated a western now by ducking while Freddie was distracted. Her flashlight fell and went rolling as she flattened her body onto the filthy floor. Shots rang over her head, the stone walls of the tunnel echoing with the deafening sound. Dirt and bits of stone rained down on her head.

She lay still for a moment until the air cleared. "Jarl!" she screamed, and she was as loud as the shots.

"Here, baby," he said, and she ran to him in the darkness.

She held on to him with all her might.

"It's over," he whispered. "You're safe and I can go home."

It wasn't easy to do but she pulled away from him. "Yes, you must return to your country and I must remain in mine. It will be better this way. Will you get a guardsman to see to my cousin?"

"Yes, Your Royal Highness," he said mockingly as he turned away and left her in the darkness.

Chapter Twenty-two

Aria walked erectly as she left the limousine and made her way to the field behind the Lanconian Academy of Sciences building. The white plastered walls glared in the sun and hurt her swollen eyes. Even though she wore a little veiled hat, she knew the redness of her eyes was still visible.

It had been two weeks since the encounter in the underground passage between Jarl and Freddie. Freddie had not been killed, only wounded, but the Royal Guard had given him time alone in the library with a loaded pistol and Freddie had taken the honorable way out by putting a bullet through his head. The official story had been that he had had an accident while cleaning his gun. Only Aunt Sophie had questioned that statement. *"Freddie* clean his own gun? Balderdash! I never heard of anything so ridiculous. What *really* killed him?" No one who knew answered her.

Lieutenant Montgomery had left Lanconia the next morning without a word of farewell to anyone.

Immediately after his departure, Julian had become so possessive that Aria had told him to leave Lanconia and her life. She wasn't sure if he wanted her kingdom or the uranium. He certainly hadn't wanted *her*.

Young Frank Taggert had remained in Lanconia to help with the engines, but for all his size, he was just a boy, and a sudden long rain had left many vineyards with moldering grapes and no way to get them down the mountains fast enough.

Hours after J.T. left, Aria was in her grandfather's house and raging at him for not telling her about the uranium. He said she was more angry about that cowardly husband of hers leaving than about any secrets he had kept. She had defended J.T. but not for long. She had gone back to the palace to hear the news of Freddie's suicide. She gave orders that a royal funeral be arranged for him.

She had met with the people involved in putting Kathy Montgomery in Princess Aria's place in the War Room. Not even the groveling and apologies of the Lord High Chamberlain had cheered her from her deep depression. Lady Werta had looked as if she might faint and had whispered that she would like to resign from Her Highness's service. Aria said that whatever her ladyship had done, she had done out of faithfulness to the true princess. She awarded the woman the Order of the Blue Shield for her patriotism.

She also met with her cousin Cissy and thanked her for what she had done for Lanconia. Cissy was glad Aria was alive and unhurt and all she asked in reward was a banquet. She had been put on a semifast by both the Lanconians who had switched her and later by the American government who had held her as prisoner. Everyone except Cissy believed she needed to lose weight. Aria ordered a feast that took Cissy three days to eat.

Then, as if Aria didn't have enough misery in her life, a committee of Lanconians presented her with a petition asking for the return of the American, Lieutenant Montgomery, so he could continue helping them with the grapes. She explained to them that his return was impossible, that his own country needed him. To her horror, they wrote to the American president and, somehow, the story got into the American newspapers. The short article made the Lanconians look like incompetent, backward peasants and said that they needed a red-blooded American to run their country for them. Aria crumpled the paper in disgust. She would find someone else to teach her people about dams and wells and vocational schools and car engines and whatever else needed doing. She just had to find someone who could figure out what needed doing and where to start looking for that person. If she only had someone to ask for help—if she weren't so completely alone.

Julian had been gone for three days now, Gena saw no one but her young American, and Aria had no one to talk to or laugh with. She had never felt lonely before she went to America and met that odious man, so what was wrong with her now?

She went about her duties without feeling. Now she was never tempted to break through crowds and drink goat's milk, and she accepted every engagement proposed to her so she never had a chance to be alone to think—and to remember. The people of Lanconia noticed her dreariness and attributed it to the loss of her fiancé, Count Julian.

Today Aria was to unveil yet another statue of Rowan the Mighty, a twenty-foot-high stone sculpture of a square-jawed man sitting on a chair with lions' heads for arms. She had not slept well last night or the night before, or the one before that for that matter, and her eyes were tired and red and her head ached.

There had been built a raised stand that held a podium with a microphone (newly imported to Lanconia) and six chairs containing the sculptor and his guests. Three hundred people stood in the audience.

Aria mounted the three steps up, opened her piece of paper, and began to read the prepared speech. She was halfway into the part about Rowan's magnificent accomplishments when a noise to her left distracted her.

J.T. slouched in a chair in the big living room of his parents' house on the coast of Maine. Outside he could hear the wind and not far off a ship's horn sounded, but he had no desire to go see what ship was docking. In fact, for the last ten days he hadn't had much interest in anything. He had caught a ride out of Lanconia on the first plane leaving with vanadium. He knew he was being cowardly in not saying good-bye to Aria, but he had said good-bye to her before and once was all he could bear.

He didn't really have orders from the navy as to where he was supposed to be, so after landing in Virginia, he had thumbed a ride to Key West. There he had found his Uncle Jason doing a better job than he ever could have. He saw Bill and Dolly that night, but they reminded him so much of Aria that they made him feel worse than he already did. Everything seemed to remind him of her, and Dolly's hundreds of questions about Aria didn't help any. He ended up leaving in the middle of dinner and walking along the beach all night.

The next morning Commander Davis received word J.T. was to report to General Brooks in D.C.

On the long train ride, J.T. stared out the window and thought of the things that could be done in Lanconia. With the money from the uranium, schools could be built—maybe even a university. The countryside was so beautiful that he was sure there was some way to attract tourists.

The more he thought, the more depressed he became. He wondered if Aria was having a good time with Count Julian.

In Washington, General Brooks said J.T. was a disappointment to America, that America needed him in Lanconia.

J.T. made a halfhearted attempt at explaining that Aria could not put an American on the throne beside her, that the people wouldn't accept an American. She would have to abdicate. "Unless the people asked for me," J.T. mumbled.

"And you didn't stay there to fight," the general said with disgust. General Brooks sent him home to Maine until he could find a "suitable" assignment for him—which J.T. guessed was going to be either the front line or the worst desk job in the military. J.T. didn't care which.

He went home but he wasn't glad to be home. Nothing seemed to cheer him, not seeing his family or the sea, not rowing out to an island alone, nothing.

"Get out of the way."

J.T. looked up to see his brother Adam wheeling his chair toward him, Adam's healing leg stuck out straight in front of him. He had very little sympathy for J.T.'s sulks and moodiness, especially since J.T. refused to talk about what was bothering him.

"There's a special delivery letter for you from

General Brooks," Adam said, tossing an envelope in J.T.'s lap.

"Orders," J.T. mumbled, not caring much, not looking at the letter.

Adam leaned over and snatched the envelope. *"I'm interested in where you're going. Maybe they're sending you to hell to use your sunny disposition to further punish the occupants."* He opened the envelope. "It's a clipping of a newspaper article. Hey! It's about you. It says the people of Lanconia petitioned President Roosevelt for your return to their country. I'm glad *somebody* wants you."

It took J.T. a moment to react. He snatched the paper from Adam's hands. "They *asked* for me," he said softly. "The people of Lanconia *asked* for me."

Adam knew the basics of what J.T. had been through in Lanconia. "It says they want you to tell them about raisins and cars. They did *not* say they wanted you for their king."

For the first time in many days there was life in J.T.'s eyes. "But maybe there's a loophole in their constitution, maybe there isn't a constitution, maybe the people wouldn't mind an American king." J.T. stood.

"I thought you didn't *want* to be king. Bill Frazier told Dad you hated the idea. *I* would. No freedom, always shaking hands, some tight-lipped queen for a wife, tea parties."

"You don't know *anything!*" J.T. shouted at his brother. "You don't know what it's like to be needed, to be necessary. That place needs me and"—he paused—"and I need Lanconia—and Aria." He started out of the room.

"Where are you going?"

"Home," J.T. shouted. "Home to my wife. They

may not let me be king, but I'm going to die fighting for the right."

Adam laughed and tried to scratch under his cast.

Aria turned to see Lieutenant Montgomery standing at the edge of the platform.

Anger filled her so she could barely speak, but she continued reading, a tremor in her voice.

He walked to the podium and put his head between her and the audience, his mouth close to the microphone.

"People of Lanconia," he said, ignoring Aria, "I want to make an announcement. A few weeks ago your princess went to America. She was gone a long time and you were told that she had been ill. She was not. What took her away from you so long was her marriage to me."

Aria tried to push him away but he didn't budge as the crowd began to murmur in disbelief.

"I know I'm an American," J.T. said, "and I know I'm not of royal blood, but if you'll have me, I'll be your king."

The crowd was so stunned that no one spoke until one man yelled, "What does Princess Aria say?"

"No!" Aria said, and J.T. looked at her. "You went off and left me. I could never trust you to—"

J.T. pulled her into his arms and kissed her and the crowd began to cheer. "I couldn't bear living without you," he shouted to her over the din the crowd was beginning to make. "And the people asked for me, so you don't have to abdicate. And have you ever heard of Warbrooke Shipping?"

She was a bit too dazed to understand. "No. Does it have to do with boats? Jarl, we don't *need* boats. We need schools and wells and—"

He kissed her again.

"Long live King Jarl," the crowd shouted.

"Prince!" Aria yelled into the microphone. *"Prince Jarl,"* she said, but no one heard her.

"Come on, baby, let's go home," J.T. yelled. "I brought some members of my family with me. We're going to bring this country of ours into the twentieth century."

She slipped her arm around him, forgetting she was in public and that she was a princess. "Ours," she said, smiling. *"Our country."*

Jude Deveraux

*America's favorite historical
romance author!*

The James River Trilogy
____COUNTERFEIT LADY 67519/$4.50
____LOST LADY 67430/$4.50
____RIVER LADY 67297/$4.50

Enter the passionate world of the
Chandler Twins
____TWIN OF ICE 50049/$3.95
____TWIN OF FIRE 50050/$3.95

The Montgomery Saga Continues
____THE TEMPTRESS 67452/$4.50
____THE RAIDER 67056/$4.50
____THE PRINCESS 67386/$4.50
____THE AWAKENING 64445/$4.50
____THE MAIDEN 62196/$4.50

POCKET
B O O K S

Jude Deveraux

A Unique New Voice
In Romantic Fiction

Jude Deveraux is the finest new writer of historical
romances to come along since Kathleen Woodiwiss.

The Montgomery Annals

____The Velvet Promise 67040/$4.50
____Highland Velvet 67470/$4.50
____Velvet Song 67226/$4.50
____Velvet Angel 67521/$4.50

**POCKET
B O O K S**

**Simon & Schuster, Mail Order Dept. MON
200 Old Tappan Rd., Old Tappan, N.J. 07675**

Please send me the books I have checked above. I am enclosing $_____ (please add 75¢ to cover
postage and handling for each order. N.Y.S. and N.Y.C. residents please add appropriate sales tax). Send
check or money order--no cash or C.O.D.'s please. Allow up to six weeks for delivery. For purchases over
$10.00 you may use VISA: card number, expiration date and customer signature must be included.

Name _____

Address _____

City _____ State/Zip _____

VISA Card No. _____ Exp. Date _____

Signature _____ 302-01